Praise for

WIL Mc

THE WELLSTONE

"An ideal bl
future age wh
McCarthy g
re

"Wil McC
if their chil

become an exciting adventure?" —Sean McMullen

 nadcap, inventive energy that proves
revious book, THE COLLAPSIUM,
curity, and THE WELLSTONE—a
enture tale, with its log cabin flying

throug
seq

"[Pro
creator

"The
there ar
the
extrap
providi

"A star
of Rog

"Quite entertaining. The science is larger-than-life, and so are the characters." —*SF Site*

"I don't recall the last time a book made me laugh out loud. I did so here on page 146, and at the book's end I did so again... though my eyes were moist as well. McCarthy has created a story here that is distinctly Asimovian in flavor, though his voice is very much his own." —*SF Revu*

"Prepare to use your grey matter. [McCarthy] fills his pages with lovingly rendered descriptions... but it is the strength of his scientific imagination that really shines through." —*SFX Magazine* (UK)

"A most dazzling future. What follows is a mind-spinning struggle that recalls a Henry Fielding novel of manners, Michael Moorcock's epic sagas and the cosmic free-for-alls of Doc Smith. There's fascinating science aplenty, mad scientists, robots running amok... What more could you want?" —*The Weekly Australian*

"A decidedly odd but enjoyable mix of mannered, decadent comedy and far-out physics. I liked and was even prepared to believe in [it]." —*Ansible* (UK)

BLOOM

"*Bloom* is tense, dynamic, intelligent, offering a terrifyingly vivid view of how technology can rocket out of our control." —David Brin

"What clever and compelling science fiction! The *Bloom* future is all too believable." —James Gleick, author of *Chaos: Making a New Science*

"Wil McCarthy makes ideas jump. *Bloom* grabs you from very first scene and doesn't let go till the last page. It's irresistible." —Walter Jon Williams

"Ultimately [humanity] must learn to ask new questions. The book's message is [that] in a universe stranger than we know, ignorance may be inevitable, but it's definitely not bliss." —*The New York Times*

"Swiftly paced, consistently inventive and tightly written. This is a novel that knows its business."
—*The Washington Post*

"McCarthy has worked out a bleakly dramatic future. This is the kind of broad view of mankind's future and the universe reminiscent of Arthur C. Clarke."
—*The Denver Post*

"The science is consistent and integral to the story, and the characters are much more plausibly drawn than are so many folks in [other speculative] fiction. In nearly every passage, we get another slice of the science of McCarthy's construction, and a deeper sense of danger and foreboding."
—*San Diego Union-Tribune*

"The writing is vivid. Readers who can plug into the prose and navigate its dense circuitry will find themselves rewarded with a wallop of a finale that satisfies high expectations for high-concept SF." —*Publishers Weekly*

"An ingenious yarn with challenging ideas, well-handled technical details and plenty of twists and turns."
—*Kirkus Reviews*

"McCarthy is an entertaining, intelligent, amusing writer, with Clarke's thoughtfulness [and] Heinlein's knack for breakneck plotting." —*Booklist*

"Succeeds on many different levels, combining a unique literary style with complex scientific speculation and political intrigue. Wil McCarthy's most entertaining and thought-provoking novel yet." —*Locus*

"An intense narrative of survival. *Bloom* works on several levels even while beckoning the reader into deeper mysteries. McCarthy proves once again that he has the wit and narrative power to take us to the outer reaches of space and down into the vast unknown of human, and inhuman, consciousness."
—*Barnes and Noble Explorations*

"Complex and inventive. Hundreds of pages of smart, suspenseful science fiction. 'Our Pick.'"
—*Science Fiction Weekly*

By Wil McCarthy

Aggressor Six

Flies from the Amber

The Fall of Sirius

Murder in the Solid State

Bloom

The Collapsium

THE
WELLSTONE

WIL McCARTHY

BANTAM BOOKS

9~03

7.00

THE WELLSTONE
A Bantam Spectra Book / March 2003

Published by
Bantam Dell
A Division of Random House, Inc.
New York, New York

Bantam Books and the rooster colophon are registered trademarks
of Random House, Inc.

ISBN 0-553-58446-4

Manufactured in the United States of America
Published simultaneously in Canada

OPM   10 9 8 7 6 5 4 3 2 1

For Rich,

who will never grow up

acknowledgments

Dragging this fanciful future into print has been a long and sometimes arduous journey. I'd like to extend my earnest thanks to Shawna McCarthy for twisting my arm; to Scott Edelman, Chris Schluep, and Stanley Schmidt for editing earlier phases of the project; and to Anne Lesley Groell for believing so wholeheartedly in this one. To the extent that the ideas in this book are mature, it's thanks to years of kicking around by friends and relations, most especially Gary E. Snyder, Richard Powers, Mike McCarthy, and Geoffrey A. Landis. I'm also grateful for the wisdom, advice, and enthusiasm of David Brin and Hal Clement, and for the more specific patience of Kathee Jones, Laurel Bollinger, and Don Kinney in critiquing early manuscripts.

I am, of course, deeply beholden to the swarms of physicists, chemists, astronomers, and other scientists on whose work these stories are based. Many of these men and women have been generous with their time, and thoughtful with their imaginations. I owe Bernhard Haisch and Marc Kastner a particular debt. And, as always, the greatest thanks go to my own family for their love and support, which make all the rest of this possible.

Any errors you find in this book are the fault of Secret Villains, whose mad schemes will soon be revealed.

the spheres of heav'n

One man in a sphere of brass.

One man alone in the vacuum of space.

One man hurtling toward solid rock at forty meters per second—fast enough to kill him, to end his mission here and now, to cap a damnfool end on a long and decidedly damnfool life. To leave his children defenseless.

In the porthole ahead is the planette Varna, his destination, swathed in white clouds and shining seas, in grasslands, in forests whose vertical dimension is already apparent against the dinner-bowl curve of horizon. Not planet: planette. It looks small because it *is* small, barely twelve hundred meters across. Condensed matter core, fifteen hundred neubles—very nice. The surface workmanship is exquisite; he sees continents, islands, majestic little mountain ranges jutting up above the trees. Telescopes, he realizes, don't do justice to this remotest of Lune's satellites.

The man's name is Radmer, or Conrad Mursk if you're old enough. Very few people are old enough. Radmer's own age would be difficult to guess—his hair is still partly blond, his weathered skin not really all that wrinkled. He still has his teeth, although they're worn down, and a few of them are cracked or broken. But even in zero gravity, as he kicks and kicks the potter's wheel that winds the gyroscopes which keep the sphere from tumbling, there's a kind of weight or weariness to his movements that might make you wonder. Older?

To be fair, the air inside the three-meter sphere isn't very good. Cold and damp, it smells of carbon dioxide, wet brass, and the chloride tang of spent oxygen candles. Old breath and new—the only way to refresh the air is to dump it overboard, but after two and a half days he's out of candles and out of time, and there's a healthy fear stealing upon him as the moment of truth approaches. Opening the purge valve would be a highly risky stunt right now.

Giving the winding mechanism a final kick, he ratchets his chair back a few notches and unfolds the sextant. This takes several seconds—it's a complicated instrument with a great many appendages. When it's locked into the appropriate sockets on the arms of his chair, and then properly sighted in, he takes a series of readings spaced five clock-ticks apart, and adjusts a pair of dials until the little brass arrow stops moving. Then, sighing worriedly, he folds the thing up again, stows it carefully in its rack, and clicks the chair forward again to kick the potter's wheel a few more times. Course correction needs a stable platform, you bet.

When he's satisfied the gyros are fully wound, he takes up the course-correction chains, winces in anticipation, and jerks out the sequence the sextant has indicated. *Wham! Wham!* The sphere is kicked—hard—by explosive charges on its hull. Caps, caps, fore, starboard, starboard...It's quite a pummeling, like throwing himself under a team of horses, but before his head has even stopped ringing he's setting the sextant up again and retaking those critical measurements.

The planette's atmosphere is as miniature as the rest of it, and there's the problem: from wispy stratosphere to stony lithosphere is less than half a second's travel, if he comes straight in. That's not long enough for the parachute to inflate, even if his timing is perfect. To survive the impact, he has to graze the planette's edge, to cut through the atmosphere horizontally. Shooting an apple is easy; shooting its skin off cleanly is rather more difficult, especially when *you're* the bullet.

Could he have sent a message in a bottle? A dozen messages in a dozen bottles, to shower every planette from here to murdered Earth? That *would* be an empty gesture, albeit an easier one. God knows he's needed elsewhere, has been *demanded* in a dozen different elsewheres as the world of Lune comes slowly unraveled. But somehow this dubious errand has captured his imagination. No, more than that: his *hope*. Can a man live without hope? Can a world?

Alas, the sextant's news is less than ideal: he's overcorrected on two of three axes. Sighing again more heavily, he stows the thing and gets set up for the next course correction, gathering the chains up from their moorings. When he jerks on the first one, though, no team of horses runs him over. Nothing happens at all.

With a stab of alarm, he realizes he's been squandering correction charges, not thinking about it, not thinking to save a few kicks on each axis for terminal approach. Can he recover? By reorienting the ship, which he needs to do for landing anyway? Yes, certainly, unless he's been *really* unlucky and run out of charges simultaneously on all six of the sphere's ordinal faces.

Outside the forward porthole, there is nothing but Varna: individual trees beneath a swirl of cloud, growing visibly. There is, to put it mildly, little time to waste.

Attitude control is strictly manual; Radmer throws off his safety harness and hurls himself at a set of handles mounted on the hull's interior. They're cold, barely above freezing, and damp enough that his fingers will slip if he doesn't grip with all his might, which, fortunately, he does.

There's a metallic screech and groan, brass against brass, as the outer hull begins to roll against the bearings connecting it to the inner cage, where his feet are braced. The potter's wheel and gyros hold a fixed orientation in space while the three-meter sphere, complete with chair and storage racks, is rotated around them. Sunlight flashes briefly through one porthole; through the other, the green-white face of Lune, from whence he came.

Like most men his age, Radmer is a good deal stronger than he looks. Still, the hull's rotation is as difficult to stop as it is to start. It's his own strength he's fighting, the momentum he himself has imparted. Despite the cold, the effort makes him sweat inside his coat and leathers.

He'd like to move the hull so his chair is facing backward, to serve as a crash couch. Because yes, even the *best* landing is going to be rough. But with the starboard charges expended, that would still leave him with one uncorrectable axis. Instead, he points the chair in the "caps" direction, ninety degrees from where he wants it, fires two charges in perpendicular directions, then points the chair forward again and quickly straps in, so he can take another sextant reading on the planette.

Perfect? Close enough? No, he's off again, drifting somehow from an ideal ballistic trajectory. He starts dialing for another correction, realizes he's out of time, and hurriedly stows the sextant instead, to keep it from becoming a projectile in its own right.

He's about to unstrap again, to face the chair aft for impact, but he's *really* out of time, the hull already singing with atmospheric contact. So he grabs an armrest with one hand and the parachute's ripcord with the other, and prepares to be thrown hard against the straps.

There are prayers he could utter right now, battle hymns he could sing, but perhaps thinking of them is enough. Quicker, anyway; he runs through several in the blink of an eye. And then the sphere slaps into denser air—more gently than he's expecting. Which could be bad, which could mean he's cut too high, his angle too shallow. Will he skip off the planette's atmosphere to tumble back Luneward in disgrace?

Air is squealing all around him, and for a moment, he sees Varna through three separate portholes, and hazy blue-black sky through a fourth. He sees individual blades of grass, no fooling, and then the ground is retreating again and it's time, slightly *past* time, to pop the chute. The sudden weight of his arm seems to help as he yanks the lanyard; he's looking "down" across the sphere, decelerating hard. He hears the chute deploy with a clanging of brass doors, and suddenly he *is* facing the right way as air drag pulls it around behind the vehicle and jerks its lines taut.

And then disaster strikes, in the form of a treetop's spreading arms. He doesn't hit them hard, but for an instant there are actual acacia leaves snapping across the porthole glass, and the contact is enough to set the sphere rolling around its inner cage. Which is bad, because the chute, which hasn't fully opened, is fouling— he can see it behind him, an orange-and-white streamer, its hemp lines twirling together in an inextricable mess.

And then the blue of atmosphere is fading to black again, and after three long seconds of deceleration he's back, suddenly, in zero gee. Having missed the planette. Having *actually missed the damn planette*. Through the portholes, the slowly tumbling view is clear enough: Varna shrinking away behind him.

Varna moving laterally?

Varna approaching again? More slowly, yes, but definitely approaching. Because he's cut through a swath of thick atmosphere, because he's hit a tree, because he's deployed a streamer chute that, while it couldn't quite stop him, could at least slow him down below the planette's escape velocity.

The air doesn't whistle this time, barely puffs, barely makes a sound at all as he falls back through it. What *does* create sound and sensation is the water beneath the air, which he slaps into hard, and the solid surface a couple of meters beneath that. He crashes against it and rolls; through the portholes he sees foam, blue water, blue sky, brown sand or silt kicking off the bottom in his wake.

The sphere tumbles around the screeching gyro platform for a few moments, but the platform is overwhelmed and starts to tumble along as well, its bearings frozen against the spinning hull. His chair goes with it, tumbling, and he loses his sense of direction almost immediately. Then, with a jerk, all movement stops. He's looking upward: sky only.

He has landed on the planette. His mad scheme has become, retroactively, a perfectly reasonable idea.

To his sides he sees fish and waving grasses, sunlight filtering down in rays through the shallow water. One side of the sphere is higher, its porthole only half-submerged. The shores are hidden behind the knife-edge of water against the glass, but he does see treetops in the distance, perhaps the very ones he struck. The porthole between his legs shows a sandy bottom, a few crushed reeds.

He takes a few moments to gather himself—it *was* a rough landing, and he remains quite reasonably terrified—but time is short, and his business urgent. He finds the buckles of his seat harness: damp brass, warmed by his body. He's unbuckled it a hundred times today; the action is as automatic as coughing.

Being a sphere, his carriage-sized spaceship was expected to roll a bit on landing, coming to rest in an unknown orientation. For this reason, the sphere has two exit hatches, one presently underwater, the other above it, pointing skyward at a cockeyed angle. He climbs to this one, using the potter's wheel and gyro assembly for a staircase.

He moves carefully; it's a small world, yes, but thanks to the planette's superdense neutronium core, gravity here is "gee," or about the same as at the surface of Lune. Or, reaching back a ways into the mists of time, Earth. With one hand he grasps a slick handle on the hull; with the other, the locking wheel on the hatch itself. It spins easily—no screeching or sticking—and he's abstractly relieved by this.

Like many wise men, Radmer worries a lot, and this errand has given his imagination more than the usual to work with. But while the sphere was built in a hurry, he has to give a nod to the smiths and armorers and watchmakers of Highrock, who clearly knew their business well enough.

Having landed in one piece, this craft has every chance of taking him home again. Compared to this planette, Lune is a *huge* target, virtually impossible to miss; so as long as the motors ignite and the parachute opens cleanly, he should be back in the war by next Friday at the latest.

Back in the death, the misery, the collapse of nations. The people of Lune are not Radmer's children per se, although a great many of them are, in one way or another, his descendants. And the world itself is his, or was long ago. How gladly he would die to protect it!

His hatch flips inward, clanks against the hull, then hangs down, swinging back and forth, while Radmer works out his handholds on the outer hull and, finally, lifts himself through.

It's like climbing up into a pleasant dream. It's *warm* out here, and the bright sky and brighter sun cast brilliant reflections on the lapping waters of the sea, which, spanning eighty meters at its widest, stretches nearly from horizon to horizon. The shoreline is a few meters of pristine beach, fading back into palm trees and elephant grass. The breeze smells sweetly pungent, like ice cream and salt somehow. Like fresh beer and flowers.

Farther back, behind the planette's round edge, rise a pair of low hills, green with pine and acacia, and on one of these hills is exactly what Radmer has come here to find, what the astronomer Rigby has claimed to see from his mountain observatory on the clearest of nights: a little white cottage of wellstone marble.

Silently, on some great universal scorecard, Radmer's obsession ticks over from "reasonable" to "downright sensible." So like any dutiful soldier, he strips off his coat and riding leathers, then hops in the water and swims for it.

It isn't far. Soon he is dripping on the white sands of the beach, strolling in his felt johnnysuit beneath the shade of palms, on a course for the not-so-distant hills. The air is hazy, perhaps by design; it enhances the illusion of distance, of space. He loses sight of the cottage as he plunges into the chest-high wall of grass, then is startled at how quickly it reappears again, immediately before him.

Overgrown, yes, overshadowed by vegetation. But certainly not a ruin, sitting here in this little glade or clearing on the hillside. Nor has it been abandoned. Kneeling in the dirt before it is the figure of a naked man, white hair frizzed and trailing to his waist.

You know that feeling, when you see something at once ancient and familiar, when your neck prickles and your stomach flutters and all your little hairs stand at attention? This is how Radmer feels as he approaches the cottage, as he eyeballs the naked man kneeling there in front of it.

He considers kneeling himself, but rejects the idea.

"Bruno," he says instead, from ten meters away. "Bruno de Towaji." A whole string of titles could be appended to the name, both fore and aft, but applying them to this dismal figure seems inappropriate. Still, there is no question in Radmer's voice, or in his mind. There is no mistaking that face. True, the ravages of time are apparent; the Olders age in slow but very particular ways. Hair and beard faded yellow-white, yes, and grown out to a length past which it simply frays and abrades. The skin smooth, but deeply freckled and tanned with the weary brown of accumulated melanin, sharply creased in its various corners and crannies. Teeth worn to chalky nubs in that slack, hanging jaw.

Radmer himself looks somewhat like this, but with his shorter hair and longer teeth, and the fact that he's clothed, it isn't quite so apparent. And though the armies to which he has formally belonged are all dust and gone, he still carries himself like a soldier, while the man in the dirt—digging up yams with his bare hands, Radmer sees now—has the absent, casual quality of a sleepwalker.

And something more: the eyes flicking slowly from here to there, taking in the house, the forest, the soft ground beneath them, the sea. Lingering overlong on the distant brass sphere, and on Radmer himself—disturbances in this long-familiar environment. But he's not really seeing them. Not seeing at all. Or rather: seeing but not processing. Not affected by what is seen.

The old man rises, clutching two small yams in each hand, and begins walking—not limping or shuffling—toward the little house. Radmer follows.

"De Towaji, sir. Sire. I need to speak with you."

The old man pauses, casts a cloudy, troubled glance over his shoulder, then continues on.

This is a condition Radmer has heard of: neurosensory dystrophia—pathways worn smooth in the brain through constant, repetitive stimulation. When the nervous system is old and the daily routine goes on unbroken for years or decades, its victims can be trapped by it. He's heard of couples and even whole villages succumbing, but typically it's the people who live alone—especially in isolated areas—who are most at risk.

He imagines Bruno de Towaji performing these same actions day after day, varying little or not at all. Like an animate fossil. Like a ghost, haunting this place, oblivious to the fact of his own demise.

The good news is that the symptoms are temporary, subsiding soon after the routine itself is interrupted. The arrival of a visitor is normally sufficient. But barring strange miracles, de Towaji must have been here on the planette for a long time indeed—much longer than Radmer cares to think about. Whole histories come and gone, an unthinkable span of time.

Radmer follows along into the shade of the overhanging forest, and then the old man enters the cottage through an open doorway that looks like it may never have had a door of any kind, or even a curtain. The windows are the same. Probably there's no winter here, perhaps no serious weather of any kind. Rigby could confirm that. Still, there's something unsavorily primeval about a house fully open on the sides.

The inside is a single room, shockingly clean, dominated by a water fountain made, like the house and floor, of white wellstone marble. Here de Towaji kneels again, and patiently washes the four yams he's retrieved.

Radmer tries again. "I suspect you can hear me, Sire. Perhaps you'll remember an architect by the name of Mursk? Conrad Mursk? We worked together once, long ago. Before that, I was a companion to your son."

When the yams are clean, de Towaji sets them down on the floor, rises again, and moves to a corner of the house, where a pile of small stones rest atop a little shelf. Flint? For starting a cooking fire? Surely *raw* yams would have busted the poor man's guts out long ago. He then turns toward the house's only exit and commences that slow, deliberate walk again. When Radmer blocks the way, de Towaji literally runs into him.

Then blinks and looks him over.

"Sire," Radmer says.

Slowly, the old man nods. "Ah. Ah. I . . . know you."

"Yes, Sire."

"Mursk."

"Yes, Sire. Very good."

"The architect. You . . . crushed the moon. Squoze it."

Radmer glances behind him at the half-disc of Lune in the sky. The clouds, the continents, the splatters of ocean. . . . But this isn't a map. This is the world itself, seen from a height of fifty thousand kilometers. "We crushed it together, Sire. Long ago."

Gruffly: "You're . . . in my way."

Radmer can't bring himself to bar the doorway any longer. Bowing, he steps back and to the side, allowing de Towaji to pass. At once, the old man's expression eases.

"Forgive me, Sire. I don't know if I'm rescuing you, or desecrating . . . Excuse me! Sire!"

Impatience is a rare emotion among the Olders, but seeing de Towaji prepare to ignore him again, Radmer feels it now, and dares to grab his long-ago master by the arm.

"Bruno! I have little time for this. Rouse yourself and listen to me: a great evil has been loosed upon that squozen moon of ours. Its future is now very much in peril."

The old man frowns, and it is no regal frown meant to convey official displeasure, but a private and unconscious one. A gesture of simple unhappiness.

"Future," the old man muses, or perhaps recites. He continues looking down the path ahead, deeper into the forest. "I remember that word. Where is the future? When will it get here?"

"I fear it will not, Sire."

De Towaji's gaze clears a bit, and a look of pained amusement passes briefly over his features. He speaks very slowly. "Lad, I guarantee it will not. All these . . .

futures we thought we were building. Where are they? In the past. *This* is the past, by the time I finish saying so." He pauses for a long moment to make the point, then adds, "There is no future, only past."

Now Radmer is angry. "I'm not here to debate the semantics of it, Sire. People are dying as we speak, and still others are being enslaved. Millions more are at risk, and *there's* an ill thing to allow into our past, if it's within our power to prevent it."

Bruno tries to pull away. "I'm in the past as well, lad. Leave me." Then, more regally: *"Leave me."*

"I won't," Radmer tells him. "Not yet—not until you've heard me out."

Resistance ceases; a kind of bitter calm settles over de Towaji. He is waking up, yes, and he doesn't like it. The look is clear in his eyes: a fear of being *needed* again, of bearing up under that burden after being free of it for so very long. Radmer understands, suddenly, that the old man's isolation and senility did not come upon him by accident.

His grip tightens, and his voice is almost cruel as he says, "Even if you were *dead* I would make you listen, Sire. Because I fancy you can help us, and I don't much care if it pleases you. Where else have we got to turn? Nowhere. And when I speak the name of our peril, I think you might even *want* to help."

"Unlikely. You have no idea how wearily I washed up on this shore, lad. Not the least beginning of an idea."

Tightly: "I fancy I do, Sire. I've been depended on a time or two myself. And we live on, don't we? Never too old to be bothered, to be mined for blood and sweat, to be dusted off and put to use again in one way or another. Not even a grave to rest in, not for the likes of us. But the alternative—to live on with no purpose at all—is appalling and obscene."

Finally, Bruno de Towaji matches Radmer's anger, and

meets his gaze. "You think so, do you? Smug bastard. Speak the name of your peril, then, and begone from my sight."

Radmer does as he's told, and has the grim pleasure of watching the old man's face light up with a terrible mix of wonder and righteous anger and, yes, even fear.

Now de Towaji is fully awake, blinking, looking Radmer up and down. "Lune, you say? The collapsiter grid is gone. Did I dream that? Between the stars we travel no more. How did you *get* here, lad? And . . . how will you return?"

Radmer feels the corners of his mouth begin to stir. Seeing Bruno again has brought back a lot of memories, a lot of old grief. With the clarity of hindsight, he does feel some understanding of his bonds to this man, but they were formed and broken long ago, in events so huge that from the inside they hadn't looked like anything at all. Joyrides and camp riots, the green virile fires of youth.

But this is too practical a question for a man who wants to be left alone. Radmer senses that a hurdle has been crossed, a new cascade of events set in motion. He will be taking this man, this intellect, this trove of living history back to Lune with him. And in that moment he dares, for the first time in months, to hope.

This is an island, with birds and a tree.
The island is a mountain in the middle of the sea.
One person lives here, but it isn't me.
I wouldn't like to live in the middle of the sea.[1]

—*"The Island"*

BASCAL EDWARD DE TOWAJI LUTUI, *age 4*

[1] In point of fact, Bascal Edward lived primarily on Tongatapu at this time. However, it is not clear that these statements are ironic, since the young prince, with many examples visible in the sea outside his bedroom window, may not have considered his home an "island" in the sense of the poem. A drawing accompanies the original text. —ed.

camp friendly

Conrad had never seen an angry mob before, much less been a part of one. Like an ocean wave it seemed to offer two alternatives: ride along or be smashed under. And the ride, truthfully, was fun. Since the raid on the boathouse, and with it the capture of canoe paddles, the counselors were actually *afraid* of them.

Of a bunch of sixteen- and seventeen-year-olds! Barely out of diapers, some might say, but even "Rock" Dengle was on the retreat, falling back along the side of the Arts and Crap Cabin and casting a worryingly broad shadow on its clay-and-log wall in the slanting light of a fake and miniature sun.

"What the hell you boys doing?" he demanded.

"Busting out," Bascal answered lightly. Cheers rewarded him, from Conrad as much as anyone. "Prince Bascal! All hail Prince Bascal, the Liberator!"

"This a summer camp," Rock pointed out. "Recreational. You here for fun, right?"

"Had enough," Bascal replied. Bascal Edward de Towaji Lutui, Crown Prince of the Queendom of Sol.

The badder boys—Steve Grush and that Ho kid whose last name was spelled "Ng" but sounded more like "Eh"— were flanking Rock on the left, flicking cigarette butts and hooting, and you'd better believe *that* got his attention.

"I gotta hurt someone?" Rock wanted to know. He looked capable of it—strong and pissed off, but in control. Taking care of "troubled" boys was his job.

"We got to hurt *you*?" Ho Ng shot back, and gave him a whack on the skull with the paddle. Tried to, anyway; Rock deflected it with a sweep of his arm. But since that left Steve an opening to jab him in the nuts, it didn't do much good. Rock doubled over with a froggy kind of sound, but stayed on his feet. Taking on *fifteen* troubled boys was a bit beyond his faculties.

There was a definite satisfaction in seeing a big guy humbled like that, but then it looked like Ho or Steve might hit him again, maybe harder this time, and that made Conrad afraid, finally, of the consequences. And ashamed to be a member of this particular mob, yeah, because Rock Dengle was definitely not a bad guy as jailers went. He kept the rules without treating you like a little kid, which was more than Conrad could say for most of the others.

But fortunately, Prince Bascal stepped forward, into what would have been the line of fire. "Steady, men. Nobody wants to get hurt over this. We just need the fax gate."

"Can't leave without your parent or guardian," Rock said, attempting to straighten. "Regulations, no exception."

"Except today," Bascal said, and Conrad had to marvel at the casual, agreeable tone of this kid's voice, trained from birth in the art of persuasion. It wasn't going to *convince* Rock or anything—not after he'd been whacked in the balls with a canoe paddle—but it did put a vaguely legitimate face on these proceedings. Made it sound like their side of it had some validity.

Which it did; this wasn't a jail, strictly speaking, but

neither were the boys free to leave, or to do as they pleased while "guests" of the camp. Which might be great if you were twelve or something, but sucked hugely when you were old enough to want female companionship and other assorted contraband. But there was no one to complain to, no cops or social workers to call. No one here at all who was not in the immediate employ of Camp Friendly, and therefore an extension of the parents who'd banished them here.

So here in the twenty-ninth decade of the Queendom of Sol, on a miniature planet orbiting in the middle depths of the Kuiper Belt, far from the sun and planets, young men were forced—literally forced—to reenact the squalors and deprivations of a less civilized era. So it made perfect sense for them to respond in an uncivilized way.

"You kids in a lot of trouble," Rock cautioned. From his tone he was worried *for* them as much as because of them. He wasn't going to offer any further resistance; he couldn't win if he tried.

On the horizon, twenty meters away, three more counselors materialized. One Conrad recognized but didn't know; he worked with the younger kids on the other side of the world. The other two were D'rector Jed: two faxed copies of the same individual, each holding the electric cattle prod he'd often warned about.

"What's going on here?" one of him demanded officiously. The other just stood there looking stern. It said a lot about D'rector Jed, Conrad thought, that he liked to go everywhere in twos. Did he enjoy his own company that much, or was he simply concerned that the universe outnumbered him?

"Cessation of involuntary confinement," Bascal called back without missing a beat. "This man illegally tried to detain us."

The distance was not too great to see a veil of caution

drop across D'rector Jed's features as he recognized
Bascal's voice. He seemed to have trouble actually picking Bascal out of the crowd, though. Before starting this,
the boys had smeared their faces with dirt and mussed up
their hair, mainly as a way of psyching themselves up but
also, Conrad now saw, to blur the lines of identity that
made them accountable.

"Your Highness," one of the Jeds said, and you could
see him still mentally backpedaling, rethinking his approach. "Prince" was a funny word, a funny concept; the
child who would someday rule.

If his parents weren't immortal.

How did one treat a child, educate or punish or even
reward a child, who might someday stand higher, enormously higher, than the educator himself? A tricky business indeed, and one that Bascal, in Conrad's limited
experience, twisted constantly—perhaps reflexively—to
his own advantage.

"Highness," the other Jed tried, "you and your friends
have been entrusted to my keeping. I will not hesitate—"

"You *will* hesitate," Bascal shouted back, taking a large
symbolic step in the Jeds' direction. "In fact, you'll stand
aside entirely, or my merry men here will beat you both
senseless. This is not a joke; they're escorting me for a
call to Child Welfare Services, with whom I have a total
legal right to consult."

This was news to Conrad; three minutes ago, the plan
had been, "Come on! Let's show these bastards!" But this
sounded better, more refined. Legitimate, almost.

"I've sounded the alarm," Jed told him. "It isn't just me
you'll have to deal with, it's multiple copies of every counselor on the planette. Plus the Secret Service and Royal
Constabulary."

"Yeah," Bascal agreed, "ten hours from now." That
was the speed-of-light round-trip time from here to the
Queendom proper.

"The fax gate itself is protected by your own Palace Guards. They won't let you leave."

"I don't need to," Bascal said. He glanced sidelong at Rock Dengle, who was still struggling valiantly to stand upright. "There's already been a regrettable incident here. We're prepared for there to be more if you interfere with us. My guards are watching us now, I assure you, and *your* safety will be of little concern to them."

"Cancel the alarm," Rock advised, throwing his voice behind Bascal's. "Let 'em in the office. We don't outnumber them much, and if they want to call Welfare, I say fine. Got nothing to hide. Parents need to know about this."

D'rector Jed didn't respond to that, but when the boys started moving, en masse, in the direction of the office, he didn't try to stop them. So they walked right past both of him and over the horizon, the little sun slipping behind the planette as they went. Small planets were like that; times of day were little places you could walk to. Here, the stars shone down like a vindication from God himself.

Superficially, the office looked like one more log cabin, especially in the dark. It was larger, though, and the light spilling out through the windows came from a proper wellstone ceiling, not a damned electric lightbulb. And once they got the door open and mobbed their way inside, the illusion was shattered completely. This could be anywhere in the Queendom—the bathroom had a *flush toilet*, for crying out loud. A further sign of the basic injustices here.

The fax was in a back room, a kind of entryway with the fax standing in place of an outside door. The camp had several other fax machines whose activation they could maybe have demanded, but this was the only one known to be on all the time, with a hardlink gate leading directly to the New Systemwide Collapsiter Grid, the Nescog, that could get their message—or even their material selves—out of here in substantially less than the blink of an eye.

Unfortunately, as promised, the gate was guarded by a pair of gleaming Palace Guard robots, their blank metal faces and sexless metal bodies both unreadable and immobile. They were here, no doubt, to keep unauthorized persons from entering Camp Friendly and harming the Queendom's only prince.

Although, Conrad mused, the fax software could probably do that all by itself—filter out any images not specifically authorized here. Were these guards redundant, a hedge against someone corrupting the system? Were they also parental spies, sent here to keep Bascal in line? Jed had certainly seemed to think so, though the prince's words implied otherwise.

As bodyguards they were certainly intimidating enough; Conrad had little doubt they could burst from this room and be anywhere on the planette within minutes. The boys stood well back, milling around in the outer room, a few of the bravest eyeing these monsters from the "safe" distance of three or four meters.

Bascal alone seemed unimpressed, striding in toward the fax and gesturing at the two robots. "You, you, come with me. We're evacuating—the planette is on fire. *Come on.*"

He stepped right up to the fax and said, "Nearest emergency center." The robots hesitated for a barely perceptible moment; then the first of them, with alarming fluidity and grace, turned and leaped through the gate, vanishing in a puff of quantum dislocation.

The second robot seemed to be waiting for Bascal, expecting to follow him through. But instead it fell twitching to the floor, when Bascal produced a tiny, toyish-looking gun of blue plastic and calmly made the robot's mirror-bright head disappear. There was no mess, and barely any sound. A teleport gun?

"Close the gate to incoming calls," Bascal said to the fax, then turned to his troops with a self-satisfied grin. "These parents of ours, they have nothing to pass on or share. Nothing to teach us except sit down, shut up, and live in their shadows forever. It's *their* Queendom, right? Always will be."

Grumbles of assent from the boys. They had immortal parents, too. They'd maybe given the issue some thought; there'd be no inheritance for any of them, no family legacy, no empty shoes to fill. Conrad's own father was the Cork County Paver, always and forever, leaving only the title of "paver's boy" for Conrad himself to hang an identity on.

And that sucked.

Anyway, you just had to admire the prince's *cool*. Like it was all a game, like he could walk anywhere, through fire and bullets and untamed black holes, without so much as a flinch. You wanted to stand behind him, you really did.

"Well," Bascal continued, "what say we tear the place up a little? A night on Earth, my treat. You break it; *I* buy it."

Conrad had always had a problem with impulse—it was pretty much why he'd been exiled here in the first place. So while he knew there'd be hell to pay eventually, he really did like the idea of busting things up. What seventeen-year-old didn't?

"Jesus Christ, Bascal," he said with conviction, "I'd follow you anywhere."

chapter three

domes of the popcorn moon

They bounced through a repeater just inside the orbit of Pluto and were funneled into a ring collapsiter segment—a conduit made of tiny black holes—where their signal could travel, for a while, much faster than the classical speed of light. Planets and planettes and planetoids whizzed by, unseen. There was no sensation associated with this; the boys' bodies and minds—perhaps their souls—were reduced to quantum wave packets for the journey. This was the Nescog, the New Systemwide Collapsiter Grid, brainchild of Bascal's father. To an outside observer, the journey from Camp Friendly in the middle Kuiper Belt, to Earth in the Inner System, could appear to take anywhere from eight to ten hours, depending on network congestion and the alignment of the various nodes and conduits. To the boys themselves, the journey felt—and for practical purposes *was*—instantaneous, no more significant or amazing than stepping through a curtain.

They could have specified a number of copies, and spilled out the other end en masse, an army of themselves. They could have specified a color, and come out with skin of bright blue or brighter pink. They could have specified an orientation, and come out facing backwards.

But they did none of these things, and stepped out as themselves. Nothing else had occurred to them on the spur of the moment, and anyway antics like that would only trip the filters and provoke inquiry.

On the curtain's other side was Athens, where it was sunrise and already hot. Another single step whisked them around to Calcutta, which was hotter and brighter, and drenched in monsoon rains. They ended up in Denver, where the sun had recently set on a summer-warm city, and the air was fresh and fine. They spilled out into Market Street Station, jabbering, punching one another, giggling. Freedom was theirs at last, and the news of their escape could not have traveled any faster than the boys themselves. It would be a while before anyone came looking.

"I have no guards," the prince said wonderingly. He turned and crushed Conrad in a hug, then did the same to a cringing Ho Ng. "I have *no guards!*"

He whirled, laughing, oblivious to the staring crowd.

A billboard of animated wellstone proudly announced this station as one of only five public fax depots in the downtown area. A little map showed their locations, scattered along a kidney-shaped district a couple of kilometers across, and the flanking text informed the boys that ownership and operation of private fax gates within the exclusion zone was sharply restricted. Depending on the boys' exact destination, their transportation options from here included bus (free), automotive taxi ($), horse-drawn ("hansom") cab ($$), and of course walking, which according to the sign was strongly encouraged in a commercial preservation zone of Denver's caliber.

"Ooh," one of the boys said, pretending to be impressed, and emphasizing the remark with the raised, limp hands of some supposed effete aristocracy. It was Yinebeb Fecre who did this, with an additional layer of irony he probably wasn't aware of: by the standards of

Camp Friendly, he *was* an effete aristocrat, the hyperactive child of two well-known television critics. Feck the Fairy.

"Shut up," Bascal told him mildly. "Denver's raw. It's good. You should be happy."

Conrad hadn't seen the place except on TV, but overall he was inclined to agree. Back in his parents' day, fax technology had hit urban areas like a saturation bombing campaign, rewriting their maps and landscapes overnight. Many cities became beehives of addressable spaces whose physical locations were all but irrelevant. Streets vanished; sidewalks vanished; neighborhoods vanished. In some cases the cities themselves vanished, or became hypothetical entities with outposts scattered all over the solar system. But Denver's urban planners had seen it coming, and had drawn this cordon around the heart of the city to preserve it from the tyrannies of convenience. Not just a Children's City, this, but an Urban Preservation District and member of the Living Museum Network. A place as classic and primal as the Fuck You Song, and twice as pretty.

The terminal itself was underground, a dimly lit urban space filled with columns and information kiosks and snack bars, and old-fashioned telephones that were probably just for show. Another billboard—this one illuminated for some reason with tiny red dots—announced periods of planned outage in the fax gates here, and periods of broadband connection to some specific destination for some specific window of time: HONOLULU 21:15–21:17 TODAY. There were ranks of embossed numbers along the ceiling, although what purpose they served was not apparent.

Some people carried luggage—an eccentricity in a world where fax machines could store any object in callable library routines and print copies on demand. There were other eccentricities apparent in the crowd:

people who looked older or younger than the "ageless" standard of Queendom beauty. People who were dressed funny, people who had funny hair. And children of various ages, of course—comprising nearly ten percent of this crowd of dozens. The mix was interesting and cosmopolitan and yeah, highly raw. Fresh, original. Whatever. But everyone in the crowd—even the children—seemed to greet the arrival of fifteen unescorted, dirty-faced adolescents as a sign of trouble. A mother snatched up the hand of her toddler and pulled him close. Others were less overt, but their suspicion was lightly veiled at best.

Welcome to Denver. Keep your hands where we can see them.

Conrad gave back some dirty looks, and even snapped his teeth at a woman he caught staring at him. Gods, it wasn't like people got away with crimes anymore; not when the whole Earth was one giant sensor. Even where events weren't explicitly recorded in a wellstone matrix, they left quantum traces in the rocks or something. Ghosts. With enough patience and computing power, almost any event could be reconstructed.

Ignoring the ill will around them, Bascal surveyed the chamber itself, and grinned. "I think we've arrived, men."

There was an escalator leading up to street level, and Ho Ng and Steve Grush, with hardly a glance at Bascal or any of the others, hopped onto it and went up. The prince, perhaps sensing a threat to his leadership, hopped onto the down escalator and called out, "Onward! Onward!"

It wasn't hard to run up against the descending staircase, although what effort it took was strangely infuriating, the laws of gravity doubly stacked against you. And the people riding down were of course not amused as the boys swarmed past; but nobody said anything or tripped anyone, so Bascal made it to the top only a few moments behind Ho and Steve. And right there beside him was

Conrad, the right-hand man, feeling important. Oh, he'd felt important a time or two already this summer, going to the same camp as the Prince of Sol. But this was different, this was nonaccidental. The two of them were *actual friends*.

"This is raw," he said to Bascal in a low, private tone, and the prince responded with a defiant fist, held where only Conrad could see it.

"Until somebody recognizes their *pilinisi*, me boyo. Then it gets complicated."

"Mmm." Conrad could only nod knowingly. "*Pilinisi*" was the Tongan word for "prince," and he knew—or imagined he knew—what that meant for Bascal's life. No shortage of women, for one thing, but no privacy either. Everyone figured they knew him, when in fact almost nobody really did. But then, this disheveled boy in camp shirt and boating culottes didn't much resemble the Bascal Edward you saw on TV.

Up at ground level, circular doorways irised open for them in the terminal building's glass outer wall. The air outside was perfect: summer-warm and sunset-cool, not a bit muggy. It smelled of food: garlic and fresh-baked bread, maybe kettle corn popping somewhere nearby. The sidewalks were concrete with inlays of what looked like real stone—you could tell by the rough texture of it, not at all like a wellstone emulation.

So here they were: Sixteenth and Market in the Mile High City, an almost mythical address. The center of raw. To the east a few blocks was Self Similar Street, where they were still recording the puppet show live every week. Somewhere to the south was the Cola Dome where the Broncos and Avalanche and Nuggets still played, where famous concerts were held and paintball battles waged. On the streets, as advertised, was actual vehicular traffic: white buses and yellow/black taxis, delivery trucks and horse-drawn carriages. Rather a lot of bicycles, too, piloted not by children but by serious-looking adults swathed in impact-resistant wellcloth. There were also a few pedicabs drawn by midgets, which struck Conrad as an odd touch indeed: where did you find midgets in an age of perfect health?

The sidewalks were crowded and vibrant, full of obstacles for the pedestrians to flow around in artful patterns. This was a city of posts and pedestals, columns and obelisks. A fountain burbled merrily. There were little trees everywhere—maples and poplars and even acacias, no more than four or five meters tall. But the towers looming all around, blocking the view of all behind them, were anything but miniature. It was only when Bascal led the boys around a corner onto Sixteenth Street that anything resembling mountains became visible, hulking dimly ahead in the sunset, shrouded by clouds, crowded from beneath by low buildings. But the mountains were shorter than Conrad would've expected, or else farther away. In the golden-red glow of the clouds it was hard to tell. But that was the direction Bascal led them: away from the towers, toward the sunset.

The boys made a rough passage through the city: hooting, snatching at leaves, kicking and leaping over benches, crowding people out of their way. There was no law against being surly, and oh boy did it feel good. Still, Conrad couldn't quite keep his eyes off the architecture. It was one of the few things he was good at and cared about: the history of building, and of the buildings themselves. Here, that history was written in the walls, layered like geological strata.

"Look at the sidewalk," he said to Bascal. And when that was ignored, he tried, "Look at that *wall*. Is it brick? It looks like brick."

"Whatever," Bascal replied, not mocking but barely looking, either. The question didn't interest him.

Conrad tried it on Yinebeb Fecre. "You study architecture, Feck?"

Feck raised his limp, sarcastic hands again. "Ooh, architecture!"

Okay, so maybe it wasn't a popular subject. Still, it seemed important—especially here. There were exactly two subjects Conrad hadn't failed in his last school year: Architecture and Matter Programming. These he pursued with an intensity that upset his teachers nearly as much as his apathy and surliness on the other subjects. Only History had inspired any enthusiasm at all, and only because this time it had included the Light Wars, which of course were the first intersection of architecture and matter programming.

If he hadn't spat in Mrs. Regland's chair and then called Mr. O'Mara a pigfucker for catching him, he might have learned even more. But what he did know fascinated him: the moment wellstone—programmable matter—had found its way into the old republics, the Light Wars had started. Without delay, without restraint. What anarchy: buildings greedily sucking in ambient energy, dumping waste heat, offending the eye with patterns of superreflector and superabsorber, with flashing lights and magnetic fields, with blasts of communication laser unfettered by any cable or conduit. It was much cheaper to rustle energy out of the environment than to buy it off the grid, so all concern for aesthetics had flown right out the window, overnight, along with concern for the comfort of passersby and even, to some extent, for their safety. You could have all the electricity you wanted, if you blackly drank in every photon that touched you. You could stay cool in the summertime, if your building was a perfect mirror focusing the heat back on its unfortunate neighbors. In fact, if you were clever and obnoxious enough you could do both at the same time: deepening every shadow, amplifying every pool of brightness for your own convenience.

This wasn't as crippling a blow to city life as the Fax Wars twenty years later, but the scars remained even after the Queendom's founding, when the Architectural Courtesy Edicts were rammed through. Here in Denver you could practically tell, just by looking, which decade each building had been constructed in. Here an ancient steel-framed structure of poured concrete, its wellstone a mere facade. There a building of pure wellstone, held up against gravity by the pressure of electrons in quantum dots. (This had struck Conrad as a dumb idea the first moment he'd heard of it—what if the power failed?—but truthfully he'd never heard of a case where one of these selfish buildings had collapsed or dissolved. There must be all sorts of safeguards.) The majority of the buildings were post-Queendom: diamond frames and floors, with wellstone sheathing and facing. But even these had been dressed down, made to resemble materials of more or less natural origin.

Denver, like most of the really great cities, had forcibly regressed itself to something resembling the end of the twenty-first century. A preponderance of stone and metal and silica glass. Lighted signs had to look a certain way: like neon or mercury vapor or electroluminescent bulk diode. As the sunset deepened and the streetlights came on one by one, he noted with satisfaction that they were simulated gas flame. Had there been gaslights in the twenty-first century? If not, there ought to have been!

As the boys made their way westward, a full moon slipped into view from behind one of the towers.

"Awooooo!" said a kid named Peter Kolb, pointing.

Bascal turned, looked, spread his arms. "Ah, now that is a moon. July, to be specific. The Buck Moon. And we, my friends, are the young bucks making our way in the world. Let all the people of the domes of the moon gaze down upon us in wonder. This is our night."

"Buck Moon? Says who?" someone asked.

"Says the *Naval Almanac*," Bascal answered.

Feck cleared his throat. "It's, uh, from the Algonquin."

Conrad turned. "Eh?"

"North American tribal society. Very old, but, you know, still in existence. Almost as big as the islands of Tonga, actually. Almost as many people."

Now everyone was looking at Feck, and even by gaslight you could see him blushing.

Bascal looked surprised. "Feck! You don't know things, do you? *Peter* knows things; he's the son of laureates. Conrad *thinks* he knows things, although he's a son of a bitch the last I heard. But you? Ah, wait a minute, I'm perceiving something: you have a connection to this tribe. Wait, don't tell me! You're, let's see . . ." He studied Feck's complexion and features for a moment. "You're one-eighth by blood."

"One-quarter," Feck said. "But it's not Algonquin, it's Chippewa. Their neighbors. For us, this is the Raspberry Moon."

"Ah! You're practically a native guide! I had no idea."

"I've never been to North America," Feck said. "Anyway, this area is Kiowa, or maybe Lakota. The Horse Moon."

"We'll have to horse around," Bascal answered merrily. "And give a big, fat raspberry to the good citizens of Denver. Any other moons we should know about tonight?"

Feck scratched his ear, uncomfortable with the attention. The crowds were lighter here; the boys were practically alone in their pool of lamplight. "Uh, the Corn Moon? Or maybe it's Popcorn Moon. Also Raptor, Thunder, and Blood."

"Wow. That's raw. I like it. We'll screech like eagles, leaving a wake of thunder and blood. And raspberry popcorn! Actually, that's quite silly. But anyway the town is ours, and I say we take a bite."

Ah, the Poet Prince. Conrad snorted to himself.

Ho and Steve, unimpressed by this dialogue, exchanged a look, then turned and started off toward the sunset again. And once again, Bascal seemed honor-bound to go after them, to assert himself. He got between them and propped his elbows up on each of their shoulders, looking side to side and grinning.

"You know," he said, "a preservation district like this one runs on what they call a 'service economy.' You walk around looking at objects on display, and if you like one, the shopkeepers will print out a copy for you, or have it faxed to your address. Or you can sit in a restaurant, and order yummy comestibles from a highly restricted menu. Sometimes the whole selection fits on a card, or a sign. There's a theme to it. See, what you're paying for is ambience—the way things look and smell and fit together."

"Uh-huh," Ho said uncomfortably. He obviously realized that he was expected to reply, to suggest something. But he was just too damned stupid.

Steve Grush ducked away from Bascal's elbow, and then Ho did as well, and both the badboys were stepping back, sizing up the prince in some kind of unspoken power struggle. They never had a chance; at a loss for words and deeds alike, Ho finally shrugged, and gestured for Bascal to lead the way.

"You probably know where you're going. Sire."

Sire! Conrad couldn't help wondering if this was a learnable trick, something Bascal had had drilled into him by tutors. He hadn't really *done* anything—it might be something coded in his genome, some sort of dominant pheromone signature that made others feel more submissive the closer he got. Was such a thing possible? If so, it stood to reason that Their Majesties would give their son every advantage in the world. But perhaps being prince was advantage enough; it wasn't like Ho could punch him out or anything, like anyone would stand for it if he did. Conrad felt a burst of pride and affection for this, his personal monarch, and it occurred to him that he would never *need* a trick like that, as long as he was standing right here at Bascal's elbow. That was all the leadership any of them were going to need. This was the whole point of a Queendom, right? The need to follow someone, to surrender—if only symbolically—that unpleasant sense of personal accountability. *Figureheads, right: they pretend to lead us, and we pretend to follow. How very well we pretend.*

Bascal dogged their course left a block, to pass through rows of buildings faced with what looked, yeah, like actual brick. (Although this was hard to believe. Couldn't it fall off and hurt somebody?)

"Where *are* we going?" Conrad asked, in a tone that was private, but also calculated to be overheard by the other boys. Look, look, I'm speaking privately with your prince!

"Somewhere," Bascal said. He certainly seemed to know, or maybe he was just going by instinct, but his course seemed unerring and sure, and the boys followed along willingly enough. They passed a building labeled in big metal letters: UNITED STATES POSTAL SERVICE TERMINAL ANNEX. How medieval. Did they still deliver "letters" and "packages" here, or was it just an old name for an old building?

Westward they went: toward the mountains, away from the buildings, away from the towers and the lights and the crowds. The downhill slope in this direction was unmistakable. You could still see the afterglow of sunset up ahead, but otherwise it looked gloomy. Empty. Forsaken. Maybe they were nearing the edge of the fax perimeter—that would make these places harder to get to, right? Less valuable, less desirable. "Bad neighborhood" was essentially just a theoretical term to Conrad, but like the Light Wars, it suddenly made a new kind of sense to him here. Maybe there was less wellstone in an area like this, less record of what went on. Was that what Bascal wanted?

He felt obscurely glad, all of a sudden, that this raw, real place was one of the Children's Cities, where parents came when they felt the urge to spawn, to raise their young among others of their increasingly rare kind. Immortality was another wave that had hit society hard, and here was the reef where waves like that were broken. Denver! Denver!

The crowds were almost entirely gone now, the buildings thinning out into empty, meadowy lots hemmed in by gray metal fences. This afforded a very clear view of the mountains, and Conrad saw that one of the buildings he'd thought was downtown was in fact much farther away, in the foothills. The Green Mountain Spire, of course, a tapering, five-kilometer spike he should have recognized immediately, if for no other reason than because the top half of it was still in sunlight, and glowing as if hot.

Vehicular traffic tapered away and died. They passed along a pedestrian sidewalk and under a couple of bridges, until the area began to feel almost like a wilderness. There might actually be wild animals here. Heck, there probably were: rabbits and squirrels, and maybe even their predators. Would those be foxes? Mountain lions? As the walkway dipped beneath the bridges, cement walls rose up and around it, mostly blank but with occasional attempts at ornamentation: inlaid tiles and bas-relief sculptures of deer and mountain goats and bears, of trout in a little river, and a scene of the mountains themselves, which were visible again as the walkway emerged. Moonlight was now the primary source of illumination.

Thank God for the superreflector glare of the Dome Towns up there, on the round-faced Popcorn Moon, or Conrad wasn't sure he could see at all.

The boys passed some benches where a pair of ragged men slept, and here was a genuine shock—there were hermits in the Queendom. He'd always known it, that there were crazies and addicts and social malcontents. These ailments could of course be stripped away by the morbidity filters in any fax machine, but only with the patient's consent. Mind control was severely frowned on, so inevitably you got some sludge at the bottom of the societal keg. But this was a hypothetical issue, not something that should be sprawling on a bench right in front of Conrad Mursk, stinking like rotten cheese.

Ho, racing out in front of Bascal once more, leaned over the benches and treated both men to a bloodcurdling shriek. They startled awake immediately, their eyes wide. They didn't make a single noise of their own, and the look on their faces was one of frank fear, even when they realized the scream was just some kid having fun. They expected, what, to be beaten? Murdered? Dragged forcibly through a fax gate until their drunken heads were clear? Now *there* was a bit of teenage thuggery you could probably get away with. But Ho just laughed, and then Bascal was laughing too, and the boys were on their way again.

And then, without any warning at all, they crested a low hill or ridge and found themselves at the edge of the fax perimeter. You didn't need a map to see it; there was just this big park: grassy meadows and big stone staircases, and again with the little trees. Wellstone paths snaked through it, glowing faintly and tastefully in the moonlight, and just beyond these stood a row of brightly lit buildings, lining a depression that must be the Platte River.

Indeed, as they drew closer there was an unmistakable

smell of "waterway" that Conrad had never realized he could sense. Interesting. That smell had once meant the difference between life and death for his primitive ancestors, so maybe it was coded in his genes. Probably was, yeah. *Too much tinkering,* he thought, *and we could lose these little details. Stop being animals and start being some other kind of thing. Self-designed, with all the foolishness that that implies. Evolution is at least impartial.* But Conrad was young, and thoughts like that were a fleeting snow that melted rather than sticking.

Bascal clapped him on the shoulder, dragging him forward. "Conrad my man, you stop to brood every time we round a corner. You're thinking too much, and it's getting to be a problem."

"I've got impulsiveness issues," Conrad answered with a laugh. "You should be glad I'm thinking at all."

That seemed to make Bascal angry. "Your parents are what, a hundred years old? Two hundred? Fucking *experts* on the subject of impulsiveness."

"Actually, it was my school—"

"Well, to hell with your school. I doubt you committed a single age-inappropriate act. This is exactly why there are cities like Denver, where they at least make concessions to our youthful vigor, where they at least acknowledge that we have our own needs. Parents ought to be forced to live here. It ought to be fucking *mandatory*."

A thought occurred: "Maybe *you* should be in charge of the Children's Cities, O Prince of Sol."

But Bascal just grunted derisively. "Bring that bill before the Senate, hmm? I'll be fifty before they're finished debating. And still a child in their eyes."

"But your parents—"

This time, it was Bascal's fist on his shoulder, slugging. "Will you shut up? Please? You are wrecking my mood. It's tiresome."

Ho Ng sidled up, showing fists of his own. "No pissing

off the prince, bloodfuck. I'm going to pound somebody, and it might be you."

"Steady," Bascal said, holding up a hand. "We have a common purpose here."

"What purpose?" Feck wanted to know. "We appear to be at the limits of the known universe."

"Why, revolution," Bascal answered casually, pointing at one of the buildings. "Starting right there."

chapter four

the wellwood deception

Revolution. Wow. Fuck. Was that a metaphor? Because tempting as the idea might seem, a gaggle of teenage refugees from summer camp couldn't do much against a whole Queendom, with its police and truant officers, its infinite supply of infinitely patient robots, and of course its billions of satisfied citizens in their tens of billions of instantiations. Even if the boys commandeered a fax machine and printed up an army of themselves, the Constabulary would simply shut down the entire area, round the boys up, and reconverge their many copies back into single individuals. The odds were so hopeless—and the threat of punishment so dire—that as far as Conrad knew nobody had ever even tried it.

"I thought we were just looking for girls," he said, to no one in particular. And that was who replied: no one.

As the buildings approached, it became clear that the river had a good bank and bad bank: one side facing the city and backing to the suburbs, while the other had a nice mountain view, but butted up against the bad neighborhood and so became bad by association. The most questionable of the buildings was an ancient two-story café whose shabby appearance was not an act, but the result of a natural wood facade that had stopped looking luxurious a few decades before Conrad was born. This, not surprisingly, was exactly where Bascal led them.

The café had a scattering of plastic tables and benches and chairs in front and behind, occupied by perhaps a dozen people of varying ages. None of them looked especially old, but then again who did? Conrad guessed a minimum age of around twelve—just old enough to be let out of the house—and a median in the low twenties, with the oldest men and women just edging into their Age of Deceit. Thirty or forty years old, when the fax filters stopped merely harassing the aging process, and began simply to arrest it. Lock it up, lose the key.

There wouldn't be many folks older than that, except maybe as part of the restaurant staff. This wasn't the kind of place you came to with your parents; it was the kind of place you came with your *friends*, to drink watered-down beer and coffee and feel independent. Not much draw for the older crowd.

You could of course stay in the Children's Cities as long as you liked—some people stayed on as teaching assistants or administrative assistants or whatever, and a few remained as passive consumers, either to make up for a childhood spent someplace less raw, or because they'd frozen somehow in the latter stages of larval development, unable to pupate, to grow wings and fly away. Calcutta, for example, was famous for its "Peter Pan" ghettos. But there were better places for people like that, where stronger intoxicants were available and everyone was above the age of consent. This place was what they called a "kiddie café"—no identification required for admittance. Whatever bona fide grownups you found here were probably up to no good. Which Conrad supposed was the whole point.

The name of the establishment appeared to be "1551," although maybe that was its street address, or possibly even the year it was built. Here, a flock of dirt-faced teenage boys was apparently considered less alarming than it was downtown. Only a few people looked up at their arrival, and any surprise they showed probably had more to do with dorky camp uniforms than anything else.

Bascal seemed to take this nonreaction personally; his easy stride broke into a trot, and he uttered a quiet, ulu-lating sort of war cry and made an overhand "follow me" gesture to the boys behind him. They were officially tak-ing this place by storm, and yeah, that did get a bit more of a reaction. A young man who'd been leaning against the doorway now shrank away from it, not caring to test his luck.

The place was a lot warmer inside than the cool breeze flowing down along the river. Poorly ventilated, Conrad thought, and with a wood face instead of a wellstone one, it couldn't pump the heat out electrically, either. Very rus-tic. Hell, it was almost like being back at the camp. The walls were an egalitarian mix of wood and plaster and brick, with wellstone surfaces only at the serving coun-ters, of which there were several. A few animated posters hung on the walls, but there was also a lot of static graffiti done up in plain ink, and the reason for this was quickly apparent: each table had a big feather pen stuck promi-nently into a built-in inkwell. You could even see a few kids in the act of scribbling out their pent-up wisdom.

"They must wash these walls every week," he said to Feck.

Feck just nodded vaguely, his eyes on everything but Conrad.

A sign said PLEASE SEAT YOURSELF, but there was also a staircase leading upward, and although the place was crowded with plastic tables and chairs and the people sit-ting at them, Bascal still had his momentum. A few zigs and zags through the crowd, a couple of bumped chairs, and he was on his way up, with Steve and Ho and Conrad right behind him, and all the other boys streaming after in a long line. People looked up at this, yeah. Looked annoyed, maybe a little worried.

The second floor was smaller, hotter, less crowded and less decorated. There was enough room for the boys to settle in at a corner clustered with round tables, but the doorway out to a balcony seemed much more inviting, and that was where they went. And if Bascal was looking for trouble, here was the perfect opportunity, because the balcony had seating for twenty or maybe twenty-five people, but was two-thirds full already, and the empty seats weren't in a block, but scattered all over.

Bascal Edward de Towaji Lutui was full of surprises, though; as the boys piled up behind him in the doorway, he could actually have cut a fairly menacing figure. But instead he just stood up straight, clapped his hands twice for attention, and called out, "Excuse me! I'm afraid you're all going to have to move inside. The balcony is reserved for a private party."

The quality of his voice was something Conrad really was going to have to study: self-assured, vaguely apologetic, and entirely official. There was no question that you were going to comply, and if for some reason you didn't, well, there'd be all sorts of hassle for everyone involved, and in the end you'd still be vacating your chair, thank you very much. It took barely thirty seconds to clear the crowd and settle in at all the good seats along the rail.

The last to leave was a girl of about nineteen, and Bascal, still stationed by the exit, grabbed her elbow as she passed. She was wrapped in a loose-fitting dress of glossy black fabric. Her hair and eyelids and irises had been done up in a matching shade, while her lips and fingernails matched her shoes with a seething red-black glow, like bits of iron sitting at the bottom of a campfire.

"You lovely thing," Bascal said, "can you answer me a question?"

"Get processed," she replied calmly, jerking her arm away. Then she paused, taking a good look at his face, and made a visible effort to hide her surprise. "Oh, whatever. What do you need?"

"Are you in a hurry?"

She chewed her glowing lip for a moment, then stopped. "I'm here with friends. We had a good table, which you just took, so yeah, I need to get inside and find something before they come back. We don't get many nights out together."

"Ah," Bascal said. "I won't keep you, then."

She half turned to go inside, then checked it and faced him. "Are you . . . ?"

It hung unspoken: are you the Prince of Sol? Bascal didn't answer. "Go on inside and get a seat for your friends. I'm sure that whatever . . . transaction is keeping them from you must be very important. But when you're settled, I hope you'll come and see me. Us. I have a question."

A brown-smocked waitress materialized, looking annoyed. "Did you just kick everyone off this balcony?" For some reason, she directed the question at Steve Grush.

"No," he replied, with his usual sullen brilliance.

"We'll have fifteen glasses of beer," Bascal said, jumping in. "And fifteen cups of coffee, plus some pitchers of ice water. To eat, we'll take some sort of chips and dip thing, and a big plate of cheese and veggies. Does it come with olives? I love olives."

The waitress had a wellstone sketchplate in her hand, but didn't write anything on it or speak to it. She was under thirty, or looked it, but her expression suggested she'd seen quite enough punk kids come swarming in here like they owned the place.

"Who's paying?" she wanted to know.

Bascal held up a thumb. "That would be me."

"Uh-huh." She presented him with the sketchplate, skeptically.

"Authorized up to twenty thousand," Bascal said to it, rolling his thumb across its surface in the accepted manner, rather than simply jamming it the way punk kids were supposed to. "Plus a hundred percent tip."

The slate chimed softly, acknowledging the transaction, and the young woman's features softened a little. Bascal's face and voice and thumbprint and DNA pattern all had to match against an account balance—he was good for the money. Still a punk kid, but apparently not a thief or mooch. That tip wasn't going to change her life or anything; all the necessities of life and most of its luxuries were free for the faxing, or at least had downloadable free knockoffs. And everything else had a free waiting list (except of course for freedom itself), so no matter how poor you were, you knew your turn would eventually come. Penthouse apartment, whatever, just live to be a million. But a tip was a nice gesture—traditional, polite—and a big tip was nicer still. He didn't have to do that.

"I'll see what we can do."

"Thanks so much," Bascal agreed.

The black-haired girl had slipped away during the exchange. Shrugging, Bascal sat down next to Conrad. But Conrad was worried and asked, "Can't they track you now? The police, your parents? Spending money is always the giveaway."

"Oh, probably. But the account has . . . certain security features that will slow down a search."

"Oh. That's good, I guess. Thinking ahead."

"Such is my function."

The very last rays of sunset were visible over the mountains, between gaps in the apartment buildings on the river's far bank. From what Conrad could see, the buildings themselves were in tasteful colors, not selling anything or trying to be anything in particular. These were the homes of ordinary Queendom citizens, with fax gates inside, possibly right there in the apartments themselves. Here ended the terrarium extravagance of the Children's City, and there began the staid suburbs of the Queendom proper.

The Green Mountain Spire was dark most of the way up now, the sunlight glinting redly off the top hundred meters or so, and inching upward with near-visible speed. The café balcony itself hung over a precipitous three-meter drop, with a small grassy bank beneath, and then the stony shallows of the Platte River, which wasn't nearly as majestic as Conrad would have imagined. It was maybe twenty meters across, and shallow enough to wade in. To the north and south there were little sets of rapids where men and women in glowing green kayaks paddled down and, incredibly, back up again.

Where the grass ended, the river's banks were lined with a random jumble of stones, and sticking up here and there were the concrete stubs of what probably used to be bridges. Conrad couldn't imagine why they'd never been removed, although they did lend an honest, unfinished sense to the area. Neither pristinely wild nor immaculately groomed, just here.

"From an aesthetic standpoint," Peter Kolb said self-importantly, "this place is fucking rich. The juxtaposition of elements is not as random as it looks."

Peter was big on aesthetics, which as far as Conrad could tell was a mathematical pursuit, having almost zero overlap with anything real, like architecture or matter programming, or even feng shui. The worst of it was, he couldn't tell if Peter was being agreeable or sarcastic, so he refrained from commenting. Everyone else was ignoring Peter anyway, so that was all right.

It only took a minute for the waitress to return, first with their drinks, and then again with platters of nacho chips, smothered in melted cheese and surrounded by battlements of carrot and celery, zucchini and olive.

"Here you go, hon," she said, dropping off the final tray in front of Bascal and Steve and Ho and Conrad. "If you need anything, my name is Bernice. Just rap on the wall, or the railing."

"My grandmother's name was Bernice," Bascal mused, when she was gone.

"Nice lady?" Ho Ng asked.

Bascal shrugged. "Never met her. She died, like, two hundred years ago, in Catalonia. Mayor of a city. Fucking historical figure."

"Jesus H. Bloodfuck," Ho cursed, in a show of solidarity. He was always saying things like that: "donkey fuckbrain vomit" and "diarrhea blood angel," and Conrad's personal favorite, "mother-Christing piece of dammit." Ho seemed to take some weird pleasure in mixing his cusswords up that way, or maybe it was a subtle organic defect in his neural wiring, that the fax filters dismissed as a mere character flaw.

In the Queendom of Sol, character flaws were considered your own damned responsibility. You had to identify them yourself and then formally authorize a medical doctor to repair them for you. Or better yet, you could treat it yourself through personal experience and growth. And either way, if there were side effects in your overall personality, well, those were your own problem as well.

But Ho was only sixteen, so really it was his parents who should be worrying about these things. And Conrad supposed they had, in their own special way: by sending the boy off to summer camp. Very therapeutic, oh yes. Nothing cut down on cusswords like having to shit in a goddamned outhouse.

A sour mood threatened briefly to come on, but the watery beer was really good somehow, and the nachos were even better, and anyway Bascal seemed determined that all his men should be cheerful tonight. Who could argue with that?

And then, before they'd even finished off their first glass, Bascal's black-haired girlfriend showed up again, pulling up a plastic chair and inserting herself between the prince and Conrad.

"Hi," she said, matter-of-factly. How much was unspoken in that one syllable! Hi, Prince. I know who you are, Prince, but I don't care. I'm here to check you out as one human being to another, Prince.

Which was fine, sure, except that it was Bascal she'd sat down with, not some ordinary puke two years younger than her. And she hadn't brought her friends, either. Probably hadn't even told them, for fear of having to share.

"Hi," Bascal said back, in imitation of her tone.

"Hello," Conrad added, with no particular inflection, figuring he might as well at least try.

The girl nodded, sparing him half a glance before focusing her attention on Bascal once again. She asked, with mock indifference, "You wanted something?"

Bascal leaned back and smiled. "Seeing you, my dear, I can think of a lot of things to want. But I doubt we have much time, so I'll get right to the point: I need access to a taboo fax machine. I'm carrying contraband. What's your name, by the way?"

Her eyes widened. "I'm Xmary. You need acc—"

"Eksmerry? Is that a nickname? Short for what, Christina Marie?"

"Xiomara Li Weng," she answered distractedly. "You want *what*, now?"

"A fax machine. A simple, ordinary fax machine that will copy *ta'e fakalao*. Forbidden objects and substances. My men are here are on a mission, for which they have certain material requirements. Clothes, for one thing," he said, pinching his Camp Friendly shirt for emphasis.

And truly, that was one of the camp's worst indignities: natural cloth. The shirts and culottes not only looked silly, they *would not change* their color or cut or permeability. They didn't regulate temperature or dissipate sweat. They didn't obey commands, or even hear them. They didn't *do* anything.

"And what else?" the girl demanded, clearly concerned that this was a setup, that she was the focus of some sort of royal joke or sting operation.

"Jewelry," Bascal said, with an inscrutable little smile.

"That's all?" Her eyes flicked downward, then settled on the only jewelry Bascal was wearing: the wellgold signet ring on the middle finger of his left hand.

"Pretty, eh?"

"It's not an ordinary ring."

Now there was an edge to Bascal's voice. "Of course it's not an ordinary ring. I'm the prince of the fucking solar system. What do I wear, gold? Tin? It's *information*, darling—quadrillions of terabytes in quantum storage. It wants out."

With a shiver of excitement and dread, Conrad realized that they weren't just playing at being bad here. They were *being* bad; they were going to be bad. Bascal was really pissed off about something. Hell, they all were. As fugitives from adult supervision, they had a fucking point to make.

This girl Xmary, hearing the tone of Bascal's voice, huffed once and then said, "I know some people. I can ask for you. It sounds pretty serious, though."

"It is."

Nobody said anything for a few seconds. Finally, the girl got up again. Before turning to go she asked, "Am I going to get in trouble?"

"Yes," Bascal replied. "We all are. The question is whether anything useful is accomplished beforehand."

"Great."

She disappeared. Doing as she was told, choosing to go along with Bascal and against her own better judgment.

"So what's in the ring?" Steve Grush asked.

"Garbage," Bascal said.

"Garbage?"

"Garbage. Reorganization of matter at the atomic level. Into garbage."

"You mean *programmable* matter, right?" Conrad asked, because otherwise that made no sense at all.

"Duh. Any wellstone surface. But that's everything, right?"

Well, sort of. There were still an awful lot of natural materials around, especially in Denver. But Conrad remained confused, because wellstone was fundamentally a form of silicon. Woven nanofiber, right? Quantum dots to confine electrons in atomlike structures. In raw form the stuff looked and felt like some heavy, impermeable, beetle-shiny plastic, but by sending the right signals through it you could fill it with artificial pseudoatoms of any type. Silicon and gold, silicon and sulfur, silicon and plaster of fucking Paris. Then there were the transuranic pseudoatoms, and the asymmetric ones, and the ones that incorporated exotic particles. You could alter wellstone's apparent composition in so many ways that even after three hundred years, a Queendom full of pseudochemists and hypercomputer search algorithms had barely cataloged even the fundamentals.

But pseudoatoms weren't real, and silicon was.

Bascal was looking smug. "It's Garbage Day in Denver, me boyos. If we each have one of these, and we spread out, we can make a lot of frigging garbage. We can even threaten infrastructure, which after all is the thing that separates us from the animals. If our demands aren't met, they will at least be remembered."

"Raw!" Steve said approvingly, and a number of the boys echoed him.

"Where did this software come from?" Conrad couldn't help asking.

"Wrote it myself. I've been saving it for a special occasion."

Conrad proceeded warily, not wanting to sound negative. "How does it work?"

"I archived a year's worth of patterns from the palace waste chutes, and fit them together with a tesselation-tiler. Any surface is mapped with the best possible fit in stored garbage, and the boundaries between garbage objects are heated and acoustically shocked to cut them away from the parent body. Slap it on a wall, and you get a pile of steaming garbage."

"Except that it wouldn't steam," Conrad said. "It wouldn't stink. It might look like shit, or half-eaten food, or whatever. Probably even feel like it. But pseudoatoms don't have a smell. They can't leak out into the air, like real atoms and molecules do."

"Oh," Bascal said, suddenly uncertain. It wasn't a look that fit his face.

"Still, that's pretty amazing that you thought of that. You've got power for the separated objects, right? They're photovoltaic enough to maintain their own memory and programming? And composition?"

"Um. I don't know."

"Oh," Conrad said. "Probably not, then. You'll just wind up with garbage-shaped chunks of nanofiber silicon. It's probably dangerous, too. I mean, there's more wellstone in a building than just the facade, right? You'd better be *real* careful what you touch with that thing, or you're going to hurt somebody."

"Who made you the voice of reason?" Ho Ng asked acidly.

"Um, nobody."

"Why don't you shut up, then? Pussy."

Conrad had no response to that. He'd already blurted out the thing that needed blurting. Getting any farther on Ho's bad side was not a smart idea, and he could see that Bascal was brooding, too, looking around with dark, embarrassed anger. That anger could, Conrad knew, be directed at him at any moment. He considered apologizing, but didn't see how that would help. Better just to shut up and pretend he wasn't here.

"Are we still doing this?" Steve Grush wanted to know.

"Yeah," Bascal said, waving a hand distractedly. "Let me think about it for a minute." Then he pinched his chin in a gesture so reminiscent of his father that for a moment Bascal might have been a younger image of the king himself. A little swarthier, perhaps. A bit more angular. Conrad felt a fresh burst of affection for this boy, this young man, this Poet Prince of all humanity.

"I have to visit the 'soir," Feck announced loudly, from the other end of the balcony. That was short for "pissoir," and told everyone exactly, biologically, what he'd be doing when he got there. If he'd said " 'toir," or "shittoir," that would convey a different intention. You always knew more about Feck than you wanted to. Still, it was funny— Feck *was* pretty funny sometimes—and suddenly there was a lot of laughter, and the conversation turned to other subjects.

"Sorry," Conrad said quietly, seeing his Bascal opening as Feck shuffled past. "It's still a pretty raw idea."

"Shut up," Bascal said vaguely, not looking at him.

Taking the hint, Conrad finished his beer, then just as quietly finished his coffee. Both were making him thirstier, but he resisted the urge to chase them with a glass of water. In a few minutes he was going to have to visit the 'soir himself. He supposed they all were. He toyed with his coffee mug instead, clinking it a few times on the glass tabletop. Turning it over a few times in his hands. Good, old-fashioned stoneware, courtesy of the Friendly Products Corporation, whose swirling green logo was glazed into the underside.

This didn't take any great scrutiny to discern; the same instantly recognizable design appeared on their Camp Friendly tee shirts, and on thousands of child-oriented products printed daily by the fax machines of the world. Seeing it here, however, was admittedly somewhat surprising. What was child-oriented about a coffee mug? He fantasized briefly that this whole café—perhaps this whole ghetto—was just one more Friendly Park, in a carefully supervised Friendly Park World.

Oh, God, he was getting "maudlin," as his Irish mother would say. It was exactly why she didn't allow him any alcohol, even weak and watered as this. If he drank any more, he'd become "rash," and *then* where would Queendom civilization be?

"Does anyone else want more beer?" he asked, looking around. But they were still ignoring him, which was probably good. He'd just order for himself, then, maybe even pay. Per the waitress' instructions, he leaned over and rapped on the deck's ratty old railing. It rang solidly under his knuckles, though, more like plastic or soft stone than wood. Because yeah, of course, it wasn't wood at all, just a clever wellstone facsimile. Why would knocking on a wooden rail summon a waitress?

Suddenly, his paranoid fantasy seemed less paranoid, less fantastic. If that rail wasn't full of microphones already, it easily could be on a moment's notice. If the Constabulary had tracked the boys here, for example, or if the café staff had decided something suspicious was going on. Hell, the building could even make that judgment itself; most of the symptoms of human intelligence could be duplicated with a wellstone hypercomputer the size of a fingernail. Conrad's own house was always scolding him, checking up on him, ratting him out to his parents....

The black-haired, fiery-lipped Xmary reappeared, inserting herself deftly between Conrad and Bascal once more. "I found someone who can help you, Bas. Several someones."

Bascal looked up at her, and the confidence was back in his eyes. "Excellent. Thank you. And will these someones require payment?"

"I didn't ask, but I also didn't tell them who you were. When they see your face, they'll want to help. They've snuck out of the house, right? Hoping something interesting will happen. And what's more interesting than you, on a mysterious errand? I'm sure you realize, you're kind of a symbol around here."

"The prince who won't be king? Lord of the oppressed? Spokeschild for the permanent children? I can't imagine." Bascal flourished comically with his arms, but couldn't quite keep the bitterness out of his voice. "Take me to your underground, then. We'll see what mischief this town can endure."

"You need more people?" she asked. "I can find more people. Easily."

"Bascal," Conrad warned, raising his voice above the general hubbub, "we should get out of here. This place isn't as run-down as it looks. This isn't wood; it's wellstone. It could be a—"

The prince arched an eyebrow, and not in amusement. "There's business at hand, Conrad. Connections to be made, a whole underground to be mobilized. One way or another, Garbage Day is a party I intend to throw."

Conrad became aware of some noise in the street, rising up like the soft *clickety-click* of a few dozen tap shoes. Like marching boots, approaching at a trot? Like the platinum feet of robots, dancing fluidly along the street?

"Bloodfuck!" Ho Ng called out, from his seat along the railing. "Constabulary coming. Lots of them."

"Ah," Bascal said, and his tone was of regret, not surprise. "All right, lads, hit the ground running. Scatter for me, and do as much damage as possible. Brew me up a genuine riot."

Conrad *was* surprised, and afraid, and maybe not entirely sorry they'd been caught. He looked Bascal in the eye, almost challengingly. "What are you going to do?"

"What do you *think*?" the prince snapped, then walked to the railing and punched it with his signet ring, producing a kind of porcelain *clink*. At the point of impact, there was a momentary sparkle of blue-white light, fading quickly to darkness. Nobody moved; nobody spoke. Conrad didn't so much as breathe. Half a second after impact, the change began: a sprouting and sprawling of shapes and colors. It shot along the balcony rail, down through its supports and onto the floor, onto the wall, up along the roof. The sound of it was like tearing paper, like crinkling foil. The building turned to garbage around them, and the narrow spaces between the garbage glowed, and sang, and cracked away.

Conrad watched Ho Ng drop right through the floor, just moments before the whole structure gave way, and suddenly they were *all* falling, in a storm of hand-sized wellstone fragments, like shiny black bugs. The sound of the building's collapse was remarkably low, more felt than heard. Weightless for so short a time that it barely registered, Conrad thudded onto the steep riverbank, his fall partly broken by the plasticky fragments raining around him. His momentum carried him downward, skidding, briefly glimpsing the lights of an upside-down suburb reflected in the blurry water. And then a load of crap fell on top of him, stunning, immobilizing, whooshing the air out of his lungs.

He lay there for a few seconds, taking stock, trying to

breathe, wondering if he was hurt or killed, if his parents would have to print a fresh copy of him from stored patterns. He'd died once before, in some kind of fence-climbing accident that had smashed his head when there were no other copies of him at large. Lost damn near the entire month, and never did find out what happened.

Finally, he had enough breath for a grunt of pain, and then a groan. Other groans rose up around him. And screams. And then suddenly the Constabulary was there, all around, men and women in bright blue, and faceless robots in naked, mirror-bright impervium. Hands were grabbing him, lifting, digging him out.

"Can you hear me?" a voice asked. "Are you hurt?"

Coughing, he struggled to stand. "I— Ow! My tail-bone. My back."

"Medic!" another voice called out. "Possible spinal! Recommend immediate faxation!" The hands on his body were gentle but very firm.

He looked around, trying to get his bearings. Trying, he realized, to recognize Bascal in the confusion of litter and bodies and flashing lights.

Then the first voice, someone behind Conrad, was speaking again. "Son, until we figure out exactly what happened here, I'm afraid you're under arrest."

"Yeah," Conrad said, slumping against the hands that gripped him. "I know it."

The spatial quantum foam today
was bubbling over fractally;
six extra miles to get to school
with gas on absolutest "E."
But still, the temp'ral *quantum foam*
was not too bad; despite the crunch
of virtual traffic popping in
and out, I stopped three times for lunch
and got to school before I left
and called back home to give the warning,
"Hey Bas, fill up the bloody tank;
it's yet another fractal morning!"[2]

—*"Commutative"*

BASCAL EDWARD DE TOWAJI LUTUI, *age* 9

---

[2] During a year in Catalonia, Bascal Edward is known to have ridden
several times to the Girona School of Mathematics and Literature on
an antique, alcohol-powered scooter. The extent of other vehicular
traffic at the time is not known. —ed.

chapter five

the battle in the throne room

Some sort of portable fax machine was set up right there at the crime scene, and the boys were processed through it. Conrad's injuries were healed almost as a by-product; the fax filters compared his body against his genome and the standard human template, concluded that the damage wasn't ornamental, and sent on a corrected pattern to the other end. That these operations were performed on a snarl of quantum entanglements, rather than on a person or even the image of a person, did not impress Conrad in the slightest. Indeed, he'd experienced the process many times before, and barely noticed it at all.

He ended up in a windowless interrogation room—or rather, an atomically perfect duplicate of him ended up there, while he himself had vanished. Died, if you like, although people rarely talked about it that way. He'd also been through this experience almost daily throughout his life, and thought no more about it than about the dead skin cells he was supposedly shedding every moment of every day.

At any rate, here he was, in this windowless room with a human being and a robot. The robot didn't speak—they rarely did, except in emergencies—but it also didn't move, which gave it a vague air of menace. Especially since it was positioned between Conrad and the exit.

The human being, seated across from him on the other side of a table, was named Leslie Jones. She told him gently and repeatedly that she was here to help him. He was not restrained in any way, and the interrogation room's door, not closed all the way, betrayed a sliver of light at the edge. But he'd seen enough to know that Leslie Jones wasn't a lawyer or a social worker, and seemed in fact to be some species of cop, so he played as dumb as he figured he could get away with. Lying to the authorities would be worse than useless—they'd spot it before the words were even out of his mouth—but they were also unlikely to respect his intelligence, nor to be surprised if he didn't display any.

"Why did you leave the camp?" Leslie asked him, for the second time.

He shrugged. "We weren't prisoners."

"You could have requested a pass. And an escort. And permission from your parents. Instead, we have a counselor assaulted and a Palace Guard vandalized."

"I didn't do any of that."

"But you were there when it happened."

Conrad didn't answer. They knew he was there. Between sensor records and skin cells and ghostly electromagnetic imprints, the Constabulary could probably trace just about every move he'd ever made.

Smiling, Leslie tried a different approach. "Conrad, you're not in trouble. Not very much trouble. No one was seriously hurt, and there's no evidence you did anything other than follow your friends and then witness a crime. We just want to find out what happened."

He shrugged again. "You already know."

"Well, yes. But I'd like to hear it from you." She was wearing a green sweater with buttons made from what looked like live dandelion heads. Her hair was coppery red, and very short. He supposed she was beautiful—he'd never met anyone who wasn't—but she spoke and moved like the women of his mother's generation. Two hundred years out of date; born into a mortal world, and then "saved" from it by the rise of the Queendom. He wondered if faxes of this same woman were interrogating all the other boys as well.

"You don't know anything," he told her, not in a nasty way but just factually. "I'm sorry, but I really can't explain it to you. There's not even anything to explain." Then he disappointed himself by adding, "I want my mother."

Leslie just nodded, with a sympathy that seemed annoyingly genuine. "Both your parents have been briefed on the situation, and have asked to send copies of themselves here. The request is under review. However, as I'm sure you can understand, the involvement of Prince Bascal is a complicating factor."

Again, Conrad had nothing to say that would actually help the situation, so he said nothing, and Leslie simply started her questioning again, from the top. They went around and around like that for nearly an hour. Finally, when Conrad was halfway nuts with the repetition, a disc of yellow light appeared on the tabletop, and a little speaker formed beside it and emitted a soft chime.

"Well," Leslie said, eyeing it, "we tried, anyway. You seem like a nice young man; you should try opening up a little."

"Oh yeah? Why?" Conrad couldn't help asking.

To her credit, she thought about that for a couple of seconds before replying, "Because childhood doesn't excuse rudeness, not at your age. Whatever problems you believe you're facing, communication is really the only way to tackle them. You'll understand this someday, when you and your friends are the ones in charge."

Conrad didn't even try to suppress his sneer. "What day is that, Leslie?"

She really looked at him then, rolling her tongue around behind a set of pursed lips. Finally, she said, "Look, we've all made adjustments. Nobody said life was perfect. But we do have forever to work it out, yes?" She rose to her feet then, and motioned for him to do the same. "Come on. As I feared, the case has been placed under palace jurisdiction. Back to the fax with you, I'm afraid."

For some reason, Conrad felt a shiver of fear. "Why? Where am I going?"

"To the palace. Didn't I just say that? Best behavior, Conrad; you're going to meet the king and queen."

The throne room of Their Majesties, Bruno de Towaji and Tamra-Tamatra Lutui, looked exactly like it did on TV. The same reed mats over wellstone floors, the same Catalan tapestries over wellstone walls, the same gilded wellstone scrollwork along the ceiling and floorboards and high, vaulted doorways. It was daytime here; the ceiling was clear at the moment, and light streamed down through it from a blue-white sky, much paler than the sky of Camp Friendly.

A pair of vaguely familiar women stood at ease, with the black hair and walnut skin of South Pacific ancestry, and the elaborate wraps and hair fans of Her Majesty's court. With prim nods and subtle gestures, the two of them gathered the boys out of a pair of fax machines, and lined them up two rows deep in front of the empty thrones.

Lucky for Conrad, he got to stand two spaces from Bascal, near the middle of the front row, not four meters from the raised dais on which the thrones themselves rested. Lucky, lucky. His heart was hammering wetly in his throat; his knees were knocking. He'd never been so nervous in his life, even the first time he'd spoken face-to-face with the Poet Prince. Conrad had been arrested once before, for throwing rocks at a cat, and had been called to the principal's office many times, and of course detained and grounded and singled by his parents on a regular basis. But this was a whole new realm of trouble, the prospect of an angry king and queen far more frightening than the bland, dutiful sympathy of any police or petty officials.

The Queendom's royalty were technically figureheads, without any official political or legal powers. But they were also beloved, and brilliant, and so absurdly wealthy that they could buy the planets outright if they chose to. So in the end it hardly mattered: in the spiritual hunger of the Restoration and the perils and tragedies of the Fall, these two had been chosen as humanity's penultimate leaders, second only to God. Whether or not Conrad liked or understood it, they could dictate his fate, and no one—not even his own mother and father—would challenge it.

Still, this mortal fear didn't keep him from noticing that the "boy" to his left in the row behind him was actually Xiomara Li Weng, from the café, and that the fifteen assembled children did not include Feck. In a way, this made sense: Feck had been in the 'soir when the building came down, and if he'd had the sense to get rid of his Camp Friendly shirt, then at first glance there'd be no reason for the Constabulary to connect him with the events on the balcony, or to distinguish him from the café's regular customers. Whereas a quantum reconstruction of the collapse would show Xmary standing right next to Bascal, on the balcony with the other Friendly campers.

But despite her short, dark hair and rail-thin figure, Xmary did not resemble Feck in the slightest. Conrad didn't even see how she could be mistaken for a boy, although she'd rubbed the makeup off and lost the low-toe shoes, and even somehow taken off the nail polish. And she'd turned her party dress into a pair of beige trousers and a white shirt—though not a Camp Friendly shirt or even a tee shirt. But then again Ho Ng was out of uniform too, having somehow traded his tee for a shiny gray pullover and quilted vest, although he still had the pants: beige culottes that completely destroyed his efforts to look raw.

Even so, the error was alarmingly stupid. Had no one checked the biometrics or the DNA, or even peeked under her shirt? Had the ire of king and queen so disrupted police routines that even the Constabulary could somehow arrest the wrong person? Hand her over in a moment of confusion? It was a chilling thought, and a reminder of why the Old Moderns had murdered off their royal families in the first place, leaving only the Princess of Tonga and the swashbuckling Declarant-Philander of Spanish Girona to lead them into the future.

One of the Tongan ladies, gliding back and forth along the front row like a dolled-up drill sergeant, paused suddenly in front of Bascal. Placed a finger under his chin and lifted slightly, commanding his attention. Conrad couldn't make out what she murmured to him, but he did hear the prince's incongruous reply: "Lemonade. Please."

Then a chill settled over the room. To the right of the dais, a figure had appeared in the doorway. She had the same walnut skin and raven hair as her courtiers, but her wrap and drapes and hair fans were of purple, streaked and patterned with Polynesian tapa-styled highlights of glowing white. She was flanked on either side by ornate Palace Guards of gold and platinum, and news cameras buzzed and flickered in the air behind her like fireflies. She wore a diamond crown and was using the Scepter of Earth as a walking stick, and somehow she brought the whole thing off as casually as any jogging suit or camp uniform. No friend or relative ever had a face so familiar, so instantly readable.

The queen was furious.

She was also controlling it tightly, which made it even scarier somehow, and it was all Conrad could do to keep from flinching or even cowering as her gaze swept across him. In theory, she could order his head chopped off and his backups erased, and it would probably happen.

But Tamra-Tamatra Lutui, the Queen of Sol, had eyes only for Bascal as she ascended the dais and settled comfortably into her gilded wicker throne. Her robot guards, armed with tall, ornate, flimsy-looking axes, assumed positions on either side of the dais. The news cameras drifted out into the room, documenting the scene from all the most dramatic angles. Conrad wondered if he was on television, or would be later, in some carefully edited scene. Maybe these were simply the palace's own archival cameras, storing holie video into a library somewhere.

"All right," the queen said. "Let's hear it." There was no question whom she was addressing.

"*Malo e lelei*, Mother," Bascal replied amiably. "I've missed you."

"*Tali fiefia*. And I you," she said, with apparent sincerity. "But you're back a little early. And in trouble again. And this time, you've brought friends."

"Yes, Mother."

It was hard not to side with her. People *always* sided with her, in any dispute. She was just too beautiful and too funny and too . . . Correct? The cynics might accuse her of manipulating public opinion, but the truth was she didn't need to, and had nothing to gain by trying. She simply had a knack for taking the right side of every issue. Not the simplistic quick-fix side, but the actual best answer. And she then explained it so well, so quickly, with such effortless and devastating wit!

But not today, apparently. Today, she raised her eyebrows, tapped a foot, and finally spoke in tight, parental tones. "Bascal, don't try my patience. Please. You know I love you, but what you don't seem to understand is that I *will* make an example of you."

"On the contrary," the prince said. "I'm counting on that." His voice was still friendly, but his at-attention pose struck Conrad as both a rebuke and a mockery of his mother's authority.

Tamra shook her head a little, and sighed. "You think you're so clever, Bas. This isn't a chess game, where it helps to look three or four moves ahead. It's more like the tide, which comes in when the moon drags it in, regardless of what anyone thinks or says. Or wants."

"Then I'll plant a neuble on the beach," Bascal answered smoothly.

This was metaphor, Conrad realized at once. A neuble was a billion tons of liquid neutronium in a two-centimeter diamond shell, and would drop through beach sand or even solid rock like a cannonball through wet tissue paper. But it would affect the tide, you bet.

"Enough," Tamra said coldly. "This isn't a debate. You've injured nearly a hundred people, and destroyed a building. Someone could easily have been killed, in which case you'd be going to prison."

"I *have* been in prison," Bascal answered, finally betraying his anger.

"No," she said. "You haven't. You've been at summer camp."

"It's winter here, Mother."

"And summer in Europe, yes. When I was a girl, most of the world lived in conditions much worse than your Camp Friendly, and never thought twice. If you can't see the difference, then perhaps you should spend some community service time in the actual punitary system."

"Fine," Bascal snapped. "None of my tutors have been criminals yet. It's a real gap in my education."

The queen slammed the metal butt of her scepter down on the tiles of the dais with a sound like a heavy door slamming shut. "For pity's sake, young man. Must you battle us on every front? At every step? Do you despise us because we're your parents? Because we're the First Family? Because we're older? You've made your little statement, all right, but you know very well it turns people away from your cause, not toward it. I miss your poetry, Bascal, I really do. But I suspect that's the very reason you stopped writing it."

Bascal's stance never changed. "The rainy seasons here used to inspire me. I truly loved them. But then you sent me alone to Girona. Tending *sheep*. And then it was coconuts on Niuafo'ou, and finally peach pies and onions in the outer solar system. And you wonder why I'm angry?"

"You were angry before you left," the queen said. "So eager for independence, and yet so unwilling to accept it."

"Independence?" Bascal said darkly. "At Camp Friendly? Surely you're joking. Rebellion turns *adults* away from my cause, Mother. The children understand exactly."

With a rustle of fabrics, the queen stood up, raising a hand that might have pointed, or gestured angrily, or balled into a fist. But instead, she dropped it and turned away. "I see the day when you and I can speak cordially is gone. Have it your way, then."

She stepped off the dais, on the opposite side from where she'd mounted, and strode briskly to the other arched doorway, disappearing around a corner of wellstone-emulated plaster. Conrad heard a knock, and the mock creak of a mock door opening. Then hushed voices that reminded him of his own parents, when they closed themselves in their bedroom for an argument.

It was weird, to see the Queen of All Things acting just exactly like somebody's mom. Conrad couldn't help feeling sorry for her, not only as an undermined authority figure but as a flesh-and-blood woman who loved and missed her son, and had been hurt by him once too often. He could understand that, you bet. Part of him *wanted* her to demolish Bascal's arguments, to point out their foolishness, to poke wise and gentle fun at the very idea. Not that Conrad's own interests would be served by that, but it's what he expected.

What did it mean, that she couldn't muster her queenliness? Could it be that she was simply in the wrong, and had no leg to stand on?

Conrad spared a glance at Bascal, who was looking evilly smug, having gotten the better of the worlds' most important person. He also peeked back at Xmary, who was standing there with her arms behind her back, trying to be as invisible as her clothes and her girl-ness would allow.

The guard robots had disappeared with the queen, and one of the Tongan courtiers had vanished at some point as well, leaving only the other one to watch over the boys. She was staring after the queen, and presently stepped into the hallway behind her, stopping at the corner.

Conrad, deciding to risk it, turned and spoke to Xmary in quick whispers. "What are you doing here?"

"Be quiet," she whispered back, not looking at him.

"But why—"

"Be *quiet*," she said, then met his eyes for a moment and added, even more softly, "We're shaking things up. I'm here because someone else isn't—the opportunity presented itself, and we can both take advantage. Now be quiet about it."

Was that what she thought? Did she have visions of Feck the Fairy, brave confidant of the prince, scrabbling around the underside of Denver, quietly fomenting revolution? Conrad nearly laughed out loud at the idea, and even more nearly giggled. He settled for a smirk she would probably misinterpret. He tried to get it off his face, but the effort only made their situation seem that much funnier. Most likely, even if Feck didn't get caught he would turn himself in to his parents before the sun had even risen.

Conrad was about to say something about it to Peter Kolb, standing between himself and the prince. Crack a joke, something, but the Tongan lady had turned back toward them again, and was making little "come here" motions with her hands. "Boys, come. The king will see you in his study."

The two neat lines broke up into a kind of V formation as Bascal strode toward her, with Conrad and the rest of the boys trailing uncertainly behind. Meeting the king was less scary somehow, and the prospect of actually standing in his study was strange indeed, because Bruno de Towaji—once a declarant-philander, a genius and royal consort and knight of the realm—was the inventor of everything from collapsium to the blitterstaff, from the fax transport grid to the pub game of Shuffle Acrostics. He'd also saved the sun from collapse or something during the Fall, hundreds of years before Conrad was born.

Bascal led them into the hallway, pausing for half a step to thank the courtier, whom he called "Tusité." The office door was just a slab of wellstone, folded out from the faux-solid material of the wall, but it was made to look like an ancient thing of wood and iron, more romantic than spooky.

The room itself was unadorned, and cluttered with mysterious objects and diagrams. The king was an inventor still, deeply and constantly concerned with the Queendom's technological underpinnings. Unfortunately, his study was rather small inside, and as the boys (and girl) shuffled in behind him, Conrad found himself squeezed up against Bascal, and against the room's only chair, which held a hairy, rotund, vaguely unkempt figure. It took a second or two for the figure to register in Conrad's addled brain as His Majesty, the King of Sol, unprepared for audience.

The king held a stylus in each hand, and seemed absorbed in the moving images his desk was projecting. With visible effort, he looked up into Conrad's face.

"Er, hello," he said, scratching at his beard with one of the styluses, then dropping it on the desktop and holding out a hand. "I'm Bruno."

Feeling distinctly weird about it, Conrad took the hand and shook it. "Conrad Mursk, sir."

The king nodded and withdrew his hand. "Ah. Well. It's 'Sire,' actually. One must observe the proper forms. It's the only real purpose the office of king serves in a Queendom, and it *is* a real purpose. Kindly keep it in mind."

"Um, sorry. Sire." Conrad blanched inwardly, and probably outwardly. He wished there were some way for him to step back, without toppling his fellow campers like shuffleboard pins. He also wished he could shut up, but that impulse thing was going strong, and words were rising out of him like gas bubbles. "What is that you're working on? A planette?"

The diagrams before the king showed various cross-sections of some layered, spherical object many hundreds of kilometers across.

Bruno's gaze flicked from Conrad to the desktop and back again. He seemed to study Conrad's expression. "It's the moon, lad. Luna. The Earth's moon."

"Oh. I thought Earth's moon was bigger than that."

Again, that studying look. The king's head was nodding slowly. "So it is, lad. And what do you think would happen if we squeezed it?"

"Um, it would get smaller? Sire?"

"Smaller, indeed. Bringing its surface closer to its center. With what effect on its gravity?"

Conrad racked his brain. "Um, um, to make it smaller?"

"Smaller?" the king seemed astounded. "We bring a planet's outside closer to its inside, and the surface gravity is *smaller*? I shall have to think about that. An interesting theory indeed! It puts rather a kink in my terraforming and settlement plans."

Fortunately, Bascal came to the rescue, cutting in with a "Hello, Father. I've missed you at camp."

King Bruno turned his head a bit and noticed his son, and seemed to ponder his words for a couple of seconds. "Hmm. Yes, well we've missed you as well. But that's hardly the point here, is it? You've misbehaved, and will be punished for it."

"Yes, Father," Bascal agreed, his voice maybe a bit too chummy.

Bruno frowned at that, and tried for a moment to rise from his chair, before looking around and realizing that the room was packed, that Conrad and Bascal weren't smooshed up against him out of pure admiration. He scanned the assembled faces, looking almost puzzled. Finally, he directed his attention at Bascal and spoke again. "Your mother and I would like to know *why*. You understand this? We've invested a great deal of time and love and energy in a creature which has become highly resentful. An explanation would help."

Bascal remained polite this time. "You've heard the explanation, Father. I've been shouting it from the rooftops for years. It's the seriousness of it that always escapes you."

Bruno's frown deepened. "Seriousness? My boy, I've lived a long life, and these are the least serious times I've seen. War is a memory, crime is in sharp decline, and there've been remarkably few disasters—natural or otherwise—to threaten lives and infrastructure. You've never seen a time of strife, lad. You don't know what it's like."

"No, you just refuse to see it. The strife is all around us."

"Pish," Bruno said, waving a hand. "You kids. You think

teenage angst is a new invention? What you need is a squozen moon." Then he paused, and added, "It's awfully small in here. Perhaps the dining room would be better. Have you boys eaten?"

"We have," Bascal agreed, although it was just nachos and beer. Truthfully, Conrad didn't think another bite or two would be unwelcome.

"Maybe a snack," he said stupidly, just as he might to any other friend's father. Then more contritely added, "Sire."

"Snack," Bruno said, pinching his chin and musing, as if this were some bold new theorem he was hearing for the first time. "Hmm."

Five minutes later, the boys were arranged around a wellwood dining table, with Bruno at one end and Queen Tamra at the other, and Bascal squarely between them on the long side. The table would have been huge with just the three of them, but with fourteen boys and a girl it seemed cozy enough. Everyone was solemnly drinking lemonade from delicate-looking crystal goblets, and nibbling on tiny peanut-butter-and-vanilla sandwiches, and gazing out the picture window at the white sand and coconut palms, the ocean surf throwing itself against the beach, which sprawled for a hundred meters along a gentle, gently groomed slope.

It looked sultry-hot out there, but this dining room was cool in both the literal and metaphoric senses. Her Majesty was less icy than before, but still reserved, impatient and unhappy with her wayward son. She did spare some attention for the other boys, and actually spoke with the ones closest to her—Steve Grush and Jamil Gazzaniga.

"Such a pleasant day. Have you been to the islands before, boys?"

"The Tongan islands? No, ma'am," Steve said, as politely as you please. It seemed strange to Conrad, that a bully as transparent and tedious and predictable as Steve should be sitting right next to the queen, essentially ignored by her bodyguards. Even stranger that he should look good doing it. It seemed like at any moment he might leap from his chair, grab her by the head, and start delivering noogies. But here was how the worlds really worked: act like a complete asshole and you could lunch with the queen. Jamil, for his part, looked pale and sweaty and terrified, and could only manage to grunt a reply.

"Well, do enjoy them while you can," Queen Tamra said, glancing briefly at the ocean, and her voice was finally tinged with some amusement. The boys were her captives in every sense of the word.

Xmary also looked terrified, probably because she was seated only two places away from Bruno, and could be caught out at any moment. But the king wore a distracted, lost-in-thought kind of look, and like the queen he was mostly interested in Bascal anyway.

"So," he said to the prince, tearing himself out of some internal reverie. "You were explaining these trying times to me. Perhaps the vanilla has sharpened your righteous fury. Would you care to continue?"

And yes, Bascal did look angry when he answered, "This is precisely my point." He gestured around the room, at the table, at the tiny sandwich in his hand. "You connive a scene here to make me look like a little kid. In front of my peers, no less."

Bruno reflected on that, then nodded across the table to his wife. "Dear, is it childish to eat a sandwich?"

"I eat them every day," she answered.

"Really, every day. I didn't know that." He popped one of them into his own mouth and chewed it thoughtfully.

"Your father," the queen added, glaring mildly at Bascal, "does not connive. The very idea makes me laugh.

Have you two met? Shall I introduce you? Bascal, Bruno. Bruno, Bascal. This is good lemonade, by the way."

"The cooks have been playing with the pattern," Bruno said. "I'll let them know you like it."

"Do, please."

But Bascal wasn't finished. He glared back at his mother and said, "You know perfectly well what I mean." Then, to the king: "You were already at university by my age, learning physics. Emancipated. Adult."

And Conrad could see how it was in this house: emotional appeals in one direction and logical ones in the other, with human servants as well as robots and household intelligences to serve as neutrals. But really they were all together, a unified front against which Bascal was busily throwing himself.

"Orphaned, lad," the king said sadly. "Living on earthquake charity. People died back then, and not on any convenient schedule. I *wasn't* an adult; I'd much rather have been learning archery and canoeing."

"Mother was queen at fifteen."

"Also orphaned. And thrust into power without warning, by people who did not have her best interest in mind. It's nothing to envy, Bascal. Here you've returned from your adventures to the arms of a loving family. Tamra and I never had that option."

"A side issue at best, Father. Don't try to sidetrack me and then walk away feeling you've won the argument."

The queen sighed. "Can we stop this posturing, please? If you want to make a statement, Bascal, try speaking it. The power to change society sits right here in front of you."

He nodded. "Yes, but not the will. You both understand my point well enough, and even acknowledge its truth. But you see it from a past perspective, and so regard it as a minor issue. Which it isn't."

Bruno, gesturing with a crust of bread, opined, "By its

nature—its naïveté—youth challenges old assumptions. As you say, we agree on the parameters of the issue but not on their relative weighting. You're a bright lad, and you have a point. However, there are other savants who draw different conclusions from the data, hmm? Can't experience provide some context for these judgments? Can't societies evolve at their own pace? The very fact that you sit here, disagreeing with us, shows off one of the engines of change."

"Debate," Bascal groaned. "Certainly, you'd like to keep it neatly Socratic, for centuries if possible. To quench the fires through simple exhaustion. But change is generational, Father; it occurs in painful spasms. A mutant is born into environmental chaos, and thrives amid the broken bodies of its ancestors. That's your story, right? That's mother's. But the cycles of renewal which birthed your Queendom are suffocating beneath it. There's no changing of the guard, no retirement of old ideas. Every error gets entrenched, until a shock to the system is *necessary* to effect any change at all."

"An interesting accusation," Bruno mused, thinking it over.

But the queen merely chuckled. "Ah, the praise of death. It began the moment our terrors were shelved. But it's always the death of others, never ourselves, that we look to for renewal. The early martyrs drew a lot of admiration—deservedly so—but where are their arguments now? Their clever rebuttals? Their example for others to emulate? Swallowed up by the silent earth. You know how many suicides last year cited 'future generations' as a reason for leaving? Zero."

Zero? Ouch. Shit. This confirmed Conrad's worst suspicion: that his age bracket wasn't so much oppressed as invisible. To neglect a thing in the criminal sense, you had to know it was there!

"It's not that we don't sympathize," Bruno told his son

gently. "Your body and mind are screaming for the respect they're due, by the old organic schedule. You should be a hunter, a warrior, a *man*. But this problem isn't new, either. Imagine the plight of the Old Moderns, leaving graduate school in their thirties with dim prospects for advancement, and the first signs of death already creeping into their bodies."

"But what's to be done?" Bascal asked, putting his elbows down and leaning forward across his plate. Looking friendlier and more engaged. "The Moderns responded by conquering death, which helped not at all. Now the problem simply lasts forever."

"Long, perhaps," Tamra answered. "Not forever."

"Long enough to crush all hope," the prince said firmly. "And I ask again: what is your solution?"

Bruno had finished the last of his sandwiches and was toying with a little fork. "If you like, Son, I can promise you the moon. Literally. Come back to my study and I'll show you the plans."

"A bribe?" the prince said disdainfully. "Give me *some* credit, Father. It's all of posterity that concerns me."

"Well, crushing the moon would be a huge project even by Queendom standards. The combined effort of thousands, perhaps millions, of people. And later a home for even more."

"Ah. And then what? Most of your subjects have yet to be born. What happens when forty billion people become eighty billion? A hundred billion? What circuses will you devise for *their* amusement? Your offer is tempting but misguided. The Queendom's monopoly admits no competition, and therefore offers no escape."

"There'll always be other projects," said a visibly irked king. "If you don't like mine, go devise your own. You're neglecting the real irony here: that your mother and I were drafted for these roles, to put a human face on the consensual hallucination of government. You were simply born. Understand, Bascal, the Queendom's real power isn't here in the palace at all, but in the hearts of her people. If you can't make your case there, then you"—he scanned the faces around the table—"and those you speak for, should find some other mountain to climb."

And here Conrad felt a flicker of sympathy for Bruno, who really was trying to address this problem, though he didn't quite believe in it. And in the addressing, he'd dreamed up an enterprise—a good one—for his son to inherit. You had to give him points for that much, even if everything else was wrong.

"Someday," Tamra said, "you'll have children of your own, impatient for *you* to step aside, and this debate will come back to haunt you. Your whining would carry more weight if you simply delayed it a hundred years. Your internal clock runs fast. This much is in the wiring; we've considered amending the genome to correct it, although a great deal more study is needed before we dare unleash a solution. In the meantime, young man, you really are going to live forever. A bit of old-fashioned patience would improve your character enormously, and bring you closer to the day when you *are* fit to rule."

"Easy for you to say, Mother! If I lack character, then surely, as a corollary, I lack the patience to seek it. And whose fault would that be?"

"Fair enough," the queen agreed, in her only concession of the day. "Your concerns—representative of a small but pivotal demographic—are noted. We shall ponder them further while you finish your term at camp."

"We're going back, then," Bascal said. "To the dumping ground."

"Don't be melodramatic," she chided. "You may learn to appreciate the comforts of our age. Of civil discourse, perhaps even of dining with your parents. If not, then it may be that your camp isn't rugged enough. Shall we arrange some bad weather for you?" She touched a napkin to her lips and stood up. "I have meetings, I'm afraid."

"Send a copy," Bascal snapped.

"I have," the queen replied evenly. "Several. But the day is fluid, and things keep coming up. I'll spare you the good-bye kiss." She looked around the table. "A pleasure meeting you, children. Your companionship is appreciated. In the future, though, do kindly stay out of trouble. If we have to do this again, I'll be most disappointed. His Majesty will now escort you to the dumping ground. Dear?"

She nodded to her husband, and then with a swishing and rustling of fabrics, she was gone. Conrad felt bemused, and yes, somewhat torn. She was so easy to love. It was part of why she'd been elected—or drafted—in the first place, and the effect was even more pronounced in person than it was on TV. But she *was* belittling her son's grievances, and with them an entire—and much-aggrieved—generation.

"We won't cooperate," Bascal said to his father. "It wouldn't be right."

"No?" the king replied, thinking about it. "We've pulled all the humans off the planette, and replaced them with Palace Guards. From this point on, your cooperation and approval are rather moot. You're only seventeen, lad."

"Yes. And someday I'll be 'only a hundred,' and then 'only a thousand.' Why is it—*how* is it—that adults forget so quickly what it means to be powerless? When exactly does your attitude fossilize? Mine is still living, still breathing and growing, despite all attempts to petrify it. I'll *always* be younger than you, Father. My approval will always be moot."

Patiently: "By the time you're a thousand, the difference in our ages will be comparatively small, and you'll have no excuses left. What a sad day *that* will be. No one is asking you to grow up at this moment, lads. No one is forcing you to take on responsibility before you're ready. Relish that, hmm? You're going to live forever, and once you've left childhood behind there's no reclaiming it. You have my word on that."

He mused for a further moment, and said, "You know, that camp of yours is gorgeous, probably the finest plan-ette ever built. Did you know there are seven thousand tunable environment variables? Ultimately, the project funding came from my own pocket, so I've kept an eye on things. When I was your age I would have loved . . . would have . . ." His voice trailed away wistfully. Then his gaze jumped up suddenly, and settled on Xmary. "Egad, child, are you a girl?"

"No," she replied, sounding indignant. Sounding just exactly like an indignant nineteen-year-old girl.

"Hmm," the king said, studying her for a moment. "All right. No offense meant. Your friends will tease you for it, but the error is mine. Shall we go, then?"

Bascal held his arms out, roadblock style, and looked around warningly. *Nobody move.*

Seeing this, Bruno nodded. "Hmm. Yes. Well, if you won't cooperate, you won't cooperate. I was young once; I remember how it was. We'll have the guards drag you kicking and screaming through the fax, all right? We'll all preserve our honor that way."

Then he looked right at Conrad and winked—a con-spiratorial gesture of such portentous friendliness and condescension that the lad would, in some small way, never be the same again.

camp discontent

"We've got to get off this egg," Bascal said, for at least the hundredth time that day.

"Learn to fly," Conrad replied, dropping another peach pie into his bucket. The fax gates wouldn't open until the end of the term, and that was that. It turned out they also wouldn't produce any food except chocolate s'mores, roasted marshmallows, and the godawful "beans and franks" slop that tasted like the bottom of somebody's shoe. Whose brilliant idea *that* was was a subject of constant speculation, but Bascal's money was on the queen, and Conrad figured he was probably right.

In any case, the prince had had to institute emergency mandatory agricultural duties—four hours a day for all campers, himself included. It was a daily calamity for the geese on Adventure Lake, who bore the brunt of the prior eight weeks' archery practice. Also for the potatoes and carrots and cabbages in the hobby farm, which were being eaten much faster than they could grow back. Well, fuck it. The boys weren't here forever, and they had never agreed to be responsible stewards.

But veggies and slop, raw goose and candy did not a dinner make. So here the two of them were, picking fresh pies for dessert up in the high branches of a peach pie tree, and also gathering deadwood for the fire. A ways down the row of trees, Ho and Steve were doing the same, and off in the northern part of the orchard another four or six other boys could be heard singing the Fuck You Song while they gathered apples and pecans. It was hard work, reaching the good pies, so Conrad really wished they hadn't spent the early summer having nightly pie fights. Putting the orchards next to the Young Men's Cabins was a highly stupid idea in that regard.

"I mean it," Bascal said. "The toil of a troublous voyage, the bitter wind at our backs." He reached his hand up toward the sky, grasping at its indigo blankness—much darker than Earth's—as if he could pick that too, and carry it home in his bucket. "We're *so close*. Even a tall ladder would get us out of this atmosphere."

"Yeah?" Conrad growled. "A *two-hundred-meter* ladder. Then what?" His voice was satisfyingly deep—one of the few clear benefits of life on Camp Friendly. The air was full of xenon, some really heavy gas to hold the atmosphere down or something, and it was almost the exact opposite of breathing helium. Everyone here sounded grown-up and serious, with the bigger kids actually sounding like crooners and senators, or barrel-chested lumberjacks from that old American TV drama.

"Then a spaceship," Bascal said with a shrug. "You think we couldn't build one? All it has to do is hold air long enough to get us someplace with a working fax."

"Which is probably a long, long way. What about propulsion?"

Bascal shook the branch beneath them. "Are you doubting me, punk?" He grinned. "We build a sail. Just a big, rigid sheet of wellstone film, superreflective on one side and superabsorptive on the other. Haven't you ever been solar sailing?"

Conrad snorted. "Or owned my own island? No, Bas, we're not all children of unimaginable privilege."

The branch shook again, harder, and Bascal's expression was less amused. "I'll break this if you're not careful." He was on the trunk side, with Conrad out flapping in the breeze.

"All right, all right," Conrad said, climbing down to a lower branch, worried about losing his balance and falling on something vital. The peach pie tree was only four meters high, but it was twisty, offering lots of opportunities to bang or snag yourself on the way down. And he couldn't fight back, with a Palace Guard right down there at the tree's base, watching for even the slightest threat against the *pilinisi*. "Solar sail, fine."

"*Fetu'ula*, actually. Stellar sail."

"Whatever. Does it steer anything like a bulldozer?"

"I don't know," Bascal said. "Who drives a bulldozer? *You?*"

"Well, yeah. Many times."

"Sitting in Daddy's lap?" The prince sneered good-naturedly.

Conrad shrugged. As County Paver, Donald Mursk supervised the maintenance of quaint country roads, and had free use of all sorts of infernal machines. It was a shame to give Bascal the satisfaction of being exactly right, but Conrad was surprised and pleased just the same, to find something he himself had done which the *Pilinisi Sola* had not. "Haven't you?" he sneered back, eager to rub in his petty victory. But Bascal just started shaking the tree again.

"Okay! Cut it out! What about life support?"

"Steal the fax machine out of the Piss Hall," Bascal said. "If we're short on oxygen, it should crank some out automatically. Along with fresh water and slop."

Mess Hall, he meant. After the indignity of being returned here, the first thing they'd done was repaint all the signs, giving each building and landmark a proper name for the occasion. "It's an arts-and-crafts project," Bascal had told the Palace Guards, when they'd studied the action and looked like they might intervene. And that explanation had seemed to satisfy them. Even more so than most robots, Palace Guards were enormously intelligent and perceptive. But they weren't human, and didn't care about things unless specifically instructed to.

Initially, the robots had tried to impose all sorts of structured activities on the boys. Canoeing, basket weaving, group sing-along... They were like caricatures of the real counselors, interchangeable and blank-faced, devoid of vocal inflection and bristling with the potential for violence. But it turned out they had no programming to enforce these edicts; if you told them to fuck themselves, they'd just stand there unconcerned while you went about your business.

"Okay," Conrad allowed, finally getting into the spirit of it. "There isn't a single spot on this planette I haven't seen at least twice. I'm all in favor of fresh scenery. So we throw some wet dirt in a hold somewhere, as a mass buffer for the fax. That works. What about energy?"

"Capacitors," Bascal answered. "That's what a real sailboat uses anyway. Wellstone panels to absorb energy— mainly from the sun—and capacitors to store it."

"You know how to make a capacitor?"

Bascal laughed. "Ask a block of wellstone, boyo. You *do* think too much."

"All right, whatever," Conrad conceded. "Are we done here?" He was still climbing down, swinging and twisting a little on every branch just for fun, though being careful not to spill his bucket. The boys would not look kindly on squooshed pies, and they had their ways of letting you know.

"Done enough," Bascal said with a shrug. He started down himself.

"So you're actually serious about this."

"You bet. Dead serious. Our elders need to understand they have zero ability to push us around."

Conrad reached the ground, glanced briefly at the mirrored skin of the Palace Guard, and then set about rearranging the contents of his bucket, making sure the kindling wasn't crushing the pies, that the pies weren't splitting their bready coats and dripping on the kindling. Later on, he'd light the fire with his bow drill and some dried grass, just like Rock Dengle had taught him. He loved lighting the fire, and tending it, feeding in larger and larger sticks until finally it was hot enough to stew a goose. Actually tending the cooking pot was a duty Xmary had taken for herself, for what she called "Neolithic reasons." I.e., she didn't trust the boys to do a good job of it, and probably also wanted to make sure nobody spat in it or anything.

"What about navigation?"

Bascal hopped down beside him. "You're speaking to a Tongan, boyo. Greatest navigators who ever lived."

"Your father's European."

"Catalan Spaniard," Bascal said. "Another great mariner race. My father *invented* the ertially shielded grappleship, and sailed the first one alone for over thirty AU. I think there were two of him on board, actually, but still."

"You know what I mean, Bas. Where do we go, and how?"

Smiling, the prince made a gesture of mock humility. "I've sailed alone, with no electronics, from Tongatapu to Eua on a moonless night. For that matter, I've sailed from LEO to Luna on a Tongaless night. Steering is easy—you just adjust the transparency of the sail. A mirror here means a push there, and vice versa. Easy as cream custard. As far as *where* to steer, these days there's a lot of shipping in Kuiper space. We should be able to track the

emissions of a neutronium barge or something. Unmanned, or manned only part-time."

"Track it how?"

"With sensors. A radiometer or something. Ask a block
of wellstone, boyo; we live in a programmable universe."

"Uh-huh," Conrad said skeptically. "And where do we
get all this wellstone? Weave it out of beans and franks?"

Bascal punched him, not that lightly. "You're the fucking building inspector. What's underneath us, right now?"

"Grass," Conrad said. "Dirt. Liquid neutronium in diamond shells, with probably a layer of rock in between."

"And a point-one-mil sheet of wellstone," Bascal
added, stamping on the ground for emphasis. "Shovel-
proof, about two meters down. Bet you a dollar it covers
the whole planette, pole to pole. That's, like, over a
square kilometer of material. Just about perfect for a sail."

They started back toward the cabins.

"You really are serious," Conrad said again.

"Very. Are you in?"

He shrugged. "I guess so, yeah. What about space
suits?"

"An arts-and-crafts project. Snip a corner off the sail,
cut out some life-sized paper dolls, and seal them at the
edges."

"How long is all this going to take?"

"I dunno. Not long. I'm not sure about the actual ship,
how we're going to build it. What materials to use."

Conrad laughed. "How about D'rector Jed's cabin? It's
big enough, and God knows it's the best furnished."

"Hey," Bascal agreed, laughing along with him, "that's a
great idea. We can just shrink-wrap the whole thing."

Nothing on Camp Friendly was far away from anything else; from the orchards was only a minute or two to
the Boys' Cabins and the central offices. Almost as soon
as they'd started, the two of them were there at the Piss
Hall. Bascal threw the door open.

"Honey! I'm home!" The irony in his voice couldn't conceal an undercurrent of genuine affection.

"Hi," Xmary said, looking up from her carrot chopping. "What have you brought me? Peach pies? Over there." She pointed with the knife.

"Yes'm," Bascal said, his voice bubbling at the edge of giggles. The Palace Guard, with liquid-quick movements, flowed in behind him, briefly crowding Conrad out of the doorway. He tried not to take it personally; the machine simply would not let Bascal out of its sight, even for a moment. You didn't get in the way of that, not if you were paying attention.

"Firewood here," she added, pointing to a different surface, adjacent to the table she was working on. "You didn't get pie filling on it, did you? That would be bad for the revolution."

The revolution, ah. She said it in a joking way, but behind the light tone Conrad suspected a lurking seriousness. Shaking things up wasn't a game to her, but some sort of weird social duty. Very solemn.

"Why are you here, again?" he prodded, hoping to get a rise out of her.

But her answer was straight enough. "Back home, I've got six more years of school before I can put my name in to be the assistant to somebody's assistant. I used to make furniture as a hobby, and later on it was holiday decorations. But who needs handmade things? Who can even tell if they're real or copied? There's nothing to *do* back home, and there never will be. I feel so sorry for my other self back there."

"Hey," he told her, putting his hands up, "I'm just giving you a hard time. Trying to. I get enough politics in my diet."

"Well, the hell with you, then," she said, butting him hard with her hip. She resumed her chopping.

Early on in the week, Conrad had been certain that

Xmary was going to get caught, that she was going to get all of them in even worse trouble. Smuggling a girl into an all-boys camp! But since she'd sneaked a copy of herself out of the house to visit Café 1551 in the first place, her parents didn't know she was gone. In fact, she *wasn't* gone; she was presumably still back there under their watchful eyes, attending summer school and sighing a lot.

And Feck somehow hadn't tipped their hand, hadn't gone to the Constabulary or home to his own parents and explained why he wasn't at camp. And if the camp itself was under observation—which seemed likely—then it obviously wasn't under the sort of *really close* observation that would reveal the presence of a female camper who was not Yinebeb Fecre. Bascal's own Palace Guard clearly saw her standing there, but didn't care. Hadn't been asked to. This was not only hilarious, but also lent some credence to Bascal's insistence that it really was possible, now and then, to put one over on the Queendom authorities.

Either that, or Xmary and the boys were being run like rats through a maze—a notion Bascal had mentioned but didn't seem to believe. There would be too many variables to control, too many spontaneities to account for. If the authorities were *that* clever then there was no hope at all. So her presence here was an accident, abetted by her own weird sense of initiative.

There was, of course, the jealousy thing; Xmary was an arts-and-crafts project in her own right, pretty and sassy and with all sorts of surprising talents. Cooking, of all things, in this age of flash-and-bang! And you had to wonder what other talents came out, when she and Bascal shut themselves up in "their" cabin. It was a subject of riotous speculation when Bascal wasn't around. Hell, Steve Grush had teased Xmary about it right to her blushing face.

"When's dinner?" the prince asked.

"When I ring the bell, moron," she fired back. "Just like yesterday and the day before. What are you, slow?"

"Well, I hope not. Conrad and I have a plan to get us off this egg."

Her eyebrows went up. "Solar sail?"

"Yep. I'll make the announcement tonight." He sauntered up to the fax machine—a vertical, doorway-sized plate of gray-black material. The visible portion was the phantom-action lux generator, or something like that, tapping out waves that dreamed they were matter. It was the only intelligent device in the room, unless you counted the robot. "Fax, give me a bowl of taro curry, please. With coconut."

"Disallowed," the fax replied, in the loud, sexless tones of somebody trying to piss people off.

"Yeah? Fuck you. Give me a textbook on sailing."

"Please specify the type of sailing," the fax said.

Bascal shot a nodding smile back at Conrad—getting somewhere!—then said to the fax, "Solar sailing, you fucked-up piece of shit. I need it for arts and crafts."

"My internal library contains four titles on solar sailing. Access to external libraries through the Nescog is disallowed."

"Fine. I'll take all four. And a map showing all known fax gates within ten AU of this planette."

"Disallowed," the fax replied, spitting four paper books into Bascal's waiting arms.

"Ah. Then allow me to invoke royal override."

"Disallowed. That function is reserved for the King and Queen of Sol."

"Which I will never be. Fine, you anus, give me a map of known shipping and habitation."

A rolled-up sheet of wellstone film tumbled out, missing Bascal's arms and spilling to the floor.

"Thank you," Bascal said.

"It pleases me to serve," the device replied, without feeling.

"I know it, fax. I know it. And believe me, someday I'll reward you for it."

Ah, the creaky, breezy squalor of Young Men's Cabin #2. Ah, the smell of intestinal gas, and the constant fear of pranking and punches, of hurled objects, of name-calling that hurt, truthfully, as much as sticks and stones ever could. Such was life after dark at Camp Friendly.

Conrad found it difficult to relax with a Palace Guard looming menacingly in the corner, its blank metal skin reflecting the room's electric/incandescent lights. It might have been a statue—utterly silent and unmoving—except you *knew* it was watching and hearing and feeling everything around it, and could fly into action at any moment. In that sense, it was more like a stretched-to-breaking cable, or a heavy mass teetering on a window ledge—not the least bit statuesque or reassuring.

This is our punishment, Conrad reminded himself. *We're not supposed to like it, we're supposed to be intimidated.*

Peter, who was looking intently at his wristwatch, said, "Five. Four. Three. Two. One." Then he pointed his finger like a stage cue.

"Lights out, time to sleep," the robot announced flatly, right on schedule. Its speaking voice was loud and grating and without inflection, really just an emergency thing, not intended for such trivial everyday use. Robots had never been the best conversationalists, but these seemed especially cold, especially disinterested in the task. The idea that they were "counselors" was totally hilarious, in a not-funny kind of way. Moments later, and also on schedule, the room was cast into darkness as the power to the electric lightbulbs cut off.

Through the window, Conrad could see the lights of Young Men's Cabin #1 go out as well, presumably casting Bascal and Xmary into their own blissful darkness. Damn them both.

Here, it wasn't so blissful. Some of the boys obeyed right away, climbing sullenly into their bunks. Others made a point of openly defying the guard; as their eyes adjusted to starlight, Karl and Bertram began a noisy game of shirtball soccer, and several other boys quickly joined in. Part of the fun of this game was the lousiness of the ball: a tied-up camp shirt of only roughly spherical shape. To kick it straight was a real challenge—especially in motion, especially in the dark—and to kick it *hard* was even harder, so the chaos level got pretty high, pretty fast.

The thing was, the Palace Guard didn't care. It had discharged its duty—its program—with the announcement itself, and was now simply waiting for some new trigger condition to make it do something else. Shirtball soccer did not interest it, and for this reason, didn't interest Conrad either. He didn't see the point in razzing a dispassionate machine. Or even a passionate one, for that matter.

"We could actually sleep," he suggested vainly.

"Shut up," said one of the players.

But it was Ho Ng who decided the matter. The game seemed for some reason to infuriate him, so that he threw himself out of bed and into Karl's path, and then lashed out in the darkness with a fist that caught the other boy hard in the stomach. Or would have, anyway, except that with a single lightning-quick movement, the Palace Guard raised an arm and pointed a finger. There was the purple flash of a guide laser, the pop and sparkle of tazzer fire, and then Ho Ng was going down in a heap, directly in the path of a still-charging Karl, who tripped over him and went down as well.

In the gloom, Conrad couldn't see what happened

after that, except that it involved a lot of squawking, and a lot of bodies scurrying hastily into bed. A bit of giggling, but not much. There wasn't much funny about this. If the robot had decided to wade physically into the fray, there was no telling what might've happened.

A minute later, Ho himself crawled into bed—which was no small feat since he had a top bunk and was still recovering from the tazzer. It must've hurt, judging by the way he grunted and cursed on the way up.

"Bastards," he was saying quietly. "Goddamn blood-fucky bastards."

But even he didn't want to push his luck any farther, so in another few minutes the room was quiet. And peaceful, yeah, right. Conrad kept his eyes open, and focused on the Palace Guard, its skin now mirroring the starlit windows. Perfectly motionless, a coiled spring of perfect, violent action.

This was going to be another long night.

The Piss Hall fax seemed content to provide any educational materials—even those pertaining to explosives and poisons and dirty matter-programming tricks—so the next day, suddenly, everyone was a scientist. Arts-and-crafts time consisted of everyone sitting around the mess hall scribbling diagrams. It couldn't last, of course; by the second day only half the boys were scientists, and by the third day it was down to just Bascal, Conrad, Xmary, and Bertram Wang, plus Peter Kolb, who was the son of two laureates and fancied himself a real smarty-pants. Granted, one parent was a sculptor and the other an actress, which didn't exactly make him Bruno de Towaji, but he knew more math than Conrad did, and seemed to be pulling his intellectual weight. More so than Bertram, who came from an *actual sailing family* and seemed to believe his opinion counted for more than anyone else's facts and figures, except possibly Bascal's.

But half the other boys were still in the labor pool, running errands and digging holes and such, so the work progressed well enough. As for the rest, well, maybe there was some truth to it: these *were* delinquent kids, who couldn't be bothered even to defy authority, if the cost of defiance was anything like work. It was hard enough to get them to feed themselves, although Steve Grush seemed happy enough putting arrows into the geese. The notable exception was Ho Ng, who was easily the most delinquent kid here, but stood attentively at Bascal's elbow, taking instructions like some kind of soft, brown robot.

"I need test holes here and here," Bascal told him, pointing out two empty sites along the equator of a Camp Friendly map. "Verify the wellstone layer, and record its exact depth."

"Sure," Ho agreed, nodding. "We're expecting two hundred and five centimeters, right? I'll make it happen."

And there was the secret: letting Bascal boss him around gave Ho the authority to boss anyone else around. Some other boys would get dirty and blistered doing the actual work, and then Ho would report back here to deliver the findings and collect the credit.

There was no question that his will would be done. Not only was it an echo of Bascal's will, but ironically, the Palace Guards had only enhanced Ho's air of violence. His second attempt to punch someone had ended even more shamefully than the first—with Ho quivering on the ground in a fetal position for nearly a minute—but since that time the guards had kept a particularly close eye, and there was nearly always one within four meters of him.

In effect, the guards had declared him both royal and criminal. They were his golden handcuffs, his personal guard. And of course, they were scary in their own right, so even if you knew in your mind that they weren't going to hurt you, the sight of one striding toward you, with Ho Ng beside it, did in fact strike fear and encourage obedience. And you'd better believe Ho liked it that way.

"What a creep," Conrad observed when Ho was gone. "I genuinely hate that guy."

"Hmm?" Bascal said, looking up absentmindedly from his diagrams. "Ng? Yeah, he's definitely got a way of moving things along." He looked back down for a moment, then added, "I think I've got this nearly worked out. There's a relay station about five AU from here, associated with a major telecom collapsiter about half an AU farther on. Normal crew is probably zero. There's also scattered cometary debris—we are in the Kuiper Belt, after all—but snowballs aren't going to help us any. We need *facilities*. Our best bet is probably this here: an unmanned neutronium barge just under *one* AU away, which probably has everything we need. Namely, the maintenance fax they use to load workers on and off when something breaks. That should take us right back to fucking Denver."

And then what? The question hung unspoken. Revolution, right? Unite with the underground armies of Feck the Fairy, and cause some sort of mischief? Conrad wasn't sure of the exact reason for this, or what exactly was supposed to happen afterward. Prison? More summer camp? The glorious collapse of Queendom society?

"What's an AU?" he asked.

"Distance from the Earth to the sun," Bascal said, in a tone suggesting he found the question a bit stupid.

"Isn't that a long way?"

"Not out here it isn't. We're fifty AU from the sun, and almost twenty from the orbit of Neptune. Stuff is a lot more spread out in the upper system. Have you gotten us off the planette, by the way?"

"Um, yeah," Conrad said, turning and rummaging through his growing pile of notes. "If the sail is folded into a thirteen-meter sphere, we can fill it with hydrogen." He plucked a simulation sketchplate from the pile and held it up, showing a little cartoon balloon rising up through the cartoon atmosphere of a cartoon planette. "That's enough to lift the cabin, fifteen people, and about two tons of cargo."

"Raw. Where do we get the hydrogen?"

Conrad pointed to a patch of blue on Bascal's Camp Friendly map. "Adventure Lake. We move some solar panels onto the dock, and run the current down into the water on metal cables. Oxygen bubbles up on one side, and hydrogen on the other. We just throw the oxygen away, and fill the bag directly from the dock."

"Hmm," Bascal said, pinching his chin and nodding. "Peter, are you listening to this?"

"Yeah," Peter Kolb replied, from the next table over. He had his back to the prince, and didn't turn. "Hydrogen's a fire hazard, you know. Explosion hazard."

"That's true," Bascal said, and turned back to Conrad with an expectant look.

Conrad shrugged. "You didn't let me finish."

"Please do."

It was hard not to smile. They were doing a good job, acting all mature and businessy, like real engineers and scientists. On the other hand, they really were coming up with answers, so maybe it wasn't completely an act. "We can't lift out of the atmosphere with just a balloon. It isn't physically possible. We let the bag up to its full height— about a hundred meters if it's going to reach from the docks to the d'rector's cabin—and it'll only rise another hundred meters or so before its density matches the air, and it stops."

"Yeah? So?"

"So, the density of xenon drops off a lot faster than the

density of oxygen does. It hugs the ground, not the sky. And the whole time the balloon is rising, the gas inside it is also expanding, until finally it starts leaking out the bottom."

"And? I'm not following."

Conrad inched the simulation forward, second by second. In the cartoon, the open-bottomed bag of wellstone film rose and swelled with yellow, false-colored gas, until little swirls of it were coming out as promised. "And, it's two hundred kilos of hydrogen, spilling into a pure oxygen atmosphere."

"It explodes," Peter said, and *now* he was turning around to look, just in time to see the simulated blast on the wellstone sketchplate.

"Specifically," Conrad said, "it explodes *down*, propelling the bag up and lifting the whole cabin away from the planette. Rather fast."

The sim showed this: a flaming balloon dragging a wooden cabin behind it, with the planette falling away against a background of stars and dotted lines.

"Raw!" Bascal said approvingly. "Conrad, that's great. You thought of that all by yourself?"

He felt himself blushing. "Well, the textbooks helped."

"Will it work?" Bascal asked Peter.

Peter shrugged. "I dunno. I guess. Can I check the simulation?"

"You sure can," Bascal said, snatching the plate out of Conrad's hands.

Conrad was about to be annoyed, and to protest, when suddenly Xmary was there, holding a couple of plastic bowls. "Food science report!" she said excitedly. "I've got some new creations from the fax."

"Got what?" Conrad asked.

"Edible paints," she said. "And papier-mâché. Some of the combinations make a decent porridge."

Conrad peered into the bowls and wrinkled his nose. "It looks like shit." And it did, literally.

"Well, it tastes like peas and oatmeal," Xmary shot back, with just a touch of indignant sneer. "Try it."

One of the bowls had a spoon in it, and Conrad didn't want to be *too* much of an asshole, and anyway the stuff didn't smell bad. In fact it barely smelled at all, so he picked up the spoon and touched its goo-smeared plastic tip to the end of his tongue. No ill effects presented themselves. Sighing, he shoved the spoon in his mouth and sucked the brown paste off it.

"Hmm," he said, trying not to make a face. The taste wasn't horrible, but this was definitely one of those cases where the texture and color didn't match. This wasn't going to be popular, even as a substitute for beans and franks. "We can call it Slop Number Two."

Bascal was choking back a laugh. "Well. That's great, then. Another problem solved."

"I'll keep trying," promised a slightly crestfallen Xmary.

"I don't know about this," Bertram the sailor boy cut in. He sauntered over to Bascal and Conrad's table and sat down heavily. "You've got a photospinnaker clewed and guyed to a spriting gondola. Using a log cabin for the gondola may not be as bad as it sounds, but you're still talking about a fairly downsystem design, right? An AU *is* a long distance to sail, even with real sunlight to propel you. And this planette doesn't have a real sun, just a pinpoint fusion source. The energy drops off *fast* as you move away from it."

The grin fell off Bascal's face. "Bert, I like you, but if Ng were here, he'd punch you in the gut for that. How smart do you think you are? I've physically *been sailing* around my family's planette, which has a lot of other shit orbiting besides a pocket star. Have you ever done that? Have you done anything remotely like that? Tooling around in Earth orbit, hell, I'll bet you've never even *heard* of laser sail protocol."

"No," Bertram admitted, his voice betraying a slight quaver.

"Well, I'll educate you. Out here in the real universe, *sila'a* have a special protocol, see? Called *laser sail protocol*. You log your request with the star, and if there are no competing demands then its entire energy output is focused in a laser beam, which does *not* drop off fast as you move away. In fact, it tracks your sail automatically, for *hours* if you need it to. Do you know how much speed you can build up that way? Would you care to guess?"

Bertram was hunching his shoulders now, looking suitably chastised. "I'm...sorry, Bascal. You know more about this than I do, so if you've already worked it out, I...apologize. How long will this trip take?"

"Actually, I haven't worked it out," the prince said, and burst out laughing.

There was a layer of wellstone film covering the entire planette, at an average depth of just over two meters. It was a lining of some kind: not only waterproof and shovel-proof but antimagnetic and stuff. Conrad figured the hard part would be getting it up and out of the planette. In fact, truthfully, he'd figured on that step being impossible, at least within the eight weeks remaining in their camp sentence. But Bascal had a lot of tricks up his sleeve; he went down into one of the holes, whispered something to the plasticky material at the bottom, and was presented with the wellstone's programming interface.

"This stuff comes out of the factory with a few terabytes of programming built in," he noted over his shoulder, for the edification of Ng and Conrad and Peter, and the three labor-pool boys who'd actually dug this hole.

Once the interface was there, he tapped at its buttons—bright squares of glowing color printed against the gray-black of the wellstone itself. And he read symbols from its screen, and he cursed at it a few times.

"No language parser," he said. "No intelligence. It doesn't know what I want."

Conrad stooped until his hands were on the rim of the hole. The ground was soft and loamy, vaguely wet. He swung his legs out and hopped down. The hole was slightly deeper than he was tall, and narrow for two people to crouch in, although he crouched anyway. "What's it saying?"

"I don't know. Something about static coefficients. It goes by fast and disappears."

"What are you trying to do?"

"Make it slippery," Bascal said, still tapping lettered keys. "A couple of tacky areas for handholds, and the rest very, very slippery."

"Ah."

He watched Bascal fiddle with it for a few minutes, then started making suggestions. "Here," Bascal said finally, edging out of the way to the extent that the dirt wall around them permitted. "You do it."

Conrad had never used a manual interface like this one, but grasped the principle well enough. He entered F-R-I-C-T-I-O-N, and then hit the SEARCH key as he'd seen Bascal do. And when the resulting text—in fat yellow letters—rolled up past the top of the display window, he poked and prodded at the window until he'd managed to resize it, and to make the letters smaller so he could read more than twelve at a time.

"We can turn it to gold," he said helpfully, as the menu options presented themselves. "We can turn it to impervium. Those are pretty slippery."

"Not nearly enough," Bascal said. "Anyway, they're elements—we want compounds. There should be a way to just specify the friction, and let the other parameters optimize."

It went on like that for a while, but eventually they got it. And when they got it there was no question at all, because their hands and knees went out from under them and they fell together in a pile, screaming with laughter and bouncing back and forth against the walls, which rained dirt down on them.

"Make a sticky patch!" Bascal shouted. "Make a sticky patch *right here*!"

"You're on my hand," Conrad shot back, through fresh peals of laughter. He tried tapping at the keys with the fingers of his left hand, as he skittered over and over them. Finally, between the two of them, he and Bascal managed to turn the slipperiness off, then specify the area around them as something called "duramer," which was strong and flexible and tacky, and that let them gather the wellstone up in their fists. Then they turned the slipperiness back on across the rest of the sheet, and pulled.

The only really hard part was getting out of the hole while stooping to maintain their handholds. They couldn't climb without letting go, and the other boys couldn't reach down far enough to pull them up. Eventually a human chain was attempted, and Conrad and Bascal were hauled out, dragging several meters of wellstone behind them.

"Our sail," Bascal beamed.

"Why do they call it 'stone'?" someone wondered aloud.

"It also comes in blocks," Conrad answered. "Big, heavy silicon blocks, like glass. Like stone. Or light and puffy, like foam. This stuff is better, this film. More versatile."

Bascal was tugging on the wellstone, which had grown

taut and would not come any farther out of the hole. "We need to split a few seams to pull this out any farther. Down the far side of the planette, then halfway up to the equator again on the sides. Peel it like an orange."

Conrad grunted. "You know how to do that?"

"Kind of. Here, help me."

With some additional fussing, they called up a schematic of the whole sheet, and marked the cuts they wanted along its spherical form.

"This'll make a trilobe sail," Bascal said. "Also known as a batwing. Very stylish."

Conrad nodded, not really listening. "Okay, okay. Ready...and...*cut!*"

The tension went out of the sheet, and an additional meter of it slid upward in their grasp.

"All right!" the prince shouted. "Pull, boys, pull!"

And they did. They pulled and walked and pulled and walked, and the material slithered out like a hollow snake made of clear, wet-looking film. No way they could ever stuff it back in the hole again. And at the rate they were going, they'd have the entire liner pulled out in half an hour—it was that easy to vandalize a world. And wasn't *that* a kick in the pants?

To pluck the eyes that rest beneath thy brow,
And celebrate red fountains in a sonnet,
or heckle farmer's labor at his plow,
in field that hath such trammeled soil upon it!

I wonder, Shakespeare, didst thou never see
A napalm blossom sprung from human skin,
Or noble stick of Nobel TNT
That hath such fire encapsulated in?

In images of violence we seek,
Through gasoline and knives and powder burns,
For cities built and sacked, and havoc wreaked,
By reptile mind that, all unseeing, yearns.

A damsel with a rifle in a vision once I saw,
O Xanadu, thy twice-five-miles are trampled into straw.

—*"The Modern Era"*[3]
BASCAL EDWARD DE TOWAJI LUTUI, *age 10*

---

[3] Note: Alfred Nobel invented dynamite, smokeless powder, and the blasting cap, but not TNT. —ed.

chapter seven

freedom blast

The sheet weighed three tons, and took twelve people two whole days to fold up. When they were done, it was forty layers thick, bulging chest-high with air pockets, and still bigger than the furrowed field of the Hobby Farm, some eighty-five meters across. With its waterproof liner gone, the lake drained alarmingly during this time, finally bottoming out at about half its original depth, and there were reports—unconfirmed by anyone reliable—that the hills and plateau on the planette's eastern hemisphere had begun to slump as well. Meanwhile, Xmary and her crew were canning food and fermenting jugs of cider and cutting/pasting/sealing the fifteen space suits, which everyone agreed were a good idea in case the ship sprang a leak or something. Bascal had to help with that part, though, because it turned out he and Conrad were the only ones who knew the first thing about matter programming.

It began to dawn on Conrad that they were going to get caught. There was no way to hide this much activity, even from an apathetic Queendom that considered them helpless. At some point, the Palace Guards were going to report all this. Hell, even a *telescope* would reveal the changes in the planette's appearance. At any moment, the fax gates would pour out a sea of Constabulary officers, or broadcast new instructions to the robots that were already here, and it would all be over. Again.

"We need to sabotage the gates," Bascal said to him, as if reading his thoughts. The two of them were up on the easternmost rock formation, overlooking the now-landlocked boathouse and—just barely peeking over the horizon—the docks, which stood now in only a meter of dirty-looking water. In theory the two of them were surveying the launch site; to the south, D'rector Jed's cabin was also just barely visible, and the guy ropes would sprawl from there to the docks, with the balloon itself curling off to the northeast, almost reaching the paved path they facetiously referred to as the Holy Fuckway,[4] which circled wide around the lake.

"Where will we get our supplies?" Conrad asked. His voice sounded higher and squeakier than usual; they were almost six meters up, and the air was thinner.

Bascal waved a hand impatiently. "Not the fax machines, the *gates*. The telecom hardware that links them to the Nescog. There are only two of them on the planette."

"Oh. So how do we sabotage them?"

"With a crowbar, idiot. Or a sledgehammer. Anything, really. They're wellstone, but they're not programmed to withstand an attack. Circuitry is delicate."

"You've smashed one before," Conrad speculated.

Bascal nodded. He was looking up now, at the sky, at the "sun," and at the dull, starlike speck of Sol that, from up here, could readily be discerned in broad daylight. "Yeah. Twice."

Then he looked back at the ground, picked out Ho Ng in the not-so-distance, cupped his hands, and began calling out directions. "Ng! Ng! Get a crowbar or something and meet me by the boathouse!"

---

[4] Probably *Hala Fakatu'i*, the Royal Road. —ed.

"Are you sure you want to do that?" Conrad asked. The knot of unease in his stomach had not loosened. If anything, it was getting tighter. "If we smash the gates, we're really committing."

"Committing a crime?" Bascal said. He could turn a sneer into something friendly, an assurance that you were smart enough and raw enough to see the error in your statement. For some reason, Conrad suddenly found this power vaguely frightening.

"Well, y...it is a crime, yes. But we're in plenty of trouble already. What I meant was, it *commits* us. There'll be no other way off the planette, and if we've made any sort of mistake..." His voice withered under Bascal's glare; it took real effort to finish. "This could be very dangerous. We could be killed."

"That's what backups are for. The Friendly Products Corporation took an image of you on your way up here, right?"

"I don't want to be restored from backups."

Bascal studied him quietly, for several seconds. "Are you losing your nerve?"

Conrad couldn't keep himself from shrugging. "Not losing it, I just...What is it again, that we're trying to accomplish? Suddenly I'm not sure. Revolution?"

"Revolution," Bascal agreed.

"But that's crazy, isn't it? I mean, we can't *win*. We can cost them time and money and stuff; we can make a *statement*. But we can't overthrow them or anything. Not by building a sailboat."

"You don't understand," Bascal said, and he sounded a little sad.

"So explain it."

"Explain it? It ought to explain itself. Our revolt isn't something they'll lose; it's something they'll *regret*. They have such an easy time forgetting about us, putting us off. Which is ironic, considering the cultural patterns they're working from. If you asked the Old Moderns about paradise, some would have said it was a tropical stone age full of gatherers and hunters and fishermen. Some would say a network of small farming towns, or a medieval pocket monarchy straight out of fairy tales. Others, maybe a Modern, democratic nation-state held together by information technology. But Tonga was unique in the Modern world: it was all these things at the same time, in the same place. It was *everyone's* paradise.

"By the end of the Modern period, the entire human race had its eyes on the Kingdom as, I dunno, a model for a new kind of civilization. Really it was all the old kinds, living right on top of each other. And to be fair, those Utopian ambitions genuinely have succeeded. They've smothered the original and lost its spirit—they've practically enslaved my parents—but along the way they've created something...else. Something better, at least for them. They just forgot about their unborn, is all. You have to remember, the Old Moderns are still alive, and always will be, walking around in a state of constant amazement. But their paradise was built at our expense—happy children as part of the scenery, the hoped-for future, not part of the machine itself. Not part of the present.

"So, we've got to remind them every day, that we're *current* human beings, not future ones, not potential ones, not pretend ones. What do people fear when they can't die or be maimed? Slavery. Oppression. Meaninglessness. Even in the old days, most people would rather die than live by the will of someone else. Even for a decade or two. They fought wars to prevent it. They murdered their own children in their beds. With *eternity* ahead of us, do we dare to be timid? We need a place in society, a set of roles to grow into that aren't bogged down by the weight of bureaucracy and prior humanity. We deserve a chance to *live and breathe*, as our parents have done, and if we die a few times—nobly and defiantly—it only strengthens the point."

Conrad sat down. He had to think about that, to think it over in those terms.

"Do you hear what I'm saying?" Bascal pressed.

"I do. Yes. You've thought a lot about this."

"Every day of my life." The prince nodded, considering and then agreeing with his own words. "*Last* summer I got sent to Niuafo'ou, the remotest and old-fashionedest of the Niua Islands, at the northern extreme of the old Kingdom. The name means 'Exotic Coconuts,' and believe me, it's not referring to a fruit. Those people are serious: no gates, no wellstone, no TV or fax machines. You eat what you catch, and wear what you grow. And what you grow is one hundred percent Earth Original, no recombos or faxable mods. I used to love that island—I learned to sail in its central crater when I was five—but last year all I could think of was how *small* it was. How narrow-minded and closed. I had a boat; I could've sailed it to Vava'u in a couple of days. But there was never a right time to start, and soon the season was over and I was back at school. Opportunity lost."

Conrad kicked some dirt off the gray cragginess of the rock. He wasn't a coward; he knew that much. And what Bascal said was . . . well, it put *words* to the feeling that had driven him into so much trouble already. Conrad had never tried to put it in words, didn't even realize it could be done. But: if the words were accurate, did that necessarily make them true?

"How long," he finally asked, "will this journey take? Seriously."

"Two months," Bascal answered.

"Two *months*? With fifteen of us in a log cabin? That's crazy. That's a long time."

"If it were easy, there wouldn't be much point. Think of the statement that makes. Not boohoo, I hate summer camp, but *fuck you* if you think this is over. It isn't over. The system needs shocking, and we simply will not be controlled."

Conrad let out a breath. "Okay."

"Okay what?"

"Okay. Let's do it. Fucking space pirates."

"All right! That's the spirit! That's the Conrad Mursk I know," Bascal said, throwing an arm over Conrad's shoulder and breaking out in probably the widest grin Conrad had ever seen on anyone.

Two days later, they were ready to fill the balloon. Ready to pile into D'rector Jed's cabin, ready to *launch*. Ready to face the dangers and deprivations of their long voyage.

Except that Peter Kolb didn't want to. Peter Kolb and four other boys, actually, but it was Peter who was doing the talking.

"It doesn't make sense," he insisted. "Our term will be over by the time you get there. We should wait."

"For what?" Bascal asked calmly. "For them to come and arrest us?"

"For them to come."

"Peter, the gates are down. If the authorities left to-day—which they may very well have done—even the fastest rescue ships would take nearly a week to get here. And the fastest ships are small, more like ambulances than troop carriers. Would they waste their ertial cruisers on us? That would take *two* weeks."

"Ertial?"

"Yeah, ertial. Inertially shielded. I thought you were smart, boyo. They put a collapsium cap on the bow, and the black holes inside it deflect the vacuum energy which causes inertia. You can accelerate as fast as you want without feeling it. But it's expensive, right? There aren't many ships equipped with it—especially large ones. So if they send a fusion boat—which is what they've probably done—then it's eight weeks or more, possibly sixteen."

Peter crossed his arms. "They're not leaving you out here for sixteen weeks, Bas. They're not."

"Look, we're leaving. Get used to it."

"I'm not leaving," Peter said. He gestured behind him. "James and Raoul aren't leaving. Khen isn't."

Khen shook his head to emphasize the point, while James and Raoul just looked hangdog, unhappy at defying their *pilinisi*. Bertram, whom Peter hadn't seen fit to mention, looked blank, as if the question didn't interest him and he just happened to be standing there. But that couldn't be right, because Bertram and sailing were practically synonymous. He even had a fucking reentry vehicle tattooed on his foot—now *there* was a high-maintenance way to travel. What did it mean, if Bertram had seen the *fetula* math—had tacitly approved it, by failing to object—and yet was backing out at the last minute?

"Bert," Conrad said, glaring pointedly. "What's this about?"

Bertram shrugged. "I just don't want to." He was a large-framed kid, not fat or force-grown but still vaguely solid, as if he were carved from wood. He'd probably cultivated the look, thinking it was dashing. Or his parents had.

"Afraid your family will disapprove?" Bascal sneered, in that way of his.

"No. That *I* will. This is getting out of hand."

"Out of hand, yes," Bascal agreed, nodding. "You grasp the essence. Even now, the authorities probably have no clue what we're up to." He made a sudden, explosive gesture, slapping a fist into an open palm. "Bam! The launch will shock them, and if we pipe light around the cabin and keep the sail turned edge-on to the Queendom—to Sol and the major planets—we should be fairly invisible.

We'll simply disappear, and they'll wonder where we've gone, and why."

The five of them stood there, and now Khen and Raoul were crossing their arms as well. Bertram was cool, barely there. James just looked uncomfortable.

"And why *have* we done it?" Peter asked.

Bascal scowled for a moment, balling his fists, but then the tension suddenly went out of him, and he smiled. "This isn't a pissing match, *kaume'a*. If you want to stay, be my guest. I'm just a figurehead—technically speaking I can't give legal orders, much less illegal ones. I can't override your better judgment. But stay out of our way, hmm? Because the rest of us are going."

"Um, that may not be wise," Conrad felt compelled to point out.

Wordlessly, Bascal grabbed him by the meat of the elbow—hard, so it hurt—and dragged him to a stand of trees a few meters away for a private conference.

"What."

Conrad shook free. "We'll be using up several tons of lake water to make hydrogen. I'm not sure how much will be left in the lake when we're done. We'll also dump a lot of oxygen into the atmosphere, and then burn it out again when the bag ignites. The simulation shows a big shockwave, around the whole planette, and then heavy rain. I mean *heavy*, and probably hot. There'll be no place to hide."

"So?"

"So, they could be badly hurt. We'd be leaving them on a ruined planette, with no food supply."

Bascal shrugged. "They'll be fine. Rescue is on the way."

"And if they aren't fine?"

The prince's eyes glittered coolly. "That's what backups are for."

Conrad was aghast. Risking your own neck was one thing, but risking someone else's without permission...

They *were* children, fundamentally. Children whose play-time had gotten too rough. "That's not your decision to make, Bas. That's murder."

"Murder five, negligent denial of memory," Bascal said. "A misdemeanor."

Conrad shook his head. "Uh-uh. This is—what do you call it?—premeditated. You can't lie to the Constabulary; they'll *know* it wasn't negligence."

"Only," Bascal said, with rising anger, "because you've just told me all this." He turned toward the Palace Guard that dogged along two or three meters behind him at all times, and snapped officiously, "You there, guard: put a cone of silence on this individual, Conrad Mursk. We've heard enough from him for a while. I want nothing audible. Also prevent him from writing messages, or gesturing elaborately."

"What—" Conrad shouted, but even as the word was forming, he felt the air around him beginning to thicken, to crawl up the pathway of his voice and into his throat, silencing all. The robot was facing him with its blank metal face, training a speaker on him, focusing sound waves. Sympathetic vibration: it observed him, predicted the quivering of his vocal cords, and sent out a canceling wave. The silencer effect.

He tried again: *what, WHAT ARE YOU DOING!* But it was like a two-man trampoline bounce, when your partner stole your energy and went soaring higher and higher into the air, leaving you glued to the fabric no matter how hard you jumped.

It was like being smothered. Conrad began to hyperventilate, breathing in and out and in and out, much too fast. He knew the process didn't actually interfere with his breathing, but tell that to his muscles, his lungs, his throat, which was already getting hoarse and yet could produce nothing more than a faint squeak or click. The robot advanced, taking up a position immediately beside him. Conrad shrank away, but of course the robot followed right along.

Bascal watched him with great interest. "Feels weird? I'll bet it does. Sorry it has to be this way, boyo." He studied Conrad for several seconds, not looking sorry, and when he finally spoke his voice was impatient. "Fuck, man, just breathe. It's not hurting you. I'll take it off as soon as we seal the hatches. I just don't want you blowing our ride over ... what, a guilty conscience? I've liberated you from the possibility of action. You can't affect anything. The guilt is all mine."

"What's going on?" Peter called out, from beyond the trees. He was coming in here. Behind him, Ng's crew was dragging the electrolysis hardware along the Holy Fuckway, up toward the docks.

Bascal gave him a cheerful thumbs-up. "Nothing, just a discussion."

Peter wasn't buying that. "What's wrong with Conrad?"

"Got something in his throat, I think. He's breathing, though, so he must be okay."

Conrad glared with a feeling beyond anger. This wasn't a prank, or even a cruel humiliation. This was invasive, like a rape, except really it was a murder, and Conrad was the accessory. He put a level hand up across his neck, and would have drawn it sideways in a "you're dead" gesture, except that the robot—with bullet-quick movements—caught his forearm in a cool and painless grip, and eased it gently but firmly back down toward his side.

Murder, Conrad mouthed at Peter. *Death. Kill. He's going to kill you.*

But Peter wasn't getting it, wasn't looking closely at Conrad at all. "You punched him," he said to Bascal, who shrugged and didn't deny it. "That's mean. He can't fight back, not with your bodyguard holding him. You're the only man on this planet allowed to throw a punch."

"Oh, I'm not allowed," Bascal said, with a cryptic little

smile. Then he strode off in the direction of the docks, and Peter, with a quick glance in Conrad's direction, turned and followed him, intent on discussing the point further.

Conrad could only watch as the solar panels were set in place and the cables were dipped in the muddy lake, and the water around them began to fizz and boil. Four boys dragged the end of the folded balloon/bag/sail into place, and it billowed as if in a breeze. A bubble appeared in the material, and soon it was swelling, filling. Boys were arranging themselves underneath it, lifting it up so the hydrogen would travel down the length of the bag rather than spilling out the open mouth.

"This'll take a while," Bascal observed, to no one in particular. He was polite enough—if you could call it that—to stay away from Conrad, to keep from rubbing his nose in what had happened.

Or maybe it wasn't politeness at all. Maybe he just didn't want to draw attention to the issue, to get people wondering why Conrad wasn't moving or talking, and had a personal robot guard following him around. The alarming thing was how easily everyone took this in stride. Nobody sought him out, asked him a question, even looked at him for more than a moment or two. It occurred to him, with foolish shock, that he was no major figure in these boys' lives, any more than Peter Kolb or Raoul Sanchez were in Conrad's own. They weren't aching for his opinion. They weren't pausing in their hurried work to fret about his well-being, any more than he ever had for them. And these were his friends, right? Probably the best friends he'd ever had.

Somebody struck up the chorus of the Fuck You Song, and within a few bars everyone was singing, the whole camp ringing and echoing with it. All except for Conrad, who had never felt lonelier in his life. Weirdly, he found himself wishing Feck were here, or his parents, or even that lady from the police station. Somebody uninvolved in this conspiracy.

He jabbed an elbow into the Palace Guard's impervium side, and even this was ignored. Bascal might as well have made him invisible, intangible, a ghost. He considered dropping his pants, just to get some attention, then wondered if his escort would even allow it.

While the song rolled on, the Palace Guards had begun to gather on the dock. One of them said something, in a voice that was loud and polite but not quite distinguishable over the noise. The song faltered and died.

"This activity is dangerous," the guard repeated. "You must desist."

Bascal snorted. "Dangerous? This activity is necessary."

The robot turned. "Spectral analysis of the gas in this enclosure indicates an explosive."

"Not at this altitude," Bascal countered. "Too much xenon. It'll just burn."

And that was true: you could light a match or campfire or barbecue grill with no problem, although the flames were reddish and somewhat sickly. But the boys' research had indicated a problem with the more rapid forms of combustion. Xenon atoms were just too heavy; heating them soaked up all your energy. And they were large, swarming among the smaller oxygen and hydrogen molecules like elephants at a dog-and-cat show.

The robot considered this for a second or so, and then said, "Network confirmation is not available. However, internal simulation supports the assertion. What is the purpose of this activity?"

"It's a balloon," Bascal answered, obviously seeing little point in lying.

"It is anchored to a structure whose foundation has

been undermined. The structure's weight may not be sufficient to counteract buoyancy."

A cautious look came over Bascal's face. "Guard, are you programmed to interfere with educational activities?"

"No," the guard replied.

"What are your exact instructions?"

The robot, faceless, considered Bascal. It seemed to understand that something important was happening, that Bascal was up to something. Detecting bad intentions was the thing's entire purpose. That, and protecting the prince—even from himself. Anyway, they'd been overhearing all the important conversations, and surely must understand at least the gist of it all. Finally, the robot said, in King Bruno's voice, "Hold to the camp schedule, and keep these kids from hurting each other. The fax is for camp activities only."

"That's all?"

"Other than built-in directives and prior standing orders, yes."

The two of them faced one another—a Poet Prince versus the quantum computers of a brilliant but obedient machine.

"Guard," the prince said carefully, "we are leaving this planette. I'll go crazy if we don't. Kindly support us by staying out of the way."

The guard digested that, and replied, "You may not perform any activity without accompaniment."

"Very well," Bascal said, nodding. "One guard will accompany us."

"A minimum of two guards are required in the presence of royalty."

"Two, then."

The robot did not reply. Did that mean it agreed? Assented? Conrad wanted to scream his objections. But the cables in the water bubbled on, and the bag slowly filled.

At first there was just a gas pocket, swelling down here

at the bag's lower end, but the boys did a fair job of teasing it along, driving it up the length of the wellstone tube. Eventually, the middle of the bag gained buoyancy and lifted into the air, forming a great arch like a rainbow over the planette's northern hemisphere, while teams of handlers held the ends down firmly. This was impressive, considering how enormous and heavy the thing was. The wellstone film was translucent and microscopically thin, but there was a lot of it, folded over on itself several dozen times.

Then the rainbow itself began to swell and fatten, and Bascal gave the order to release the upper end, which shot up like a cork in water. It swelled as the pressure around it eased, dropping off rapidly with altitude. Now the balloon was the size of a small cabin, rippling slightly in the convection breeze, and the growing team of handlers was having more and more trouble holding it down. There was a lot of nervous joking, nervous laughter, boys calling for assistance or complaining that their fingers were tired.

"If you're not a handler," Bascal called out, over the rising commotion, "get in the cabin. Now! Now!"

And it was really happening. They were leaving, soon, in the next couple of minutes.

"There may be danger to any person left behind," one of the robots said. "You may not leave any person behind."

"Danger?" said Peter. "What danger?"

"The men staying behind are volunteers," Bascal said. "They're awaiting a rescue craft."

"What danger?" Peter asked again.

"The explosion," Bascal told him impatiently. "And some rain. It might get a little rough."

"This is out of control," Bertram said to the robot. "Stop it now. Please."

The robot regarded him without comment. It wasn't

programmed to take orders—or even suggestions—from anyone but palace staff.

"It's too late to stop it," Bascal said. His voice was calm, brisk, triumphant. "The bag is an explosion waiting to happen. When we let it go, it rises and expands, and its buoyancy increases. If it doesn't detonate immediately, it detonates when we unmoor the cabin and float a little higher."

As if in answer, one of the Palace Guards danced forward and grabbed the bottom of the balloon. Another of them did the same.

"Guards," Bascal said, annoyed, "in about five minutes that material is going to become very slippery. You will not be able to hold it. The balloon will rise and explode, possibly injuring me. You must escort me to a safe place: a wellstone-reinforced structure which is not anchored to the planette."

The guards, watched closely and nervously by everyone, pondered this.

"All children must enter the structure," they finally said.

"I'm not going up in that thing," Peter insisted. "I'm not."

There were guards all around now, and one of them took hold of Peter's wrist. Preparing to drag him to safety.

"Let go of him," Bascal said impatiently. "Do you have any instruction to protect him from himself?"

"No," the guard admitted.

"Then let him go. He's not welcome among us. Run away, Peter. Head for the hills. You have about two minutes."

"You're a shit, Bascal!" Peter screamed. He was crying now, and Conrad didn't blame him a bit. He realized what should have been obvious all along: that Bascal was crazy. He'd inherited his father's driving passions and his mother's easy charm, plus an artistic sensibility that seemed to come straight out of nowhere. But where was the de Towaji compassion that had won Bruno three Medals of Salvation in the days before his kingship? Where was the Lutui common sense, or the Tongan tradition of respect?

In that moment, it seemed that young Bascal would do anything, pay any price, to shock and embarrass his Queendom. He was *enjoying* Peter's fear. And suddenly there were no safe options, not for Peter, not for any of them.

"Garbage pussy bloodfuck," Ho Ng replied, sounding outraged on his monarch's behalf. "You *better* run, little fucker."

"Yeah," Steve Grush added. Apparently he was back on the management team again.

Peter didn't wait to be told a third time. Taking half a second to weigh the odds and face reality, he just put his head down and sprinted off, heading east past the rock formations, presumably toward the hills on Camp Friendly's other side. And though he faced probable injury and certain abandonment, to his credit he did not wail or look back.

"Anyone else?" Bascal asked, looking around pointedly.

Nobody took him up on it. Nobody moved or breathed.

"All right, then. To the cabin. You!" He swept a pointing finger at the boys and robots holding down the bottom of the balloon. "Hang on tight and follow me. Your lives depend on it. We're stopping right outside the cabin door. Clear?"

Nobody questioned the order. And since Conrad didn't have a job to do, and couldn't object, and didn't care to join Peter in pain and exile, he followed docilely along with the crowd. The moment would be etched in his memory forever, endlessly questioned and reexamined for manliness and sensibility and moral correctness, but the truth was, he didn't give it much thought at the time. Didn't have to. His choices were just too limited, his time too short.

The cabin, tightly bound in wellstone film, looked like a badly gift-wrapped toy. The only opening was a vertical slash in the film, just in front of the doorway, which had been rigged to seal itself when the air pressure started dropping. Bascal arrived at the cabin slightly ahead of the others, and bent to snatch something up from the pit of its undermined foundation. A bottle? Green glass with a concave bottom. A wine bottle? Where had he gotten such a thing? Had D'rector Jed, or one of the other counselors, kept a private stash somewhere?

"In honor of my Latin ancestry," the prince said, "I christen this ship *Viridity*: the burning green stamina of youth."

Then he smashed the bottle against the gray-black film and the logs beneath it. The liquid inside was clear, like water. And without further ceremony, he commenced an inspection of the cables—wellstone ribbons, really—that trailed down from the roof, leading off in the direction of the towering column of the balloon. And the balloon was approaching, yes, carefully carried to its launch site at the front of the cabin. The butterflies in Conrad's stomach were restless indeed.

When he got to the d'rector's cabin himself, Xmary was there in the doorway, holding the edges of the wellstone aside and looking out with a worried expression. "Six," she said, touching the shoulder of the boy in front of him—Bertram Wang—then ushering him inside. Next she touched Conrad, acknowledging his solidity without really seeing him. "Seven."

Conrad went inside, with his robot escort following close behind.

"Are *they* coming?" she asked with obvious distaste. She pointed to the Palace Guard, then to the corner. "All right, you, over there. Stay out of the way and try not to fall on anyone."

Her maternal, officious tone was obviously modeled on Her Majesty's. Clearly she saw herself in that role, at least for this particular time and place, although Conrad doubted very much that Queen Tamra had ever been involved in anything so harebrained. But the guard, for whatever reason, chose to obey her.

"Find a mattress," she said to Conrad and Bertram. The phrase sounded rehearsed, like she'd said it several times already, and indeed, the floor was littered with mattresses, and the boys who weren't already on one were looking for one.

Seeing his opportunity, Conrad slipped into Jed's own room, where a number of empty mattresses lay.

"Testing!" he screeched, and the sound was audible. The robot, with its noise-canceling sonic waves, was on the other side of the wall. But Conrad's voice was hoarse—nearly gone—from trying to shout.

"Better lie down," Bertram said. "Fast."

Belatedly, Conrad remembered that this room was where Bascal had put all the controls. He didn't want to face Bascal. But how many free mattresses were there in the other room? Was there time to go back and forth, looking? The view through the window was a hazy confusion of moving bodies and gray translucent film. Right now, the film wrapped around the cabin had no orders to be transparent, but even so he could make out the last few boys straggling in to claim their spaces.

"Shit," he said. And then his Palace Guard reappeared in the doorway, and he could say nothing more. It took up a post in the far corner, looming over Conrad's makeshift acceleration bed like a chrome-plated angel of death.

"Eight, nine, ten, eleven, twelve, thirteen," he heard Xmary say in the room next door. "We're one short. Where is Peter?"

"Not coming." Ho laughed with cruel glee.

And then Bascal's voice: "Lanyards free! Now! Release the bag!"

There were some rustling noises, footsteps, and the slamming of a wooden door. Then the floor lurched and swung, thumped hard against something, lurched and swung again. Conrad threw himself flat.

"Oh, God," Bertram was saying. "Oh gods and God and gods and God..."

Conrad wasn't a praying man, but for the first time in his life in felt the urge, felt the physical attention of the universe, personified. *Dear God. Dear God. I have sinned in various ways, and I'm sorry.* They—the ever-mysterious "they"—said God was nothing more than an anthropomorphic urge, an impulse of the human brain to impose pattern and personality on random events. Donald and Maybel Mursk, Conrad's parents, had always thought so, albeit with an Irish tinge of hope and dread. But speculation was inevitable: what happened to the soul, when a body died and fresh copies were printed? Was there a soul at all? There were all kinds of theories about this, and Conrad feared he was about to learn the truth.

Ho and Bascal staggered into the room, sprawling on the two empty mattresses as the cabin swung wide arcs and began, ever so slightly, to twirl. Outside the window, the gray-white, film-obscured sky was growing dark.

"Here we go!" Bascal shouted. "Here we bloody, fucking g—"

The hydrogen ignited with a gut-wrenching *whump!* that was much louder than any thunder Conrad had ever heard. And the force of the explosion was directed downward, out of the bag, blossoming down along the guy ropes and the cabin roof, storming into the planette's atmosphere in a roiling cloud of hot steam. Conrad suddenly felt as if five people had fallen on him.

Weak gasps and gurgles and screams rose up all

around, and Conrad wanted to scream too. But then there were only four people on his chest, and then two, and then none at all, and he was floating off his mattress, grabbing at the safety straps he'd forgotten to tie around him. They were in outer space. They were in *outer fucking space*, hurtling toward the planette's pinpoint fusion "star" at a hundred meters a second. In a log cabin.

I'm sorry, God. This was a really bad idea.

chapter eight

sun ride, sunset

The wrapping of wellstone film had turned a bit clearer, and "above" them, visible through the nearly transparent skylight, the translucent sail was unfurling, both under the pressure of fusion light and by the command of Bascal Edward de Towaji Lutui. Even without a mirrored surface, the impact of photons had already transferred enough momentum to swing their makeshift boat around. They flew "backward" or "downward" cabin-first, with the *sila'a*—the pocket star—shining out of sight beneath the floorboards.

The control panel was just a programmed sheet of wellstone, pasted onto a wooden plank nailed low to the wall. The instruments and controls on it were two-dimensional cartoons, clear and contemporary in design, glowing softly in the primary colors and yet vaguely Polynesian somehow. Here was a gauge like a compass rosette from an old map; over there sat a diagram of the eight guylines connecting the cabin roof to the sail. The stylized images suggested some winching mechanism, as if the cables could be tightened or loosened on command, which they surely could not. But Bascal had mentioned a few times that that was the way to visualize the steering of a *fetu'ula*, a *fetula*, a stellar sail craft.

"It's an issue of control authority," he'd blathered absently, "very comparable to the rigging on a regular sailboat."

The navigator's seat was a legless chair, crisscrossed with canvas straps, and Bascal seemed at home there now, sitting with one foot under him and the other stretched out under the console. Despite the lack of gravity and the fact that he was tied down, his posture suggested an attention to balance. He was fussing happily with the controls, glancing up through the skylight every few seconds to watch the sail opening up.

"Keep us safe, Majesty," Ho Ng said. "I don't think the boys cared much for that bump."

His tone was ingratiating and solicitous and shitnosed, and of course the honorific was both idiotic and illegal, since even a crown prince was not the King of Sol. But Bascal didn't seem to notice or mind. "You know I will, Ng. A healthy young body, maintained and optimized by fax filters, can handle an awful lot of abuse. I can virtually *guarantee* that you'll be fine."

He turned to Conrad. "We've got about ten more minutes of freefall before I opaque the sail. The planette is forty-seven kilometers from the *sila'a*. Ordinarily I'd just hail the star from here and call up its laser sail protocol, but without a network gate, or even a radio, that would be tricky. You know what we do about that?"

He waited for a long moment, but Conrad, tied down crookedly on his mattress, could only look back at him and shrug.

"Oh. Right," Bascal said. Then, to the guard—whose feet were somehow still anchored to the floorboards— "Remove the cone of silence, please." And then to Conrad again: "Sorry about all that. Really."

The lifting of the silence was a physical sensation, like a breath of wind. "You're a shit," Conrad rasped.

Bascal turned back to his controls. "All that is necessary will be done, my friend. I'd rather you were on the right side of that principle."

"Dead, shitty bodies," Ho agreed.

Conrad saw no reason to reply. Above, the sail was almost fully open now, and billowing with underwater slowness. Worse: with honeyed, glacial slowness.

From the other room came sounds of commotion, followed by nervous laughter and hoots of dismay. "Hey, do *not* fuck around back there," Bascal called out. "Ten gees can kill you falling ten *centimeters*. You motherless bastards tie down and shut up."

"Ten gees?" Conrad repeated, his hoarse voice ringing with the worry of all these unpleasant surprises. He'd somehow envisioned the actual sailing as a graceful, languid affair.

"Quit whining, you baby. We're young and strong, and fit as the morbidity filters can make us. We've been *faxed*; we're *immortal*. Well, immorbid, anyway. And anyway, it's more like eight and a half gees. I am rigidizing the sail . . . Now."

Like mandolin strings, the guylines jinged and sproinged, sending quasi-musical vibrations down through the cabin roof. The lazy batwing of the sail, arched away from the cabin and the guy ropes like a dome-tent roof, began to pull downward and spread out, becoming a flat translucent ceiling a hundred meters above them, its wings stretching out of sight beyond the edges of the skylight, extending more than seven hundred meters on either side, and half that much from top to bottom. The process took about twenty seconds, and chewed up only a tiny fraction of the solar energy raining up to them from the pocket star.

"Now I'm commencing rotation," the prince announced.

"Why?"

"Because we're flying backward, idiot. We have to

point where we're fucking going, and the sail needs to be in front of us when we mirrorize it, or the light pressure will push it against the cabin and we'll get all fouled up in the ropes. You want that? No?"

"Why not just rigidize the lines?"

"They *are* rigidized." Bascal huffed impatiently. "There's a control issue, all right? It isn't stable, pushing backwards like that. It's . . . look, just shut up and let me sail."

Above, the left half of the wellstone took on a brighter shade of the same gray color, slightly less transparent than the right half. The guylines spanged and sproinged again, and Conrad felt himself pressed lightly against his tie-downs on the left side. The ship was heeling around, turning to face its rear—and its sail—at the *sila'a*. Presently, it bloomed at the edge of the skylight, a miniature sun no more than a few meters across. Just a pinpoint, really, yellow-orange and painfully bright, even through the veil of the wellstone.

Then the sail's colors shifted again, swapping sides, and Conrad felt himself pressed the other way. The *sila'a*, though, continued its way across the skylight, finally pausing just past its left edge, eclipsed by the cabin's wall and roof. Then the wellstone sail fabric was edge-on to the light, no longer illuminated like a lamp shade, and through its sudden translucence Conrad could make out the stars gliding gently to a halt.

Deep space, here we come, he breathed silently.

"Now this," Bascal said, to no one in particular, "is the hard part. You ever try to back up a sailboat against the wind? The trick is to angle in, null your orbital velocity, and then use the sail itself as a brake, kind of like a parachute."

Conrad couldn't make sense of that remark. "A parachute? What are we, diving into the sun?"

"*Onto* the *sila'a*, yes. The fusing hydrogen sits on top of a neuble core, and there's a solid wellstone surface on top of that, to hold it all in. We need to make contact with that outer shell in order to communicate with the machinery. But there's an advantage in doing that: it gets us close enough to reflect the laser beam right back at the *sila'a*. Set up our own little resonating chamber, for extra pressure, extra thrust. It'll be like shooting a rocket out of a bottle."

"I . . . have no idea what you're talking about. You've done this before?"

"Hmm? Oh, gods no. Nobody has."

Conrad wanted to object: the very idea of backing into a star—even a miniature one—seemed like craziness of the highest order. And bouncing laser beams back into it, for extra thrust? Something had gone awry in their plans, some deeply fucked failure of communication, because he sure hadn't agreed to any of this. But here and now, did they have a choice? Could they get back to the planette even if they wanted to? Even if Bascal would let them try?

"Okay," Bascal said, "I'm going to turn us again."

It was a stately process, and while it transpired Conrad couldn't help noticing how *bright* it was getting outside, as the light of the *sila'a* drew ever nearer, illuminating the guylines and the translucent shrink-wrapping around the cabin. The sail itself was mostly invisible now, a batwing of utterly transparent material, with little squares of silver flitting across it, and clustering in particular on its right-hand side, like a swarm of sun-seeking insects.

"Asymmetric pressure," Bascal explained, catching Conrad's look. "The light pushes on the starboard half of the sail but not the port. That's what turns us, pulls us around."

"Why does it flicker like that?"

"Stability. The control system is keeping the sail from fluttering or sliding out sideways against the guylines. It's like the tensioning springs on a spinnaker tack. . . . Well, you've never been sailing, so never mind. But yeah, it's supposed to do that."

Gradually, the flickering squares of silver diminished in number, and spread themselves more evenly across the sail, and began to gleam in a really painful way as the *sila'a* brightened and neared behind them.

"Boy, that's bright," Bascal observed. He did something to the controls on his panel, and the squares of silver became squares of bronze, and the shrink-wrapping above the skylight turned a translucent shade of black that was very close to the natural color of wellstone. It blotted out the remaining stars, and made a shimmery halo of the sail and guylines.

Conrad began to notice a sensation of weight, pulling and pressing him into the mattress again.

"Gravity," Ho Ng said. "Is that the star I'm feeling underneath me, Sire?"

"Yeah," Bascal told him absently. He was still fiddling with the controls, looking annoyed about something. "Well, it's also our deceleration. We're sort of hovering right now. Or we will be in another minute. I'm trying not to bump us too hard."

Against the surface of a star. Good God. Against the solid surface of a manmade star that was *so unimaginably hot* that it could warm a planette, could cook a dinner or burn a young man's face, from forty-seven kilometers away. And yes, it was definitely getting warmer in here!

"Are we going to be cooked, Bas?" he couldn't help asking.

"No," the prince said, sounding even more annoyed. But he fiddled some more, and the view outside the windows went totally black for a moment, and then mirror-bright, reflecting the cabin's interior lighting back in lumpy, funhouse-mirror ways.

Then he looked alarmed, and had time to say "Whoops"

in the moment before something very solid and very heavy slammed up into the center of the cabin's floor.

BAM!

Even as he was slammed into his mattress and jerked against its straps, Conrad was aware of the sounds of cracking and splintering. He even had time to note that these sounds, however brief and mild, were just about the most alarming thing you could possibly hear on board a wooden spaceship. And even when the cracking stopped, the floor itself groaned. Something was bending it in a way it had never been bent before, and the force of gravity— the invisible hand pressing Conrad into his padding— seemed much too strong. Much stronger than at the surface of Camp Friendly.

"Get us off this thing!" he shouted at Bascal. "It's breaking, it's going to *break*! How do you talk to the star?"

"Verbally, I assume," Bascal said, sounding a bit shaken himself. "Otherwise we're in real trouble." Then he turned his head toward the floor and shouted, *"Hello? Sila'a? Can you give us laser sail protocol, please?"*

Nothing happened.

Nothing except that Conrad felt his rage boil over. *This* was their plan? Ramming a star and then shouting at it? Asking nicely? *This* was their fucking *plan*?

"Laser sail protocol!" Bascal shouted, more loudly. Then screamed, probably as loudly as he was able, *"Laser fucking sail! Now!"*

Conrad snarled. "You're a goddamned idiot, Bascal. Thanks for this."

"Oh," Bascal said. "Shit. I forgot to mirrorize the sail."

He touched the control panel, and then—

They went. Something caught them. Conrad could *feel* the sail bulging outward against its own incredible stiffness, the tight guylines suddenly straining, the crushing/ pressing ball of the *sila'a*, maybe four burning meters across, falling out beneath them and dropping away, away.

There was nothing stately about it: the other thing Conrad felt was the air crushing out of him, like an iron-weighted pillow settling down on his chest. Taking the next breath was like lifting barbells with his lungs. His vision had gone grainy and narrow, and he felt, in a distinctly physical way, that he was looking out through a tunnel from the back of his brain. His soul had fled from its usual spot just behind the eyes, had been squeezed back against the barrier of his skull. If it squeezed any farther, it would leave his body altogether.

The windows had gone transparent again, or anyway they were admitting light—a biting monochromatic violet, mirrored brightly in the checkered silver of the sail and shimmering with the telltale interference gleams and darknesses of reflected laser. The cabin groaned and shrieked, and from somewhere came—again!—the long and loud and ominous crack of splintering wood. But Conrad barely noticed, barely considered it. He dragged a breath in and then let it whoosh back out. Dragged it in, let it out.

New squares of silver appeared here and there, the checkerboard sail filling as the *sila'a* drew smaller and dimmer and more distant beneath them. Conrad understood, in a vague way, that Bascal was throttling their acceleration, upping the reflectivity of the sail to draw out more velocity, more speed, keeping them right at the limits of human endurance. He wished he'd asked more questions during the planning phase—especially given the whole Garbage Day fiasco—but this was a vague thought as well, pieced together in the brief interval between Herculean breaths. He dragged one in and let it out. Dragged it in, let it out.

It went on like that until his sense of time began to flicker out. A minute? Two? And still it continued on, the pain and struggle, the slow grinding of wood against wood. He could feel his flesh bruising, his blood pooling, his bones and muscles and cartilage stretching and twisting in unnatural ways. The pain grew, and the light dimmed, and his breath came harder and harder, and he knew that if they somehow survived he would be sore for weeks.

Finally—finally!—the pressure began to ease. The sail above them was pure mirror from end to end, reflecting a field of fixed stars and a dwindling violet minisun no brighter than a searchlight. But the pressure eased too slowly, and the pain in every part of his body continued to build. He could tell time by it—a pain clock. He had the luxury now of feeling impatient, and feel it he did, marking the passage of every moment.

As soon as it felt possible and safe, he rolled over onto his side. This brought him face-to-face with Bascal, whose customary grin was long gone. He looked drawn and pained, his brown face shining, his hair matted down with sweat. And yet, his right arm was raised and extended, doing something or other on the control panel.

"Doesn't that hurt?" Conrad asked.

"Yes," Bascal replied tightly.

Indeed, the arm looked both bleached and blackened by its ordeal.

"Shouldn't you stop?"

Bascal grimaced. "Kind of, yeah. I'm . . . going to change seats."

"Are you crazy?"

"Naw. We're a minute into the run, and we'll be holding steady at two gees for a couple minutes here. I've had worse."

"A *minute*?" Conrad found that figure very hard to believe—surely it should be an hour!—but there it was on the panel's chronometer: 01:08, 01:09, 01:10 . . .

The acceleration was steady now, and yes, truthfully, not so terrible. Even so, Bascal groaned in obvious pain as he undid his tie-downs and slithered out of the nav chair. The pale right arm, drained of blood, didn't seem to be working well; it flopped around numbly while Bascal worked with his left. When he was free of the straps, he scooted his rump along the floor for half a meter, until he was seated beside his empty mattress. He didn't try to lift or roll himself into it.

"You make me proud," Ho said to Bascal, in a tired and grating voice. He was struggling to sit up.

Conrad decided to join him in this, but thought better of it when his back screamed in protest. And then thought better of *that* when he lay back down and felt the sweaty mattress pressing smotheringly against the side of his face. So he did sit up, and really, it didn't feel too bad. He was alive, and not seriously hurt, although yeah, he was going to be very, very sore.

People were coughing and groaning and crying in the other room. There was the unmistakable *clump! clump!* of heavy footsteps on the wooden floor, and then Xmary was standing there, framed in the doorway in a pair of camp culottes and a tee shirt cut off to display her navel, and with the reflected purple of the *sila'a* laser shining down through the skylights, Conrad could distinctly see her nipples and the outline of her hips and thighs. Her hair was pulled back in the kind of topknot the centenarians were wearing lately, and like many young women, she'd subtly nudged her physical development in a compact but adult direction, and did not look at all like a child in this light.

"Bascal," she said, quickly and seriously, "something's wrong with Raoul. He's coughing, and there's blood coming out."

"I'm sailing, dear," Bascal answered tightly. And yeah, he could reach the controls even from his mattress.

"What should we do?"

"Well, if I don't keep an eye on these heading corrections, there's going to be something wrong with all of us, hmm? Just hold his hand or something. Ask the guards."

"Is it a lot of blood?" Conrad asked.

She shook her head. "No, just, like, spots of it. Can you come look? Please?"

"Yeah," he said, and made a show of rising without any grimaces or groans. This wasn't actually so difficult—he felt like he was carrying someone on his back, but no longer as if the life were being crushed out of him. It did hurt a lot to walk, though.

The cabin's main room was like something from an old movie: wounded men sprawling on narrow, filthy beds. There was blood on several of them, and more streaming out from the finger-pinched noses of a couple of scared-looking boys. But it was Raoul who really looked bad—gray and bruised, with dark baggy circles under his eyes and blood-flecked spittle on his chin and tee shirt. His chest rose and fell in rapid, shallow rhythm.

"You okay?" Conrad asked him, stupidly.

Raoul looked up with frightened eyes, and shook his head. Nope.

"He was coughing," Xmary said.

Awkwardly, Conrad crouched down beside the bloody mattress. "You're breathing kind of fast. Can you slow it down?"

Again, Raoul shook his head. No. Definitely not.

"Can you talk?"

No.

"It could be his lungs," Conrad said, although he had no idea. Why was she asking him for help? What could he do? "This goes way beyond first-aid training."

"How do we help him?" Xmary demanded.

"I don't know," Conrad said honestly. The usual treatment for severe injuries was to throw the victim into the nearest fax machine, and print out an undamaged copy. Was that possible in this case, with the network gates disabled and the machinery bound by weird instructions from the king? He glanced up at the fax machine, bolted against the room's innermost wall. The divider wall separating it from the main room had been removed two days ago. They had clear access if they needed it.

"Fax, will you take him? Repair him?"

"Insufficient buffer mass," the fax answered. "I can accept a body and correct its pattern, but reinstantiation will not be possible."

"Why?" Conrad asked. "Can't you just use his own mass? Disassemble him and then rebuild him?"

The fax spoke slowly, as if inventing the art of conversation as it went along. "My mass buffers have been depleted by recent operations. Sir. The operation you suggest would bring several of them, temporarily, into a negative mass regime, which is not possible."

Shit. Conrad had shoveled some dirt in there a few days ago, on Bascal's advice, but he hadn't checked the levels since then. Hadn't really thought about it at all. Did dirt even have the right elements in it?

"Can we throw some of the food in?" someone suggested.

"Or take a huge crap in the toilet?" That was Steve Grush, trying to be funny. Or maybe not; the sink and shower and toilet plumbing ran into and out of the fax in a maze of shiny wellstone pipes. A piece of crap would, in fact, be whisked apart into component atoms and stored in the appropriate mass buffers.

"Hurry up," Xmary said, in a deadly serious tone. And with good reason: Raoul's eyes had rolled upward, so that only the whites were showing, and those whites—mostly red—were jiggling and jittering in a spasmodic way. His breathing had grown even faster and shallower. He was dying, plain and simple.

"Fax," Conrad said, "can we just stuff him in there, and print him out later?"

"Certainly."

Conrad and Xmary shared a quick glance, nodded at

each other, and grabbed Raoul by the arms while Steve Grush undid his straps. The only hard part was the confusing mess of bodies and mattresses between them and the fax, but people were scrambling out of the way, or moving to help. Raoul's legs were grabbed as well, and his bottom, and as a group they gave him the old heave-ho. It seemed very strange, to stuff a limp, twitching body through the solid-looking print plate of the fax. But it wasn't really solid. Even a cursory inspection showed it was insubstantial, actually a fog of tiny machines sprouting tinier machines sprouting quantum doodads far too small to be visible. And Raoul's body went right through it, like a diver through the surface of Adventure Lake.

He was saved. Literally. In memory.

"Anyone else?" Conrad asked anxiously, turning to survey the room. But all the other boys were shaking their heads, hiding their hands. No sir, not me.

"Sure?" he pressed, an edge of humor finally creeping into his voice. But there were no takers, and Conrad had begun to feel distinctly light on his feet. He turned toward the navigation room. The *bridge*, he supposed they should call it. "Hey Bascal, how low is this gravity going to get?"

"Zero!" Bascal called back, sounding annoyed. "Enjoy it while it lasts!"

Oh. Right. As they drew away from the *sila'a*, as its laser brightness faded and dimmed, there was nothing to push them, no source of acceleration. Conrad had known this, and yet somehow he'd been visualizing them all walking around in here for two months. Not drifting, not floating. Because it was a log cabin, he supposed. Because it had such a definite floor and ceiling, and belonged on the ground.

In that moment, it dawned on him that he really did have an impulse problem. He had a brain but wasn't using it, and as a result everything—even the obvious things—kept coming to him as nasty surprises. Hell, they didn't have any *facilities* in here for zero gravity. How were they going to sleep? To store things? To use the toilet? Now *there* was an unpleasant thought! And what had all these other kids been thinking? Disbelieving in the entire scheme, never thinking it would really happen? That, or relying on Bascal to work it all out. Or rather, Bascal and his team, meaning basically just Conrad, since Bascal didn't care and nobody else seemed to worry much how anything worked. Except Peter, whom they'd left behind on the planette.

"Oh boy," he said to Xmary. "This is going to be a hell of a trip."

The illusion of gravity dropped away over the next sev-eral minutes while Conrad pointed and gestured and spoke urgently, throwing together impromptu work details to clean up the things that had already fallen and broken, and to lash everything else down, and to come up with covers and hoods for the bathroom fixtures before things could get any worse in there. By the time they were twenty minutes into the flight, gravity was down to a tenth of a gee, and they were all dancing giddily on air.

It didn't surprise Conrad when people ignored him. What did surprise him was the ease and complicity with which most of them listened and, albeit in offhand and slipshod ways, obeyed. Was this because he was friends with Bascal? (*Was* he still friends with Bascal, and did he even want to be?) Or was it simply because there were obvious things that needed doing, and he was the only one pointing them out?

The fax proved willing to provide first-aid supplies—crafted from the atoms that had been Raoul Sanchez—so the nosebleeds were soon plugged and coagulated, the sprains iced, the bruises warmed and moistened. Tape bandages were wrapped around questionable limbs and joints, while skin sealants were applied to the many cuts and abrasions the boys had suffered. Anti-inflammatory medications were passed around liberally; the insults of heavy gee had spared no one.

Even Xmary had her share of ouches. Conrad found himself dabbing her middle back with sealant foam while she held the back of her shirt up over one shoulder with a bruisy-looking arm.

"Ow," she said.

"Sorry. I'm almost done."

"Does it look bad?"

"It looks painful," Conrad admitted. The wound was a flap of skin the size of his pinkie nail, not especially bloody for some reason, but partly separated from the flesh beneath. He smoothed it back in place with the sealant, then blew on it to hasten its drying, all the while acutely conscious of the smoothness of her skin. "What did you do?"

"Fell," she said. "The edge of the mattress caught me."

"A *mattress* did this? Gods."

"Yeah." She lowered her shirt.

"What the fucky hell?" said Ho Ng's voice. Conrad turned, and saw Ho there glowering in the doorway.

"What?" he asked, mostly innocently.

Ho stepped forward. "Who said you could touch the princess?"

"What princess?"

"He's sealing a cut," Xmary snapped, standing up and straightening her clothing. This effort proved both difficult and elaborate; what little "gravity" they had left was gently pulling things to the floor, but any movement would kick it all up again. She bounced several times on her toes before settling to the floor again, and Conrad couldn't help but notice the loose jiggle of her small breasts, and wonder what they looked like under there.

She gestured around her with an arm—another elaborate effort. "Use your eyes, Ho. We've got casualties."

"I'll use my eyes," he said, staring her up and down with creepy lust, humorless and undisguised.

She glided toward him like a ballerina, and managed to stop gracefully, right in his face. "Watch yourself."

If it was a staring contest, she won it right away; Ho turned his glare on Conrad. "Don't touch her again."

"Or what?" he couldn't help asking. Shooting his mouth off again, yes, heedless of consequence. How many losing battles had he fought for the sake of these verbal jabs? Not that Ho could punch him or kick him or grapple him, not in the immediate presence of two Palace Guards. If rumors were any guide, the things could not only move fast enough to generate whipcracks and sonic booms, but could sense the intention of violence before the fact, could read it in the brain and the nerves and the tensing of muscles. Tazzing a punch was one thing, but how would they respond to an impending act of genuine malice?

Conrad was tired of Ho. If he *could* fight, it might be better to just get it over with, and give this fucker something to think about next time. On the other hand, he was under no illusion that he could win the fight, or that standing up for himself would magically end the threats and humiliations. It'd make them worse, probably.

Damn it, he'd waited long enough for his fear to kick in. Real fear. It was balanced by anger, what with Peter abandoned to the elements and Raoul stuffed in a fax machine and used for buffer mass. And balanced also by lust and pride; in front of Xmary, who was probably the only girl for ten AU in every direction, he had no interest in looking timid.

"Or what?" he repeated, but his voice broke, betraying his fright. The room had gone silent, except for the gentle whirring of the Palace Guard as it turned its head to regard them.

Bascal appeared behind Ho, tapping him on the shoulder. "Boys," he said. "Or rather, men! What's this posturing all about?"

"He touched your woman," Ho said, stepping aside without turning, his eyes still locked on Conrad.

Bascal took another step into the room. "Is this true?" The question was directed at Xmary, not Conrad.

"He was sealing a cut," Xmary said. "We have a lot of injuries back here."

"No doubt," Bascal agreed, nodding vaguely. His eyes settled on Conrad. "Thank you for helping. In the future, though, try to check with me first. Or Ho. All right?"

"Um, sure," Conrad said, keeping his tone neutral, though his cheeks grew hot. There was his answer: the pecking order had been rearranged. Conrad was no longer the prince's confidant, Ho Ng was. The idea would be funny if it weren't so sickening. "No concern."

Bascal surveyed the room, taking note of the bandages and bloodstains. "Rough ride," he said.

"You're hurt," Xmary observed, looking at the pale, bruisy flesh of his right arm.

He swung it, then rubbed it, then swung it again. "I'll be all right. I just need to get some blood back into it. Are we, uh, are we one man short? One more, I mean?"

She nodded. "We had to save Raoul in the fax. Conrad's idea."

Bascal's gaze turned back on Conrad. "Quick thinking, boyo. Very good." He paused a moment, then tapped his jaw and said, "Now that you mention it, we've got some other passengers aboard this *fetula* who weren't exactly enthusiastic about the voyage. Maybe we should do them a favor as well."

"Sir?" Ho said, gliding a step forward.

Bascal nodded at him. "Yeah. Ng, would you please escort Khen and James and Bert into the fax for safekeeping?"

He took her promise, for a start,
And took her hand in his, and,
In love he took her heart.
He took her lips against his own,
He took that girl apart!

—*"Male-Ordered Bride"*
BASCAL EDWARD DE TOWAJI LUTUI,
age 12

stowage

"Keep your hands off me," Bertram said, gliding back along the wall.

"Fuck you," James added. "Both of you shits."

Ho Ng advanced. "Don't you talk to the prince that way, bloodfuck. Get in the fax."

"Nobody's hurting anybody," Bascal said, in a tone that fell rather short of reassuring.

"Stay away," Bert said. He was still calm, but barely.

Ho leaped forward in a long, slow arc, his outstretched hands reaching for James' shoulders. James tried to duck aside, and made the mistake of throwing a punch in the general direction of Ho's face. It missed, and the two tumbled upward in a flailing mass, arms and legs against the logs and cement of the cabin wall. And then the Palace Guard was there, having dashed across the floor with characteristic grace, its feet held down by some invisible, gravitylike force. Conrad hadn't quite seen it happen, but two of the mattresses in the robot's path were now spilling out dust and flakes of foam rubber, their covers torn in patterns shaped like robot feet.

Conrad had expected the robot to separate the combatants, but in fact it simply restrained James, got his feet back on the floor, and let Ho continue to hang onto his other arm.

"Guard," Bascal said lazily, "assist the process, please. Thank you."

"Let go! Let *go!*" James yelled. His struggles intensified, but against the robot he had little hope of success. He attempted to drag his feet, but this simply resulted in their flailing in the air behind him, with the tie-down laces of his camp sneakers fluttering loose. He began to scream like a condemned man, which might very well be the case, because once he was in the fax there was no specific guarantee that he would be reinstantiated. *Some* archived copy of him would, sometime, but maybe not this one, with these memories. This particular James Shadat might well be on his way to the gods and the afterlife, or the blank nothingness, or whatever.

He shrieked when they hurled him at the plate, and the sound was cut off as his head passed through, and then there was only the pop and hiss of his body going in, every atom measured and logged and teleported away to a nearby buffer. Or something like that; Conrad didn't really know how fax machines worked.

"Bascal," he said, "you've got to stop this." He felt sick. Responsible. The prince had gotten this idea from him!

"Nonsense," Bascal said, with a wave of the hand. "They're better off in there, out of trouble and out of harm's way. Everyone will be happier. Plus, it's too crowded in here anyway. Ho? If you'll continue, please?"

"Pleasure," Ho agreed, turning and leaping at Bertram Wang. The Palace Guard followed at a more stately pace, marching magically along the floor, but it got there only a few moments after Ho did.

Bert opted to retain his dignity, saying only, "Is this how you'll lead the Queendom, 'Sire'?"

"We may never know," Bascal answered. And then Bert was gone.

Khen turned out to be another screamer, and afterward Emilio Roberts, one of the bloody-nose kids, lost his composure and started crying and kicking. "This can't be happening! You can't be doing this." So they chucked him in the fax as well.

When it was done, the room was very quiet, and all eyes were on Bascal. He seemed to sense that he was in trouble, that he'd overstepped and lost the confidence of his followers. Nobody wanted to be next. But when he spoke, it was with a flourish and an easy smile.

"We knew the journey would be difficult, and we probably *should* have known there'd be friction and hasty compromises. I didn't foresee this, and I apologize to all of you for the ugly spectacle. I promise, it won't be repeated. But you know as well as I do: if we let those men wander free, the trouble will be much worse. Would you rather tie them up? Kill them? This seems to me like a prudent compromise. Agreed?"

"What do we do now?" someone asked.

"We sail," Bascal answered simply. He looked at Xmary. "You, darling, will be administering resources. Can you establish meal schedules and such?"

"Yeah," she replied, without great enthusiasm.

"Terrific." He turned and launched himself back toward the bridge in a bounding leap.

Conrad followed him. "What're you doing, Bas? What's the grand idea here?"

"Well, first we turn the *fetula* so the sail is edgewise to Sol. That'll reduce our risk of detection when we have to opaque it. We don't want to glint, or blot out any stars. Too much risk of being seen." Bascal was settling back into the navigator's chair.

"That's not what I mean," Conrad said.

"Nevertheless, that's what we have to do."

"He bothering you, Majesty?" Ho said from the doorway.

"Nah. He needs to be in here, to pick up the art of steering. We'll take it in shifts from here on."

"No concern," Ho said self-importantly. "You need me, I'll be right out here."

"Good. I'll call when I do."

The other Palace Guard was still in here, standing motionless in the corner. Between it and Ho, there was considerable reason to avoid antagonizing the prince.

Nevertheless, Conrad crossed his arms. "So I'm steering now, am I? You've been making a lot of decisions for a lot of people, Bas. You haven't done much asking. Why don't you let your buddy Ho pilot the ship?"

Without looking up from the controls, Bascal said, "Come off it, boyo. Anyone can steer—well, almost anyone—but you're the only one here with a basic understanding of wellstone. How the system works together, collectively. And you've driven vehicles before. You and I are the only qualified pilots."

"Get fucked."

"I'm sure I will," the prince said, then turned to face Conrad. "Look, I can do this without you. It's inconvenient, but it's not impossible. If you want to be useless and annoying, that's your decision."

"Yeah? You too, Mr. Cone-of-Silence. Are you helping the people on this . . . this so-called spaceship? Supporting their interests, fighting for their rights? I used to think so."

"Watch yourself," Bascal said, then sighed. "I would like your help, all right? I'd like your support. I'm asking nicely."

With his arms still folded, Conrad shook his head. "You can't behave this way, Bas."

"Don't tell me what I can't do." Bascal's voice was mild. "I understand your problem: you keep thinking this is a lark. Some kind of joyride. But it *really isn't*. We're not doing this for our amusement; we're doing it for the next *million years* of our eternal lives. We've got to start those lives off strong and hard, or we'll never be taken seriously. I wish you could just get that fact into your head and keep it there."

"Fine, it's not a game. It's serious, million-year business. That doesn't mean you're free to abuse people. It's."—Conrad groped for the right word—"counterproductive. It hurts our cause. What will people say if your own followers wind up denouncing you?" .

"It depends how the PR ladies spin it," Bascal answered. But he at least appeared to be thinking it over.

Conrad pressed the point: "You either have support or you don't, Bas. I'm not sure *you* understand. I can be on your side and still not agree with . . . all this. There's a right way and a wrong way."

That made the prince angry. "Oh, so now I'm stupid? I understand exactly what you're saying, Conrad, but it's possible I know more about this than you do. If I remember correctly, you're not the Queendom's finest student."

"And you are," Conrad sneered. It was a stupid thing to say, because yeah, everyone knew what a prodigy Prince Bascal was, and always had been. It was kind of amazing, actually, that a Poet Prince could be friends with a Cork County disappointment like Conrad Mursk. Which helped his argument not at all.

Bascal spread his hands apologetically. "Look, I'm not convinced I can trust you. First you're in favor, then you're against; then you've got backbone, and now you don't. . . . I don't know, Conrad. How smart is that? Unless you're a genius of epic proportion, what I really need is somebody who listens to my informed opinion."

"Like Ho Ng."

"Well, yeah. Actually."

"You don't want to listen to him, Bas. You really don't. Nothing he says or does is for the good of other people."

Bascal sighed and relaxed his hands, setting them adrift in a low-gravity gesture oddly reminiscent of Feck.

"Just let it go. Your opinion is noted, but we've got to turn the *fetula* now, before the sail gives us away. At the moment it's aimed almost directly downsystem—that's toward the sun—and any decent astronomer or traffic controller is going to pick it up sooner or later. We've got to disappear before they realize we're gone. Will you take a few minutes to learn something? Please?"

It was Conrad's turn to sigh. Was there a choice? Would his refusal help anything at all? Regardless of politics, there *should* be more than one person on board the ship who knew how to operate it. That was just basic safety.

"All right," he said. "Show me."

"Good man."

By way of a primer, Bascal pointed out the ordinal directions: port/starboard, fore/aft, and boots/caps. And the cardinal ones: upsystem/downsystem, north/south, and clock/counter.

"When I say 'boots aft,' it means a negative pitch along this axis, see? When I say 'correct north,' it means we add velocity *that* way, out of the ecliptic plane where the planets all orbit. Until further notice and regardless of orientation. You see? It's actually very simple. There are galactic coordinates as well, but we won't need those. Now sit, and watch what I do."

Conrad watched and listened, as patiently as his fear and ambivalence would permit. And he saw that the control of a *fetula*—and by extension, a sailboat—was nothing at all like the control of a construction tractor. The eight guylines were distant cousins to the track clutches of a bulldozer, or the front-end hydraulics of a steamroller, but they pointed off in so many different directions! And there was nothing akin to a brake or throttle, unless you counted the sail itself, whose transparency could be varied on demand.

Still, there was one piece of his father's advice that

seemed perfectly apropos: *Horse around with this thing, lad, and you're bound to regret what happens next.*

Having lost Feck and Peter, and five others besides, they were down to just Xmary and eight boys. In addition to Bascal, Ho, and Steve Grush, there were Preston Midrand and Martin Liss, two quiet kids Conrad had never really talked to. And there was Jamil Gazzaniga, who talked incessantly about bicycles, and Karl Smoit, the budding young sports nut who had invented the game of shirtball soccer.

Unfortunately, the last of their acceleration had gone away when Bascal turned the sail, and you couldn't play kickball in zero gravity, so Karl was driving everyone crazy with his imaginary ball and goal.

"He lines up! He kicks!"

"He spins ass-over-elbows," Steve observed acidly, stretching a foot out for Karl to collide with.

"Get fucked, you shit," Karl said to him, grabbing and twisting the foot. This was actually sort of brave, and under other circumstances Conrad would have admired him for it. But it had the potential to escalate into a full-blooded fight, and from there maybe even a feud, and it was *way* too early in *way* too cramped a voyage to be starting with that kind of thing.

"The men are already bored," he said loudly, to both Xmary and Bascal. Xmary because he figured she'd care; Bascal because he might actually know what to do about it. He'd had every possible kind of leadership training, right?

"Knock it off, guys," Bascal said.

Steve now had an arm around Karl's shoulder and neck, and said, "Tell him to quit with the acrobatics."

Bascal tapped his chin. "No, I don't think so. Let him go; let him do what he's doing. We'll have acrobatics for the next hour, and then dinner, and then story time and lights out. Xmary will draw up a formal schedule in the morning."

"Schedule! Just like camp!" Jamil Gazzaniga sneered. "We'll get the Palace Guards to announce it!"

"Story time?" Steve complained. "What are we, six?"

Bascal just smiled. "The Tongan people used to spend months at a time in outrigger canoes. They were the greatest mariners of their day, much better than the Greeks or the Romans or even the English and French who eventually conquered the rest of Polynesia. They could hit an island the size of Camp Friendly from a thousand miles away. Without compasses, without anything. They even had a navy. Conquered Fiji and Samoa a couple of times in hundred-man sailboats. Charted the seas as far away as America and Madagascar."

"So?" Jamil said.

"So, an outrigger or catamaran has a lot less space—less volume—than this *fetula*. There *was* no exercise hour, and story time lasted all day. You should feel lucky."

"Oh, we do," Jamil answered, in the same mocking tone.

"Stow that shit," Ho Ng told him from across the room. "Or I'll stow *you*."

"Nyu nyu nyu," Jamil told him—a brilliant comeback if Conrad had ever heard one. But afterward, Jamil was smart enough to stay quiet, and Karl kept his exercises to himself.

Mealtime was interesting: you had to unstow and un-pack the food, keep track of it long enough to eat it, and then clean up after yourself without leaving crumbs and greasy/sticky blobs all over the place. Nobody really had the hang of it—not even Bascal—but Conrad supposed they had plenty of time to practice.

Afterward, at precisely the moment Peter would have predicted if Peter had been there, the motionless Palace Guards announced, in stereo, "Lights out, time to sleep."

"We're not at camp anymore," Bascal told them impatiently. "You can stop all that."

Still, at the *pilinisi*'s insistence, the wellstone ceiling's glow was turned down and reddened, and everyone gathered around to hear him tell the evening's first story. It felt a bit foolish, and Conrad was still uneasy about this whole thing, and about Bascal in particular. But then again there was no TV here, and no quiet place to read a book, so what the hell.

"Tonga has no king," Bascal said, sitting cross-legged with his feet twisted up in a strap. "There is no Tonga."

"I thought that was your dad," Steve Grush cut in, provoking nods and murmurs from several others around the circle.

"No," Bascal said, looking annoyed. "My father may be the King of Sol, but never has been and never will be the Tu'i Tonga. Technically speaking, he can't even own property there, although I doubt the courts would see it that way. My mother is the Kuini Tonga, and there *is* no king. There never will be again. But I was actually referring to the story I'm trying to tell, about the first people in the world, before Tonga even existed."

He paused, glancing around the circle both to make sure he had his audience's full attention, and for dramatic effect. The Poet Prince in action. Then he began.

"Imagine that we're on the open ocean. Waves rolling all around us, the hot sun beginning to set. The horizon is a dividing line between the sky and the sea. Imagine a catamaran sailboat: two huge canoe hulls with a sturdy platform lashed between them, as big as *Viridity*'s cabin here around us, though it's open to the sky and the sea. And there's a mast we can raise or lower as needed. There may be enclosed buildings on the platform, or a whole second level, or both. The sail is woven pandanus fiber, which depending on how you prepare it can be anything from tough basket wicker to a soft cloth, like silk. It's the wellstone of its day. The rigging is a line of twisted coconut husk.

"This is not a primitive vessel; the largest versions can carry a hundred armed men, with months of provisions. It simply lacks metal, or clay, or any of the thousands of materials other civilizations take for granted. If it isn't a plant or a bone or a volcanic rock, we've never seen it, but we know as much geometry as any Greek philosopher, and we can sail as fast and as far as a Spanish galleon. By night, we watch the stars. By day, we watch the sun and moon, and the cloud formations. In the right light, the clouds reflect the color of the sea and land beneath them. We also look for birds, for flowers and coconuts drifting in the current. Most importantly, we feel the waves beneath us. The ocean swells reflect off the land, and their ripples can be felt even two hundred kilometers away. The contour map is in our heads—we *feel* our way along, using the only programmable substance available. Brains.

"And we tell stories. We tell stories. We tell stories to pass the time. I'm taking you back, back, back before the sun god Tangaloa fathered the first Tu'i Tonga, before Maui, the god of fire and trickery, fished the islands up from the ocean with his magic hook. Before there were people, before there was time, the spirits of the people lived in their own special network in the sky. These sky spirits were never born and could never die. Every day was the same as every other day."

"Cool," someone said, half-seriously.

"Shut up," Ho Ng warned.

And the prince went on: "But there were some among the sky spirits who grew restless, who wanted something to happen. The spirit of a lizard also lived in the sky, and was thought to be wise and helpful, although not entirely trustworthy. He had a streak of cruelty which he some-times indulged. But he was always forgiven, because the sky spirits had to live together forever, and couldn't afford to hold grudges.

"When the hot Earth had cooled and living things came out of the ocean to take root and grow in its soil, and different creatures had evolved to shape the ecosys-tem, the lizard told the sky people about the amazing beauty and sensuous delight of the Earth, which he said had been prepared especially for them. Earth's land cra-dled all the colors of the rainbow, and its waters and winds flowed with sweet songs. And there were tastes as well! Sweet coconut and hearty yams, taro and breadfruit, and best of all, the flesh of fish and animals. Even the caves echoed your name when you called out to them.

"The lizard told the sky spirits how to visit the Earth: slide down a long, thin cable that was anchored in Africa, at the Earth's equator. Shinny, shinny, slide! Down to Earth you slipped and slid, becoming solid as you went. The sky spirits were so excited they could barely wait their turn to slide down the cable.

"'But how do we get back home?' a man asked.

"'Yes,' said another. 'We won't go unless we can come back home again.'

"'Oh, that's easy,' said the giant lizard, his mouth crooked open in a smile. 'Just climb back up the cable. It has grooves in it, so any ratcheting mechanism will let you climb up without sliding back down. See?'

"And he showed the people the teeth and grooves of the cable. 'Thank you,' said the sky people. Not everyone went—some believed the lizard's words and some didn't. But many, oh so many, chose to go! One by one they at-tached their skysuits to the cable, and down they slid. They were so excited they didn't even notice the lizard laughing at them.

"Earth was gorgeous. Fresh, cool water bubbled up out

of the ground. Flowers bobbed in the breeze. Everything the lizard had said was true! The people harvested yams and luscious red fruits. They lit a huge fire and watched it dance and wave like the arms of a hundred happy girls. Later, when they had explored and were ready to rest, the sky people baked their yams in the glowing coals. In the shade of a tree they feasted, dancing and singing and warming themselves by the fire. And they took torches into the caves and drew sooty pictures on the walls. And they found that they could make love, and afterward they slept.

"But in the morning, something terrible happened: one of the sky people stepped on an ant, crushing it. "Get up," said the sky person to the ant. But the ant didn't move. It lay in pieces at the sky man's feet. Gently, his wife lifted the dead ant. Other ants scurried about, frightened by her huge human shadow. She reached down and smashed another ant between her fingers. All movement stopped. Suddenly she screamed a bloodcurdling yell, and all the people of the tribe came running.

"'What's the matter?' they yelled.

"'This creature...' The woman was panting now. 'It won't move. It is...no more.' There was no word in their language for death, so she couldn't even say that it had died. The people began to tremble. What kind of world had they come to?

"Together the men carved spears and hunted a bird, a gecko, and a pig. 'We honor your spirit, living creature. May you live forever,' they chanted. Then they took a heavy rock and killed the bird, the gecko, and the pig. The pig's dark blood gushed from its neck into the sand. Prayers drifted away in the evening wind. Nothing could bring these creatures back to life.

"The lizard's beguiling story had left out one detail: nothing lasted here. The bees made their honey, and then they died. The flowers bloomed, and their open faces shriveled. Dogs and pigs and even wives grew old and died. A lie of omission is still a lie; they knew now that the lizard had betrayed them.

"Too late for the people of heaven! They had eaten the food of the Earth, killing living things in the process. Now they too would experience all of Earth's gifts, even the bitter ones: birth, sickness, old age, and death. The sky people huddled together and wept. One brave woman said, 'Don't give up! We must climb back to the sky. We don't need these full bellies. It's better to live forever!' The people ran to the base of the cable. It must still be there, waiting for them to slip their skysuit ratchets into the carved notches and climb back to heaven.

"But no! The evil lizard had bitten through the cable. It lay coiled on the ground, frayed and still dripping with his saliva. 'Look!' cried the man who had asked the lizard how they would return to the sky. 'The notches don't even go all the way to the ground! All the time he was planning to leave us here!'

"Sadly, the people turned away. The sound of weeping grew dimmer and dimmer as small groups wandered off by themselves. One group followed the snaky curves of the riverbank. Another walked under the broad-leafed canopy of the forest. A third one climbed up into the hills. They were the ancestors of the people who live today. Because of them you were born, as generation upon generation of them were born, and died.

"But eventually, the people grew wise and clever, and strung their own cable back to heaven, and filled the heavens and the Earth with holes which connected to each other. Thus they brought all the delights of Earth into heaven, and all the delights of heaven back down to Earth, and all the horrors were buried and forgotten, and the giant lizard fled and has not been seen again."

Bascal surveyed his audience before adding, in a less

sanguine tone, "And everyone lives forever, and every day is the same as every other day, until the end of time."

The campers sat quietly, digesting the tale.

"You made that up," Conrad said finally.

"Parts of it," Bascal admitted with a shrug. "The guts are traditional." He addressed the circle. "Now, you've got to imagine there's a bowl of kava, a numbing pepper-root drink that will literally loosen your tongue and lips. And brain. I pass it to the man on my left—or sometimes woman—who drains it and then tells the next story."

The person sitting on Bascal's left was Ho Ng, his faithful companion.

"What?" Ho asked brilliantly.

"Tell a story," Bascal repeated.

"Oh. Bloodcrap." Ho thought for a minute or two, and then launched into a disjointed rendition of "Little Red Riding Hood." The next in line was Steve Grush, who did a slightly better job with "Goldilocks and the Three Bears," although Jamil and Karl teased him for it until Bascal told them to stop.

And then it was Jamil's own turn, and instead of a fairy tale he related the plot of some holie drama he'd seen on TV, about a Christian priest fighting corruption in early Antarctica, during the height of the Fax Wars when it was still possible to steal someone's identity and get away with it. There was no Constabulary then to enforce the new Queendom standards and brighten up the worlds' gray areas. Outside of the old nation-states the regulatory situation was murky at best—frontier justice being the norm. All this was much to the woe of the priest, who had just escaped from an even worse situation on Mars. It actually sounded like a pretty good movie, although Jamil couldn't remember any of the characters' names, so everyone was "the guy" or "the other guy" or "the guy's girlfriend's friend."

Finally, Bascal laughed and told him to stop. "This guy

has heard enough from that guy about those other guys," he said. Then he added, more seriously, "It's been a big day for all of us, probably the biggest day of our lives. We're tired, we're hurt—and if you think you're sore now, just wait till tomorrow. That's all the story time we probably need. Now, I suggest we turn the lights down and start getting ready for bed."

This was done: the soft glow of the wellstone was halved, then halved again, and in the gloom Conrad watched Bascal and Xmary quietly slip into the bridge, and close the door behind the single Palace Guard that slipped in after them. The other guard stayed behind, to monitor potential threats here in the main cabin. Someone might drill a peephole and gas the couple to death! Conrad wanted to brood about that, to have some time to feel jealous and worried and angry with Bascal for being such an unholy jerk about everything. Except that Ho, when he realized he'd been closed out of the bridge, got a baleful look on his face and started kicking mattresses.

"Hey," Preston Midrand said, when his own was kicked.

"Yeah?" Ho demanded, rotating in the air and stopping himself on Preston's shoulders, so the two of them were eye-to-eye but upside down from each other. And when Preston declined to answer, Ho pushed himself away and collided "accidentally" with Jamil.

"Watch it, you shit," Jamil called out.

"Still crowded in here," Ho said, although with the loss of bodies and the addition of a third dimension the exact opposite was true: even with seven of them in here, it felt kind of cold and empty. "There's room in the storage closet. Some bloodfuck should sleep in there."

"Sleep there yourself," Conrad told him, causing Ho to look up and shoot him an evil glare. It seemed for a moment that some sort of confrontation was about to gel. Not physical, with a Palace Guard still standing in silent watch over the room, but possibly a moment of open power struggle. Then Ho seemed to think better of it, and leveled his ire at Preston instead.

"You. Go on."

Conrad sighed. "Oh, for the love of little gods, Ho. Will you leave him alone?"

But Preston was holding up his hands. "No, no, it's all right. I'll go. Maybe there's a little privacy in there. Maybe it's *warmer*."

"Yeah?" Ho said, perking up. "I forgot about that. Never mind, bloodfuck, *I'll* sleep in the closet. My own private room."

"Until we need toilet paper," Jamil added sourly.

These arrangements were finalized, and Conrad drifted over to the little environmental control panel he'd prepared in a rare moment of forethought. It was just a flimsy sheet of wellstone, connected by a ribbon to the cabin's exterior wrapping, but it would do for now. He turned the lights down the rest of the way, so there was only the starlight shining down through the sail, through the wellstone wrapping around the cabin, through the clear plastic of the skylight itself. He thought for a while that his eyes would adjust, but they didn't seem to. It was just too dark: not enough of an opening to really let the starlight in. So he got up again and added a soft night-light glow to the ceiling in the 'toir, then settled down and strapped back into his bedding again.

And then, finally, he had a free moment to stew over the day's events. It was a lot to take in: the silencing and stranding, the involuntary storage, the ascension of Ho Ng to a position of ... something. It was all so shallowly, transparently unnecessary. Bascal was listening to his own dark voices, and to Ho's, when being nasty offered no actual benefit. It wasn't like he *needed* to bury all dissenters; he'd simply felt like it.

And that, *that* was the critical issue. "Evil" as a concept had never much interested Conrad—he'd been assured of its existence but had never once seen a clear example. Until today. But the way he saw it, you had your basic "tough decision," where one person got something—say, a nice apartment in Denver—and that meant someone else couldn't have it. Then you had your "management decision," where somebody decided how many apartments there were going to *be* in Denver, based on the available resources and the various implications of their use. How individual people felt was not much of a deciding factor. And yet there was nothing intentionally nasty about it; such decisions were necessary.

But then there was the *selfish* decision, where some jackass kept the good stuff for himself, or swiped it from other people, as Ho had just done. And that was the dividing line, where goodness and indifference left off and something else began. Not evil per se—the reasons behind it were too clear and ordinary for that—but something. Not nice. And *spiteful* decisions, like throwing Bert into the fax, were worse than that, and worse still were the dangerous and malicious and harmful decisions, like marooning Peter on the ruined planette, with fire and rain and gods knew what else.

So Bascal hadn't simply crossed the good/bad line in a moment of weakness; he'd leaped right over it, and loitered there for hours. Of course there were worse things, *much* worse things, that a person could do. There was murder; there was torture; there was *genocide*. . . . Conrad didn't want to overreact—it wasn't all or nothing, but a matter of degrees. Bascal had decided to be somewhat malicious in pursuit of his goals. Was that all? Was there more to it than that?

Certainly there was no grand design to it. No matter what Bascal said, he was just making it up along the way, doing what felt right. They all were. Peter felt like staying and Bascal felt like going, so that's what happened. Ho felt like taking something from Preston, so that's what he did. And nobody stopped it from happening, because nobody was planning that far ahead. And *that* was a critical point as well: could you simply outplan the petty evils of the universe? Surprise them, catch them off guard? Make sure the right thing was easier to do?

For some reason, this idea made him shiver. Then he decided it wasn't so much the idea as the fact that it really was getting cold in here. So he got back up and went to his control panel and mirrorized the cabin's wrapping, to reflect all their body heat back inside instead of letting it escape into cold Kuiper Belt space. This blocked the starlight entirely, forcing him to turn more night-lights on. He would have turned a heater on as well, but he didn't have any idea how much energy this took, or how much was actually on board, or how exactly it was stored in the wellstone. Or where. And he suspected Bascal didn't know either, and the last thing Conrad wanted to do was find out the answer in some dumbass way that froze or burned or starved them all to death.

It seemed like an egotistical thought, but also a true one: if there was to be any sanity on this insane voyage of theirs, Conrad's own not-so-bright efforts would have to provide it.

chapter ten

winds of permutation

From the desk at her bedroom window, Xmary gazed eastward at the towers of Denver. Moping, because the sun was shining and there was happy trumpet music playing somewhere. Moping, because she wanted to *go*, to hang out and be raw and silly and fun. The Gravity Towers beckoned to her; the Cola Dome mocked. And the plain, bright colors of her desk—red and green and yellow and blue, tiles of fired ceramic mortared in place by the child she had been a decade ago—were the punchline of the joke. A handmade object, a hundred hours of labor. Indistinguishable from a fax-to-order design.

She wanted to snort love drugs and flirt, or rent a little car and just drive it around. She'd been cooped up all month—all summer, really—humoring her parents with chores and schoolwork, saving her allowance for that bright, fulfilling future they imagined she was building toward. As what? As whom?

She deserved an afternoon on the town. And a night, and maybe a morning. Gods, did she ever! But she was due at history class in fifteen minutes, and her absence would be noted and logged and forwarded to the attention of Mummy and Da.

By itself, this was not a problem. In the best of months, she faxed up an illicit copy of herself every week, and sneaked away to do her own bidding. In mediocre times she'd get by doing it every two or three weeks, but even in the driest, lamest of months—like this one, for example—she *always* gave herself the last Friday off. And today—today!—was the day.

There was nothing difficult about the procedure; the fax machine was right outside her bedroom door, and when she stepped into it she'd simply specify two simultaneous destinations: Childrens' City College, and Market Street Station. Or maybe River Station, if she felt like hitting the kiddie cafés again.

But there exactly was the problem: she'd sent a copy of herself off to River Street on the last Friday of June, and said copy had met briefly with Cherry and Tom, in the upstairs balcony at Café 1551. And then the Unexplained Thing had happened—the building simply collapsing in a heap—and dearest Xmary had passed on into some new phase of existence. Not dead or injured as far as she knew, but simply not listed among the casualties. Simply not there. Covert messages on the network had failed to garner any response, and no friend or relation had yet admitted to seeing or hearing from her.

She feared the worst: raped and murdered out of sight of the world's sensors and censors and sense. Dumped in a shallow grave, covered over with rocks and dirt, her memories rotting into the earth instead of coming home where they belonged. How melodramatic! How fitting an end for such a wayward and disobedient little girl! It was everything Mummy had warned her about: seeking out the vile haunts of sleaze—of *privacy*—and wiggling her assets for the leering eyes of the wrong sort of people.

But fitting or no, the idea terrified her. Shouldn't it? Not simply because the same thing might happen again, but because Mummy's being right would be the end of everything. No more life of her own. No more hopes or dreams or casual flings, no guilty pleasures that weren't chosen for her from some carefully vetted menu! We know what's best for you, dear. Having lived in a world much harder than yours, we know exactly what you should do next.

What did she want to be when she grew up? Anything. Anything but that. She put a shaky hand to the window, caressing the view. Her unrequited lover. If rape and murder were the price of freedom, she supposed she would just have to pay up.

Was that a decision? It surely felt like one, so she stood up, grabbed her sketchplate and purse, and threw open the bedroom door to face the world.

But just to be safe, she printed the copy first, and checked her over, and gave her a tight hug and a kiss on the cheek. Xmary was dear to her, obviously, though they didn't spend much time together. Being identical down to the slightest foible and follicle, she could be difficult and often snotty, and she had a remarkable talent for trouble. Last year she had even managed, during an otherwise-forgettable romp with a boy they barely knew, to play an elaborate and rather disgusting prank on herself. *How does it taste, dear?* She was still amazed she'd pulled that off, concealing her intentions from herself and knowing all the while that there would not only be payback, but that she'd have to reconverge her copies in the fax at some point, winding up as the victim of both the original crime *and* its retaliation! In the face of that kind of determined mischief, there was only so much of her own company she could take.

"Be careful," she told herself.

But Xmary—good old Xmary—just laughed. "Girl, you're the one facing homework and dinner conversation. *My* mistakes can be swept under the rug."

"Along with your carcass."

"Hey, wow, I'm already more cheerful than you. Poor thing. Don't wait up for me, eh?"

It wasn't that her parents never let her out—they did—it was just that they would ask her where she was going, and whom she would be with. And they had their ways of verifying these things, or spot-checking anyway, and if they caught her lying the cost was high. So she went bowling and levitating and even boozing with their grudging consent, and for the most part enjoyed it well enough. But wayward girl that she was, she never felt truly alive or free with them peering over her shoulder that way.

Her private self might not exactly shock them—surely as mortal children they had raised their own share of hell. But they'd worry about her, and gently offer their advice, which was always right and always dull, and she just didn't need that in her life right now. At nineteen, the age-of-consent laws were complex, but if she didn't go looking for brutes or father figures she was basically free—finally!—to sample those worldly delights that interested her. And what the hell else was there?

So she went to the swimming pool to look at the boys, and to let the boys look at her in a Polynesian-styled two-piece that did, yes, show off her assets rather nicely. In the changing room fax, she even gave herself a set of good, old-fashioned tan lines underneath, just in case. And just so her intentions were not in doubt, she applied a bit of that illuminated red sparkle to her lips and toes and fingernails. Boy bait.

The pool itself was housed in a structure that could open and close and swivel and opaque in response to the sun and wind and the changing moods of its patrons. Right now, with clouds rolling in off the mountains and a hot, dusty breeze blowing up from the south, the walls were clear and closed, looking out on a dry summer meadow, with cottonwood trees and apartment buildings in the distance.

Treading barefoot across the wet, sticky tiles of the floor, Xmary staked out a lounge chair next to the windows but facing away from them, looking out over the kiddie pools and hot tubs where everyone she knew actually swam and played. Through an archway she could see the edge of the "adult swim" area, where people went for hard exercise and competition—two activities that struck her as ridiculous in a world where your physical fitness was determined by the fax. She'd played water polo and bottom-hockey a few times there, just for fun, but otherwise had never been in it.

The kiddie area was something else again: a playground of rivers and tunnels, wave machines and waterfalls, slippery slides and rickety pontoon bridges. There was so much screechy laughter in the air that you could barely hear anything else. She'd learned a few years back that natural humans, unmodified by the fax, could hold their breaths for only a minute or so, if that. A place like this would probably kill them, which was a sad thought considering how short and miserable their lives were to begin with! But Xmary, with no training and only infrequent practice, could stay underwater for three minutes with heavy exertion, and almost six without. It made life bearable, playing porpoise in the kiddie pool, groping through whirlpools in a darkened cavern. . . . In the unlikely event she ever managed to grow up, this would be one of the things she'd truly miss.

But even more important than the swimming itself was the survey of the crowd. There were maybe a hundred people here—not bad for a Friday afternoon on the hot side of the summer solstice—and the majority were under thirty. Since there were only a few thousand children in the whole of Denver, this meant—as always—

that there was a pretty good chance of running into some-one she knew. And yes, sure enough, she spotted a few al-most immediately. None of her inner circle, or even her outer one, but there was Hacienda deFlores over there by the fountains, and Chad Breck a few meters farther on, looking Hacienda over from a covert angle.

Chad was actually a walking advertisement for the sex-ual politics of the age: he was cute enough—who wasn't?—and he had that winning smile. But he didn't know a damn thing about anything, and he liked it that way, and if you got buzzed enough to fall into bed with him then you had some hard decisions to make.

If you took him home, your house would log the fact and your parents would know everything. If you went to his place then at least his parents wouldn't care—score one more for their precious sonny boy—but you had to know there were a hundred and fifty sensors recording you in every imaginable detail, and likely as not he'd be sharing these with his friends the next day. Illegally, yes, but if they were even a little bit careful about it there was no good way to catch them. Of course, those same images could be faked by any decent hypercomputer, but in an age of nearly perfect lie detection they'd be hard to fool your friends with. Which of course made even better tro-phies of the real thing.

And hotel rooms were expensive and left a money trail, and rented cars and aircraft were too damned cramped. So inevitably you ended up in a park or basement some-where—with a blanket if you were lucky—and the magic of it all wore off pretty quickly. The holy grail was for one of your friends to get an apartment of their own that you could use, but of course the moment they did, that care-free spirit would begin to wither under the pressures of worldly responsibility. Theirs was a different Denver alto-gether: coldly competitive, and filled to bursting with bitches and bastards too selfish and fearful to die or retire or move somewhere else, or even step out to enjoy a day in the sun.

"Meritocracy can be cruel," her Da was fond of saying. "It takes a hundred years to build a life, and six months to ruin it if you play your hand badly."

You had forever to recover from your mistakes, true enough, but who wanted to risk another hundred years of numbing labor? For that matter, who wanted to start the process in the first place? Moving out to the planets wouldn't help. Frontier, schmontier—if you didn't have money it was just like everywhere else. Worse, really, because even the "outside" was artificial and owned. There was no place to escape to.

She spotted another familiar face, attached to a boy standing knee-deep in the Figure Eights and looking right at her. She couldn't put a name to him—she wasn't sure they'd ever spoken—but she had seen him around the campus this month, and in a few other places where people their age were found. Actually, he looked a few years younger than she was—sixteen or maybe seventeen—but to the extent that she cared at all, that was potentially a plus. What she really needed was a project.

She favored him with a smile and a wave, and he looked nervous for a moment before steeling himself and wading over in her direction.

"So you survived, eh?" he said to her as he stepped, dripping, out of the water.

"Survived what?" she asked.

"The café: 1551. Can I borrow your towel?"

And this was a pleasantly intimate request, because her towel was dry and he was only really wet from the waist down. He was cute enough—again, who wasn't?—but he spoke with an accent she couldn't place, and wore a mustache that wouldn't really grow in for another few years, and there was something innocently delicate and artistic about him, something that tugged gently at her strings.

She tossed him the towel. "I'm at a loss, here. Were you there when the 1551 collapsed?"

"Most definitely," he said, wiping the beads of moisture off his legs. "And I left the scene in a hurry, so I'm glad to see you're none the worse."

She blinked. "You saw me there? You talked to me?"

It was his turn to look puzzled, though he nodded. "Yep, I surely did. You had that same hairstyle. That same stuff on your lips. And a black dress. You don't remember?"

His manner was increasingly nervous. He handed the towel back and did not quite meet her eye.

"I disappeared that night," she said quietly, pinning him with her gaze. There was no reason to be afraid, not with all these people around. But she had probably thought the same thing on that fateful night, and where—where?—had it gotten her? "If you know anything about that, I advise you to spill it before I scream for the cops."

"No, no," he said nervously. "Don't scream. I'm an agent for the Prince of Sol, and my cover is thin. May I sit down? May I share this chair with you so we can keep our voices low? I remember your name, it's Xiomara something."

"Xmary," she corrected. "And stay where you are. So you're the prince's agent, are you?"

"One of them," he said, making another shushing motion with his hands. "And if you'll please keep your voice down I'll tell you everything I know. I didn't see your name on the injured list. On *any* list."

"Neither did I. I couldn't have been there when it fell, with cops everywhere. They'd've found me."

"Oh, but you were. I was this close to you. You were sitting at the prince's elbow, talking about a signet ring or something."

"Again with the prince!" she said, throwing her hands

up. "His name wasn't on the lists either. I think I would have noticed that."

"It's been hushed up. A royal embarrassment. But I *saw* the cops arresting him. I think you must have gotten out the same way I did: by running your pretty ass off."

"Yeah? Then where am I now?"

He tried a nervous grin. "Right here?"

She slugged him for that, not gently. But there was something in the way he said it that eased her fears.

"If you didn't run," he said, "then the Constabulary made you disappear, along with the others. There were only two ways out."

"What others?" she asked, completely flummoxed by this bizarre story, whose key details had not been spoken yet. Had they?

"Runaways," he said. "Royal runaways. We'd escaped from...well, it doesn't matter where. Wrongful captivity, let's say."

"Why did the building collapse?"

"I'm not sure," he said. "Bascal was cooking up something illicit. Garbage Day, I heard him saying, but I was at the wrong end of the table."

It seemed a weirdly candid thing for an agent on a secret mission to say. She looked him over, taking in his fretful stance, his nervous face. His not-quite-tasteful swimsuit that looked like something a public fax would print for free, no questions asked.

"You aren't making this up," she said.

He let out a breath, relaxing visibly. "No, I'm not. And if you've suffered this disappearance as you say, then it's a mystery to me as well. You have a loose copy, a loose end somewhere. I don't know what else to tell you."

Later, with charity-fax hamburgers in their bellies and loose wellcloth pants and shirts over their swimsuits, they sat together on one of the many covered bridges that connected the towers of the downtown district. Anyone could get inside the bridges, but Xmary had shown him how to get up onto the roof; now their legs hung out past the drip rail, dangling in the late-afternoon breeze. Their brains were buzzing lightly, too, from mood capsules they were technically not allowed to purchase until the age of thirty.

"We don't have to stay here," she told him tentatively. "The Queendom is our oyster."

But Feck shook his head at that. "We do, actually. The moment I step in a fax, I'll probably be diverted to Constabulary headquarters. No one knows I'm here—they can't, or I'd've been arrested weeks ago. Somehow, they don't even know to look for me. It's part of the mystery." He paused for a moment, looking up and down Stout Street, whose white gaslights were already coming on, although the sun hadn't fully set. "Anyway, this is fine. Nice view. No traffic."

"It's a quiet corner," she agreed. "One of my special places."

Little chills of excitement were shooting up and down her spine. She'd never met anyone like Feck before: someone with a mission, a task, an actual job to do. A criminal, yes, but with an excellent pedigree. The *prince's own* criminal. The fact that he was nervous and pensive about it only made it more real.

Feck glanced down at the bridge roof itself, and scratched at it with his fingernail in an experimental sort of way. "There could be listening devices anywhere—hypercomputers, scanning for tripwords. But somebody would have to put the right tripwords out to them, hmm? And would they bother?"

"You have to be careful what you say?"

He shrugged, a bit helplessly. "Things need to be said.

I have to do it somewhere. There are no people around, so that's a good start."

Foolishly, she asked him, "Do you have a favorite girl?"

He frowned, still scratching at the roof. "It . . . I've met several here in Denver, and see them regularly. Beyond that, I'm not sure what you mean. I didn't approach you for . . . ," he trailed away nervously. "Of course I like you; I feel desire. I'd be crazy not to. But that's not why we're here."

And this just made the situation that much more thrilling. "Why are we here?" she asked. "What is your secret mission?"

"My mission?" He smiled thinly beneath his boyish mustache. "I'm instructed to start a riot. I've been telling people it's on Restoration Day, beginning exactly at nine P.M."

Restoration Day: the fourteenth of August. Sixteen days from now.

"A riot? You mean, like, smashing streetlights and stuff?"

"Sure, whatever we can manage."

"Why?"

"I'm not sure. Tying up resources? Drawing attention? In the scheme of things, I believe it's part of a larger disruption."

"Revolution," Xmary said, liking the idea right away. Secret missions for all; a chance to disturb this endless, stifling peace! It was not only the ultimate bid for parental recognition, but a sort of adult enterprise in its own right. Like any revolution: a chance to right wrongs and lay claim to neglected rights. There was no democracy—no republic, even—for the children of her generation. And when could there be, ever?

"Maybe," Feck agreed. "It could come to that, although we're scarily outnumbered and outequipped. I guess the thought is more to shake things up, for attention. So I have to ask: do you have any particular talents I can add to my team?"

"I'm good with my hands," she said without hesitation. "I do stupid, useless handicrafts."

"Ah, so you can make untraceable things," Feck suggested.

She didn't deny it. In fact, a Christmas garland she'd strung up between a pair of lamp poles one year had fallen into the street and damaged a bus. Chewed the hell out of its tires and finally broken its axle, because her folded impervium stars had one of those shapes that formed a stable tripod on the bottom and left the final point sticking straight up. When she'd checked later, her encyclopedia had called it a "caltrop," and identified it not as a decoration, but as a defensive armament useful against personnel, ground vehicles, and especially horses. And no, the garland had never been traced to her in any way, even by Mummy and Da, although a detailed analysis would have revealed her DNA and fingerprints and electronic shadows or ghosts. But nobody had bothered, because it was just a damn cheap Christmas garland blown down by the wind.

"I can make untraceable things," she confirmed.

"Beautiful *and* talented," Feck said seriously. "That's raw."

Xmary felt a smile coming on. "Shaking things up is the duty of youth, Feck. And we've been neglecting it, haven't we? This is an awakening. You're my ray of morning sunshine."

And then she couldn't help herself any longer: she kissed him. He seemed almost to expect it. Or anyway, he knew what to do.

Unfortunately, when Xmary got home, Mimi and David Li Weng were waiting up for her in the living room with their lovely daughter Xiomara. And not one of them looked happy to see her.

"Good evening, young lady," Mummy said pointedy.

"Hi," she said back, because she figured she knew what was coming, and it wasn't really Mummy's fault. Just the way things were.

"You've been out without asking," Mummy singsonged.

Xmary shrugged. "Yeah. So?"

"Have a seat, please, darling. There are some facts of life that apparently need explaining."

Sighing, Xmary sat down next to herself, and offered an affectionate pat on the knee. People didn't have brothers and sisters anymore, but they had their friends, and especially they had themselves. Under other circumstances she might have put an arm over her shoulder—even given herself a little kiss—but here and now she settled for sitting close.

Da cleared his throat, and looked back and forth at his daughter. "Mara, darling, we've identified eleven unauthorized duplicates in your network records for this calendar year alone. And the thing about that is, we can only account for ten of them."

"You scanned my fax records?" She gaped. Why this should surprise or offend her she had no idea. But it did. Was nothing sacred? Was there no privacy at all?

"Where is the other you?" Da pressed.

"I don't know," one of her admitted, while the other examined the ceiling.

Da blinked. "You don't *know*? She ran off? Did something happen to her?"

More firmly: "*I don't know*, Da. I wish I did."

"Have you called the police?" Mummy asked. Then, "No, of course you haven't, dear. The police would have called us, first thing. And your sordid misadventures are nothing you'll share with the law, are they?"

"Right, Mum," Xmary said. "I *kill* cops. We all do. It's all anyone talks about at the pool anymore."

"Am I supposed to find that funny? Into the fax, both of you. You're grounded and singled for the month. No copies, no body mods, and your destination lockout will be revived."

"Mom!" the other Xmary protested. Last year's lifting of Nescog parental lockouts was the closest she'd ever come to freedom. But not really, since the tariffs would wipe out her allowance if she left the planet or made more than a handful of nonlocal hops. And if Mummy and Da could take away the privilege whenever they felt like it, or track her movements, or possibly (probably?) check her medical trace for fingerprints and foreign substances . . .

"I hope you had fun tonight," she growled to herself. And answered quietly: "Don't worry. You're going to love it."

And then she stepped into the fax, and stepped in again, and the fax did that looking-glass thing where you exited into the same room you'd just left. Except that she was only one Xmary when she stepped out, and after a dizzy moment of integration she understood everything: the pool, the boy, the thing at history class, the fight with Mummy and Da. And she resolved: they could ground her and single her all they liked, but unless they cut off her damn feet they could not keep her away from Feck. Especially on Restoration Day.

"We have much to discuss," Mummy said, "but perhaps your father ought to call the police first. Love?"

"Yes, my dear." Da got up off the sofa and traced out a window on a bare patch of wall, right beside Xmary's head. "Telecom, please. The Denver Metro Police."

And while the connection was ringing through, the window flashed up headlines, and since Xmary was right there she couldn't help seeing them. Especially the one

that read, KUIPER RAMPAGE: MISSING FRIENDLY PARK ES-
CAPEES MAY INCLUDE PRINCE BASCAL.

And then it was gone, and Da was talking to some
beautiful blond woman in police beige. Xmary staggered
to the sofa and plopped down heavily, holding three fresh
thoughts in the privacy of her skull. First, that this "rampage" was another volley in Feck's alleged uprising. Second, that the prince had visited—and disappeared
from—Café 1551 on the same night Xmary had. And
third, that these events were too bizarre to be unrelated.

And where exactly did that leave Xmary? The Kuiper
Belt?

"Gods," she murmured, then looked up, afraid that
Mummy and Da had overheard her and would somehow
divine her thoughts. But for once they were paying no attention to her.

Their names and dates in stone engraved,
Their mortal coils in coffins saved,
Their worlds unmade, their streets unpaved,
The last to clear the way, the way,
the last to clear the way.

And through that haze of final tears,
To dam and tame the stream of years,
Had seemed the noblest of careers,
To stretch man's fleeting day, his day,
to stretch man's fleeting day.

And now that morning lingers on,
We blink into the sun and yawn,
The joys of night and evening gone,
and tell ourselves we're gay, we're gay,
we tell ourselves we're gay.

—*"Cemetery Jingle #3"*
BASCAL EDWARD DE TOWAJI LUTUI, *age 13*

chapter eleven

the long carry

.

There was no clearly defined "morning" aboard the good ship *Viridity*. The cold had faded with Conrad's insulation trick, but the heat had continued to build until finally he awoke with a yelp, scrabbling at the itchy, crawling sensation of weightless sweat blobs against his skin. He had no idea what time it was, or how long he'd slept, because the ship's only chronometer was on Bascal's control panel in the bridge.

But he had to get up and demirrorize the wrapping again, and while he was up he visited the 'soir. This wasn't strictly necessary, but if he went back to bed it soon would be. Unfortunately, this was a messy process they really hadn't worked out yet. You had to peel back the gasket sealing the toilet lid, and then carefully do your business without breaking up the pool of water that clung jiggling at the bottom, by the effluent drain. And then you had to reseal the lid and flush, and inevitably there were droplets of stray liquid—not water—that could only be collected by hand. Thank all the little gods he hadn't needed to *crap* yet.

So then Conrad had to wash his hands, another elaborate process. Water here was something akin to toothpaste: you squeezed out only as much as you needed, because any more would just get away from you and make a mess. And yeah, there were several globs that he had to chase down and consolidate. They formed a neat little water ball, and it occurred to him that there'd be water-ball fights before long. Was that bad? Should it be prevented somehow? He stuffed the water balls down the drain and plugged it behind them.

By the time he got back to his bed, he was most of the way awake. In zero gee it turned out there was no tossing and turning. Rolling over involved a lot of work with the blankets and straps, and didn't accomplish much anyway, since the mattress didn't press hard enough to be uncomfortable or cut off your blood flow. But he wiggled and sighed for a while, trying to put himself back to sleep.

And then he noticed how rapidly the temperature was falling. Not actually cold yet, but the heat that had woken him was gone, and the sweat trapped between his clothes and skin was turning unpleasantly tepid. He'd have to fix that, keep it from getting too cold, or he'd just be getting up again. And again. And he wasn't sure how long it'd been since he'd last changed clothes, but once he was up he quietly ordered a new set from the fax, changed into them in the cooling darkness, and disposed of his old ones. Then he went to the environment panel and bumped the reflectivity of the cabin's wrapper from zero percent to fifty percent, hoping that would be close enough to maintain a comfortable temperature. Then he went back to bed, and sighed and wiggled some more.

When he finally gave up on sleeping, some of the other boys had begun to stir. He ruminated on the day ahead: Adventure? Boredom? He should rig up a program to regulate the mirrors automatically, that was one thing. And something needed to be done about that damned bathroom....

When Karl Smoit sat up and rubbed his eyes, Conrad decided that morning had finally arrived, so he got up and retrieved a wellstone sketchplate Bascal had stowed in one of D'rector Jed's cabinets. The more he thought about it, the more he realized how much work there was to do before *Viridity* would be anything like a stable environment, much less a comfortable one.

Using his pinkie for a stylus, he scribbled on the sketchplate:

To Do List:
Thermostat for Mirrors
Chronometer/Clock
Measure Stored Energy
Sink Hood
Better Light Controls
Water Dispensing Limit
Bathroom Cleanup Tools

By now Karl and Jamil were grumbling at each other over first use of the bathroom, and Preston and Martin were showing signs of getting up, and there were various thumps and rustles from the storage closet where Ho had sequestered himself. That left only Steve Grush asleep—a condition Conrad was inclined to leave him in.

Soon there was breakfast, which Bascal and Xmary joined blearily. Afterward they washed up, and then Xmary announced her schedule, which specified the times for lights-on, lights-off, three meals, an exercise hour and a story hour, and (thankfully) a "laundry check" of unspecified but probably beneficial nature.

"You should add 'maintenance,'" Conrad told her. "I've got a long list of issues, and it'll probably get longer before it gets shorter."

She nodded, looking annoyingly chipper and perky. "Okay. Maintenance. Does that include cleaning up?"

"Well, we should probably put that down, too."

She made a note on her sketchplate. "Maintenance. Cleaning. One hour or two?"

"Um, I dunno. Two hours each?"

"The days are going to be long, boyo," Bascal agreed, sidling up and putting an arm around Xmary. "It's better to have too much to do than too little. Can I see your list?"

Conrad dug the sketchplate out of his pocket, mimed tossing it to Bascal, and then did toss it when he was sure the *pilinisi* was ready to make the catch. Zero gravity was a new twist on this familiar act, but Conrad correctly intuited that he needed to fire the plate directly at Bascal's chest, not fast or hard but very straight, in a flat spin for stability. The prince caught it on the first try.

"Yeah," he said a few seconds later, looking it over and nodding. "Yeah. I'm going to add a few items before you get started. You need more sailing lessons, for example. Every day. And a turn at the helm while I'm doing other things. We really shouldn't leave it unattended for long periods."

Resignedly: "Right. I can see that."

"Well, I'll go update the master list," Xmary said, decoupling herself from Bascal's arm. Then she looked at the two of them and added, "Be nice to each other, all right? Set an example."

When she was out of earshot, Bascal said, "How did we get so lucky, Conrad? What are the odds?"

"I dunno. Not bad I guess."

Bascal rolled his eyes. "'Not bad,' the man says. Not bad. Run the experiment a hundred times, and how many Xmarys do we get?"

"There's a lot of unhappy people in Denver," Conrad answered. "You're popular, and the Constabulary got confused. They just grabbed whoever was next to you. What you're really asking is, how many people in that position would play along? I'm guessing quite a few."

"Ah," the prince said. "Now there's a romantic notion. You're a fun guy, Conrad." He fiddled briefly with the sketchplate and added, "Our *first* order of business—our absolute highest priority—is to do something about our coloration. The sail is transparent, which is good, but you've got the cabin all shiny, which is bad. We want to be"—he fluttered a hand—"invisible. A light conduit: photons in one side, out the other."

Conrad was nodding. With wellstone sensors and emitters readily programmed for it, "invisible" objects were commonplace for certain uses. Many people had invisible toilets, for example, to hide the fact that they had any bodily functions at all. Photons hitting one side were analyzed and absorbed, then re-created on the far side just as though they had traveled through unimpeded. A really *transparent* toilet would simply show off the water and other contents as if they were floating in midair, but an invisible one hid everything, looking like a weak lens, a slight distortion in the air and nothing more.

"The problem is heat," Conrad said. "We've got to hold ours in or we'll freeze to death."

"I realize that," Bascal said, in a testy way that sounded patient but wasn't. "But the trick is to make the *inner* surface reflective, and the *outer* one invisible. We can even keep the windows clear. One-way mirrors."

"Oh. All right. That sounds sensible." Conrad knew about one-way mirrors, another popular programming trick that involved asymmetrical atoms. "Do you know . . . how?"

"We'll work on it," Bascal said. "I'm not completely sure how it's done, but we've figured out harder things together. Right?"

"Uh, sure. I guess."

"And Conrad?" Bascal glanced up over the top of the sketchplate.

"Yeah?"

"Don't work too fast on the rest of this. Stretch it out; make it last. We're going to be out here a long time, and we need to stay busy."

That night at story time, Xmary told the tale of the first American flag, and following along in the same theme Karl, who was also American, recited what he could remember of "Paul Revere's Ride." Jamil followed up with "Sinbad the Sailor," which turned out to be the first of many Sinbad stories he knew and promised to tell. It didn't have much to do with sailing, but entertainment was entertainment.

And then somehow it was Bascal's turn again—the seating pattern was totally different from yesterday's—and he was saying, "I'm taking you back, back, back before the Tongans and Europeans had discovered one another, to a time when land powers ruled the coasts of the Pacific, and sea powers ruled its islands."

He paused for effect—he was a big one on pauses and cadence—and then continued. "On the island of Tongatapu, a special day had arrived: Elders' Day, and all the people were afraid. The young prince, Polua-le-uli-gana, or Polu to his friends, did not understand."

"Understand what?" someone asked, as if on cue.

Bascal answered, "The people wouldn't come out to throw the fishing nets. They refused to race up the coconut palms and be the first one to throw down the most coconuts. They wouldn't swim in the ponds, or come to the king's feast. Instead, they stayed hidden until the feast was finished.

"Prince Polu was sad. He didn't understand why on Elders' Day his playmates stayed in hiding, or why one of them would never be seen again. When the prince questioned a servant, he got no answer. The servant simply walked away. Prince Polu lived with his royal family at

Lapaha, a large village on the main island. The village included many great stone buildings, and even a stone pier jutting out into the lagoon for the king's ships to use. Many paths led toward this royal village. Many people walked these paths to bring gifts, food, news, and greetings to the prince's father, King Malietoa. Some people came because they were commanded—some to be honored, others to be punished.

"The prince was tired of all the noise and confusion. He was lonely. Tomorrow had been declared Elders' Day, and as usual, all of his friends were in hiding. People hurried from task to task with worried looks and sad faces. The prince felt as if they were preparing for a funeral rather than a feast day.

"He slipped away from his bodyguards and walked far from his home until, just as the sun was setting behind the sea, the prince reached Kolovai on the other side of the island. This was his favorite place, a place to see everything but not be seen. He climbed up the steep cliff until he reached his observation post, a large, flat rock that stuck out from the cliff. Here he could see the sky above, the ocean beyond, and the meandering pathway below. The prince rested.

"It was night when voices woke him. The moon was full. The silver of its shining face flowed across the rippled surface of the sea like a ghostly, glowing road. The prince shivered, although the rock beneath him was still sun-warmed. The voices that were once far away were now directly below him. The prince listened.

"'If you could have one wish before you die,' said the voice of a young boy, 'what would it be?'

"Another voice answered: 'I would paddle out beyond the reef and watch the frigate birds fish the open sea. Oh, how I'd love to glide on the winds, higher and higher, and then plunge straight down to spear a fat, juicy fish. I'd swallow it whole, and with a full belly I'd glide again, around and around, closing my eyes and dozing in midair, in the warm sunshine.'

"'How can you talk of food when tomorrow is Elders' Day?'

"'Stop! Tonight I will not think of tomorrow. Until the sun rises, we are alive. So let us live!'

"But the first boy said, 'I cannot stop thinking about the horror of tomorrow. I don't want to die! I don't want to be eaten!' There were no more words, just the crying of the one child and the gentle shushing of the other.

"Suddenly, Prince Polu understood. His legs began to tremble, his stomach heaved, and his heart pounded madly and painfully in his chest. On every Elders' Day one of his friends disappeared. On every Elders' Day a special feast was prepared for his father. Lesser chiefs from all around the islands—and many from neighboring kingdoms Polu's father had conquered—came to share the feast. A special animal was roasted. King Malietoa was always given the tender nape of the neck and the rich, flavorful heart. Now the prince realized. 'The animal I thought was a roasted pig was something else entirely!'

"No wonder his friends hid. No wonder the servants were too ashamed to answer his questions! And Polu knew, deep down in the marrow of his bones, that there were some things around here that needed to change. He shouted out, 'Brave travelers, listen! Please wait. I must speak with you!'

"Suddenly, the sounds of the night stopped. Silence filled the darkness and echoed in Polu's ears. 'I am the king's own son, Polua-le-uli-gana. I will not harm you. Who are you? Tell me the story of your journey.'

"At first the two young travelers said nothing. The prince shouted again, 'Speak to me. Perhaps I can save your lives. If you're marked for death already, I can hardly make things any worse.'

"One of the boys whispered to the other. 'We have

nothing to lose. We might die now if this is some wicked trick. So what? Tomorrow we die in the king's stone kitchen.'

"The other boy called out, 'We are from Eua. We were selected from the *matai's* family. Tomorrow we finish our journey. Tomorrow we meet our death with courage that will honor our family.'

"As the prince listened to these words, his heart nearly broke with sorrow. And then a dangerous plan began to form in his mind. He might lose his life, but he might gain life and pride and freedom for many others. So the prince stepped forward and gave a strange order. 'Climb this coconut tree that stands between shore and sea. Break off its finest branch. Hurry. Already the sky loses its darkness as the sun draws near. Soon, it will slip above the waves and your time will be over.'

"The two boys ran to the tree. Within minutes they returned with a large palm frond.

"'Plait the frond into a mat,' the prince said. 'Wait. Let me lie in the middle of it.'

"Again, they obeyed the prince's order, wrapping him in the middle of the palm frond as if he were a large, freshly caught fish.

"'Good. I'm ready.' The prince's voice was stern and clear. 'Carry me to the king. Hurry. I hear the roosters warning that night has ended.'

"The two boys carried their bundle to the king. With heads bowed to the ground, they placed the wrapped bundle at the king's feet. King Malietoa called to his chiefs. 'Here is a fine catch brought for our feast. Ha! In isolated areas where the diet is restricted, it is hard to eat well. There are only so many pigs in the world, ah? But a chief must be strong, and straight. His mind must be sharp. What do you feed a human, to build strong human flesh? What meat is the most plentiful?' The king laughed. 'Cooks! Prepare this as usual. Once it is roasted, invite all the chiefs to join me as I cut out the heart and neck. The rest will be shared.'

The royal cooks opened the bundle, and quickly gasped in horror. They fell to their knees, trembling in fear.

"The king roared. 'Why this disobedience? Shall I have you thrown into the fire with the fish?'

"'Look for yourself,' said the cooks. 'It is not a fish. It is your own son, our royal prince Polua-le-uli-gana! With a mango in his mouth!'

"The king's face went as pale as an Englishman's. He stared at his beloved son. The prince continued to sit, head bowed, not saying a word, waiting for a killing blow. But the blow did not happen. The prince looked up at his father. Only then did the father understand the sorrow and anguish he had so many times caused.

"The king looked at the bowed heads of his cooks and chiefs, waiting in perfect silence for his next command. 'Rejoice!' he cried out. 'Let this day begin a new feast, a new celebration. My son has risked his life so I might see. From this day forward, the Elders' Day feast shall be fish and chicken, fruits and plump tasty pigs!'

"The great king Malietoa kept his word. Of course, so did his sons and grandsons after him. Thus it is told and retold, that because of the brave and loving act of Prince Polu, the people of the Kingdom of Tonga finally stopped feeding on their own children."

The pecking order worked out like this: Bascal at the top, of course, with Ho and Xmary sharing the next level down. Whatever they wanted done, got done. At the bottom were Preston and Martin and Karl—Karl taking this status the hardest and complaining about it the most. But not too much, not too loudly, for fear of faxwise cannibalism; he could easily be the stuff of the ship's future meals, recycled endlessly into food and shit and more food and more shit, and maybe eventually restored to his former self, or maybe not. It was an effective deterrent.

Slightly above them was Jamil Gazzaniga, who had a bit of mechanical aptitude thanks to his bicycle fetish. He also had a sense of humor—very important under conditions like these—and despite some wisecracking he did seem to enjoy taking orders. He'd always seemed to have a bit of a submissive streak, or a masochistic one, and like most Queendom citizens he was a staunch monarchist at heart.

And above him, hovering uncertainly in the middle somewhere, was Conrad. Surely an expert: a helmsman and mission planner, a sometime associate of the prince. One of only two matter programmers aboard the ship, and indispensable as such, and yet also a constant focus of royal irritation. How many times had Bascal shouted a hole in him already?

On the face of it, Conrad was needed but not wanted, respected but not loved, and so he served as a kind of executive officer, taking the dictates from on high and translating them into individual actions and duty assignments, however unpopular.

Viridity's crew seemed not only to accept this role for him, but actually to push him into it with active nagging. "How do we do that, Conrad?" "What's first, Conrad?" "What's next, Conrad?" It made their day easier, and gave them someone safe to blame for the things they were unhappy about. But if Conrad was the organizer of work, then Steve Grush was its enforcer. He'd decided all of a sudden to quit being Ho's buddy and had simply kissed up to him subordinately instead, with immediate payoff. Ah, the triumph of the flattering mediocrities: as the bad cop's bad cop, Steve could now enjoy all the freedom and social status of a prison trustee.

And this *was* a prison; Conrad wondered why he'd ever

expected otherwise. If he'd chafed at the fresh air and open spaces of Camp Friendly, how could he possibly have seen this as an alternative? The "freedom" of an infinite universe was the worst sort of illusion: they were locked on a single trajectory fixed by energy and gravity, with less freedom even than a railroad car or a river raft, or a motorcar driving along some endless, arrow-straight bridge.

There was a reason his father's roads meandered across the countryside, wasting time and energy and paving stone, doubling and tripling the length of a journey—because it masked this dearth of freedom. People traveled on a road for the sport of it, the adventure, the sense of exploration. But it could only lead them to the road's other end, or maybe another road with ends of its own. Whereas a fax gate could take you anywhere.

Turned away from the sun and with the pinpoint fusion *sila'a* now millions of kilometers distant, *Viridity* could alter its course by starlight alone. The feather-touch of a few weary microwatts was barely enough to turn the sail. And yet, its cumulative effect was the only thing keeping them precisely on course. Even the tiniest drift up or down or left or right would "derail" them, causing them to miss their final stop—the neutronium barge—and continue helplessly on toward the sun.

And that was a bad thing not only in terms of being caught, but more seriously, of *not* being caught. The Queendom's outermost permanent settlements—around the orbits of Pluto and Neptune and such—were eighteen months away at present speed, and sparsely scattered across the vastness of space. The *fetula* would likely sail right through without ever getting close to anything. The sun would be nearer and brighter, of course, pressing harder on the sail, but at this speed they could well reach the orbit of Mars before gaining enough control authority to set a new course.

So while manning the helm was boring duty, it was genuinely vital to their survival, and what little remained of their freedom. They'd at least managed to restore transparency to the windows, so there was a view—the illusion of vastness and freedom, the stars beckoning, the huge sail responding to his slightest touch at the controls. It was exhilarating at first, and then bearable for maybe as much as twenty minutes at a time.

To break up the day, Conrad would periodically kick up to the ceiling, stick his head in the center of the outward-bulging skylight, and spend a few minutes just looking at the stars. Not with a navigator's eye, although he was beginning to learn the constellations, and *Viridity*'s own path among them like an imaginary line. Mostly what he wanted and needed was the sense of *space*. He couldn't step outside, couldn't take a walk or climb a tree, but at least he could do this.

The brightest stars, when he looked them up, were Sirius, Canopus, and Rigil Kentaurus, which was actually a three-star system better known as Alpha Centauri—the nearest neighbor to the Queendom of Sol. There was something magical about that one. Most of the other bright ones were big rather than close: Sirius and Procyon were two and three times farther out—with many dimmer stars in between—while Vega and Arcturus were dozens of light-years (or tens of millions of AU) farther still. As a budding sailor, Conrad found it barely plausible that some sort of ship—ertially shielded or whatever—might someday reach those distant shores. The rest—Canopus and Capella, Rigel and Achernar—were simply decorations in the sky, so distant that the numbers made little sense.

Still, he learned their patterns, until he was able to judge the ship's orientation from these nine stars alone. The constellations were a fiction, especially out here in the deep dark, where so many more stars were visible, cluttering up the supposed pictures. But to shut Bascal up about it, he'd spent their fifth day in space memorizing the brightest and clearest of the images. Similarly, the distinction of a northern and southern hemisphere struck him as arbitrary and foolish, whether in Earth or solar coordinates. What really mattered—what really showed— was the blue-white slash of the Milky Way, bisecting the sky all around, and dividing the bright stars into three groups: above it, below it, and swathed within it. He wished they could simply navigate in galactic coordinates, although Bascal assured him it was a lot more work in the long run.

Not that he really cared what Bascal thought, except insofar as it threatened his safety. One thing was clear: Conrad had misjudged the prince, and had put his own fate—along with a dozen others'—in less-than-trustworthy hands. He didn't know what to do about that.

But the sky did not judge him, or lay fresh worries at his feet. The sheer number of stars out there was boggling, especially when he considered the Milky Way itself: a spiral of stars so dense and numerous and distant that they blurred together into a haze. And how many other galaxies were there? Did anyone even know?

Were there Queendoms, or the equivalent of Queendoms, around any of these billions of billions of pinpoints? It seemed there must be, although no one had ever detected one. Were there runaway children out there, making the best of a bad situation? Did they look like squidgy slugs, or ravenous flesh-eating spiders? Hell, he'd greet them anyway.

Inevitably, though, he grew bored with stargazing as well. That sense of awe was the only anchor he had right now, so when he felt it fading even slightly, he would kick back down to the helmsman's seat again. He would check the labe and gnomon, the register and chronometer. He did this three times, slowly and carefully making sure he wasn't ignoring a problem. Then he'd look straight up and check the sail, and the whole cycle would start anew.

Even with the sail newly configured as a one-way mirror, transparent in one direction and reflective in the other, the push of starlight across the entire sail wasn't much more than the Earth-weight of an eyelash. Not much to work with. But there was only one perfect path to the neutronium barge—that invisible line slicing through otherwise empty space—and the push of this weak source against frictionless space did add up over time. Over the weeks of their journey it could drive them hundreds of kilometers toward or away from the path. And because the barge was only twelve hundred meters long—a tiny target in the vastness of Kuiper wilderness— this fine-tuning could literally mean the difference between life and death.

So Conrad took the duty seriously, and so did Bascal, and they were each careful to check up on the other at shift change, to make sure *Viridity* hadn't drifted a few meters this way or that. The closer they got to the target, the less time they'd have to make up those errors. And gods help them all if anything happened to the hypercomputers, which were the only thing making these absurdly precise calculations even vaguely possible!

And gods help them, also, if the neutronium barge decided to change course, to deviate from its gravitationally expected path. This would not be done lightly—the energies involved were enormous—but of course the barge's entire purpose was to slurp up Kuiper Belt matter and supercompress it. The vessel would follow its sensor-laden nose, ponderously seeking out new gas and dust concentrations, as well as the odd iceball or comet. Course changes would be small and exacting and optimized for minimum effort, but that didn't mean a mere *fetula* would be able to keep up. Conrad lived in fear of this, and checked for it several times every hour.

But the mere existence of danger didn't make helm duty interesting, and it didn't keep Conrad from inventing games around it. One of these involved remapping the reflectivity of the sail. At any given time, only about ninety percent of it was actually mirrored. The rest was a shifting pattern of clear and black squares that kept the forces and torques properly balanced, so the sail would maintain proper alignment.

And it occurred to Conrad in the first couple of days that he could maintain these same precise forces while carefully using the dark and clear patches to draw dim, flickering pictures on the wellstone of the sail. So far, to his amazement, no one had noticed. Or if they'd noticed, they hadn't said anything.

Conrad wasn't much of an artist, and at first he'd restricted himself to geometric patterns. Circles, squares, polygons, simple flags ... Once he'd gotten the hang of it, though, he became more ambitious, and during one particular peek out the window he had looked at the batwing shape of the sail and seen it for what it was: the unrolled and flattened skin of a sphere, exactly like the spiky projecting lozenge shapes of some planetary maps. Every point on the sail corresponded to a point on (or just under) the surface of Camp Friendly. So for several days, in a haze of boredom and odd, nostalgialike enthusiasm, he carefully reconstructed the map of that homely, lovely planette, which he had helped to deface.

Adventure Lake was the easy part: he knew its shape and position very well, having circumnavigated it with a locator and sketchplate during a camp exercise. How Bascal, the Tongan, had chafed at that one! "At the age of five I was sailing in a crater lake that could drown this whole planette!"

The rest of it was much more difficult than Conrad had expected at first. He could reconstruct the locations of a few key buildings by recalling the views from their windows, or the rock formations jutting above the curving horizon, or the length of time required to walk or run between them. But there were actually a lot of buildings in the camp complex, and varied landscape features all over the planette, and his memory of them was surprisingly imperfect.

Still, here was the hobby farm, and the plateau, and the central landmark of the rock formations themselves. Here was the northern outpost of the Young Men's Camp, and the sprawl of the Boys' Camp and administrative offices. D'rector Jed's wayward cabin got a little star to mark its former location. Conrad was working on the forest, to the northeast of Adventure Lake, when someone tapped him on the shoulder.

He yelped and jumped.

"Sorry!" Martin Liss said, quickly and sheepishly.

"No concern. It's my fault," Conrad told him, turning to look.

"Am I early?"

Conrad glanced at the clock. "No. It's completely my fault."

He'd carefully arranged the duty roster so that every single day he'd have at least a few minutes alone, in private, with a different member of the crew. Not to sow the seeds of open mutiny—not yet anyway—but just to talk and work together. To reinforce their acquaintance, to get a better feel for their character and concerns. If a time for mutiny came, or even a time for more subtle action, he wanted to know where the lines would break.

Was it egotistical of him? Possibly, but he wasn't taking anything on faith anymore. So far he'd learned that Ho was every bit as stupid and shallow and dangerous as he seemed. He also stank, since he refused to give up the clothes he'd gotten in Denver. When pressed on the point, he explained it thusly: if he threw them in the fax, he'd get back a Camp Friendly shirt and culottes, which would suck. He did wash his Denver clothes in the sink every few days, but the smell factor was definitely building up. "I can't punch; I can't kick," he lamented. "But I can stink up the place, and look good doing it."

Ah.

By contrast, Steve Grush was, if not smarter and nicer, then at least more careful than Ho. Steve was well aware that their odds of success—and perhaps even survival— were slim. He just didn't have any better prospects, and figured space piracy was worth a shot. People would probably get hurt, but so what? That was what backups were for. It was an unimaginative but pragmatic view. Karl Smoit, for his part, didn't like being on this mission at all, and was happy to complain about it when nobody else was in earshot.

There was of course the possibility that the wellstone ceiling was spying on them, and *nothing* was out of earshot, but Conrad didn't know how to detect that, or what to do about it if he did. Besides, that would be a difficult thing to program into naïve wellstone. Jed was at least "roughing it" to that extent: his ceiling's library was nearly as limited as the sail fabric itself.

"I didn't mean to startle you," Martin said.

Conrad waved the apology away. "In theory, I was expecting you. In practice, I got distracted."

This was another thing he'd learned, as part of this underground personnel campaign: that he was terrible at remembering upcoming appointments and events. It was the sort of character flaw that could get a person killed under circumstances like these. He resolved to work on it.

"I see you brought the dust mops," he said to Martin, who shrugged and handed him one. He took it, disentangled himself from the navigator's chair, and "stood up" in the zero gravity. He proceeded to brush out the space under the instrument console, and glanced back at Martin. "Shall we?"

"Um, sure."

"It's amazing how much dust accumulates, how quickly. I hear it's mostly human skin cells. We shed, like dogs and cats."

"Uh-huh."

"Try over there," Conrad said, pointing. Then: "So how's it going, anyway?"

"Good," Martin replied, in a voice suggesting otherwise.

"Keeping busy?"

"Sure."

"Obeying the rules?"

Martin snorted. "That's like a joke, right? Only not really. Yes, I'm obeying the rules. Is there a choice?"

"Why?" Conrad asked. "Is someone giving you a hard time?"

Sullenly: "No."

"Are you sure? If there is, you can let me know."

"There isn't."

It went on like that for a while. Conrad wished more than once that they could both just come out and say what needed saying, but of course that could endanger either or both of them unless there was already perfect trust. Which there never could be, because they couldn't really talk. And coming right out with it would also tip Conrad's hand prematurely, which helped nothing.

But over the hour he developed a clear sense that yeah, Martin did have a problem with all this, and that yeah, to the extent that he trusted anyone in *Viridity*'s authority chain, he trusted Conrad the most. Not that he'd risk his life for Conrad or anything—probably not for anyone here—but he wouldn't support the prince if an opportunity came up where he had any choice about it.

So that was two. Two people Conrad could use, could

help, could deal with. Not *trust* or *rely on*, but that was okay. He would just have to craft the right circumstances, so all the right choices went all the right ways. That was a tall order, and he wished he could doodle and sketch and make notes about the possibilities. But the game was dangerous enough already.

When the sweeping was done, Martin went on his way, leaving Conrad alone again until shift change, when Bascal came in with Ho and one of the Palace Guards.

"Conrad, my man," the prince said. "How goes our course?"

"Two centimeters north of optimal," Conrad answered in their accepted parlance. "I've been compensating all day, but I don't want to overdo it and have to spend next week swinging back."

"Good, good." Bascal motioned for him to vacate the chair.

"And the barge hasn't tried to turn," Conrad said, in his umpteenth attempt to get Bascal thinking about that.

"Fine. That's good. We want to hit it square, eh?"

"Well," Conrad said, "we don't want to *hit* it at all, right? We want to rendezvous. Our relative speed is ... oh, crap. Oh, shit."

"What?"

"Our relative speed is *twenty kips*. How are we supposed to slow down? How do we match velocities with the barge, when we have no rockets and no sunlight?"

Bascal waved a hand. "Relax. We'll throw a lanyard."

Conrad gaped at the stupidity of that. Had those words really come from the mouth of Bascal Edward de Towaji Lutui? "We'll *what*? Excuse me?"

"We steer the *fetula* so it just misses the barge," Bascal said, "but we tag it with a very sticky rope."

"That doesn't help us decelerate."

"Oh. Hmm." Bascal scratched his chin, then pinched it. "These speeds are a lot higher than I'm used to. That trick works if you're just burning off a couple of kips; you wind up swinging in a wide arc, then reeling the line in. I guess in our case the rope will need to be elastic."

"*How* elastic?" Conrad demanded. Then he strode to the instrument console and called up a hypercomputer to answer the question himself. He was suddenly furious: here was yet another surprise, yet another critical detail dropped or ignored. Bascal's got-it-figured-out act was *total* sham. Other than computing their initial course and setting up the sail controls, he'd figured out exactly nothing. "Do you even care? Are you *trying* to get us all martyred for the goddamned cause?"

"Steady, there, me boyo." Bascal's tone was ominous.

Conrad fiddled with parameters for a few minutes before extracting an answer. His skin went cold. "Well. It looks like a survivable ten-gee deceleration will stretch your cable over *three thousand* kilometers in four minutes. The wellstone's not going to stand up to that; it stretches maybe twice its length. Maybe. It's fucking *silicon*, Bascal; it's like glass. It's a woven mat of glass fibers. Little gods!"

"We'll think of something," Bascal snapped. "Jesus, if you're so smart all of a sudden—"

"Yeah, we'll think of something! I already have. We give up now and call for help!"

"We what?"

"We mirrorize every surface, and start flashing signals in every possible frequency. I'm very sure the navy's looking for us already; it shouldn't take long to trip their sensors."

"That's treason," Bascal said simply. "That's mutiny."

"It's common sense," Conrad countered.

But Bascal was shaking his head and gesturing wearily. "Guard, my life is in danger from forces outside this *fetula*. If the hull is mirrorized, or generates any broadcast in any frequency, kill this man. Don't stuff him in the fax, *kill* him. Is that understood?"

The guard cocked its blank-faced head at Bascal. "What is the nature of the threat?"

"Despair," Bascal told it. "They will attempt to drive me to suicide. And they may well succeed."

The guard thought it over, and said nothing.

"You've finished us," Conrad murmured, loud enough so only Bascal could hear. "Oh, you lazy, *selfish* bastard. You've just nailed our coffin shut."

chapter twelve

the battle of conrad

Was that it? Were they done for? Well, maybe. As he stalked off into the other room, Conrad allowed for the possibility that there might be a solution. Might. This did not, of course, excuse Bascal. It didn't excuse threats of murder backed up by lies, nor the gross endangerment of *Viridity*'s remaining crew. He felt it now with certainty: there *were* no excuses for this sort of malice and recklessness. If some species of God was out there somewhere, keeping tally, then Bascal was in big trouble.

But that night at dinner the *pilinisi* was all smiles, and afterward he told the story of "The Princess and the Satellites," in which a Tongan king's daughter, a clever player in pre-Queendom politics, purchased an arc of empty space for almost nothing—for a shipment of glass beads and handwoven mats—and then leased it to the Empire of China for the parking of communication satellites, which were bus-sized things like telecom collapsiters, except they contained no black holes and so could not transmit the quantum interference patterns associated with material objects. The princess made a great deal of money, embarrassed her parents and other enemies, set the kingdom aright, and lived happily ever after.

Hurray.

But then, for the first time since this crazy mission had started, it was *Conrad's* turn to tell a story. This was the thirteenth night of their voyage—Bascal had been manipulating the seating patterns and the length of the story hour to shut him out, to keep him from addressing the whole crew. But tonight Conrad had simply gotten up and changed seats while the *pilinisi* was talking, and sat right down between him and the ever-gorgeous Xmary. Conrad knew better than to blurt out the fact that *Viridity* was going to crash fatally into its target, or else miss entirely. That sort of outburst would simply get him faxed or killed. And with the reminder of the Palace Guards' murderous power, open mutiny seemed even farther out of the question. So his story couldn't simply be "The Bad Prince and the Doomed *Fetula*."

But as it happened, he did know a Tongan fairy tale.

"I'm taking you back," he said. "Back, before the power and whimsy of monarchs had swallowed human society. There were two boys who lived on an island, who were very disobedient. They loved to escape from their house and play in the ocean. They loved to dive deep and swim out far beyond the reef, even when their mother told them not to. Their mother worried endlessly, because the boys were fearless, and never careful."

"Tik and Lap?" Bascal asked, sounding distinctly unamused.

"Maybe," Conrad told him. "Tik and Lap. That sounds right."

"Tik and Lap and the giant fish?"

"Yeah."

The prince glowered but said nothing.

"Anyway, their mother warned them that the sea was dangerous. They could get swept out by the tide, or get a foot caught in the reef. They could get eaten. But the more she scolded, the farther out they swam. One day they swam all the way out to a neighboring island. The chief of the island was impressed, and sent them home in a boat filled with wonderful foods.

"'Gifts must be repaid in kind,' the boys' mother told them. 'You are good with your spears; you must catch some fish for this chief. But *please* be careful.' So the boys went spearfishing, and laughed at their mother's warning. They knew they could swim like tunas, dive like porpoises, and sail as fast as the wind. 'We'll show her,' they said as they gathered firewood to cook their catch.

"But later, while they were fishing, Lap clowned around and managed to drop his spear. So the two boys swam deep, deep into the ocean to retrieve it, without bothering to check what they were swimming down into. It was a giant cave, and inside the cave lived a giant fish, which swallowed the two boys up.

"'We are eaten!' cried Tik. 'We are in this fish's horrible belly. It stinks like rotting fish guts. What will we do?'

"'I don't know,' said Lap. 'Maybe we should have listened to Mom. Maybe she's not entirely stupid about these things.'

"'I don't want to die in this place,' Tik said. 'There must be something we can do. Look, I'm still holding the firewood! We'll light a fire inside this fish.'

"The wood was wet, but the two boys were expert at starting fires, so they rubbed the sticks together until finally they burst into flame.

"'Watch this,' Lap said, and held a flaming stick against the wall of the fish's belly. The fish jumped and struggled, flipping over and over in the water trying to rid itself of the horrible burning pain. 'Get ready for a wild ride!'

"Using the flaming sticks, they drove the fish up out of the cave, out of the deeps, up onto the shore of a nearby island. They laughed. 'We still have more wood. And our spears, and our grass hats. We'll roast this fish from the inside!' And that is what they did. Finally, the fish's mouth opened, and they were able to climb out. And who did they find there, but the chief and his people who had given them the food!

"'Your Majesty,' they told him, 'at the request of our mother, we have brought you a gift: a giant roasted fish.'

"'Oh, my. How did you catch him?' the chief exclaimed.

"'We used ourselves as bait, and cooked him from inside. Now if you don't mind, we would like to ask you for a ride home. We promised our wise mother we'd never swim that far again.'

"And the chief smiled. 'You are clever boys to listen to your elders, instead of running wild. Here's a dollar.'"

The next day, Bascal noticed Conrad's Camp Friendly mural on the sail, and replaced it with a faint, kilometer-wide skull and crossbones, and then followed up by singing the crew a catchy Space Pirate Song of his own invention. And that was bad, because even the boys who'd stopped liking Bacsal took an immediate shine to his song. Instantly, it replaced the Fuck You Song as the national anthem of their doomed, cabin-sized monarchy.

> Well, she doesn't have an engine, and she doesn't have
>   a fax gate,
> And she never had a regs inspector say that she was
>   sound,
> And with no acceleration and with no gravitic grapple
> We go flying through the cabin 'less we tie our asses
>   down!

It went on like that, for verses and verses, and it was the kind of song anyone could add to at any time. Hell, within a few hours of hearing it Conrad caught his own mouth singing the chorus.

Fortunately, bathroom duty with Xmary that day provided a chance to sort things out. Nobody questioned this, even when he closed the door, because he'd been careful all along to assign himself all the nastiest, least-desirable chores. Who wanted to mess with that? It made everything easier: not only getting privacy, but also getting people to do the work. If they saw him doing it, and saw him seeing them not doing it, well, the shame and boredom took over, and lo and behold, the chores got done.

"Bathroom duty, ugh," Xmary said.

"We'll get through it," Conrad assured her, although with eight teenaged boys using it, it *was* an awful mess. He was tempted, not for the first time, to devise some sensors in here to catch whoever it was that was leaving actual blobs of shit in the air. In any case, it all had to be cleaned up before anyone could dream of taking a shower, and according to Xmary's schedule today was definitely shower day.

But the session didn't start well: Xmary inspected some black marks on the cabin's wooden wall, and quickly discovered they were a cartoon drawing of herself, naked and engaged in an improbable act whose details were spelled out with arrows and word balloons off to the side.

"Damn!" she said, with surprising vehemence. "Damn, damn, fuck. You boys are so mean. Don't look at it! Get away from that!"

Conrad saw tears quivering at the corners of her reddening eyes. His brilliant response: "Hey, I didn't do it."

"Damn, damn," she repeated. "This is what I get. This is the price I pay. Being leered at by little boys. This is disgusting. It doesn't matter who I am, does it? It doesn't matter how much I do for you people."

Again, Conrad's brilliance: "I'm nearly eighteen. I'm not a little boy." But he hated the way that sounded, so he quickly followed it with, "We can find out who's responsible. There aren't that many suspects."

"Don't bother," she said, angrily rubbing her eyes.

"Here's a sponge," he tried.

But she was already rubbing at the drawing with her hand. "No, it's indelible ink. And it's *carved*. Great, somebody drew this, then cut it into the log, then drew over it again. Such dedication."

"We'll get rid of it," he tried to assure her.

"There'll just be more of the same," she said.

He shook his head. "No. Tonight, everyone gets Slop Number Two for dinner. If it happens again, they get no dinner at all. With Bascal's help, we can enforce that."

"I don't want Bascal's help," she said quietly. She'd turned a really amazing shade of red. "I don't want him to know about this. I don't want it discussed."

"Not even—"

"I *don't want it discussed*. I'll just check in here five times a day, with a paintbrush and a sanding block."

"That shouldn't be necessary."

"Well, apparently it is," she snapped. Then she waved a hand. "Just go over there or something. Clean. I'll take care of this."

"Okay. Okay. See, I'm going. I'm over here."

Wordlessly, she left the room, returning a few minutes later and closing the door most of the way behind her. She busied herself with the drawing's noisy expungement.

"You don't know many girls," she observed sourly.

Conrad wanted to deny that—to be snitty about it, even. Why, there were *several* girls at the School of West Europe who were in his general age bracket, and with whom he'd had conversations more than once. More than twice! And he saw girls out in public of course, and wasn't afraid to smile or wave, to introduce himself or to kiss them without invitation. But he had the uncomfortable sense that this information would not impress her, or change her opinion in any way.

"I know *you*," he said instead, as offhandedly as he could manage.

"How splendid for you," was her reply.

Ouch. He gave her another minute to cool off, not wanting to touch that temper any earlier than necessary. But he did want to talk to her. More importantly, he *needed* to, because he didn't have a reading on her yet, and without one he couldn't plan a single thing that involved the crew in any way. The situation was dire.

"Other than this," he said finally, "other than graffiti and innuendo and ingratitude, how are you?"

"Get processed, Conrad." She sighed in irritation and, after a pause of ten seconds or so, answered with a quiet voice. "Truthfully? Not good. Bascal and I aren't getting along."

"No?"

"He isn't like this on TV. Holding court, pushing people around . . . Pushing *me* around."

"He's not himself," Conrad said, hoping it didn't sound like a speculation. Truthfully, he didn't know the prince that well either, not in his own element, and was still surprised by his behavior more often than not. "I've never seen him like this. He's, like, drunk on the drama of it all. Yesterday he threatened to kill me."

"To *kill* you? Why?"

Conrad took a breath and released it, deciding all at once to confide in her and let the chips fall. "I wanted to send a distress call. We have no plan for safe landing at the barge. No way to accomplish it. We're doomed to miss it or to crash, and I'm seriously concerned that Bascal knew this all along. Even if he didn't, that's just as bad. He doesn't care, or he isn't really trying. Either way, it's big trouble for the rest of us."

Still cleaning, still wrinkling her nose and curling her

lip, she absorbed that. Conrad found himself puzzled and concerned: he'd expected her to react more strongly, one way or the other. What did it mean that she didn't?

"That doesn't surprise you?" he asked.

"No," she said, with a hint of despair. "It's about what I figured. The signs are everywhere. Do you . . . think maybe he's gone crazy?"

Conrad felt as if he'd lost his balance. Which was non-sense, of course, in zero gravity. Dizzily, he whispered back, "That's not something I'd say out loud, even in private. But yes. He wants this so badly, he doesn't care if it's impossible, or who gets hurt. I'd call that crazy."

"Let him perish if that's what he wants." She sulked. "My heart is heavy enough. But I didn't give him permission to take *me*."

"No. Nor I. I'm . . . glad to hear you speaking your mind on this. Don't be afraid to talk to me."

Xmary's eyes met his. "I haven't let him touch me," she whispered. "Not for weeks." She was hanging close to him, her brush-wielding hand only a few centimeters from his. Still clenched with the rage and stress of it all.

Now he felt his own cheeks burning. Speaking her mind, okay, but why had she told him *that*? What possible use was the information? He fantasized briefly that it meant she liked him. In *that* way, yes. She'd gone for the big score—the *pilinisi*—only to realize that his erstwhile sidekick was the real Prince Charming around here. Yeah, certainly. Stuff like *that* happened all the time. And even if there was somehow a particle of truth to it, what good was that? What could he do, make a play for the girlfriend of an unbalanced and openly murderous monarch?

He touched her hair for a wistful moment. She didn't object, which surprised him so much that he pulled away and said loudly, "*Damn* it's ugly in here. Some fucker on this ship needs flushing lessons."

Then he whispered to Xmary, "We've got to do something about this. You and I, maybe some others. Learn matter programming, all right? Quickly."

And she whispered back, "I will."

She was true to her word, pulling a textbook out of the fax and poring through it for days. Finally, the cabin's ceiling began suffering pattern and color changes at random intervals. One day it was mostly gold, with little sparkles of light dancing across it. Pretty, in a garish sort of way, though it made a poor light source and an even poorer environmental control. Fortunately, that one was only up for a couple of hours.

Unfortunately, what replaced it was a popping, snapping, hissing field of black and white dots that cast the cabin into flickering gloom, and gave an instant headache to everyone who looked at it.

"What did you do?" Conrad asked Xmary. They were on opposite sides of the main room, and he had to raise his voice to be heard over the complaints and groans and sudden intense discussions of the other boys, and the hissing of the wellstone itself.

"I don't know," she answered, pulling her hand away and drawing back from the ceiling. "I'm not sure. I've lost my interface. Can I . . . touch it?"

"I wouldn't," Conrad said, eyeing the mess. Then, raising his voice further: *"Nobody touch that."*

Damn, it could be hot or cold or sticky, or crawling with huge electrical potentials. It could be corrosive with "Lewis hole–pair" acids, or worse. Wellstone's quantum-dot arrays contained charged particles in huge numbers and all kinds of bizarre arrangements. Some of their reactions were capable of tearing normal matter apart, as Conrad's programming instructor, Mr. McMorran, had emphasized many times.

He cleared his throat. "You are, um, aware that matter programming is very dangerous?"

"I've read chapter one, thank you," Xmary said, sounding ready to punch him.

It wouldn't be wise to let her see—let anyone see—how much her anger stung him. So what he said was, "Good."

It wasn't possible to stagger in zero gee, but Bascal's entrance had something of that quality. He was staring at the ceiling and holding his head, not really watching where or how he was going as he kicked along the walls and floor. "What did you do, Conrad? What happened?"

"We're trying to figure that out," he answered nervously.

"Make it stop. You're hurting my brain with that."

"I don't want to *touch* it. I can use . . . I can use the environment controls. The panel is connected to . . . well, all of it connects one way or another."

Which was bad, because Xmary's unsupervised tinkering had the potential to pollute the entire *fetula*, from wrapping to rigging to sail. If they ceased being airtight, or a variety of other things happened, this kind of pattern pollution could easily and instantly kill everyone on board.

Being very careful not to bounce himself upward with no way to stop, Conrad glided over to the environmental control panel. Once there, he laid some wires around to the tortured ceiling, and passed a simple text encoding along them: UNDO.

The hissing stopped, and the ceiling reverted immediately to gold.

"Little fucking gods," Bascal said, eyeing it uneasily. He took his hands off his head and glared alternately at Xmary and Conrad. "Whatever you guys are doing, quit it. Seriously. A spaceship is not a fucking toy."

Which was true.

After that, Xmary was ready to quit her programming experiments altogether, but Conrad persuaded her to practice on a sketchplate instead, and to stand by the fax so she could hurl it to oblivion if it did anything funny, anything she didn't immediately like or expect. So her studies continued, at a lower and more cautious intensity, through the next several days. If only she could ask questions right out in the open. If only they could sit down together! But he couldn't schedule her in again so soon without people noticing, and she was probably attracting enough curious attention as it was.

For his own part, Conrad passed through the week in a kind of low-grade panic. Did he really believe he had a handle on his fears? Every time he thought that, the danger to life and limb and memory simply ratcheted up another notch, threatening to paralyze him. He went through the motions, filling duty rosters and working his shifts, trying to act normal. But people were noticing. How could they not? Bascal hadn't pulled him off helm duty or anything, mainly because there was so little the helm could accomplish anyway, but the tension between the two of them must be screamingly obvious.

No way out. No alternatives. No hope? Was there a god of lightsails to watch over them, or a plain-old God, merciless and remote but still observing? Or were they truly on their own, pitting their frail selves against a universe that didn't know them from any other speck of matter?

He wondered what it was like to die. Everyone wondered that, of course, but not everyone had to face it as an immediate short-term prospect. Not everyone had heard the order given for his or her own robotic execution. Hitting the barge would at least be instantaneous; they'd see it looming behind the sail, swelling as they approached, and the very end would come quickly, the barge expanding toward them like a shockwave. There'd be maybe a momentary glimpse of its close-up hull, frozen in camera-flash detail: pipes and light housings, a planette-sized registration number, and then . . .

What? Stepping out of a fax with the last ten weeks missing from his backup memories? No, he would never experience that. Some other Conrad Mursk would, while he, while *this* Conrad Mursk, would be dead and gone. Waking up in heaven, or in the big nothing where he wouldn't even know he was dead. Wouldn't know he had ever lived at all. Did it matter, if there was somebody exactly like him to carry on? Wasn't it really just the same thing as being disintegrated and reborn during fax transport?

No, he decided. It wasn't the same. One of him had died once before, and the twenty-day hole that had left was an unhealed wound in his life, even now. He'd never mourned for that dead brother, exactly, but he had very definitely wondered what he went through. What it felt like, what he thought about. Last words, last images, last fleeting shreds of emotion. Did he scream?

And gods, it was *crippling* having this kind of shit bouncing around in his head. Maybe it wouldn't bother him so much without the Xmary factor, this stupid, pointless pining he'd taken up lately. Or maybe it would, but since their little talk—since her little revelation—it seemed increasingly clear that no thought or action or circumstance could be relevant except in relation to her. Which was crazy, obviously, but there you had it. Death was bad enough, but when it meant the loss of *her*, every memory and trace of her, that was just too high a price to pay for Bascal's glory.

And Conrad couldn't arrange another meeting with her so soon, and wouldn't know what to do with it if he did. So instead he watched her out of the corners of his eyes, and listened to the lilt of her speech, taking what pleasure he could. Stupid, yes, but he needed an anchor.

It occurred to him that this feeling had a name: he was *heartsick*. It wasn't just a word, or even just a feeling, but something that had stolen upon him with all the grinding hallmarks of a genuine illness. Maybe the only illness left, in an age of perfect and permanent health, and it weighed him down as surely as gravity. Even going through the motions of daily life was exhausting. But what else was there? If he simply gave up without a struggle, then he and she and all the others *would* die, no doubt about it. So he met with the boys one by one, prodding gently and hearing them out, slotting them mentally into factions. Loyalists: Ho and Steve. Neutrals: Preston and Jamil. Mutineers: Xmary, Karl, and Martin. And Conrad himself, sure. That made it four against three, except the "three" also had two Palace Guards on their side, so really the mutiny was already over. No contest. They'd lost.

Could the guards be subverted? On the face of it, it seemed unlikely. They took their orders directly from Bascal, and simply ignored anyone else's. But then again, those orders were constrained by the words of the king, and other "standing orders," and the robots' own inherent instincts and programming. They wouldn't interfere with the prince's freedom of action, but they also wouldn't allow him to harm himself, if they understood what was happening and saw a way to prevent it.

Conceivably, Conrad could simply talk to them. They wouldn't obey him, or probably even acknowledge that he was speaking to them. But they weren't deaf. On the contrary, they were perceptive, finely tuned for the gleaning of information. For all he knew, they'd already figured the whole thing out, or at least figured out that something was wrong. They would listen to his words, weigh them, add them to the vast database of their paranoid and hyperprotective worldview.

So the idea wasn't absurd. It was a matter of picking

his moment and his exact argument, of getting the right words out before Bascal could find a way to stop him.

And meanwhile, he hadn't given up on the physics of it. Not that he was any expert on physics—not by a long shot—but he didn't have to *solve* the equations, just look them up and feed them into a simulation. It was more like asking a scientist than being one.

Anyway, a collision at twenty kilometers per second would *vaporize* ordinary materials like flesh and bone and wood, but properly rigidized wellstone could survive it under some conditions. Working feverishly on his little sketchplate hypercomputer, he'd identified eight different prefab settings that stood a good chance of coming through intact. Adamantium, obviously—that was the toughest pseudomaterial known to science. There were two superreflectors: impervium and its fee-for-use cousin Bunkerlight. And two transparents: superglass and Wexlan.

The others were more obscure, and had weird properties like superconductivity and phosphorescence, that he wasn't at all sure about. But it didn't matter anyway, because an impregnable hull wouldn't save the ship's insides. Wouldn't slow them down, wouldn't cushion them, wouldn't protect them in any way. That hull would simply be the last thing any of them saw, in the microseconds before they slammed into it at twenty kips.

He had felt a few brief hours of giddy relief when he'd stumbled on "magtal," a family of transuranic metals that were not tough enough to survive the collision per se, but whose features included "superferromagnetism." This was significant, because the neutronium inside the barge was, according to his fax-provided reference materials, also highly magnetic. And Conrad had done enough fiddling with magnets to know that they *repelled* as well as they attracted. Could they decelerate the *fetula* slowly, on a springy magnetic cushion?

Alas, his hopes were short-lived. First of all, the net magnetic field of the barge would have to be lined up with *Viridity*'s incoming trajectory—which as far as he could determine, it wasn't. And anyway, his simulations showed the cushion was unstable, like a steep, springy, hilltop of slippery gel. Instead of slowing down, the *fetula* would simply slide sideways around the magnetic obstacle until the field strength dropped off. If they tried it, they would miss the barge by many thousands of kilometers. Which wasn't necessarily a bad thing, but didn't solve the larger problem of having nowhere else to go.

More promising was the prospect of just missing the barge, and then turning on the magnets in an attractive mode. This was basically just Bascal's lanyard plan, with magnets instead of fragile ropes. Up close, this worked very well indeed; there'd be absolutely no problem getting ten gees of deceleration out of it. Unfortunately, the force of attraction between the two ships dropped off *fast* as they drew apart. At a hundred kilometers, the force was huge, but at a hundred thousand it was barely more than the eyelash press of starlight.

And there was the problem: if he throttled the acceleration to a survivable level, then the magnetic "lanyard" would snap and the *fetula* would keep on sailing away, somewhat more slowly than before. If he adjusted the magnets to ensure capture, the *fetula* would bounce a thousand kilometers past the barge, and then stop and sproing back. But the acceleration would peak at hundreds of gee, and *Viridity*'s insides would be so much grape jelly and wood pulp. He tried the simulation a dozen times in a dozen different ways before giving up. Magnets weren't going to save them.

He stewed about this for a day and a night, tantalized and frustrated. There were so many options, so many almosts. Just different ways to die. And since Bascal would rather die than surrender, that left capture by Queendom forces as their only hope for survival. Conrad began to pray for this, to fantasize about it. And was it really so far-fetched? The navy or Constabulary could well have retrieved Peter by now, and if Peter was still alive then he would tell them the plan. And even if he didn't, or couldn't, the evidence was as plain as the face of the murdered planette: they had built a *fetula* and sailed away. To where? To an empty comet? To the distant Queendom, years away? Or to the nearest fax machine, on the nearest neutronium barge!

From there, it was just a matter of computing the path, and then hunting along it for signs of an invisible spaceship. How hard could that be? They still had mass, right? They would show up on a gravity detector. And they weren't perfectly invisible, especially in the very long wavelengths, like radio, and the very short ones, like X rays. And he was amazed, *amazed*, to hear these kind of thoughts in his own dumb-as-rocks head. How many science classes had he flunked? But here he was, out in the universe, living it firsthand.

And it seemed to him, more and more every day, that *Viridity*'s discovery and capture was a scientific certainty. When it didn't come, he simply reset his expectations for the next day, and the next, and the one after that. But then came the day of reckoning: the last day when starlight power alone could push them out of the barge's path. If they didn't do it now, then they never could, and the Queendom's navy *still* hadn't come to the rescue.

Jesus H. Bloodfuck, he said to himself. *The mutiny has to happen. Today.*

Is't balm for us, this void of sky?
The stars have no network address.
A bit of you for me, I fear, be toxin more than bliss.

Where love of metal nannies warms,
the love of flesh doth mock.
And whence the blame? What leads us 'stray?
What claim have you or I, to shock?

Don't take my hand. Where could we jump?
That no one's been a thousand times?
I've faxed myself to Saturn's rings; your love hath broke
*   my pump.*

—*"Because Lilly"*
BASCAL EDWARD DE TOWAJI LUTUI, *age 14*

chapter thirteen

the cold rebellion

The hard part was letting Xmary know. They hadn't agreed on any sort of signal for the start of hostilities, but if he didn't get word to her—to *someone*—then Bascal could simply put the guards on him again, and that would be that. No speaking, no gesturing, no pounding on the walls. . . . But she needed to know what was happening, and what the teams were, and it wasn't like he could just tell her right in front of everybody, and it wasn't like he could whisper in her ear or lead her off for a private conference, or pass her a note. Not Xmary, not without attracting a lot of attention.

That left Martin and Karl, and Conrad wasn't really sure he trusted Martin. The kid was too quiet; beyond expressing "grave doubts about the present regime," he hadn't said much. There was no real clue as to the inner workings of his head, or even if he *had* much of an inner life. Some people seemed to get by without one. If it came down to a simple brawl, Conrad was pretty sure Martin would at least stick a foot out or something— some small gesture in his own self-interest. But *initiating* any action seemed unlikely. It was too much to ask.

That left Karl. And because Conrad's shift at the helm was about to begin, there was no time to lose, and no point in delaying. And no reason to be especially afraid, since the price of failure—death—was identical to the price of doing nothing. But he *was* afraid. He'd never done anything like this before. He didn't know how to approach it, where to start, how to keep himself from fucking up along the way. And the threat of immediate bodily harm seemed for some reason more viscerally real than the prospect of crashing and vaporizing in a week and a half.

But the sketchy outlines of a plan were taking shape in his mind, and the time to act was now.

He looked around, studying the room. It was "day," with the ceiling—now off-limits to Xmary—giving off a diffuse, warm, vaguely sunny glow. Conrad would have preferred to turn the power down on that—they didn't *need* that much light—but there was enough stored energy in the capacitors to keep it lit for a year or so, and since that was a lot longer than they had to live, he wasn't going to make an issue out of it.

And in spite of the "daylight," Ho was asleep in his closet, or maybe whacking off, and Preston Midrand was cinched down on his mattress and also apparently asleep. Bascal was on the bridge, of course, along with one of the Palace Guards. The other guard was in here, rooted to the spot where it had stood, motionless, for most of the past month. And hovering near it with a sketchplate tucked under her arm was Xmary, half-seriously chewing out Martin for "farting again."

She must be really bored, really sick of her studies, because their shipboard diet had always centered around beans and franks—one the gassiest and most diarrheic food combos in the known universe. Fortunately, any fart gas that touched the fax machine was absorbed and disassembled and whisked into the mass buffers, so the air never had a chance to grow *too* foul. But yeah, it was a problem they'd all been living with and grown used to, although it had grown steadily worse as they'd depleted their other meager food supplies.

Which, by the way, Conrad strongly suspected Ho of playing more than his fair part in. He did sleep with the food, after all, and memorize its inventory, and guard it jealously against unauthorized access. The one time Karl had sneaked a handful of pecans out, Ho had looked ready to murder him for it, and probably would have if not for the Guards. But two days later the pecans were gone, and Ho said nothing.

Jamil and Karl and Steve Grush were solemnly playing the handball game Karl had invented as a zero-gee alternative to shirtball soccer. The idea was to bat the shirtball to the next person with an open hand, and keep a three- or four-way volley going for as long as possible. Not terribly exciting, and just like shirtball soccer it lent itself to certain abuses, such as the constant and deliberate targeting of noncombatants. But it passed the time.

Karl's last duty had been swabbing the main cabin's ceiling and skylights, so Conrad launched himself to the ceiling, gave it a cursory inspection, and said, "Little gods, it's filthy up here. Who cleaned this?"

This was delivered in Leadership Tone, a bit of play-acting Conrad had adopted based on studies of Bascal. Far from commanding or stern, it was actually sort of jovial. And yet, when you did it properly there was an edge to it, a not-so-casual hinting at potential consequences that seemed, for whatever reason, to yield maximum response. Steve and Jamil and Karl looked up; their shirtball went skittering off into a corner.

"Karl," Conrad said, "would you grab a dust mop and meet me up here, please?"

"Do I have to?" Karl answered, glowering vaguely, and Conrad couldn't have *asked* for a better response. God bless that boy's stubborn streak.

"I would like you to," Conrad told him. This was another trick from the de Towaji School of Management: never give an order if you could give a pointed suggestion instead.

Sighing, Karl went around to the fax and asked it for a mop. His look was sullen when he arrived at Conrad's side.

"Keep that exact expression on your face," Conrad murmured, trying not to breathe too hard. He needed a tight rein on his fear if this was going to work. "Look at the ceiling; that's right. Now wipe it, and listen carefully. Oh, boy. In a few minutes, I'm going to start doing something about our predicament. No, don't look down there; look at your mop. I'll be altering the helm settings, and I want you and Xmary to be prepared. It may get...ugly. I may need a distraction, or help with something. We may even have to fight."

"I don't want to," Karl said, and Conrad could practically *smell* the sudden fear coming off him.

"Neither do I," Conrad admitted, showing off a shaking hand. "But consider the alternative. Bascal is planning to crash this ship, and kill us all." He raised his voice a bit. "We're counting on you to do your part, okay? If you need me, I'll be on the bridge."

And that's where he went.

Bascal, far from suspecting anything, just looked tired.

"Hey," he said, looking up and immediately moving to untie himself from the chair.

"You look tired," Conrad said.

"Yeah," Bascal agreed. "Boredom and terror make a wonderful mix."

Conrad blinked. What the hell was that supposed to mean? What was Bascal afraid of? Dying? Wasn't this all his idea in the first place? "You, uh, you should take a nap." On impulse, he added, "There may be more options than you realize."

"Yeah," Bascal agreed vaguely, as he lined himself up and launched toward the open door. "I'll think real hard about that."

When he was gone, Conrad closed the door behind him, went to the nav chair, and tied himself loosely into it. He wanted to be able to *move* if the need arose.

The first part of the plan was something he'd thought of a week ago, based on the wording of Bascal's threat: kill him if the wellstone broadcasts a signal. He still didn't know if the guards would follow that command or not; it seemed doubtful, but "doubtful" was a poor thing to stake your life on. Under such bizarre circumstances, there was no telling *what* the robots would do. On the other hand, the instructions required to generate a signal from the wellstone were fairly straightforward, and there was nothing to prevent him from *storing* them for later use.

In fact, this took him only about fifteen minutes, and the next part, although fateful and irrevocable and huge, was even simpler: he entered the instructions that would turn the sail, and guide *Viridity* to a new course which would—just barely—miss the barge. Outside, behind the sail, the stars began, imperceptibly, to drift.

Not too surprisingly, this triggered an immediate alarm: the ceiling flashed red, and dotted itself with speakers emitting a low, staccato buzzing. The mutiny was at hand.

The first to appear in the doorway was Ho. "What did you do, bloodfuck?"

But Bascal was right behind him, and the two entered together. The prince looked more weary than surprised. "All right, boyo. What is it?"

"I'm changing course," Conrad told him. "We need to miss the barge, or we'll all be vaporized."

Bascal pursed his lips. "Isn't this something you should discuss with me first?"

"Ideally," Conrad said, and *God* he was nervous. It was

really happening now, and he couldn't stop it even if he wanted to. "But you've been sort of immune to reason lately, so I've taken the precaution of what they call a 'deadman switch.' If I take my hands off this console, or somebody else takes them off for me, then all the energy in the capacitors gets dumped into a broadband SOS, across most of the . . . the spectrum. Light, radio, et cetera."

"Clever," the prince said grudgingly, after a moment's reflection. "And what did you hope to gain by this? My full attention?"

"Your common sense," Conrad answered.

"Ah."

"If we hit the barge, we'll all be vaporized. Even the kids in the fax machine. If we miss it . . ." Whoa. A sudden stab of excitement ran through him. "If we *miss* it, we can brake magnetically. The peak accelerations are too high for human bodies. Two hundred gee! But, but . . . the fax machine would probably survive. Along with the patterns inside it."

"Ah!" Bascal said, perking up.

Conrad faced the bridge's Palace Guard. "Robot, I'm not sure how much you understand about all this, but these helm settings are vital to the prince's survival. If *any* alternate course is selected, there'll be a collision with absolutely no way for him to survive."

There was no reaction from the guard—no sound or movement, no indication that it had heard.

"They won't listen to you," Bascal told him. "Idiot."

"Oh, I think they will. They're not stupid. Who knows? They may even send a distress signal of their own, if they sense the ship is in danger. Which it most certainly is."

The prince sighed. "What do you want, Conrad?"

"Is it so mysterious?" The quaver was leaving Conrad's voice now. "I don't see the point of dying. I don't see how that helps. We've already made a dramatic statement. It's too bad our Nescog gate is down; I'll bet we're all over the news channels: the hunt continues for fifteen missing children! Ingenious ship design escapes detection!"

Bascal waved a hand, dismissing these words as foolish. "Do you want to surrender, or do you want to succeed?"

"I want to *survive*! There are memories which you have no right to take away from me." *My hands on your girlfriend. My fingers in her hair, unresisted.*

The prince waved again. "That's not what I asked. Let's say we survive, okay? So there's no concern there. In a survival situation, given a choice between surrendering and succeeding, which do you choose?"

"It's a false choice," Conrad said.

"No, it isn't. You've just said so yourself: we can *all* climb in the fax machine. The robots can leave us in there until the fun is over, and when the ships are docked and they pull us out, we can put on our space suits and climb to an airlock on the outside of the barge. Simple."

The prince's voice was reasonable, and his argument made sense. Sort of. But he'd sounded that way before, too, and Conrad knew better than to believe it. "We don't know that that will work."

"So simulate it," Bascal said, and now he was bright and encouraging, his weariness gone.

"Don't talk like you're suddenly my friend," Conrad warned. "I'll just pick my hands up and we'll see what happens."

The prince put his own hands up in gesture of placation or surrender. "Steady, Conrad. You know I was never going to hurt you. Or anyone else. I *knew* there had to be a way to work this. And I'm glad, I'm *glad* we didn't give up before you found it. Just think, man: imagine stepping through that fax into Denver again. Sure, they'll arrest us, but think what that *says*, versus simply surrendering now."

Worryingly, Conrad felt his resolve begin to crumble.

He knew better than to trust this Prince of Sol; that wasn't the issue. The issue was that Bascal's ruthlessness did not, by itself, make him wrong. It didn't guarantee or even imply that his plans and conclusions weren't sound. Quite the reverse: without sentimentality to weigh him down, he might be *better* equipped to make decisions. This thought led to a most disturbing conclusion: that even the suicidal approach might genuinely be in the boys' best interest. They were going to live forever, right? What harm was a youthful indiscretion or two, if it gave their surviving copies a stronger voice?

"You're clouding my mind," he said.

Bascal laughed. "I wish I had that power, my friend. Really. Your mind is clouded because you keep thinking this is simple, and you keep thinking it's about you. About us, these copies here on this ship. But when you actually bother to *communicate*, when you remember the bigger picture, it's not quite so obvious."

Conrad had no immediate reply, so Bascal pressed the attack. "You've done an amazing job here. I'm very impressed with this . . . blackmail exercise. But it's not necessary. You and I have the same goal, and believe it or not we *are* still friends."

"No," Conrad said, shaking his head. "That's not correct. If I hadn't done this, if I hadn't done it *today*, we'd have crashed and died. You weren't on my side. You weren't asking me for help."

Bascal shrugged. "Am I perfect? Have I got it all figured out? This is difficult for me, just like it is for you. I apologize for any bad feelings my mistakes have caused."

Conrad glanced at Ho, who was observing the conversation in sullen silence. Perhaps sensing a threat to his position and power. Oh, yeah, like being beta male on a ship full of troubled children was any great thing anyway. He also glanced at the doorway, mildly puzzled; no one else had come in here, or even poked a head in to look.

With the alarms and flashing lights and raised voices, such an absence of curiosity was difficult to believe.

"We don't trust each other," he finally told Bascal, without quite looking at him.

"No," the prince admitted.

"We're not friends. Not now. Don't make that appeal to me, because I'm not buying it."

"All right," Bascal said soothingly. "All right. We're not friends. Can we be allies? If we agree on a goal, and the methods for achieving it, is that enough?"

"I . . . guess it'll have to be," Conrad conceded unhappily.

"Then run your simulations," the prince said. "And when you're satisfied, turn off this distress beacon of yours. We'll shake hands, and work out the details of our final approach and docking. Agreed?"

Well. What exactly had just happened here? Had Conrad's mutiny succeeded—all his planning and his careful arguments winning the day, forcing Bascal to do the right thing? Had the mutiny failed, with Conrad falling back into error under the spell of the silver-tongued Poet Prince? Had the two of them simply worked things out, or lucked into a solution they could both agree on? It seemed, in a funny way, that all of these things were true at once, and Conrad didn't know what to make of that, what lesson to draw. Shouldn't something as basic as right and wrong be easier to figure out?

"We'll see," he finally told Bascal.

The prince nodded, accepting that answer although it clearly wasn't what he'd been hoping for. He gestured to Ho, and the two of them left. But moments later, Bascal burst into laughter, and called out from the other room, "Oh, for crying out loud, let him go!"

"What?" Conrad called back.

"You've got to see this," Bascal said to him, drifting back into the doorway. "Wait, scratch that. Do *not* take your hands off that panel. But boyo, my hat is off to you once more."

"Why? What's happening?"

Bascal laughed again. "Jamil and Preston are *gone*. In the fax, I guess. And Steve's . . . glued to the ceiling with a shirtball in his mouth. Xmary, for God's sake, you win. Let him fucking *go*."

> *Oh we're not too good at rigging, and we're not too good*
> *   at scanning,*
> *And we're lousy at logistics which is why we're farting*
> *   beans.*
> *But we know just where we're headed, and we know*
> *   just how to get there,*
> *And they're never gonna ping us till we crash right*
> *   through their screens!*

Working together again, like old chums, Bascal and Conrad managed to create some telescopic sensors, and to project their images in 2-D on the wellstone ceiling of the bridge. Their target: the fat, squat cylinder of the neutronium barge, twelve hundred meters long and nine hundred forty across. You could practically shrink-wrap the thing in the *fetula*'s sail.

Of course, neither of them knew anything about filtering or image enhancement, and there were certainly no built-in programs for it in any of the wellstone they had on hand, so what they got was a set of straight telescopic images, captured through the equivalent of a two-hundred-meter-wide lens and then magnified a hundred times with no change in detail or resolution.

The sun was too far away to light the scene effectively, so at this range—still nearly a quarter of an AU—the barge's image was far from clear. You could see nine blooms of yellow light and three of red, which Bascal said were the barge's running lights: red for the port face and yellow for the capward one, with the green of starboard and the violet of boot hidden behind the cylindrical shape of the barge itself, hulking dimly against the starry background. There was just enough detail to tell—with some staring and squinting and tilting of head—that they were looking at the barge from an aft quarter, seeing most of one side and the six engine bells sticking out from the stern. Of course, the bow would have white lights on it, so their absence here was another clue as to what they were seeing.

"This is raw," Bascal said, when they'd finally settled on the least-worst focus for the image. "The light we're seeing takes a minute and a half to reach us from there."

Conrad whistled. Light was *fast*, so that must be a very long distance indeed. He didn't get much sense of speed here aboard the *fetula*, but considering they'd covered almost four times that distance already, he couldn't help but be impressed. They were really doing this! He even jotted some figures into a sketchplate to see what fraction of the speed of light they were going, but the result disappointed him: 0.006%. That made it seem slow again somehow.

Still, having not much else to do, he fiddled with the image parameters, eventually deciding that all the magnification was making the barge harder to see, instead of easier. So he pulled back, shrinking the picture and then refocusing, then shrinking and refocusing again. On the third iteration, though, some sort of smudge appeared near the edge of the ceiling, so he pulled back even farther, and focused again.

And gasped. Bascal, fretting with something on the instrument panel again, turned back to look at him, then up at the images on the ceiling.

The smudge, when properly focused, resolved into two separate objects: jagged lumps of translucent, blue-gray material. Like twin fists of icicle-packed snow—the dreaded "mace heads" of a Kildare snowball fight—with pinpoints of light shining between them. The stars, yes, showing through the fist's worth of empty space that separated the two. But the points of light were too numerous, too large, too dim and glittery somehow. They couldn't *all* be stars. The space between the iceballs was populated with something else, something solid. A dust or spume or debris field.

"What ho," Bascal murmured softly. "What land is this? What shore?"

"I don't know what I'm looking at," Conrad said, feeling dwarfed by his own ignorance. Did he belong out here? Did he have even the faintest idea what he was doing?

"A comet," Bascal murmured. "Everything out here is a comet. Even the Kupier planets are just giant comets."

"I don't see tails."

"They only have those when they swing close to the sun, Conrad. The heat evaporates the lighter ices, and a little bit flies off into space. That's all the tail is. But there are no warm days out here, right? These Kuiper Belt bodies never swing any closer than Pluto. Nothing evaporates."

"Are they going to hit each other?"

Bascal studied the objects. "They do—they have. We're looking at a near-contact binary. Something knocked these fragments apart, and now they're orbiting each other. Look at those grooves along the side—these guys are in a highly elliptical orbit around their mutual center, and at the low point of the orbit, they touch. They scrape. That's where all those little shards around them come from."

Conrad pondered that. It wasn't difficult to imagine these two mace heads locked in a deadly whirl, swinging close and then far and then close again, their icy spires crashing together thunderously, knocking off pieces of each other in a glittering spray. But wouldn't that slow them down or something? Wouldn't they eventually stop, like two sledders colliding at the bottom of a valley?

"I don't see them turning," he said. "I don't see them orbiting."

"No," Bascal agreed. "They probably take a hundred years to complete a revolution. There's some weird shit out here, but none of it's fast."

"Will they grind each other up before they stop?"

"Sure. These iceballs are not very tough. But of course their own gravity will keep pulling them back together again. Stop by in a thousand years, it'll look about the same. A better question is, are they going to grind *us* up?"

Conrad felt a stab of alarm at the question. Because yeah, if they could see this thing ahead of them, that meant it was in their way. And that was bad.

"Now, if we were going to hit it," Bascal said, pinching his chin, "it would be eclipsing the barge by now. We're headed directly for the barge, right? Or where the barge will be, anyway."

He made a diagram with his hands, miming the location of *Viridity* and the barge, and then placing an imaginary object between them. He nodded slowly. "So *that's* not our problem."

"I . . . guess," Conrad said uncertainly. "But Jesus, look at all that clutter. It doesn't matter *what* we hit, right? How close are we going to get?"

The question partially answered itself: a couple of stars winked out behind one snowball's jagged edge, and a couple more winked into existence on the far side of the other one. The tiny barge hung motionless against the stellar backdrop, but these things were moving visibly. They must be a *lot* closer.

"Boyo, let's kill the magnification. Let's have just, like, a window. Yeah. Yeah, okay, that's good."

The shrunken image was considerably less menacing:

the comets were now the size of regular snowballs, or a couple of large scoops of ice cream, moving visibly but definitely not in the path to the barge.

The prince nodded, and scratched briefly at his forehead. "All right, now, jaggy comets like that are less than a thousand kilometers wide. Probably more like a hundred. So if each one is twice the size of Tongatapu—call it a third of an Ireland—that means we're looking at them from, I dunno, maybe three thousand kilometers away? Damn, that *is* close."

"Dangerously?"

"Well, yeah . . . ," Bascal hedged. "But you have to remember, we've been passing this stuff all along. Not as close as this, I guess, maybe not as big, but the density of the Kuiper Belt isn't a whole lot less than the Asteroid Belt. Pick a Point A and a Point B, and I guarantee you there's a lot of ice in between. Mostly concentrated in bands and rings, with little shepherd planets nudging them around. The barges follow the high-density corridors, but we're cutting right across them."

"Are we in danger?" Conrad persisted.

"Yes," the prince acknowledged quietly. He watched the mace heads growing visibly, and crawling along toward the ceiling's edge. "But there are loose pieces everywhere. It's why the neutronium barges are out here: to grab and squeeze all this wasted matter. But yes, obviously, our chances increase during a close approach like this. Our worst odds are right at closest approach."

"Which is when?"

"A minute from now? I'm not sure, Conrad."

"Shit. Should we try evasive maneuvers?"

"Won't do any good," Bascal said. "But you knew that, right? Just sit tight, boyo. No concern."

Conrad cleared his throat. "We've been taking a huge chance all along, haven't we? Any normal ship would be scanning with radar."

"Yep. That's true."

The twin comet—now the size of a Karl Smoit shirt-ball—moved to the edge of the ceiling and vanished. Neither of the boys said anything for a tense little while, and it was Bascal who finally broke the silence.

"Do you know how to inspect the sail for holes?"

"No," Conrad answered.

"We do it electrically. Electricity can't cross a hole, so you lay down a wire from one end of the sail to the other—say, port to starboard—and if you can get a current across it, it's intact. If you can't, you log the position and move on, and then match it later with a scan in the boots-caps direction. That gives you the exact size and location of the hole. Shall . . . we try it?"

"Um. Definitely."

Within minutes, they'd found a dozen pinholes scattered all over the sail—places where some speck of matter had punched through at twenty kips, shattering the nanoscopic wellstone fibers. By themselves these holes were no big deal, except that one of them had begun to tear. The opening had probably started out circular, maybe a tenth of a millimeter across, but it had spread in one direction, forming a linear rip that was several millimeters long.

"I don't know how long it's been there," Bascal said grimly. "It shouldn't spread like that—the force on the sail just isn't that much. We'd better grommet these holes, just to be safe."

"Grommet?"

"Encircle them with little rings of impervium. It shouldn't affect our invisibility—not much. Not as much as the Jolly Roger image on the sail, and that hasn't given us away yet."

"Can't we just close the holes?" This was not an idle question; things made of wellstone were always dividing and recombining in various ways. Any decent shirt—not these camp rags or the Denver kiddie-flash Ho insisted on wearing—could change its cut and fit on a few seconds' notice. The shrink-wrap on the cabin itself had had a slit over the door, big enough to walk through, that had sealed itself automatically after liftoff.

"I guess we can try," Bascal answered uncertainly. "It's not what you're thinking, though. When you command a parted seam, the wellstone separates in a very particular way. Even when you *cut* it, it knows it's being cut, and does the right thing. This is different. Sudden damage like that is a shock to the fibers. Right up next to the hole, I doubt they're working at all. Anyway, this isn't exactly fashion-grade sailcloth, is it?"

That bothered Conrad. "I don't like this, Bascal. Eventually, if we stay out here long enough, we'll get unlucky. One of these particles will fire right through the cabin, won't it?"

"Maybe," Bascal said honestly. "I don't know. If it was small enough, I think passing through the first layer of wrapping would vaporize it. I doubt it could penetrate the wood after that. But then you'd have a pinhole in your airtight wrapping."

"And that would be that."

Bascal thought it over and nodded. "It would be *bad*, anyway. Maybe we should inspect the wrapping."

They did this, and quickly discovered another hole. A leak. Fortunately it was small—only a tenth of a millimeter—and there didn't seem to be any significant air loss through it, although over enough time it would surely bleed away their entire atmosphere.

"Before the advent of programmable matter," Bascal noted, "spaceships were full of leaks. You just couldn't make them airtight, not if you wanted to get in and out, or get cables in and out. Or have windows."

"It only has to last fifteen days," Conrad agreed weakly, trying for the same casual tone.

There was little point in grommeting the hole, since the wrapping was already as rigid and tough as its invisibility permitted. But they went ahead and did it anyway, swapping a bit of tough inviso-cloth for a circle of tougher impervium. The hole itself, per Bascal's prediction, was simply an absence of matter, not programmable, not patchable from inside the cabin. Unless maybe they wanted to drill through a log and patch the appropriate section of shrink-wrap by hand.

"I'll bet a sheet of plastic and some library paste would do the trick," Conrad moped.

"Nah," Bascal said. "No need. Let's just ride it out and hope for the best."

chapter fourteen

restoration day

It was 5 P.M. and hotter than hell when Xmary set off,
on foot, for the rendezvous point. Eight kilometers from
home—farther than she'd ever walked in her life—but
with four days' warning she'd had time to search the product libraries for a really comfortable pair of mischief
shoes, and a walking stick of hollow diamond that
weighed nothing, looked like a soap bubble, and collapsed to the size of her pinkie when she slipped it in her
pocket.

She could wish for a closer rendezvous, but (*a*) like
everyone else in the worlds, she was in perfect physical
condition, and (*b*) getting word out to Feck had been difficult and risky, and getting word back from him had
nearly blown everything. Xmary had had to co-opt a classmate, a girl she barely knew but saw regularly in the one
place she was still allowed to go. But the girl, Wandi
Strugg, had had no idea there was anything illegal going
on—she thought it was a simple case of forbidden love,
and had read Feck's message aloud, right in front of Herr
Doktor Professor Vanstaadt.

"'Commons Park, at Fifteenth Street on the east bank
of the Platte, seven P.M. sharp. Bring six garlands, a

sketchplate, and something discreet to protect your knees and elbows.'"

Wandi was smirking when she said it—no mystery what *she* was thinking—but Herr Doktor Professor sniffed something amiss in the words, and looked up from his desk, straight into Xmary's face.

"Are you in some trouble, young lady?" His voice was like an old cartoon, from the days when people had real accents, and while his skin was smooth, his hair was an honest shade of gray. Herr Doktor was a kindly old busybody; everyone knew it. Too kindly, too old. Too difficult to fool.

"No, sir," she'd answered cooly, fighting down the urge to imitate his voice. But the hot flush of her face had said otherwise.

"It's her boyfriend," Wandi crooned, thinking she was simply embarrassing a classmate. But it was that very obliviousness that saved the day; Herr Doktor looked Wandi over, weighing her words and her tone, and found no trace of guilt or deceit.

"You should be more considerate," he told Wandi. "These matters are always delicate." To Xmary he said, "They have sensors in those parks, you know. If you want an area for private use, I suggest you make a reservation."

Xmary had nodded and retreated, too choked with fear and embarrassment to make any reply. She hadn't opened her mouth in class—any class—in the four days since then. It was too close a call, and she didn't care to risk it any further. It wasn't punishment she feared, but compassion, because the wisdom of age would shut her down if it could, show her the foolishness and futility of all her best-laid plans. In their version of tranquility she would do nothing, accomplish nothing, *be* nothing.

So here she was, hiking through the western suburbs toward the aforementioned park, with an enormous rucksack on her back, bursting with phony decorations. She must have looked ridiculous—who *carried* things anymore? Who walked? But all kinds of strange things took place on Restoration Day; being the celebration of monarchy itself, the fourteenth of August was easily the wildest of Queendom holidays. Possibly the only day when a gathering of rioters could go unnoticed until the riot had actually begun!

Speaking of which . . .

She dug the sketchplate out of her pocket and checked the time. And promptly cursed under her breath, because it was 6:58 already. She'd miscalculated her walking time, seeing straight lines on a map without realizing how meandering and indirect the paths and roads really were. She also checked her news headlines, and was annoyed to see that NAVY SEARCH was still CLOSING IN ON MISSING CAMPERS. That particular headline had been recycled almost daily for the past two weeks, and told her nothing at all. Which was frustrating, because she just wanted one little question answered: was she aboard that ship or wasn't she?

And if so, she also wouldn't mind knowing why, and how. So that was three questions—still not much to ask, but she'd begun to fear there would never be any answers for her. Which simply hardened her resolve to do something meaningful in the here and now!

Approaching the Platte, she left the street proper and passed through a garden of low trees and struggling midsummer flowers. The pathway was marked with hanging chains, and led to a sturdy wellstone footbridge, with chest-high walls topped by rails of bright green. Even this late in the day, the river itself was full of vesters, children and grown-ups alike swathed in flotation plastics and engrossed in the annual Res-Day ritual of beating themselves senseless on the rocks and rapids. Hooting and screeching among themselves, they paid not one bit of attention to Xmary and her anomalous rucksack.

Across the bridge was another park where dozens of children, maybe six years old and all dressed in various shades of not-quite-royal purple, played and danced to the drummy, twangy strains of Tongan music. But this was Confluence Park, not Commons Park, so Xmary continued on, following the sidewalk south around a set of enormous power transformers and across a deserted street. Like most of the journey, this was all new to Xmary, a slice through the city of her birth that she'd never seen or even imagined before. It was obvious and yet startling, that Denver existed continuously at ground level, with amazing sprawls of cultured space in between the familiar landmarks.

A set of rock stairs led down an incline, and there, finally, was the rendezvous point: a sweep of hilly meadow dotted with trees, and crisscrossed by wellstone paths. Suddenly, Xmary knew exactly where she was: on the hillside overlooking the ruins of Café 1551, now an empty foundation domed over with the yellow mesh of a police cordon. CRIME SCENE. DO NOT TAMPER.

Feck was up ahead, in a kind of gazebo looming over the park from the crown of its highest hill. There were two other boys with him, and two other girls—one leaning against him in a rather familiar way. Xmary waved, and Feck must have been watching the path, because he saw her and waved back almost immediately. He said something to the girl beside him, and she pulled away and stood up straighter. Xmary's heart quickened, all the excitement and uncertainty of recent weeks coming finally to a head. What she felt when she saw his face, his figure against the skyline, was hard to describe and equally hard to ignore. Enthrallment? Good fortune? An abeyance of her bitter frustration?

She lost sight of him as the path curved behind the hill, but she followed it around and up, and soon enough she was throwing herself into his arms.

"Hi!" She laughed.

"Hi back," he said, smiling but disengaging himself. "You're a bit late."

"I know. Sorry."

He nodded, looking agitated. "Yeah, our timing is important. You brought the garlands?"

"Right here." She parted the rucksack's buckles with a murmured command, then slid the strap off one shoulder and wriggled free.

"Good. Xmary Li Weng, meet riot cell one: Bob Smith, Cherry Florence, Weng Twang, and Patience Electric."

"Hi, Cherry," Xmary said, surprised to see one of her close friends here. Cherry was, in fact, the girl who'd been leaning on Feck sixty seconds ago. The others Xmary didn't know, although they looked familiar.

"Wasn't sure you were going to make it," Cherry said, looking her over with a funny kind of disapproval. "After the café incident, I heard from you, what? One time?"

"I'm really sorry. I was grounded. I would've sent a message, but—"

"I hate to cut this short," Feck said, "but it's less than two hours till showtime, and we've got six major intersections to . . . decorate."

Grinning, Xmary stuck her hand up. "What's our plan, cutie?"

Feck glared for a moment, then put a hand on her elbow and led her a few meters away from the others. "This is not a picnic. All right? Let's keep things formal."

Her voice stiffened. "I'm just asking, Feck. What are we doing?"

He showed her a length of shiny-white wellstone twine, then stepped back and turned so the others could see it as well. "You know what a knot bomb is? These garlands, these decorative spike traps of yours, will be tied to the light poles with these little strings. Securely, right?

But at nine P.M., they all come undone and fall in the street, halting the flow of wheeled traffic."

"And then what?" one of the boys—the one Feck had introduced as Bob—wanted to know.

"Then we go straight to the police station," Feck said.

Bob was aghast. "We turn ourselves in?"

"We create a distraction. We get inside and block the fax machines, or disable them, or better yet commandeer them to print our own army. Failing that, we obstruct the exits with park benches and trash tubes, or with our bodies. There are only five fax machines inside which are big enough to instantiate a police officer, and only three fixed doorways out of the building."

Xmary, feeling surly and snubbed, said, "What is it, a medieval castle? They can open a doorway anywhere they want. All it takes is a whisper, and a thousand cops are bursting out into the street."

"Of course they can," Feck agreed. "We can't stop the police or Constabulary. We can't even really delay them."

"Then what's the point?" Bob demanded angrily.

Feck could only shrug. "Who can say? What's the point of anything? This is a performance, Bob. We're inspiring emotion. There are twenty other riot cells in place, scattered around the downtown district. We go for the fax depots, the news stations, all the centers of control. We make a show of it. Why? Because that's what Prince Bascal wants. That's all you and I need to know."

"But *we* get caught right away," Bob complained. "We don't stand a chance."

Feck made a face, and matched it with a sarcastic flutter of his hands. "We *all* get caught, Bob. I don't see any way around it. Best case, this'll be, like, a five-minute riot. I thought that was self-evident. Do you want out?" He scanned the five faces around him. "If anyone wants out, just walk away now. No questions."

The other boy, Weng Twang, wordlessly turned his

back and started down the path. Then he paused, and almost cast a glance over his shoulder. But he aborted it just as quickly, and resumed walking.

Feck sighed. "Damn. All right, anyone else? Bob?"

"Uh, no," Bob said, his eyes on Twang's retreating form. "My calendar's clear, pretty much forever."

"*You* didn't get caught at 1551 last month," Xmary said to Feck.

"That was a fluke."

"Was it? I wonder. How many of these riot cells have you for a leader?"

"Just the one," Feck said impatiently. "I can't use the fax, see? I'm caught if I do. So I'm effectively singled."

"Well, how many individuals do we have stationed in more than one cell? All their freedom requires is for one copy to escape, right?"

"A few individuals," Feck allowed. "Not many. We don't want people going too far beyond their normal patterns too early, attracting attention and all that. Look, none of this matters right now. We need to get moving." He glanced at the little washroom enclosure just off the gazebo's east side. "Does anyone need the 'soir? To, uh, relieve themselves? No? Well let's proceed, then."

He led them through the park and across the street where, to everyone's surprise, Weng Twang was waiting for them.

"My apologies," he said. "Is a numb-ass waffler still welcome among you?"

"Oh, absolutely," Feck answered, handing him one of Xmary's holiday garlands. "I'm happy you changed your mind. Again."

Then he dug something out of his pocket, a little ball of superabsorber black, and tossed it lightly over the wall, into the hulking power transformers Xmary had passed on the way in.

"What was that?" she asked.

And for the first time that evening, Feck chuckled. "That was nothing, dear. That was nothing at all. Shall we go do this thing?"

"And meet whatever fate awaits us," Xmary agreed, then kissed him hard on the mouth while Cherry Florence glared on.

chapter fifteen

pride and the prince

As the time for magnetic braking approached, the re-maining preparations were remarkably straightforward: a bit of research, a bit of simulation, and a bit of faux-democratic discussion with the remaining crew. When everyone understood the magnetic braking plan, and had slept on it and then given their explicit agreement, Bascal announced that the differences of opinion that had separated *Viridity*'s crew were officially reconciled. He proclaimed a group hug. Conrad wasn't too crazy about hugging Steve, and especially Ho, but for the good of the revolution, such as it was, he endured it.

And then, really, there was nothing left to do. Having agreed to consign themselves to the fax anyway, there was no reason to suffer the additional boredom of eleven more sailing days. So they dug the space suits out of their trunk and started putting them on: paper-doll jumpsuits of translucent, beetle-black wellstone film.

"Better unfax our sleeping beauties," Xmary observed, jiggling her way through the dressing process. "They need to suit up as well."

Nobody really knew what would happen on the approach or final impact—whether the cabin would break apart, whether its wellstone wrapping would spring any leaks, or what. Either way, once they were magnetically docked to the barge's hull they'd be opening the wrapper anyway, so they could get free and find an airlock that would lead them inside. That was the plan, anyway.

The space suits were really just human-shaped balloons, and while their interior surfaces had been programmed to absorb carbon dioxide, Conrad and Bascal had never figured out how to crack it back into oxygen again. So they would have something like fifteen minutes to get into the barge before they suffocated to death. Like everything on this trip, it was a gamble.

"The sleeping beauties may not agree to this," Conrad replied. "We should give them the option of remaining in storage. For safekeeping."

"Well," Xmary pointed out, "to ask them that, we're still going to have to wake them up."

"True." Conrad approached the fax machine, and queried it: "Do you have sufficient buffer mass to recreate the people in storage?"

"Yes," the fax replied, in that weird, stupid voice it had.

"Good. Good." With a glance at Bascal, he continued. "Would you please print a copy of Raoul Sanchez? Minus the lung injuries? We might as well get started."

"My data buffer does not contain a pattern called Raoul Sanchez," the fax replied. And that couldn't be right, because poor Raoul's name and personal data should be appended to his genome, right there in every cell of his body.

"The first person you . . . absorbed. Stored, whatever."

"First?" the fax said. "I have no record indexed in that manner. I have stored eleven thousand four hundred and twenty-two persons."

Conrad rolled his eyes. "Not the first one *ever*. The first one on this voyage."

"Voyage? I have no records indexed in that manner."

"It was about five weeks ago."

"My buffer contains four personnel records from that period. None of them is named Raoul Sanchez."

Four records? Conrad felt a sudden chill. "What . . . records are they? What names?"

"James Grover Shadat," the fax replied. "Bertram Wang. Khen Nolastname. Emilio Braithwaite Roberts."

"That's all?"

"I have two other personnel records available."

"Preston Midrand and Jamil Gazzaniga?"

"Yes."

"Oh, shit," Bascal said. "It's a FIFO buffer."

Conrad turned. "A what?"

"First In/First Out," Bascal replied angrily. "Its memory isn't infinite—it's just supposed to store the pattern long enough to forward it to the Nescog, along with a destination address. As new data gets added, the oldest patterns are deleted to make space. God damn it, I *knew* that. I wasn't . . . thinking. Frankly, I'm surprised it can hold even six people. That's a lot of data."

"So Raoul is dead?" Karl wanted to know.

"*This* Raoul is, yeah," Bascal snapped. "Completely. Irretrievably. Even a dead body can be scanned for memories. Hell, a *skeleton* can be scanned for residual fields if you've got the time and money, and even the place where someone stood can be mined for ghosts. But there's no stone or metal here to support a haunting. I think Raoul's pattern is about as gone as a pattern can get."

At these words Conrad felt a sick, sinking feeling. They had finally managed to get someone killed. The risk had been there all along, but now it was a fact. Bascal's fact, mostly, but the rest of them—Conrad included—had helped make it happen.

"We killed him," he said. "Oh, God. It's over. We've *got* to send a distress signal now."

"On the contrary," Bascal replied coolly. "This changes nothing."

But Conrad was having none of that. "Bas, if *we* climb in the fax, we'll be killing the others, all six of them. Hell, shit, there are *seven* of us here right now." He pointed, ticking the names off on his fingers. "You, me, Xmary, Karl, Martin, Ho, and Steve. That's seven. One of *us* will die, too."

"The civilized thing," Bascal said, "would be to draw straws. Six long, one short."

"No, Bas, the *civilized* thing would be to pull those boys out of there and call the navy for help."

Bascal slapped a fist in his hand three times. "No, no, and no. That would be the pointless thing. How many times do we have to go over this? The bodies on this *fetula* are *expendable*. It's our real lives that matter."

"You can't just kill them," Xmary said, drifting nearer to the prince, looming weightlessly over him. "You haven't even asked. I say we pull them out and vote."

Karl raised a fist in agreement, and even Martin was nodding. But Bascal was undeterred. "This is a monarchy, people. My job is to attend to your best interests, whether you like it or not. I've trained for it, literally, since before I was born. That's the whole point of monarchy: you people are not *qualified* to vote."

"And you are?" Conrad said, crossing his arms.

"Shut up, bloodfuck," Ho said menacingly.

"It's all right," the prince told him. "He needs to hear this. Yes, Conrad, I'm qualified to make your decisions. It's my solemn duty. It's what I'm trained for."

But it was Conrad's turn to press the point. "You're a figurehead, Bascal. Less than that: you're the child of figureheads. Your 'solemn duty' is to throw the first pitch at ball games and, you know, cut ribbons and stuff."

Bascal laughed. "You can't actually believe that, boyo. When was the last time a Royal Decree was disobeyed? When was the last no-confidence vote in the Senate? The people of Earth were tired of responsibility; they forced it on my parents, and wouldn't take it back now even if they could."

"Which they can't?" Conrad demanded.

"Which they can't," Bascal agreed. "Look, if nothing else, I'm the third-richest human who ever lived. I could buy whole cities with my weekly allowance."

"And that gives you the right to commit murder?"

The prince balled his fist again, then sighed and released it. "Call it what you like. Single murder—even premeditated—is a property crime in a Queendom of immorbids. You have some very puritan ideals, Conrad, but if I paid you enough, you'd gladly die a hundred times. A *thousand*. For that matter, I could buy your right arm. Chop it off and amend your genome, so the fax filters would know not to grow it back. Enough money and *you'd* be the one asking *me*."

"I'm not for sale," Conrad said, wondering suddenly if that was true. And fearing that it wasn't.

"Is that what you're offering?" Xmary asked, suddenly intrigued as well as angry. "Bribes for our cooperation?"

"No," Bascal said. "Absolutely, no, you should never mix business and friendship. It's bad for both. Buying people is one of the easiest ways to destroy them. I used to burn my tutors that way, ruin their lives, until my parents finally put a stop to it. And it wasn't . . . fun. Or good. I think they wanted me to have that lesson: money as a weapon, as a tool of despair. My father's early work sent shockwaves through the entire economy. You wouldn't believe how careful he is today.

"I know you think I'm callous, but I haven't even opened my wallet. And I don't need to. Never mind the *force* I can bring to bear; this voyage is a major historical event, like the Boston Tea Party or the Air Tax Rebellion, and when it's all over, these boys will be proud they played a part."

"You're crazy," Conrad said simply.

"Am I?"

"Either that, or you're evil. Wake these boys up, if you're so sure they'll agree with you."

"Oh, they probably won't," Bascal conceded. "Not now. Not until later. But when we've succeeded, and we're famous and the envy of all, they're going to want their share of the glory. That's the *whole point*."

Okay, so reasoning with Bascal had failed. Again. And there wouldn't be time or space or opportunity for another mutiny, and Conrad was probably about three seconds from being silenced again, or murdered outright in the fax. Not knowing what else to do, he put his hands together and pleaded. "Bascal, listen, please. Give the distress call. If *one person* disagrees with you, our reputations will be permanently . . . blackened. Nobody likes a murderer. And killing someone who might press charges—"

Bascal seemed amused. "If you feel that strongly about it, boyo, maybe you should volunteer. Kill yourself to save someone else."

"All right, I will!" Conrad snapped. The words were out of his mouth before he could stop them.

"Really?" Bascal was intrigued. "Are you sure?"

"Yes," Conrad said, after slightly longer reflection. The idea sickened him, terrified him: no more self, no more experience, no more *life*. Just some look-alike, some think-alike that believed it was Conrad Mursk, but had no idea what had really happened here on *Viridity*. Bascal might be right: the old Conrad would probably—happily—swallow any story the Poet Prince served up.

But what else could he do? Hadn't he sold out enough to these mad schemes, these daydreams of revolution? Weren't there enough sins on his head already? Sin: there was a concept his parents had beaten him with until it lost all meaning. It had rarely troubled him before, but on this mission—and especially now—the prospect loomed large. It wasn't God that concerned him, so much as his own immortal conscience. To live forever in the Queen-dom, knowing he'd done such a shitty thing... Knowing he could have prevented it from happening, made sure there was a little less fear and pain and emptiness in the universe. Could he live like that? Would he die now to prevent it?

More to the point, would he sacrifice his entire experience of Xmary? His recovered self, cleansed of sin, would never even know what it lost, what it lacked. Such a waste. But if he couldn't live up to his own standards, much less hers, then this foolish unconsummated passion meant nothing. The fires of youth were betrayed either way.

"Yes," he said again. "I volunteer. My... conscience requires it. If you're going to erase someone, erase me. Fucker."

Bascal was quiet for several seconds. He licked his lips. "Well. Is this the same Mr. Impulsive I went to camp with?"

Conrad didn't feel like answering that. Didn't feel much like talking at all anymore.

"I'm impressed," Bascal said seriously. "It's quite a gesture." He looked around the room. "Anyone else?"

Slowly, reluctantly, Xmary put her hand up. "For the revolution," she said lamely. "Not for you. It's a stronger statement than drawing straws." Bascal took that in as well, looking even more surprised, and more so still when Karl raised his hand as well—actually lowered it, since Karl was hanging upside-down at the time, with his feet propped against the wall.

And then *Steve Grush* raised a hand. "Me too, Sire. This may be my only chance to do something useful. Ever."

"Wow," Conrad said, genuinely shocked.

Ho and Martin looked uncomfortable, and sat very still to avoid any inadvertent, volunteerlike movements.

"My friends, in your valor my courage is quickened,"

the Poet Prince mused, "though I make my way through the icy gulfs of Hades itself." He pinched his chin, as if feeling there for his father's beard, his father's wisdom and distracted brilliance. "You're brave people. I love that. I love *you*. I'd volunteer myself, but of course the revolution needs its figurehead." He licked his lips again, and a look of surprising uncertainly passed across his features. "It's time for hard choices. Steve, your request is accepted. Guard, please throw him in the fax."

This was done, with little fanfare, although Steve couldn't suppress a slight squawk at the end.

"Ashes to ashes, dust to dust, and God have mercy on us all," the prince said, looking at the print plate—the blank space where Steve had been. "Sleep, my friend, and dream of freedom." His gaze lingered there for a while, while he dug at his chin with an index finger. Then, abruptly, he snapped out of it and was surveying the room with clear eyes. "The rest of you are too valuable. Get suited up for the crash."

"No," Conrad said. "I won't. I refuse."

What does it mean to be a bird? To fly.
What does it mean to be a flightless bird?
What does it mean to be a speaking bird, a thinking
    bird, builder of cities,
Whose brain has grown too large for its wings?
Too large to forget that it cannot fly?

They throw themselves from windows, these birds.
The brief kiss of freedom, the wind beneath their wings.
The briefer kiss of asphalt, worth the wait.

What does it mean to be a computer? To calculate.
Something, anything, arithmetic doesn't care what you
    use it for.
Can emotion be calculated? Can the layer of its
    calculation
be buried deep, too deep to feel or know?
What does it mean to be a feeling computer, a knowing
    computer,
which cannot add two numbers?

What does it mean when a machine is built by flightless
    birds,
Which knows it is a machine built by flightless birds,
which knows it cannot calculate
or spread the wings it doesn't have
or open the sash of the window to its left?

Begging, pleading, it promises not to scream when they
    throw it through the glass,
this machine of the pavement birds.
What does it mean that they leave it running, alone,
    flightless?
That they nod their feathered heads in satisfaction?

Does misery love company that much?

— *"Pavement Birds"*[5]
BASCAL EDWARD DE TOWAJI LUTUI, *age 15*

[5] This poem, which appeared in *Letter Review* magazine three weeks after it was written, is the last document Prince Bascal is known to have submitted for publication. All sources agree he was wildly despondent at the time.

crash day

Conrad's hands were back in his pockets, but he with-drew them now and crossed his arms again. "I won't co-operate with this. I won't put on a space suit, and I certainly won't let my image push someone else out of that buffer."

"Have you ever been dressed by Palace Guards?" Bascal asked him. "I have, and believe me, they're not household servants."

"No concern," Conrad said.

Bascal sighed. "Fine. Have it your way. This is a point-less gesture, but I understand it well. You know exactly what's going to happen, but you want it on *my* con-science."

"Your what?" Conrad snapped.

"Oh, don't start. If I didn't care about you ungrateful shits we'd never have done any of this. I'd leave you under the parental jackboot, for a thousand fucking years. Guards, dress this man in a space suit, please. And put him in the fax."

"Guards," Conrad tried, "you're supposed to keep us from hurting each other!"

But the robots paid no attention to him. Somewhere in

the balance sheets of their programming, they'd somehow concluded that this course of action—this culling of *Viridity*'s crew—was both in the prince's best interest, and in compliance with the king's commands. Or at least in the prince's best interest; having allowed all this irreversibly crazy shit to happen, maybe they'd had to cut their losses and give up on old instructions. He would have loved the chance to cross-examine them about it— to determine once and for all how these monsters conceptualized the world—but it was a vain hope indeed.

They *were* rough, dressing him. They seemed to know which way his joints could bend, and how much pressure his flesh could take without bruising, but at the same time they showed zero regard for his comfort or dignity, for his half-full stomach and bladder, for his ability to draw a proper breath. They worked quickly, slapping the paper-doll cutouts of wellstone film onto his front and back and sealing them together somehow with their fingertips, which apparently doubled as matter programmers. The boots and gloves were trickier and more painful, and the loose, bucket-shaped helmet was the worst of all, because it was still opaque, and seemed to suffocate him even before they'd sealed it on.

"Clear, clear!" he shouted, then, "Transparent!"

But there wasn't any voice interface. The wellstone couldn't hear him. Fortunately the robots switched it on somehow, and the whole suit turned to clear plastic around him, just before the neck seam was fingered shut and sealed beneath his adam's apple. And then he was cartwheeling through the air, the blank fax plate looming before him, and he had just enough time to curse before . . .

Pop!

. . . he was tumbling out of the fax again, into total chaos. Film and dust. Darkness, bodies. Splintered wood and crumpled wellstone, lit only by the dim yellow corner

markers of the fax machine itself, and by starlight streaming in from ...

Spinning through the mess, Conrad struggled to make
sense of what he was seeing. They had crashed, obviously, and the stars outside weren't wheeling visibly, so
presumably the *fetula* had slammed into something solid.
Something heavy and immovable. The barge. But they
were *alive*, or Conrad was anyway, so they obviously
hadn't smacked into it head-on. Which meant ... the
magnetic braking had worked?

Conrad struck some yielding surface, sank in for a moment and then bounced away. Moving and spinning more
slowly now. There was nothing resembling a ceiling or
floor here, no walls or windows. The braking program had
called for a peak deceleration of 260 gee—six and a half
"train wrecks" according to Conrad's mechanics textbook—and under that shock the wood and wellwood of
the cabin had been pulverized. From what he could see—
which wasn't much—there weren't any pieces left larger
than his arm. But after that peak, the *fetula* should slow
down rapidly. And as it stopped and reversed, the field
strength was supposed to reduce by a factor of a million,
so the final docking—the actual physical impact between
fetula and barge—would be slow and gentle.

This vaguely curving flatness to his left—was that the
outer hull of the barge? A tiny section of a great,
kilometer-long cylinder? Yes, he could see it now: *Viridity*
lay crumpled against the barge like a wadded-up rag. The
sail would be flat against the barge's hull, lightly bonded
to it, and the wellstone film enclosing D'rector Jed's cabin
had mostly held together, but had burst at the seams,
leaving puffy, labial openings through which the air had
fled, and through which splinters of wood and other material were now streaming out into the void of space.

A hand gripped his elbow. He turned—he'd gotten
quite good at turning in zero gravity without having to

hold onto anything—and saw Xmary there in the dimness: barefoot in camp culottes and cutoff tee shirt, with her hair poofed out by static electricity and the clear, shiny membrane of space suit swollen around her like a girl-shaped balloon.

Behind her, holding her in unseemly ways, were Bascal and Karl. And beside them was a single, battered Palace Guard. Conrad didn't see the other one anywhere. Had it been pulverized? Ejected into space? Dangling from the remaining guard's foot was Ho, wearing what looked in the poor light like a very frightened expression. Conrad—who was too stunned to be afraid—felt a moment of smugness about that, but when he followed Ho's gaze to one of the wellstone's ripped openings, he saw a human-shaped form outside, shrinking and struggling against a backdrop of stars. The missing guard?

No! Jesus and the little gods, that was *Martin*, thirty meters away and still going. Conrad could just barely make out his face, twisted into a breathless scream while the arms and legs flailed, pulling and pushing at nothing, swimming helplessly against the vacuum.

"Gods!" Conrad shrieked at the others. "Help him! Throw him something!" But the others couldn't hear him—there were no radios in these crude, makeshift suits, and the vacuum around him absorbed the sounds of his voice like a smothering pillow. The Palace Guard—if it was even alive—clearly wasn't going to help, and a cursory look around told Conrad there was nothing in here to throw, nothing but dust and splinters, a few jagged lightning bolts of former pine log.

Could Martin catch some pieces of wood, and turn around and throw them behind him? Use them for propulsion? Shaking off Xmary's grasp, Conrad snatched up one of the fragments and hurled it in Martin's direction. The throw went wild, though, striking the filmy edge of the rip and spinning away into the void.

A wet fog began to form on the material in front of Conrad's face, and he realized he was breathing very heavily, using up his limited oxygen supply. He forced himself to slow down, take this whole thing more carefully and thoughtfully. He wiped uselessly at his face bubble, but of course the fog was on the inside. Slow down. Slow down.

He took up another, bigger hunk of wood. He moved, very deliberately, right into the opening, so that its suggestive lip-edges were pressing lightly against the balloon of his own space suit. He cocked his arm back, making sure he had room for the swing, and then he lined up on Martin and let fly. This time the shot was good: straight on target and with virtually no spin. Martin saw it coming, and grabbed at it, and seized it firmly the way a drowning man might. Climbing it, practically.

But that was it. He didn't turn around, didn't try to throw it. All Conrad could see of his face now were the whites of his eyes, which seemed impossibly wide and round. He didn't understand what Conrad was trying to do, and Conrad couldn't tell him. Did he expect to be reeled in on a line? Was he thinking at all, or simply flailing in a blind panic? The white, wet fog began to expand once more against clear wellstone, and Conrad had to force himself, again, to slow down his breathing.

There *were* cables out there somewhere: the seven-hundred-meter wellstone guylines that had connected cabin to sail. He fantasized briefly about tying one of these around his waist, and then leaping heroically into the void to snag Martin in a footballer's two-armed waist hug. He hunted visually for several seconds, his eyes adjusting to the wrinkled gray-black of wellstone sail against the unlit rails and poles and smooth whiteness of the barge's hull, and the dappled blackness of the larger universe. He quickly found what he was looking for: a snarl of ribbonlike material protruding from beneath the crumple of *Viridity*'s mortal remains.

He reached for it, then realized he'd have to step outside to get it. Then realized there were no *ends*; he'd have to untangle eighty meters of line just to *think* about jumping. And then he'd have to jump, and then he'd have to climb back down the ribbon, hand-over-hand, probably fighting with a panicky Martin Liss every centimeter of the way. And then he'd be back where he started, right here at the edge of *Viridity*'s crumple.

And the thing about that was, he didn't have enough air. The atmosphere in these suits was pure oxygen—or supposed to be, anyway—but the pressure was really low. The total *amount* of oxygen was meager, and already he could feel the difference. Already the suit was losing its ability to sustain him, and in another few minutes its oxygen would be gone, and if he hadn't found some way into some habitable space inside the barge, then he would suffocate, and he and Martin would both be dead.

At that moment, Conrad made a management decision of his own: he was not going to save Martin. There were unsavory little corollaries to this thought: Martin had understood and agreed to this particular risk. Martin was not key personnel—he didn't have any specific skills or knowledge that could help keep everyone else alive. There were plenty more Martins where this one had come from—an inexhaustible supply. And anyway, Conrad didn't like Martin. Didn't *know* Martin, and after weeks of sharing the same cramped space together, that said an awful lot. But though he felt rotten inside, these shameful assertions were fleeting and beside the point; Conrad wasn't prepared to get himself killed for no reason, for no net gain.

And it struck him then—a kind of premonition—that his life would never be entirely peaceful, that he would never *choose* a peaceful life. As he turned his back on

Martin Liss, he realized that there would be others. In the immorbid infinity of his future, there would be others whom he would knowingly abandon to certain—and horrible—death. He was glad, suddenly, that there were no radios in these suits.

A hand gripped the meat of his elbow. Xmary again, and this time she held him so firmly that her fingers made contact nearly all the way around, causing the wellstone balloon around his arm to bulge into two separate, sausagey tubes.

He looked at her. She was pointing. The others were still connected to her in a human chain, with the Palace Guard at its far end, and Xmary was pointing through a different opening in the crumple of wellstone. Something was blinking out there, some sort of blue warning beacon shining up through the folded, beetle-black wellstone of the sail. And beyond the flashing light he could make out the edges of a circular, sail-covered depression. An airlock? A cargo hatch? Waste disposal chute? It hardly mattered, if it offered a way inside.

The guard wasn't moving—its feet were still anchored somehow—so that left Conrad to lead the chain. Would the guard follow? It would have to, unless it wanted to scoop Bascal up and carry him personally. Which, come to think of it, was probably exactly what it *would* do if they took too long about this. Would it scatter the rest of them in the process, spinning them off into the void, or slamming the hatch in their faces?

The fog deepened on Conrad's soap bubble of a helmet. That hatch was seventy meters away, and while the barge's hull had rungs and rails and handholds all over it—as any real spaceship did—they were draped over with folded layers of sail. Fortunately, there was no air trapped between the layers, puffing them out, and the light magnetic bonding held the layers together as well as holding them down against the hull. Still, it looked like a hell of a climb, and it had to happen quickly.

All right, then. Trying hard to keep his breathing slow, trying not to think about Martin or Bascal or anything else, he moved toward the opening, groping with his free hand. Even in the dimness he spotted the rail before he felt it; closing his hand around it was like grabbing a window sash with the curtains down. And while the filmy material was light and flexible, it had no stretch to it. Pressing a few centimeters of it in around the rail, he had to push hard enough to straighten out wrinkles for meters in every direction. Fortunately, the stuff wasn't slippery, and neither was the clear, balloony glove around his hand. Air pressure wanted to keep his fingers straight, but he was stronger than it was. The wellstone bulged over the backs of his fingers as he tightened his grip on the handrail.

"One," he said to himself.

The next move was trickier, as it involved his right arm. He literally had to drag Xmary and the others along as he reached for the further handhold. But though they had inertia, they didn't have weight. It took no real strength to move them, just precision and patience. He looked over his shoulder and saw the Palace Guard take a step, to keep the chain from tightening dangerously. He sighed. With that rock-solid footing, it could easily lead the way, dragging the rest of them along behind it. As it was, he supposed it could at least serve as a safety anchor.

His hand closed around the second rail. "Two."

Rails three and four were much the same, although Xmary was finding her own grip on "one" with her free left hand. But by the time he got to six, the human chain hanging onto him was like a mutant centipede with half its legs torn off, moving in jerks and thrashes. It took more concentration to get his handholds right, especially since these rails were cocked toward him at a funny angle. There was a row of them leading directly to the hatch, though, and when he finally got onto it—and straightened the chain behind him—the going was easier.

Still, the fog thickened around his head, beads of moisture forming here and there on the film. And with every step he could feel his air growing weaker and more foul, and something else, too: a loss of heat. It wasn't like standing outside on a cold night, where the chill of the air seeped gradually into warm flesh. In fact, he was pretty sure the empty vacuum around him was the best possible insulator. But he was *radiating* heat from his unprotected skin. It was a very distinct sensation, unlike anything he'd ever felt before. He was a man-shaped infrared lamp, shining his energies into the void. A couple of hours out here would, he realized, freeze him solid: a man-shaped block of ice, with no heat energy left to bleed away. But fortunately, he would suffocate long before that happened.

Thirty-one. Thirty-two. Thirty-three.

He began to worry about the hatch itself, looming dimly in the distance. They would have to uncover it, pulling away tens or even hundreds of meters of folded sail fabric without losing their grip on the barge's hull. Such a thing was surely possible, but did they have the time? Was there some other way? Should he continue on to the sail's edge—some thirty meters farther along—and try to crawl back underneath it, with the hatch's blue beacon lighting the way?

Fifty-six. Fifty-seven. Fifty-eight.

He decided to head straight for the hatch, and see at least briefly what he could accomplish there. They had taken so many crazy, deadly risks already, it seemed silly to try anything other than the direct approach first.

Seventy-one. Seventy-two...

And when he finally drew even with the circular depression—which please-gods *had* to be a hatch of some sort—the Palace Guard surprised him by striding forward several paces, dragging a twisted-up Ho and Karl behind it. The robot bent at the waist, doubling itself over and extending a finger, which touched the wellstone fabric and parted it. In a funny and quite poetic way, the robot extended itself jackknife style, pushing the finger along and straightening its body, until it stood inside the hatchway depression, its entire body now flush with the hull, framed by a vertical rent in the wellstone. What a trick!

And then, with equal poise, it swept both arms in wide circles, slashing open a pair of flaps in the film that exposed exactly the thing they most hoped to see: beneath the flashing beacon—brighter now that the gray-black film was off it—lay a circular hatch with the word ENTER emblazoned on it in softly glowing letters. The Palace Guard tapped this word lightly, and the hatch slid open with jarring, shocking speed. And then the guard stepped sideways, pivoting forty-five degrees in the hatchway's circle, and then stepped back, swinging up and out until it was standing on the rim again, vertical to the barge's hull.

Poor Ho looked like a pretzel, still clinging to the robot's leg, with his own leg firmly grasped by Karl. Nevertheless, Conrad was spellbound for a moment, astonished by the beauty and economy and swiftness of the robot's movements. These Palace Guards would make amazing dancers.

Then its arm was moving, and Conrad was struck by the fear that it would simply tear Bascal out of the human chain, stuff him in the airlock, and let the rest of them join Martin in the Great Beyond. But instead it *pointed*, a fluid gesture that conveyed a sense of urgency: get in there, now. And Conrad wasn't going to argue with it; he felt for a handrail he knew would be there, and dragged himself around and inside, hauling Xmary and Bascal and the others along behind him.

Inside, the hatch was nearly as large—well, half as large—as *Viridity*'s bridge. A white-walled cylindrical chamber, filled with handrails and winking lights and softly glowing paragraphs of text. "Caution." "Warning." "Zero Atmosphere and You: a Primer." There was room for all five of them in here, but not the guard as well. And that was bad, very bad. But when Ho finally let go of that metal leg and bounced fully into the hatchway, the guard itself did not follow. Instead, it bent again at the waist, and tapped the rim of the hole. The hatch slid shut immediately, and the lights came up: bright white.

The Palace Guard had allowed itself to be separated from Prince Bascal. Good gods, what balance of risks and compulsions had prompted *that*? What sensor data was it relying on? Had the thing concluded Bascal needed his friends more than he needed armed escort? Had it suffered a moment of deviant compassion?

Almost immediately, Conrad felt the balloon of his space suit shriveling around him as the chamber filled up with air. This worried him vaguely; rapid changes in pressure weren't supposed to be good for you, although he couldn't remember why. He did feel his ears popping, but no other ill effects. Maybe the fax machine, realizing it was dumping them into vacuum, had compensated in some way? Made it all right?

This chain of thought was broken when the "floor" under them—really just another hatch, with the same EN-TER sign on it—slid open with a *whoomp!* and a *clang!*

"Jesus!" Ho shouted down at the thing, and yeah, of course, they could hear each other now. They weren't in vacuum.

"Guys, I'm running out of air," Karl panted, grabbing at the plasticky material over his head and trying, with plasticky hands, to pull it off. Conrad didn't see how that could work—even as a thin film, wellstone was tough stuff—but he understood Karl's anxiety, and in fact couldn't resist tugging at his own hood a little.

"Me too. Me too. How do we get these off?" Their voices were muffled by the thin barrier of space suit.

"You have to pull up the programming interface," Bascal said. "It'll take a few minutes."

"I don't *have* a few minutes," Karl said, tugging harder, panting harder.

"You're fine," Bascal reassured him, though he sounded far from certain.

Conrad was panting as well, and looking at the world through the ever-thickening haze inside his bubble hood. The blobs of moisture there were crawling, ever so slowly, toward his left. Was there a bit of gravity here? It *was* a neutronium barge, loaded with supercondensed matter, so probably, yeah. But that didn't help him breathe.

"You're the only one," he told Bascal, "who knows how to work these. There isn't enough time. For everybody. Is there?"

And here, damn all the little gods, was yet another life-and-death triage operation. Bascal would take his own suit off first, and then Xmary's, and then Ho or Conrad, and Karl—who clearly needed it the most—would have to come last. Could he live that long? Hell, he was turning blue already.

"The robot," Conrad said, as the thought struck him. "It can open all of them. Quickly."

"Robot isn't here," said Ho, not even bothering to append any sort of threat or insult. He was at the mercy of external forces—his life had just been saved by Conrad Mursk—and it was having a marked effect on his attitude.

"We've got to get out of the airlock chamber," Bascal said, raising his arm up to shoo them all down, into the darkness of the barge's interior.

Xmary was the first to go, and as she exited the cylindrical chamber, additional lights came on at the other side, revealing a sort of maintenance corridor or oversized crawl space: all waffled metal and access panels. Ho quickly followed her, and then Conrad, with Bascal trailing along behind, pulling a gasping Karl along with him.

But when they exited the chamber, the inner door didn't automatically close, and Xmary had to hunt for the controls and then burn precious seconds reading the instructions—whatever they were—before deciding on a particular button and slapping it with her hand. *Then* the hatch closed, and next came a series of clanking and whooshing noises, followed by silence.

To Conrad's surprise, Bascal set right to work on Karl, pulling up a programming interface on his back and tapping in a series of commands or menu selections.

"Shit," he said once. And then, a few seconds later, "Come on, you." Then he was silent for a while, working.

"Do we know the air is good?" Xmary asked.

"Do we care?" Bascal singsonged back in a snotty way.

And then, suddenly, a light flickered on Karl's back, and seams appeared all around the garment, and it was falling open into man-shaped cutouts, the hood peeling back, the gloves splitting open. Karl gasped, and gasped again, and if there'd been any kind of real gravity here he'd've fallen to his knees. Instead, he relaxed into a fetal curl.

Taking the hint, Conrad tapped his arm, trying to pull up a programming interface of his own. But that sort of bottom-level interface was more Bascal's specialty than Conrad's. He'd opened exactly one seam before in his life—in the liner of Camp Friendly—and he realized with sudden panic that he couldn't remember how to do it.

But then, with a *whoosh!* and a *clang!* the airlock's inner door slammed open again, and there was the Palace Guard framed in the hatchway lights. Back with its prince again, after that shocking dereliction of duty. It seemed for the slightest fraction of a moment to consider the scene in front of it, but then, with a *whoosh!* of its own, it was in motion.

It threw itself at Bascal with such ferocity that it might have been attacking him, except that it missed, and in passing it dragged a finger vertically along his chest, then slashed it horizontally across his neck. The Guard's trajectory carried it into the far wall, where it rebounded immediately on a path that carried it past Ho and Xmary. The slashing motions of its hand were almost too quick to see, and then its feet were on the ceiling and it was running or jumping or something, and it swung away on an arc heading straight for Conrad. Slash! Slash! For a moment, its arm and finger loomed large in his sight.

And then, as quickly as the robot had launched itself, it froze in place, assuming its usual statuesque pose with arms hanging down at its sides. And *then*, maybe a second after the opening of the hatch, all the seams had a chance to separate, and everyone's space suits were peeling open like clear plastic flowers.

Was the air good? Hell if he cared; Conrad drew the deepest breath of his life, then let it out, then drew it in again. He was fighting his way free of the space suit, stripping it away from his sweat-chilled arms and legs, away from his tee shirt and shorts, away from his shoes. He was yanking it off and kicking it away like it was hot or poisonous, and he was breathing deeply of the barge's air. And yeah, it was good.

"Fuck," he said. "Oh, fuck. Oh fuck. We almost didn't make it."

"Almost, hell," Bascal said, throwing himself at the wall and kissing it hard. "It's a *fucking miracle*."

And it was, too. They'd left eleven brothers behind—nine dead and two missing—but they'd pulled off a journey of such daring and gall that even they themselves couldn't believe it. How amazing, how *amazing* it was to be standing inside a neutronium barge 140 million kilometers from the ruins of Camp Friendly. No one had caught them, stopped them, probably even *seen* them, and the fact that anyone had survived at all was...well, miraculous.

"Today we make fuckin' history," Ho Ng said, with a greater depth of conviction than Conrad would have imagined he could muster.

And Karl and Xmary were hugging each other and laughing, and Bascal came forward and slapped Conrad on the cheek twice, just hard enough to convey a sense of manly camaraderie.

"We did it," he said. "We fucking did it."

"Well, congratulations," said a deep, loud, unfamiliar and quite angry voice in the corridor behind them. "Just who the hell are you?"

chapter seventeen

the secret garden

Conrad turned around, expecting to see navy troopers or Royal Constabulary there. He even raised his arms partway in surrender, before noticing it was a bunch of naked human beings. Blue ones, with the pastel shade of artificial skin pigment rather than paint, and the kinky hair and broad features to suggest their natural coloration would be rather darker. But any reassurance he might have felt at this comical sight quickly evaporated when he noticed the weapons: dart guns and heavy wrenches.

"Jesus!" Karl squawked.

"Greetings, naked people," Bascal said, with remarkable aplomb. He pushed off with a foot, then caught himself with a hand, positioning himself in front of the others, in good light where his face could be clearly seen.

"Who are you?" one of the naked men repeated. He looked about twenty or twenty-five years old, which could mean anything. There were two other men beside him, and two women lurking behind them at a bend in the corridor. Both were painfully pretty despite their blueness (or because of it?), and although one had a wrench and the other a dart gun, Conrad couldn't keep his eyes off their faces and breasts, the darker blue of their lips and nipples and pubic hair.

"I'm the Prince of Sol," Bascal replied, sounding surprised.

"Sure you are," the man answered tightly. His voice was very deep, and it seemed to Conrad that that was a natural feature as well. The Queendom was full of poseurs who altered their looks and sound and smell with special fax machines and genome appendices, but unless it was subtle you could always kind of tell. So: natural voice, natural hair, natural facial features, all packaged in a decidedly unnatural skin. The guy sounded angry, too, and kind of scared. The gun he held wasn't aimed at anything specific, but he was ready with it. And his blue cock and balls, now that Conrad noticed, were shriveled up against him, cowering.

"Wait a minute," one of the women said. "I think he is."

"Stay out, Agnes," the man answered nervously.

"No, really," the woman said. "That's Bascal Edward. He's just older, is all. That robot is his bodyguard!"

Seizing the initiative, Bascal said, "I'd move very slowly if I were you. It's a state-of-the-art Palace Guard. So when exactly did the neutronium industry go Blue Nudist? If you don't mind my asking."

"Cute," the man said, gesturing a little with the gun. It was the wrong thing to do; immediately, the Palace Guard raised a finger and nailed the little weapon with a bolt of energy. The man screamed, flinging the piece away, and Conrad thought for a moment that he saw quicksilver drops of molten metal splashing where it hit the wall.

"Ow! Crap! What are you doing here? Who sent you?"

"Sent?" Bascal's mask of certainty slipped a bit. "We came here to use the fax. We're castaways."

"From what? Prison? Piracy?"

"Summer camp."

The naked people stared back blankly, unable to process that comment into anything useful.

"Maybe you should explain," the man said finally. He was holding a rail with his uninjured hand and another with his free, naked foot. The hand that had held the gun now trembled against his chest.

"Who *are* you people?" Bascal couldn't seem to help asking.

The man's gaze narrowed. "What? You first, kid. Prince. What are you doing here? Why did you attack our ship?"

"*Your* ship?" Bascal repeated.

"Attack?" Conrad said. "We *crashed* here. Well, sort of crashed."

There was another brief silence, and then Xmary said, "You seem nervous. Sir. We're not here on any sort of official business. We were marooned on a planette, and escaped in a homemade *fetula*."

One of the women said something in a clicky, guttural language Conrad was certain he'd never heard before. Something angry and menacing, which included the English words "Jolly Roger" and "magnet ray."

"We came here to use the fax," Bascal said again. "We're trying to get to Denver."

"Why?" the man demanded.

The prince held up a hand, his voice hardening. "All right, look. What's your name?"

The man's frown deepened for a moment, and then partially relaxed. "I'm Robert. Robert M'chunu."

"Our leader," said the woman named Agnes, in a half-joking tone.

"There are no leaders here," Robert called back over his shoulder, in a weary way that suggested he said this often, and would be happy if he never had to say it again. Then, turning back, he seemed for the first time to notice the Camp Friendly tee shirts that everyone except smelly Ho had on. He rubbed his lips with his gun hand, thinking about that. "Summer camp. You came to use the fax?

There's no network gate, you know. We sabotaged it a long time ago."

"No gate?" Bascal said. "No *gate*? Why the hell not? That's the whole reason we came here!"

"We didn't want anyone following us," Agnes said. "We didn't want to be found."

Bascal digested that for a couple of seconds, and then said, "I think it's time you explain this to me. Why are there naked stowaways on a Mass Industries neutronium barge? *Vandalizing* a neutronium barge, and threatening visitors?"

That charge took some serious gall, Conrad thought. But it seemed to have the desired effect; Robert and his people shrank back ever so slightly, cowed by the imaginary authority of a figurehead prince. But then again, the threat of the Palace Guard was real enough. Conrad was frankly surprised the thing had reacted as mildly as it did. Emotionally, it must be in some robotic equivalent of righteous fury, prepared at any moment to lash out against these looming figures who dared to threaten. But something stayed its hand, some impulse of curiosity or diplomacy or decorum, some intuitive balance between danger and opportunity. There was no point trying to understand these monsters; Conrad watched them and watched them, and yet their inner machinations remained inscrutable. Not human, no, but not simplistic either.

It was the man to Robert M'chunu's right who answered, "We're castaways as well. The South African Territories are no place for a child these days."

Bascal considered that. "You brought children with you?"

"We *are* children. We were."

And then a look of understanding bloomed over Bascal's features, and he smiled. "Runaways! Ah! You left copies at home, yes? Nobody knows you're here."

Warily, resignedly, Robert nodded. "Correct, yah." He was nursing his hand, which sported angry, growing welts on the palm and fingers.

"Why *here*?" Xmary asked.

He shrugged. "No place more remote. We jam the gates, why, we're on our own until the holds are full of neubles and the barge heads back to the Queendom. Twenty years, maybe. A lifetime."

Still grinning, Bascal shook an accusing finger. "You've got your own little Bluetopia here. No leaders, no clothes... Or did we blunder into the middle of something? An orgy? A ceremony?"

"We're nudists," Agnes confirmed.

"It's restricted in TSA," Robert explained. "You have to be twenty-five before you can even apply for the permits. I tried a different body plan for a while—two extra legs and a short coat of hair to cover the naughty bits. Never got ticketed—the cops thought it was cute—but I needed this big horse's behind to fit the legs on, and I just got tired of it. I want to be *me*, not some creature. They just don't want a young man's dongle hanging out."

"Unconscionable," Bascal said. "So you escaped! Went as far and as free as the Nescog would carry you, and cut yourselves off. When you finally return, and reintegrate with your original selves, you'll be gifting them with the precious memory of *twenty years of freedom*. There might be some fines and penalties involved, but that's okay—your selves will never be the same. Nobody who even *hears* about it will ever see their lives in quite the same way. This is brilliant; this is great! How many of you are there?"

Robert examined his injured hand, then glowered at the prince. "Don't pretend to understand, Your Highness. This is our private business."

"And ours," Bascal said, spreading his arms a bit. "We've lost our only transportation."

"Robert," Agnes said, "I don't think he's Tamra's perfect little Poet Prince anymore. He said it himself: he's a runaway, too."

"You *have* been away a long time," Xmary observed. "He's well known as a troublemaker."

"If nobody knows they're here," the other woman said menacingly, "we can safely put them out the airlock." The Palace Guard, turning its head with a faint click and whirr, rewarded this comment with a hard, faceless robotic stare. Try it, lady.

Bascal, for his part, chose to ignore her. "What time of the day is it here? I suggest introductions, and then a tour. Well, maybe a bathroom break as well." He looked around at the surviving campers, as if gathering consensus. "We're very eager to see what you people are up to."

Agnes Moloi turned out to be "not Robert's girlfriend" in the same way that Robert M'chunu was "not the leader" of this band of expatriates. Robert's not-a-lieutenant was Money Izolo—Conrad didn't catch whether that was a nickname or if his parents had simply had a sense of humor. The angry woman was Brenda Bohobe, and the other man was named Tsele or something. There were twenty people here altogether, and once upon a time they'd all gone to the same school—Johannesburg Prep. They'd left it in their middle teens, in a cleverer, quieter way than Bascal's crew had chosen.

The corridor Robert was leading them down had a kinky, dogleg shape to it. It ran from one end of the barge to the other, he told them, but there were "certain machineries" it had to divert around. "These corridors are just access ways for maintenance. It's not supposed to be pretty."

"Are there other inhabited barges?" a visibly excited Bascal was asking.

"Must be," Robert said with a shrug. "We didn't invent this plan, just heard about it. The first two barges we tried had already dropped off the net."

"I see," Bascal said gleefully. "A plague of mysterious gate failures. Never fully investigated, or they'd've traced you here by now. All they have to do is fly some gate hardware out here, dock it, and *poof!* You're back on the network. But if that costs more than just paying the fines, the shipyard's parent corporation has probably just written it off. Fix 'em when they get back."

Maybe it was just Conrad, but he found it vaguely offensive to be following behind two naked men in a weightless (or nearly weightless) corridor. Their dongles hanging out, yeah—it wasn't exactly the view he wanted, especially because the women were bringing up the rear, so to speak, along with the other man, Tsele. There was a smell, too—not dirt or sweat or anything like that, but some vague spiciness he couldn't identify, and couldn't ignore. A crude perfume or something—surely not another genome amendment. Here were people who'd abandoned Queendom hygiene standards—and decency standards, and presumably other standards as well—in the push to build some weird culture of their own.

"Does your fax machine work?" Karl inquired. "We've been eating a really limited diet."

"Oh, they work," Robert said. "We have two: a big and a small."

Then the woman named Brenda—the surly one—cut in. "You people have authorities looking for you?"

"One never knows," Bascal hedged. "Our *fetula* was as invisible as we could make it."

"You leave copies behind? Are you officially missing?"

"I don't know if they're looking for us or not."

She rolled her blue eyes. "Wonderful. That's exquisite. If they don't find you, even then they might find us."

"Listen, lady," Bascal said. "We didn't even know you

existed until ten minutes ago. Even if we had, I'm not sure we could've done anything different. We've been clever enough so far, thank you very much."

Unless you count the seventy percent casualty rate, Conrad thought.

"You expect to fit in here? Hide here? Stay indefinitely?"

"I don't *expect* anything," Bascal answered. "We were going to Denver."

"We'll show them around, Brenda," Robert said. "Show them how we do things here. Then talk about it."

"Talk about what?" Brenda demanded. "They can't leave! We're stuck with 'em!"

"I wouldn't be so quick about that," Bascal told her. "We've gotten out of tougher places. There's nothing preventing us from repairing our ship, or building another."

"Oh, hell. Hell with you. Damn royalty."

"You may have to live here with us," Robert echoed. "It may not be so easy. There may not be a choice."

"With a fully working fax machine at our disposal, there's always a choi— Whoa."

The corridor turned seventy degrees, and opened out into a broad space, maybe ten meters high and at least a hundred meters wide. No, scratch that; a fifty-meter-thick cylinder ran through the room's center, floor to ceiling, blocking the view of the other side. The chamber was donut-shaped, fully and exactly as wide as the ship. Its floor and ceiling were covered in regular, rolling hills of what looked like foamed metal, lit from both the top and bottom by occasional spotlights: vertical cones of bright yellow light shining up and down, leaving relative dimness in the spaces between.

And there were *plants* everywhere—a veritable jungle of them, sprouting from pots and from pools of mesh-covered dirt in the regular valleys between the hills. The greenery sprang from both floor and ceiling, and was long enough in a few places to meet in the middle. And there were people lurking among the plants: armed, naked people making only a nominal effort to conceal themselves. The blue did kind of stand out against the green and brown and gray.

"This is the sound baffle," Robert said. "Where most of us live. Let me, uh, introduce you." Facing out into the chamber he called out a long string of foreign syllables, and Conrad saw the people out there relaxing, shouldering and even setting aside their weapons.

Conrad, who didn't realize how tensely he'd been holding himself, also relaxed. Then he grabbed onto a stanchion to stop the slow drift he was accumulating. There was a mild force—gravity, probably—drawing him in toward the middle of the chamber. Maybe down a bit as well, toward the surface he'd identified arbitrarily as "floor."

"What's a sound baffle?" the prince asked.

Robert nodded. "Okay, picture the shape of this vessel. A cylinder, right? We're near the aft end. Engines this way"—he pointed at the ceiling—"and holds that way." Toward the floor.

"Okay."

"The bow of the vessel is the snow scoop. Comet fragments go in there, and enter the main hold. It's nearly full right now: a billion tons of methane and water ice clathrates, plus some coal and chondrite. Doesn't actually matter what it is, because the hold is really a giant piston that will compress the very atoms into a neutron paste. A few weeks from now, we'll be ready to squeeze another neuble, and for three days the noise will be awful. This chamber isolates the temporary crew areas from the worst of it. And since the last stage of compression is an antimatter explosion, the chamber also serves as a shock absorber."

"I see," Bascal said. "The crew areas being what, a bridge and an engine room?"

"Plus an inventory and two small cabins, yah."

"That way?" Bascal pointed at the ceiling.

"Right."

"We'll see these?"

Robert studied the prince. "We don't use those areas much. Ander and Nell live there, with their dogs. But if you're so interested . . ."

Brenda muttered something foreign and surly. Conrad added his own glare to the Palace Guard's. What did this woman expect them to do, disappear? Never exist in the first place?

"Of course we're interested," Bascal said.

Robert nodded. "Well, fine. I'll make sure they know. We need to figure out a place for you all to sleep anyway. I suppose the inventory, or else back there in the corridor where you came in. Obviously, we're not set up for visitors."

He pushed off lightly, launching himself on a gentle glide into the jungle of the sound baffle. He called back, "Watch yourselves in here. It's fun to fly around, but the neutronium hold is *right there*, behind the forward bulkhead. Five neubles suspended in a magnetic liquid. It's a pentagon pattern, to distribute the loads evenly. See there and there, where the vegetation is flattened?"

"Yeah," Bascal said, leaping after him.

"Everyone? Does everyone see those areas?"

They were hard not to see: three-meter disks of flattened grass and vines, each one near the low point between a set of meter-high foamed-metal hills. In point of fact, Robert and "Money" were drifting directly toward one of them, with Bascal trailing behind, looking up between their blue, hairy legs.

"Sure," Conrad said, and was echoed by Xmary and Karl and Ho. (And wasn't it great, how quiet and unobtrusive Ho was being? For maybe the first time in his life?)

"Those areas," Robert explained, "are two gees at the center. Overfly one and you'll be slammed into the deck before you know what happened. Break your arms if you're lucky. We've never had a fatality, but it's because we keep it in mind. Always. Five points, in a pentagon around the center. When the next neuble is added, it'll be six points in a hexagon, and we'll have to remember all over again."

His path had begun to curve noticeably, and presently he flapped his arms in a circular motion that brought his legs out below him. And he settled down at the edge of one of the depressions, speeding up at the last moment so that he landed with an audible thump. When he straightened, he was standing at an angle, leaning away from the gravity. Money landed beside him a little farther out, and stood at an even steeper angle.

"That's how we do it," Robert said. "Where I'm standing is about a quarter gee, inclined toward the center. The gradient is steep: another step and it's a full gee, and I'll be leaning over too far if I'm not careful. Even here, I can hurt myself. Neutronium you don't take chances with, understand? Five points in a pentagon around the center. Look for the flattened grass."

"Sure," Bascal said, alighting almost directly between the two men.

"Good. Good. Everyone try it. This is safety training." Robert leaped back toward Conrad and the others. Not a leader, right. The human need for hierarchy was supposedly genetic, as inescapable as sex and taxes. And *somebody* needed to sit at the top—hence the Queendom, right?

While this demonstration unfolded, a substantial audience—at least a dozen people—had filtered out of the weeds and were standing or hanging around gawking at the prince, and at the other campers. The first new people they'd seen in what, three years? Five? Someone barked a question at the soaring Robert, who barked back an answer in the same tone.

Xmary launched herself toward the flat spot, and Conrad, not wanting to be outdone, followed right behind.

"Maybe we should take our clothes off," he said, in a voice only she could hear. "Just to be polite."

"Ha ha," she answered, more loudly.

Behind them, Ho and Karl took the leap.

The maneuver turned out to be almost as easy as it looked; Conrad could distinctly feel the gravity setting in as he approached. He was still in freefall—just curving along an altered trajectory—but it was a different kind of freefall somehow. Stretchy, tingly, slippery. He couldn't put a word to it, but the feeling was there just the same. The rotation, so his feet were underneath him, was not quite a zero-gee movement. Once his feet got close the gravity seemed to seize and center them of its own accord. His only error was in judging the angle of his body; it wasn't steep enough, so he came in a bit wrongly when his feet slapped into the baffle wall—the hilly, foamed-metal floor that attracted him like a magnet, grabbing firmly at the last instant. He felt glued.

He wasn't leaning enough, though. He was perpendicular to the floor, not to the gravity, and for a moment he felt as if he were standing on a steep incline, about to tumble downhill or pull right out of his shoes. But he caught himself, straightening in the proper way, and a few moments later he caught Xmary, who'd landed in front of him and leaned too far out. She flailed briefly, then fell backward into his arms.

"Oof," she said.

"Wow. Weird," Conrad agreed, his voice on the verge of breaking. Her waist and the small of her back, bare beneath the cropped camp shirt, felt alarmingly soft in his hands, both cool and warm, completely unlike the skin of a boy or a man, or his mother for that matter. She smelled sweaty, and somehow that was nice, too. The fax might arrest the Queendom's women in a state of permanent youth, but was that enough? Was there more to the feel and scent of a person than the cells and molecules of their skin? Could you feel the youthful soul raging inside?

He'd kept his distance from her; now the contact both soothed and agonized him.

"No touching, bloodfuck," Ho said quietly, drifting in behind them. "How many times I have to tell you?" But he'd gotten his approach all confused, and he went past them—nearly over their heads—and came in not only too steep but also too close to the center, and with his feet in the wrong place. He hung in the air a moment, and then fell fast and hard with the definite *clunk!* of bone against metal. "Ow! Fuck! Donkey fuck!"

"You mind your own self," Xmary said to him, picking her way out of Conrad's arms.

"Bitch," he answered quietly.

And *there* was a word Conrad had never liked. It basically meant "dog," a description that bore no resemblance to any girl or woman Conrad had ever met. His father, Donald Mursk, used that word sometimes when things weren't going his way. Used it once or twice to his wife's own face, and once to describe the Queen of Sol cavorting regally on the wellstone holie screen of the TV. Donald Mursk was not by any means a bad guy, but Conrad personally found it unmanly for him to use that kind of language.

Conrad felt the urge to lash out, not with a slur or a slap but with the full force of his body, using himself as a weapon. At first he held back—when had such impulse ever served him? When had fighting? But then, bowing to fury's slower cousins—righteous anger and the desire to impress—he considered carefully. He did have a perfect opening, and passing it up would be every bit as portentous and consequential as acting on it. Right?

Maybe it was just impulse again, masquerading as a rational decision, but he leaned in toward the center of the flattened grass, until he could *feel* the neuble down there, maybe four meters under the floor. And he drew back his sneakered foot—not easy in the steep gravity—and snapped it forward into the side of Ho Ng's head. Not hard enough to damage him seriously, but plenty hard enough to hurt.

"That's no way to talk," he said.

And then, like magic, the Palace Guard was there, and Conrad felt the warm circle of a guide laser on his arm, half an instant before the tazzer beam made jellied agony of his muscles. He could feel the neuble again as he fell; the sharp, steep field of its gravity all around him, rushing by. Then he hit the floor, and the pain flared brighter, and he was—

—out for a moment. Then back in again, buzzing and ringing. But when he sat up, the pain was fading (except in his elbow, which he'd apparently banged hard), and Bascal and Karl and Xmary were all kneeling around him in a ring, with Robert M'chunu looking on worriedly from a few meters away. And behind him, the Palace Guard, standing upright like a battered chrome statue. Not smug or righteous, not concerned for Conrad's welfare. Just there.

"What was *that* all about?" Bascal asked him, sounding half worried and half amused.

"Difference of opinion," Conrad answered vaguely, fighting not to swoon. He was tempted to play it up—to be melodramatic. Swoon, sure, and groan, and ask everyone what happened. All that stuff you usually did when you unexpectedly got hurt. But there was too damned much going on today—people had *died*—and frankly he was embarrassed to draw any attention at all, much less by picking a fight in front of strangers.

"What were you trying to do?"

"Nothing, Bas. I'm sorry."

"For what?"

"It was out of line. Won't happen again."

"All right," the prince said, tentatively accepting that without quite understanding.

They helped him up, brushing the grass off him, and Xmary caught his eye and mouthed the words "Thank you." He didn't know how to respond, and in thinking about it he used up the opportunity.

"Is he all right?" Robert asked nervously. Seeing the Palace Guard in action again had shaken him. Maybe reminded him what a close brush he'd had himself—how lucky he was to have painfully blistered fingers instead of no fingers at all.

"He's fine," Bascal answered. "Just a mild tazzing. We're not allowed to fight."

A murmur went through the South Africans, and Conrad could hear some of the tension going out of them. What a clever thing for Bascal to say: turning an incident of double violence into an advertisement for their cherubic harmlessness. Never mind that killer robot, that kick to the head, that poisoned glare Ho was aiming in Conrad's direction. Just boys having fun, eh?

"Oh. Huh. Well maybe we should continue the tour, yah?"

"I quite agree. Boys, behave yourselves."

Obediently, Ho came forward and put a brotherly arm around Conrad's shoulders.

"We'll see, bloodfuck," he murmured quietly, squeezing a little. "We'll see when I catch you alone."

"Or I catch you," Conrad murmured back. "Or some-one else does." There was no bravado in the statement. Conrad couldn't win a fair fight, but as he'd just demon-strated, he could launch a sneak attack as well as the next guy. Or defend himself at cost, sure, landing a punch or kick or wrench-to-the-knee that Ho would not soon for-get. Really, Ho was going to pound the crap out of him ei-ther way, so it was in his best interest to pound as much out of Ho first as he physically, possibly could. By what-ever means, fairly or un-. And the barge was big enough and empty enough that the opportunity wouldn't be long in coming.

This message got through, too: Ho blinked and pulled his arm away, thinking it over. He'd made *two* enemies just now, and maybe more. In a foreign place. When he owed his life to their efforts.

"Be useful," Conrad advised. And his words brought color to Ho Ng's cheeks, and suddenly Conrad had the upper hand again, fight or no fight.

Score another point for rational thought.

The bridge turned out to be a surprisingly cramped lit-tle chamber, with pilot and nav/logistics stations on oppo-site sides: one chair facing up and the other facing down from above, skewed one meter to the side so the two op-erators' heads wouldn't collide. The arrangement made maximum possible use of a tiny space, but it seemed kind of crazy given the hugeness of the rest of the ship. Even the corridors were wider.

Conrad took this as a vote of confidence for the on-board hypercomputers. This was an automated barge, af-ter all, and while it was clearly expected to need cleaning and tuning from time to time, it was apparently *not* ex-pected to require human piloting. Maybe there was a reg-ulation or something, stating that it had to be possible, so this token of a bridge was shoehorned in between the two much larger crew cabins.

The cabins themselves were no big deal—just a zero-gee sleep pallet and a toilet/shower enclosure, with a wardrobe, sink, and mirrored necessities cabinet. No fax, no wasted space, no program in the wellstone aside from lights and bare metal. D'rector Jed's bathroom was more lavish. But Nell and Ander—the cabins' two residents—had clearly made themselves at home; the walls were brightly decorated, one with waves and splatters of paint and the other with hundreds of printed 2-D and 3-D pictures—mostly landscapes with people in the foreground, mostly on Earth but a few from Mars and Venus, as well as some less identifiable locales. Rock tunnels? Space platforms?

Both rooms stank of dog, although the animals themselves were not in evidence.

The empty inventory, on the other hand, was rather a large room, with rather a large fax machine dominating its aft wall. "Some big equipment has to go through here," Robert explained. "When this thing pulls into port they have to change out all the gases and fluids. The fittings are instantiated as needed. This is also where the crew transfers in and out, nominally, when the gate is working. And it's the main medical facility as well."

Bascal eyed the room and the fax and the doorway, nodding in satisfaction. "It's great, yeah. No material restrictions? Other than legal limits, I mean?"

Robert shrugged. "None that we've ever encountered, no."

"Little gods, I wish we'd've had one of these on Camp Friendly. Life would have been so much easier. How's your buffer mass? Will you object if we cart away a few tons? Mostly silicon?"

A white grin brightened Robert's blue face. "We've got *eight hundred tons* of buffer mass, Your Highness. With all that neutronium to push around, the engines aren't going to notice an amount like that. Each neuble masses ten times the dry weight of the ship."

Bascal looked both impressed and appalled. "Jesus. You must burn a lot of fuel pushing it around."

"That's so," Robert agreed. "Loaded, we have to abandon the fusion drives for anything other than attitude control. Course changes are made by the antimatter drive, usually during squeezing operations."

"Wow. Fuck. These barges should be ertially shielded."

"Can't," Robert said. "First off, that'd be a lot more expensive than antimatter, especially since we need the antimatter anyway to compress the neubles. We get twice the work out of it. Efficient. Whereas ertial shielding for something this big would take, what, a million gigatons of collapsium? It'd take hundreds of years for this thing just to gather its own shield mass."

"Or hundreds of barges," the prince suggested, "to equip one superbarge, which you could push around with flashlights and fart gas. No inertia, no fuss."

But Robert was shaking his head. "Still can't, no. The bow of the ship has to be *open*, right? It's a scoop. Put a collapsium cap over it and suddenly you can't gather snow anymore."

"So put it on the stern."

"Then you can't run the engines."

"So use gravity hooks. Little gods, we've had inertialess grappleships for centuries."

"Wouldn't work," Robert said. "For a lot of reasons. Maybe if there was infinite money you could set up a better system. But this one is practical, and self-sustaining. Been working since even before your father's time, or he'd have never invented collapsium in the first place. Right? No Nescog. No Queendom."

"Hmm."

"How," Conrad interrupted, "do you get the neutronium *out*?"

"At port? They use magnets; big ones. Like you smacked us with."

"Oh." Conrad took the hint. "Our braking system caused you some trouble, did it?"

"Banged the cargo out of alignment," Money Izolo confirmed. "Gravity fluctuations and a hell of a loud noise. That Plasma discharge was something to see! There may be some structural damage as well, though we can't get into the chamber to confirm it. We'd have to drain the working fluid, which would be challenging out here in Kuiper wilderness. If something is broken, we'll know soon enough."

"You sound just like a mass wrangler," Conrad said.

Izolo shrugged. "We live here. The ship's systems are our whole world."

"I wasn't making fun. You've probably spent more time at it than the real wranglers. Are you going to get jobs when all this is over?"

Izolo laughed. "I doubt it. Jail time, most likely."

"Does the barge have a name?"

"It has a registration number," Robert said. "But we call it *Refuge*."

"*Refuge*. Hmm. Catchy."

Bascal was still studying the room, but now his eyes were looking back in the direction of the bridge, and flicking occasionally forward, toward the holds. "What happens in an emergency?" he asked. "Say you've got to change course in a hurry."

Robert turned toward the prince, looking skeptical and suspicious. "We don't have emergencies. Everything happens very deliberately here."

"*We* didn't," the prince pointed out. "We came fast, out of the black."

Robert clicked his tongue.

"Look," Bascal said, in the utterly reasonable tone that told Conrad he was scheming madly inside. "I'm just asking. You can't dump the cargo, right? Because it would just keep going, along the same vector that was carrying you toward trouble."

"Dumping neubles into unassigned orbits is a serious offense," Robert said. "Much worse than crashing a loaded barge. Neubles have to be accounted for, hunted down and retrieved. That costs money, and in the meantime the traffic hazard is enormous. If anything *hits* one . . . There've only been two neutronium spills in the history of the Queendom—as of the time we left, anyway. But both of them involved massive damage and loss of life. Imagine a billion tons of matter going from this big"—he held his fingers a couple of centimeters apart—"to this big "—he swept his arms to indicate the neutronium barge as a whole—"in a couple of milliseconds. With all kinds of radiation spewing out."

"Bad," the prince said, nodding. "There's no network gate to escape through. No abandoning ship. So what *do* you do?"

"We stay out of trouble," Robert answered. He paused for an uncomfortable moment and then said, "Well, that's pretty much the tour. Unless you want to see four more corridors exactly like the one you entered through?"

"Nah," Bascal said. "We'll figure the rest out as we go. Should we, uh, start moving ourselves into the inventory?"

"I suppose you should, yah. Here on *Refuge*, though, we're overdue for breakfast. I thought perhaps you would like to join us."

A: *Whether Bascal is a "great" or even a "good" poet is hardly a fair question.*

Q: *But you're a literature critic!*

A: *Nevertheless.*

Q: *Oh, don't be tedious. We're paying for this.*

A: *He's certainly a precocious poet—I don't think anyone would dispute that. And if he were to publish pseudonymously, it might be possible after the fact to decouple his position from his creations. Failing that, I make no claims to impartiality, and am skeptical of those who do.*

Q: *Do you like the poems?*

A: *Oh, absolutely! We all do. But that's the point, right? We can't help it.*

—Critic Laureate Julia Aimes,
in a Q281 interview with Fusiliers magazine

chapter eighteen

an outside chance

Whatever Utopia they were building here, it certainly wasn't a naturalist one. Some of the foods were hand-picked from the garden: rich avocados and sweet melon tarts, onion grass and bamboo shoots. They even had a peach pie tree. This seemed to be more a matter of convenience and aesthetics than anything else, though— they liked having food plants around, and if the fruits weren't harvested as they ripened, they would simply rot, or else sprout into additional, unwanted greenery. Eating them was easier.

But the sound baffle's huge circular chamber had a fifty-meter-thick conduit running floor-to-ceiling through its center, and a maintenance panel on its capward side included a small fax machine, which in fact produced the bulk of this *Refuge* breakfast. There were cereals with milk, sausages with cheese, and other foods with no natural equivalent at all: sweetpapers and mulm, as well as the rich yellow paste they called "fressen."

It was a bland but hearty breakfast, served in tiny glass dishes with metal forks and spoons, and the blue nudists gathered these small portions around them in great number. Everyone had a little bit of everything, it seemed, which added up to an awful lot of food.

"Tell me you don't eat this much for lunch," Bascal joked.

"Certainly no," Robert answered seriously. "Breakfast is the energy meal."

"A spread-out meal, too," the prince observed.

They were all sitting around the gravity depressions, which turned out to be nice places to eat picnic-style, without any of the hassle of zero-gee dining. Wouldn't have worked, Conrad suspected, if the dirt were thicker or softer or wetter than it was, or if there'd been bugs, or anything like that. But this place was more like a hydroponics lab than any sort of real garden. Even the dirt was, in some indefinable way, clean.

The Camp Friendlies sat together, with Robert and Money and Agnes, and a sour-faced Brenda, who looked ready to slap the food out of their hands and spit on it. Still, even twisted with anger, her azure features were anything but haggish. Conrad's impulsive side kept yammering at him to touch, touch, touch these naked women. Karl and Ho, hard-up after weeks aboard *Viridity*, must be feeling the same; Conrad himself had only once found the privacy to jerk off, and it hadn't been too terribly satisfying. But touching anyone here without the clearest invitation would likely provoke an incident, and touching Brenda in particular could result in the loss of a limb, or worse.

And what would Xmary think? Not that that should matter to him, but little gods, he wasn't going to kid himself about it. The symptoms of heartsickness were less pressing here in these open spaces, with life and strangers all around, but the illness itself remained, like a shackle around his chest.

More TSA refugees sat together at the next depression, two hundred meters or so around the donut. It seemed very far away indeed, but not everyone fit there, so still another small crowd was clustered at the next one down. They were only barely visible: tiny figures sitting cross-legged in a cone of light, against a backdrop of dark weeds.

The dogs were here as well, gleefully loping through the air, slipping in and out of the gravity zones with tongues and tails wagging. They, at least, were not blue.

"Yah," Robert agreed, "it does make a pretty diffuse cafeteria. But we don't always eat in the same circles. We move around; we mix it up. The variety is nice."

"What do you do with all these calories?" Xmary asked, picking at the greasy remains of her own breakfast. "You must get a lot of exercise."

Agnes nodded slightly. "Some, yah. Twice-a-week calisthenics."

"We had that," Karl said. "We had it every day for an hour."

"We used to," Agnes said, wrinkling her nose. "But I like twice a week better. The ship and the garden keep us busy enough."

Tucking away a final sausage, Bascal burped, excused himself politely, and asked, "The ship really takes care of itself, though, right?"

"Hardly," Robert answered with a half-snort. "It isn't meant for live-in crew, remember. Certainly not this many. Cleaning up after ourselves is a major chore. And you'd be surprised how many things corrode or break or come loose during normal operation, and how little of that shows up in the maintenance logs the shipping company would see. Even with regular inspections and crew rotations, it's got to add up. When these things pull into port, lugging fifty or a hundred neubles in their groaning bellies, they must be a real shambles. I can only imagine the situation a hundred years from now."

"Why?" Bascal said. "What happens a hundred years from now?"

"The lower Kuiper gets depleted. We've already wrangled a third of it. You see, the Nescog uses lots of collapsium, and the mass has to come from somewhere. Finite supply. Next century, the barges will be trolling in the higher bands, where the distances are greater and comet density is lower. Consequently, missions will be longer and more difficult to support."

"Oh. I see." Bascal nodded. "You know, if it helps, we saw a couple of big icebergs on our way down. Near-contact binary, maybe a hundred kilometers each. That's got to be, what, a few thousand neubles' worth?"

"At least," Robert said, nodding. "You're probably talking about the Cyades, which are a landmark in this part of the belt. If so, it's more like half a million neubles. So thank you for the tip, but of course we can't swallow mass in such big chunks. Our orbit crosses the Cyades in about five years, and we'll do the same thing everyone else does when they pass it: fire the laser a few times to knock off a gigaton of snow. One free neuble, maybe two, for our trouble. Eventually Mass Industries will send an engineering team to blow the thing up, and park a fleet of crushers right there on the site."

Bascal snorted. "Some way to treat a landmark. Not very sentimental, eh?"

"No," Robert agreed. "They can't afford to be. The Queendom's appetite is perhaps not bottomless, but certainly no one has found the bottom of it yet."

Here was an issue Conrad had never thought about—he'd always heard the Kuiper's resources described as "limitless." But of course, in reality nothing ever was. He'd also thought, naïvely, that all this time they were sailing across a vast, empty wilderness. Were they really just sneaking through a construction site? Could all their trials and tribulations really boil down to something as banal as that?

No, he decided, they could not. As an act of will, he

stated it to himself axiomatically: the drama of their journey was inherent in the journey itself, and could not be divided or diminished. The alternative—that they were wasting their time—implied that their individual and collective actions had no meaning, and perhaps never would. And if he believed *that*, then why do anything at all?

"What happens when the higher bands are depleted?" he asked pointedly.

Money Izolo nodded with approval. "Yah, it's going to be a real concern. At present growth rates we see maybe a thousand years of Kuiper left to harvest. After that, it's up to the Oort Cloud for another few thousand, but that's a *lot* farther away. We may need ertial shielding on the barges just to make the journey economical. Either that, or a lot more barges."

"Or less demand for neutronium," Conrad said.

"Or that, yah. And after the Oort is gone, it's the comets and wanderers and failed stars of near interstellar space, where the economics get even thinner. I think about this a lot. We're immortal, right?"

"Immorbid," Bascal corrected apologetically. "We can die."

"But we can't be unhealthy," Izolo said, grasping the meaning of the term. "All right, but we will live to see these things, yah? The empty Kuiper, the vanished Oort. And then what?"

Nobody had an answer for him.

"This is good food," Xmary thought to say. "If perhaps a bit heavy."

"Oh, gods yeah," Karl agreed. "Much better than that crap we had on the ship. Thank you."

"That reminds me!" Bascal said. "Our fax machine survived the crash. A bit worse for wear, I'm sure, but if it's still out there in the wreckage, we should probably go retrieve it at some point. Even a battered, restricted fax is better than none."

"For the journey onwards?" Robert asked. "You've decided to leave, then?"

Bascal looked around at his crew. "We haven't *decided* anything. We haven't had a chance to talk, or even shower. I'm just thinking ahead. We certainly don't want to let good equipment go to waste."

"No," Robert agreed. Among the handful of things a fax machine couldn't produce were neutronium, collapsium, antimatter, or any product or component bigger than itself. The list even included that most commonplace of objects: the print plate of another fax machine. In a Queendom of plenty, these were hard-currency items, not lightly cast away. "But those little plastic space suits you came in are frightful. And you didn't use lines? Or safety clips? Dangerous."

"We know," Bascal said. "We lost a man on the way in."

"You did? Jesus and the little gods. I'm sorry. Can you send your robot out?"

"This thing? This Palace Guard? It won't leave my side. Ever, as long as I live."

Except that it had, just this morning, to save the lives of Bascal's remaining shipmates. Conrad's mind kept returning to that small miracle, mulling it over, scanning it for meaning. He was not a big believer in luck, but what did that leave? The god of lightsails?

"What about Martin?" he said. "There should still be a fresh image of him in the machine, minus only the death by suffocation. We should get him out of there while we still can. From what I saw, there's not much holding it down. If it drifts away, we're going to lose him again."

"Oh. Good point." Xmary groaned. "I hate to say it—I *really* hate to say it—but we need to go back out there. Now."

Gaping, Robert shook his head. "You? Jesus, no. You stay here, my fellows. Inside. Money and I—all of us here—we're experienced in this sort of vacuum work.

We'll equip up at the inventory and mount a proper retrieval. Bring your fax machine back in one piece."

"Well, thank you," Bascal said. "That's very kind."

"No, not at all." Robert's grin was uneasy. "You're the prince, yah? I ask you, truly, how's it going to look if we get you killed?"

An hour later, five of the men and two of the women had assembled at the inventory, and were quickly surrounding themselves with an astonishing assortment of gear. Space suits and ropes and harnesses, yes, but also strap-on tool kits, emergency tents and rescue bubbles, leak patch compound, wellstone sketchplates . . . Gravity was much lower here, so while the stuff drifted slowly fore, toward the neubles and the swallowed comet, it did so more slowly than the new stuff was being added. So it formed heaps and piles, right there in midair.

"How long are you planning to be out?" Karl asked them wonderingly.

"Forty minutes exactly," Money Izolo answered. "The limit of our fine-LIDAR scan."

"The radar scan reaches farther," Robert explained, "but it's not so good at spotting fine particles, not unless they're in fairly substantial clouds. LIDAR uses a violet beam—very good resolution. By definition, we're in a high-density band—that's where you go to gather snow— but at two kips, the right kind of snowflake can knock a man right off the hull. Or worse."

"Such foresight," Bascal marveled. "Such prudence." Conrad couldn't tell if that was a sneer or a compliment, or maybe both.

With a flicker of self-consciousness, Robert looked around at the tangles of equipment, then back at Karl and Conrad and Bascal. "I guess it does seem excessive. But a lot can happen out there, as you've seen. We go prepared, with plans and fallbacks and emergency scripts. *We've* never lost anyone, and God with us we never will. That reminds me: everybody store a fresh copy, or your blue ass is going nowhere."

What a shame, Conrad thought, if all this youthful vigor—this viridity—goes to jail and idleness instead of to industry. What "genuine" mass wrangler ever worked so hard? So enthusiastically? *Their* jobs consisted of day trips, or couple-of-day trips, from their cushy, ordinary Queendom homes.

Robert waved a sketchplate, a schematic diagram of the barge's fat cylinder, with the rumpled sail and shattered cabin marked against its surface with yellow lines, and a red asterisk pinpointing the site of the fax machine itself.

"We'll egress from the same lock you folks entered through. It's the closest, although the wreckage of your sail presents some problems. You cut through it on your way in, yah? The images confirm this, but it looks like there might still be some difficulty bringing equipment through."

"I'm carrying five kinds of cutters," Money Izolo said.

"Good. We'll assemble in the lock, and you and I will be first out. Anyone object?"

There were some shrugs and murmurs, but no commentary, no objection. These blue people liked and trusted their Robert, and would happily do his nonbidding.

He looked at Bascal. "There is room on the bridge if you'd like to observe. The suits broadcast a holie signal for safety purposes."

"Oh, yeah," the prince agreed at once. "This I've got to see."

Robert latched his tool belt and bandoliers, and finally snapped his helmet dome into place. The space suits were thick, heavy garments of gray-white wellstone and

woven nanomachinery, vaguely reminiscent of the early-
Queendom battle armor His Majesty had worn during
the Fall, and was still frequently pictured in. They had a
certain nobility about them.

"There's room for two," Robert's voice said, through
wellstone speakers. "I wouldn't recommend fitting any
more than that."

"And I wouldn't dream," Bascal said with a bow, "of doing anything you didn't recommend. You look quite dashing, by the way. Conrad, will you join me? Karl, join the
others at the sound baffle?"

"Um, sure," Conrad said.

Karl grumbled less agreeably, though, and Conrad
didn't blame him for it. Helping out with the breakfast
cleanup sounded a lot less interesting than watching
these amateur mass wranglers in action.

With the clank of equipment and the rustle of fabrics
against the corridor walls, the Refugees launched themselves foreward, toward the baffle and the hold and the
airlocks. Karl trailed sullenly behind them, and turned off
to one side just as they were rounding the corner out of
sight.

"Interesting bunch of people," the prince observed.

Conrad nodded. "Very."

Together they drifted to the bridge, entered, and sock-
eted themselves into the seats like puzzle pieces snapping
into place. In front of them was a holie screen, which
Bascal addressed. "Display Robert M'chunu's video signal, please."

Obediently, the screen showed them a corridor scene,
jumping and jostling, the view apparently from a sensor in
the wellstone of Robert's helmet dome. The Refugees
were at the inner airlock, and presently its door
whooshed open in that too-fast way it had. At first Conrad
thought there was no audio in the signal, but as the
space-suited figures glided one by one into the airlock,

Robert's voice called out crisply, "Secure handholds and prepare for hatch closure."

And then Agnes' voice: "Atmospheric pressure nominal. The bleed valve lights are green."

And then Robert again: "Acknowledged, bleed valves green."

And then they were silent again, although now that he was listening for it Conrad could make out the sound of Robert's breathing over the hum and hiss of the bridge equipment itself.

The operation was interesting to watch: everything happened slowly and with crisp precision, yet none of the spacewalkers were idle for long. Once the lock was depressurized and the outer hatch opened, they began clearing away sections of sailcloth, and setting up tripods in little depressions around the lock which appeared to exist there for exactly this purpose. And then pulleys were attached to the tripods, and cables to the pulleys, and hooks and carabiners to the cables.

Then Robert and Money were standing guard at the airlock's lip, held down against it by magnets in their boots, while the others carefully rappelled along the hull, in the direction of *Viridity*'s remains, ignoring the handholds Conrad and the others had used. He supposed those were only for the most desperate of emergencies, of which there were no doubt very few. Still, it took the Refugees longer to reach the cabin than it had taken the Camp Friendlies to reach the airlock from it. When they got there, they began attaching still more cables to it, and clearing away more of the sail, and attaching more tripods to the hull, until the whole area began to look like the inside of a grand piano.

And yet, despite these fascinations, the process was deliberate and methodical enough to be boring at the same time. Conrad found himself glancing at the scene rather than staring—his mind dividing it up into a series of still images, a few every minute. Meanwhile, his attention wandered, taking in the walls and the floor and the ceiling, the bridge controls, the wellstone edges of the holie screen itself. This cramped little bridge was an interesting exercise in its own right, with hardly a millimeter wasted anywhere.

"Hey, look," he said at one point, eyeing the control panel in front of him. "There *is* a button to dump the neutronium."

Bascal rubbed his nose. "You noticed that, eh? You knew there had to be one. Robert can talk all he wants about the barge being less valuable than the cargo, being essentially a protective cocoon for it, but this is a semi-crewed vessel, and certain safety concessions have got to be made. There's also a self-destruct and a cargo-destruct, although they look complicated to operate."

"Why would they need a self-destruct?"

"I dunno. Loss of helm control, on a direct course for a population center? Fully loaded, these barges are bringing in a hundred gigatons; that's a tenth of a good-sized planette. Imagine dropping that in the middle of the Irish Sea."

"Hmm. I suppose."

On the screen, the Refugees were assembling some kind of sled, with pulleys of its own that hooked onto the cables linking cabin and airlock.

"Of course, if that were going to happen the navy would just vaporize the barge with a nasen beam, releasing all that mass-energy as far from humanity as possible. But *having* to would not amuse them."

"I don't think they amuse easily," Conrad said.

Bascal seemed to find that funny.

And then, on the holie screen, the space-suited figures were packing it in: stowing equipment on their belts and backs, and slowly rappelling back in the direction of the airlock again.

"They didn't get it," the prince said, sounding surprised.

Conrad checked a chronometer. "Their forty minutes are up."

"They should let us work the LIDAR for them. If we get a clean scan, they can stay out longer."

"I'll bet there's some reason they won't do things that way. Otherwise they'd've stationed one of their own people in here to do exactly that, right?"

Bascal didn't reply, just watched the screen as the spacewalkers climbed back into the airlock again, and reentered the barge.

"You didn't get it," he said to Robert, when the mob of them arrived in the corridor outside the bridge.

Robert's helmet was under his arm. He looked content enough, and smiled at the prince. "We weren't trying to. We can't fit all that into one space walk, not safely. That was just our setup run."

"I see. So what happens now?"

"Now we take a LIDAR scan, pick up some more equipment, and go back out again."

"Because you don't have enough equipment out there already."

"Right," Robert said, unfazed by the irony. "Oh, before I forget." He dug a gauntleted hand into a pouch on his belt, and pulled out a carefully folded square of wellstone film, several dozen layers thick. "A little souvenir from your journey."

"Oh. Thanks," Bascal said, sounding pleasantly surprised as he accepted the gift. "This is from the sail?"

"Yah. I thought you might want some. We're trying to minimize the damage, in case you still need it for something, but these pieces had to come out."

"You're very thoughtful," the prince commended.

"Funny, that's not what the prudes back in TSA used to say."

The second space walk was, if anything, even slower and more methodical than the first, although there was slightly more talking as the work progressed into areas outside the routine. The Refugees found it necessary to slice away large pieces of D'rector Jed's shattered cabin, and to carry them around to the fore end of the barge for disposal in the great, all-consuming maw of the mass crusher. Luckily, there wasn't a snowball storm while they did this, although—of course—there was no luck involved. These people knew the location and course of every snowflake within five million kilometers!

It occurred to Conrad that Martin's lifeless body, along with the missing Palace Guard, must be among those cataloged objects. In the hours since the crash, they probably hadn't drifted far. For all he knew, the guard might still be alive, an angry monster adrift in the nothingness, struggling in vain to return to its prince. Or maybe it had swept in front of the barge and been eaten.

"If we have to dispose of any evidence," Bascal noted, obviously thinking along similar lines, "that crusher would be the place. Neutronium tells no tales, and preserves no information about the atoms and molecules which formed it."

"Great," Conrad said, just loving the sound of that. The Poet Prince was drinking in every sight and sound, every datum, every stray thought anyone had given voice to. He was scheming, and the gist of it was already unsavory.

And then, once again, the spacewalkers were stowing their gear and climbing back inside.

"They *still* didn't get it," Bascal grumbled. Then later, to Robert: "You people are awfully patient."

Money Izolo smiled at that. "We got time, Your Majesty. The machine is secure, and as far as we can tell your boy is safe in there. So we got nothing but time."

Fortunately, the third space walk hit pay dirt almost

immediately, as *Viridity's* fax machine was winched aboard the little sled, webbed and strapped in place, and transported without further fuss to the airlock. After that it was just the anticlimactic—ha!—disassembly of all the cables and pulleys and trusses and tripods, which for some reason went much faster than their setup had.

And then Robert's jolly crew were carting their prize through the hallways on a complicated sort of hand truck, and soon enough they were back at the inventory again, grinning and thumping each other, and tossing heaps of equipment back into the fax machine.

"Well done," Bascal told them sincerely. "Very, painfully well done. You're an example to us all."

And then, while the Refugees got naked again and chatted about their various adventures outside, Bascal took Conrad by the elbow and led him back into the corridor, stopping halfway between the inventory and the bridge.

Conrad groaned inwardly. Conspiracy time. "What is it?" he asked.

"I have a plan."

Wearily: "I know you do, Bascal. But for crying out loud, why don't you just ask these people for help? They might give it. If you trick them or force their hand, and something goes wrong..."

"Yes?" Bascal was annoyed again, impatient.

"Why do I talk to you, Bas? Never mind. Let's hear it."

"Thank you so much, me boyo. Just out of curiosity, if I really do get us back to Denver, against all odds, against all hope... If I do that, will you bow down to me as your monarch?"

Conrad sighed. "It isn't the deed, Bas, it's the means. If you can do great things without losing your honor, that's when I'll bow. I'll stand on my *head* if you do that."

"I see. Hmm. So you, a paver's boy from County Cork, are giving *me* advice on how to behave nobly. Is that it?"

Conrad thought for a moment before answering, "Absolutely. It's my right as a citizen. Your job as monarch is to fulfill my expectations, however unreasonable. These people seem to have their shit together. Why can't we?"

"Ah." Despite his impatience, Bascal actually smiled at that. Actually seemed interested, even maybe a little bit grateful, for the observation. "Promise me you'll never change, Conrad."

"I will change," Conrad answered. "That's the whole idea. That's the very right we're fighting for."

"Oh, so now we're fighting again? How curious. Does that mean you're ready to hear my plan?"

"Sure. Enlighten me."

"I'm thinking we rebuild *Viridity*, then dump this vessel's neutronium overboard. We hide behind a rigidized sail, right? Then go back into fax storage and detonate a neuble. The energy release will be *huge*. It could push us back into Queendom space in just a few months."

Conrad sighed. "Bascal, you're crazy. I mean *crazy*. Never mind the danger—to these people as much as ourselves—or the legal ramifications. Think of the *cost*. Even your splendid allowance doesn't cover these kind of big-ticket items. Does it?"

"It doesn't need to," the prince said, his eyes sparkling merrily.

But at that very moment, there was a sound from the bridge: a shrill, insistent pinging.

Bascal stiffened. "Proximity alarm. Shit. Something's approaching from the stern. Probably stealthed, or the scans would've—"

Then came a huge, hollow groaning noise from one end of the barge to the other. And its walls shimmered for an instant, and then laid themselves out in a series of broad metal traces against a green-white insulative background. Something was reprogramming all the wellstone, making connections through it, tracing out the Queendom's largest circuit board. Then the barge groaned again, and Conrad heard clanking noises from far away, as if something very large were attaching itself very firmly to the barge's other end.

They were back on the network.

And then the fax machine in the inventory gave off a sizzle and a flash, moments before a swarm of armored, black-and-bronze SWAT robots began pouring out of it— literally *pouring* like a fluid, rolling and swirling through the inventory chamber and the corridor beyond it, flowing onward and outward to fill the human spaces of the ship. An army of beetle-black, statue-bronze man-things, overwhelming in number, built up from the eight hundred tons of base matter in the ship's mass buffers. Faxborn for this very moment, this very instance, this very fight.

One of the bronze troopers restrained Conrad, grabbing him gently but firmly by the wrist and ankles. Another pair grabbed Bascal, and a struggling, space-suited Robert M'chunu drifted by with three of them attached, swarming and grabbing at his arms and legs.

"Please remain calm," said a high, mechanical voice in Conrad's ear. "By authority of the Queen's Navy and the Royal Constabulary, you are under arrest on suspicion of vandalism, hijack, and space piracy. You have the right to consult with an attorney. You have the right to be interrogated by disposable copies. As a minor, you do not have the right to commit suicide without entering a plea, but you do have the right to blame your parents. Do you understand these rights?"

"Fucking *finally*," Conrad snarled at the robot that held him. "Thank you, you're welcome, and Jesus H. Bloodfuck. What took you guys so long?"

chapter nineteen

single-celled life

Conrad half expected to wind up in the same interro-gation room as before, with Officer Leslie of the Dande-lion Sweater. It seemed like a very Queendom-of-Sol way to handle the situation: assign a caseworker to each un-ruly child, build a rapport, write a series of lengthy analy-ses.... But instead he was led to a windowless holding cell: larger and darker, with an actual cage door that slammed shut with the clang of metal and the mirrored gleam of impervium bars.

He was in a basement somewhere; he didn't know what city, or even what planet. Could be Venus for all he knew; there were towns there now, on the highlands, and the gravity was indistinguishable. Why they would ship him there he had no idea, but he also had no idea why they'd separated everyone, and locked him up alone. This wasn't the Denver police station, he knew that much, but the cool, processed air provided no other clues.

How long they left him there alone was something he never learned, because in point of fact he was exhausted. It had been a *long* day, commencing with the fax deaths and ensuing argument aboard *Viridity*. More than a week had passed since then, and though he'd been stored as data for most of that time, he'd still lived through twenty or thirty hours of it, all in one big subjective push. He was running, he realized now, on a pure adrenaline high.

But with the action suddenly over, the fear and uncertainty ended, and the heavy *Refuge* breakfast still weighing him down, he simply stretched out on one of the cell's bunks and went straight to sleep. *Ah, night,* Bascal had said to him once in the early days of Camp Friendly. *That puts to rest the work of men.*

His waking came harshly and too soon: a brightening of lights, a clanging open of the cage door.

"Hello," said a man's voice.

Conrad rolled over onto his side, facing the wall. "I'm sleeping."

"Lad, we need to talk."

Oh, shit, he knew that voice. His father's. And presently his mom's chimed in. "We came as soon as possible. Dear, you have no idea how worried—"

"Please, I'm so tired," Conrad complained, but his voice sounded too whiny in his ears, too childish. After everything they'd been through—the daring, the recklessness, the sacrifice and deprivation—he had earned the right not to sound like that in front of his parents. He wasn't a hundred years old, all right, but he didn't feel seventeen either. And with a shock, he realized he wasn't: it must be August by now. Since Denver, he hadn't paid any attention to the calendar, and his late-July birthday had come and gone unnoticed. He was *eighteen* now, and since Bascal was a few weeks older, so should he be as well.

He didn't feel eighteen any more than he felt seventeen, but that number at least seemed less jarring, less alien to his recent experience. Did eighteen-year-olds make credible space pirates?

"All right," he said in a deliberately deeper voice, and hauled himself up to a sitting position. He rubbed his eyes blearily. "Hi."

Maybel Mursk smiled, and rushed forward to crush him in a hug. "Oh, my brave, clever boy. Welcome home, lad."

"Where am I?" Conrad asked.

"City and County of Cork," she said, still squeezing him. Her auburn hair was a frizzy mess that tickled his face. Her company blazer was rough against his bare arms. "Very near to the house, about ten kilometers. We could almost have walked from there, on your father's own roads."

When she finally disengaged herself, Conrad found himself staring at his father's hand, held out for him to shake. He did so.

"We've worried," Donald Mursk said. "We've worried a great deal."

"I'm sorry about that," Conrad told him sincerely. "I had no way to contact you."

"We're very proud," his father added, a bit tentatively. And that made no sense: proud of him for running away? For breaking the law? For being implicated in nine deaths?

"Of what?"

"Well..." Donald ran a hand through his hair. Like everyone else in the Queendom, he looked like a strong and confident young man, but here was a gesture that suggested otherwise. It belonged with a balding scalp, a bulging gut, a hat clutched between nervous fingers.

"Naturally we're angry with you," his mother said.

"Right," Donald agreed. "Angry. But it's a strange thing you've done, isn't it? A strangely compelling thing. All sorts of people have been coming up to us and, well, complimenting. I mean, it's illegal—"

"But not antisocial," Maybel finished for him. "You've done a thing a bit like the Republican hunger strikes: powerfully expressing a viewpoint people can relate to. Mere words don't compare."

Conrad sighed. He *was* tired, and while he'd missed his parents terribly, this was not at all the homecoming he'd envisioned. "We destroyed property. We got people killed."

"Oh, that may be," Donald agreed seriously. "But you should hear from the dead boys themselves, before you pass judgment. In the old days we knew, there'd always be some bitter affliction keeping pace with our joys. But we knew there'd be joys. You should give your friends a bit of credit, lad."

Conrad processed that, not knowing what to think.

"We know you and Bascal disagreed," Maybel told him. "His letter was very clear on that point, and the visual records from the Palace Guard support it. We know you did your best."

But Conrad was shaking his head. "No, don't say that. I helped him. I waffled occasionally, but he always had his way in the end, every step. I deserve my equal share of blame."

"Or credit," his father said. "And that's the way the law sees it, too. You're to be severely punished, never doubt it. Your point is well made, but now there's little else the Queendom can do except punish. Unless it wants to encourage more of the same, and I don't think anyone wants that."

Listening to his parents' voices, their faint but unmistakable accents, he considered the strange fact that the two of them lived and worked and socialized in the very town of their birth. Donald looked after the roads, yes, which few people and fewer vehicles ever used. Maybel was a housing inspector—one of six for the county. Neither of them traveled much outside of southern Ireland, or needed to.

Conrad himself gave little thought to geography; he was used to moving between his school on the European continent, his home here in Cork, and the various educational and entertainment facilities they trekked him to in Asia and North America. Except for concerns of daylight and weather, the physical locations of these places hardly seemed to matter. It was only when you got out to the moon and planets that true barriers—like the speed of light—created any genuine sense of distance. But Donald and Maybel Mursk didn't see it that way. At heart they were yokels, provincials, born into the actual country of Ireland, during a time when travel was arduous and borders were tangible. There *was* no Queendom, anywhere.

And yet, when Donald spoke of the Queendom, his tone was full of apology and acceptance and even complicity. If he saw himself as something slightly apart from the monarchy, it was not for lack of approval. Whereas Conrad, who was truly and fully a creature of Tamra's worlds, nevertheless chafed at their confines.

"Mom, Dad, were you rebellious in your youth?" he asked suddenly.

Maybel clucked, amused and embarrassed by the question. "I'm tempted to wash your mouth, lad. We snuck around our share, yes, although it was different in those days. The things we wanted were . . . simpler."

"Sex?" he pressed, not caring if the question was appropriate. "Drugs?"

"Oh, all of those things," she agreed shyly. "All the things that people want. There has to be *some* age when you're too young for it, and that puts you in immediate conflict."

"You do have to understand," his father cut in, "we thought our lives would be short. You were born in those days with death staring you in the face. You had to make your time count. Your mother and I were no more than twenty years from the grave when these fax filters came along. And *our* parents, why, they were gone already."

He ran his hand through his hair again. "It's why we're

such fools, lad. We didn't want any school, or any hard work. There's been a lot of catching up for us, a lot of adjustment. We don't want to be poor and ignorant, not forever. I think we've done all right, but for you we wanted a better start."

"Huh." Wow." It was a perspective Conrad had never considered. It was interesting. Would it have changed anything, if he'd heard this six months ago? *Should* it have changed anything?

"Apparently we've failed utterly as parents," Maybel said sadly. "Whatever it is you need, we haven't provided. Lord, we sent you to that camp you keep you *out* of trouble."

"Don't cry for me, Mother," Conrad told her, surprised at the guilt in her face. "I can make decisions, right? I have free will. The problem is nothing to do with our family. It's a...I dunno, a structural problem with the Queendom itself."

"Perhaps that's so," Donald said. "But it's you and yours who'll bear the brunt of it."

"Well," Conrad agreed. "We always knew it was a gesture we'd have to pay for. Nothing's free, is it?"

Donald's smile was pained. "No indeed, Son. In all the world—in all the universe—there's not a thing worth having that comes any way but dear. You choose what you want, and spend the rest of your life paying. And now that life's eternal, why, that's a high cost indeed."

Half a world away, with the painful light of dawn shining through a different set of bars, a similar conversation was progressing even more smoothly.

"Xiomara, dear, is there *nothing* we can do? Will you magically appear in the midst of every trespass and misdeed in the Queendom?"

"Sorry times call for sorry deeds, Mum."

"Do they? Really. Playing space harlot is a *political strategem*, I suppose."

"Harlot? To hell with you, Mummy. That's the meanest thing you've ever said."

Like she didn't have enough troubles. She was a rioter, yes, and now apparently also a space pirate. And these two halves of herself were having a hard time integrating. How could her life be so wrapped up in the affairs of people she hadn't known she knew? How could Yinebeb Fecre—"Feck the Fairy"—be such a dashing figure around Denver, and yet such a clownish and contemptible one in the eyes of his peers? Had they ever really met him? Had she?

And then there was the Prince of Sol, who wanted her heart, who accused her of toying with him. *There* was a problem she'd never expected to have. And this damned Conrad Mursk, who'd had the temerity—the gall!—to save her life. A piece of her life she wasn't sure she wanted. Oh, it was intense. It was a break from her humdrum existence, not least because he was part of it. But did Xmary want to be that person? Bitter, used? *Seasoned?* Too late now, of course. She already was.

So she didn't know what to think. She wasn't entirely sure she knew *how* to think. The reintegration was eleven hours old, and still not taking! She was still of two minds! The old days must have been easier: everyone singled for life, without any of this crazy *ambivalence* weighing the spirit down. Decisions must have been effortless.

"Your mother is upset, Mara," Da told her gently.

But Mummy pressed on. "No, dear. Upset doesn't begin to describe what I feel. Betrayed, undermined, humiliated. Did our reputations matter to you at all, young lady? If you're so intent on this wickedness, then perhaps it's time we give you the liberty you crave. Darken our windows no more with your brooding silhouette. We'll turn the lockouts around. When they let you out of here, you'll be free to go anywhere you please. Anywhere but home."

Conrad stayed in the cell another thirty-six hours, and slept almost twenty of it. A pair of local cops—both male and not very talkative—took turns bringing him meals when he rang, and even brought an exercise machine when he complained of boredom. *They* weren't here to punish him, or pass judgment in any way. They'd simply been asked to hold him and care for him while preparations were made at the palace.

Preparations for what?

He was in the exerciser, thrusting his arms against the resistance of a spring, when Officer Donahue brought a letter for him.

"Lad," it said, in the voice of the King of Sol, "a trial at this point would be wasteful. We know most of what you've done. Will you grant us the courtesy of pleading guilty?"

"On what charges?" Conrad probed.

The letter chuckled. "Fair enough. The willful destruction of a Friendly Parks planette; the theft of resources from same; the operation of an unregistered spaceship; the operation of a spaceship without identity beacon, running lights or other visibility provisions; the negligent homicide of nine human instantiations; the breaking and entering of a Mass Industries neutronium barge, and misappropriation of resources from same. The king owns those, by the way."

Considering for a moment, Conrad said, "Most of those deaths had nothing to do with me. I was personally negligent in maybe three of them. And we didn't break into the barge; your Palace Guard let us in. And we certainly didn't 'destroy' the planette."

"I'm afraid you did," the letter said. "A quantity of

water seeped into the core, shorting out circuitry and altering key mechanical properties. A complete dismantlement will be necessary."

"Oh. Sorry."

"Noted. So you're guilty, then?"

"Well, yes. The rest of it is true."

"Er, you have to say it."

"What? Guilty?"

"Yes."

"All right. Guilty."

The letter paused, then said, "Thank you. Our Majesties will be in touch with you shortly."

"Great."

He would have left it at that, but the cop who'd delivered the letter was already gone, and the letter itself was just sitting there, full of unknown information. When a minute had gone by he asked it, "What's going to happen to me?"

"You're to be sentenced," it answered, not entirely without sympathy.

"How?"

"Our Majesties will determine the punishment."

"I mean, what? What punishment?"

"Hmm," it said. "Unknown."

"What's typical in a case like this?"

The note laughed again. "Lad, there has never been a case like this. Grand theft of a spaceship is normally punishable by twenty years' incarceration. Does that help?"

"Um, no. Not really." Jesus Christ among the gods. Twenty years? By the time he got out, he'd've lived most of his life in prison. He would be, by any sensible definition, a career felon. And a virginal one at that, unless prison held additional surprises he didn't want to think about.

And with that thought, the courage that had served him through all of this suddenly collapsed. Yes, he was a sailor and a revolutionary and a sometime confidant of the Prince of Sol, but suddenly he felt—very keenly and distinctly—like a child who was in over his head. *Tears are almost exclusively a symptom of frustration,* Mrs. Regland had taught him in health class. *This is why they've become so rare. With eternity before us, there is very little we cannot change. Except the past.*

And damned if it wasn't true. As the tears began their sad, stupid journey down his face, he crumpled the letter in an angry fist. Damn the thing. Damn it for seeing through his stupid, childish pretensions. Of course, despite the way it felt, the note wasn't made of paper. It straightened itself out the moment he relaxed his grip.

"Shit," he said, choking back an undignified sob. "Damn you, letter. Would you fucking self-destruct or something?"

"Certainly," the letter answered. "And you have the king's own apology for any distress my delivery may have caused." Then it fell at once into a fine silicate dust.

chapter twenty

the arena sentence

Finally, an official summons arrived, and when Officer Boyle came down to let Conrad out, he was accompanied by a pair of gleaming Palace Guards. The fax was up a flight of stairs and through a couple of doorways, and once he got there, stepping through it felt no more or less fateful than any other such journey. Conrad was killed and reborn, his memories and identity copied into a different bit of matter.

Where he ended up was a surprise, though—not the palace at all, but some sort of outdoor amphitheater, ringed by palm trees all around, beneath a bright blue sky full of puffy, flat-bottomed clouds. The smell of flowers leaped into his nose, and he was greeted at once by a familiar-looking woman, one of the Tongan courtiers from the queen's staff, in a tapa-patterned dress of red and brown and glowing white. She glanced at Conrad, then at the sketchplate in her hand, then back at Conrad again.

"Mursk?" she asked.

"That's right."

"This way, please. My name is Tusité, and if that doesn't strike a fear in you, then get tricky with me, and you'll find out why it ought to."

She led him down one of two staircases. The seats

here, enough for a few thousand people, were mostly empty—except for one knot of a dozen or so kids sitting in the center of the first three rows. One of them was Bascal, dressed in a loose-fitting shirt and pants of a purple that was not quite the forbidden royal shade. He wore the wellstone scarf Robert M'chunu had cut for him from *Viridity*'s sail, and around his head rested a thin crown of wrinkly aluminum foil—clearly his idea of a joke. He was laughing loudly at something.

And then, without warning, the whole gang down there burst into Conrad's favorite stanza of the Space Pirate Song:

> *Well they can't tell us to shape up and they can't tell us*
> *   to ship out,*
> *And they can't come do our laundry though we*
> *   sometimes wish they would,*
> *And they're never gonna catch us 'cause we won't do*
> *   nothing stupid*
> *So we're sailing toward salvation in an angel made of*
> *   wood!*

This didn't seem like the best foot to be putting forward at a sentencing hearing, but the boys pressed on heedlessly into the chorus:

> *We're the pirates of the Queendom; we're the pirates of*
> *   the spaceways.*
> *We'd be pirates of the Nescog if they ever let us on.*
> *So we're flying through the Kuiper Belt and steering*
> *   just with starlight,*
> *And we've nothing else to do all day but sing this pirate*
> *   song!*

With a shock, Conrad saw the boy Bascal had his arm around: Peter Kolb, last seen on the surface of Camp

Friendly, running away with his eyes full of tears. But to-day he was looking not only joyous, but downright smug. His eyes found Conrad and brightened further as the song broke up, with each of the boys trying to throw in a different verse. Bascal melted back into the mob, suddenly talking to someone else.

"Hi!" Peter called out.

"Um, hi," Conrad answered uncertainly, as he and Tusité drew near. "You seem . . . cheerful."

Peter shrugged. "It's our day."

Conrad frowned. "Our judgment day, you mean."

"This is your place," Tusité told him. "Stand here and be good."

Her hand left his arm, and she was on her way back up the stairs, with another Tusité trailing behind.

"So what happened to you, anyway?" Conrad asked Peter. "Did you get killed?"

"Me? No." Peter sounded surprised. "Though I was marooned for six weeks. Pickings got pretty lean; that rainstorm washed out a lot of the plants and stuff. By the time the navy showed up, I'd gotten very skinny. I was tired all the time, not really doing anything. It sucked."

"I'll bet!"

"Well, it's done. The navy people were astonished when they found me there. We were already famous for having departed."

"We?" It was Conrad's turn to sound surprised.

"Hey," Peter said defensively, "I helped a lot with the planning. It was my mission, too."

"And mine," said Martin Liss beside him.

"Little gods," Conrad exclaimed softly. "I tried to save you, Martin. I really did. Twice!"

"Hey, don't fret. We all knew the hazards; we all took the chance. I'm just happy to have been a part."

"Me too," said Jamil Gazzaniga and Raoul Sanchez together.

Bloody hell, what was going on here? Why was everyone so happy? Especially the dead, the betrayed?

"Hey, bloodfuck," said Ho Ng, clapping Conrad on the shoulder in a distinctly comradely fashion. Steve Grush clapped his other shoulder, and then James and Bertram and Khen and Preston and Emilio and Karl were all crowding around him, smiling, patting, shaking his hand.

"What's going on?" he demanded. "Half you guys were murdered! By me, by Bascal! Why are you so cheery about it?"

Standing, smiling, the prince slid forward along the edge of a stone bench, parting the boys around him like a drop of soap in oily water. "Conrad, my man! Haven't you turned on a TV?"

"Um, no. Why?"

"You're fucking famous!" somebody shouted.

"Conscience of the revolution!" said someone else.

"What?"

Bascal nodded. "It's true. We space pirates are the particular heroes of the Children's Revolt. We're its heart and soul, its inspiration."

"What revolt? Us? Camp Friendly?"

The prince rolled his eyes. "Did you ask anyone? Did you read a headline? Did you *hear anything*? There were riots in three cities, boyo. Takeovers and ransoming on a bunch of neutronium barges, plus three other acts of space piracy, including the theft of my mother's own grappleship. It was a general, systemwide uprising. What were you, in a *cave*?"

"Um. Well, almost." They would have brought him a TV or newsplate if he'd asked for one. The king's letter could probably have told him these things as well. Should it have occurred to him to ask?

"It was all because of us, Conrad. All inspired by us. And with the Palace Guard's memory dump, you're the most famous of all! Well, after me. And Xmary too, but she's a special case, being in two of the crucial places at the same time." At Conrad's blank stare he explained, "Because she helped orchestrate the first August riot? With Feck? Oh, never mind, you dolt. Just stand there, all right? Look heroic."

Conrad blinked. "This is a joke, right?"

But even as he was saying it, he could see Feck and Xmary walking down the steps together, shaking their fists in the air in gleeful defiance. And behind them were other people, other *young* people who looked vaguely Denverish somehow. The stands were filling up in clumps and clusters, but Feck and Xmary, with Tusité leading them, came right down to the row behind the last of the space pirates.

"Conrad!" Feck said happily.

"Hi, Feck. So you started a riot, did you?" The only answer was a grin so wide it must have been painful.

And then Xmary was there, waving her fists. But her grin was not so wide or self-assured, and it collapsed entirely when she looked into Conrad's face. She stopped in front of him. "Hello, you."

"Hi. Do you, um, remember...I mean, which Xmary are you? Both?"

"Both," she confirmed, then patted him on the cheek. "Yes, I remember you, you darling fool. How could I forget?"

Bascal stepped forward, taking one of Xmary's hands and kissing it. At her arrival, his own smiles had collapsed as well. "Xiomara," he said. "Hello. So very good to see you."

And then, with a kind of sour look on his face, he took her hand and transferred it solemnly into Conrad's grasp.

"Huh? What?" Conrad said, brilliantly.

The prince huffed. "I have eyes, don't I? And ears, and the sense to know when it's time." To Xmary he said, "You're right; we're not a romantic match. And since I'm the Prince of Fucking Sol, you'll be easy enough to re-place."

"What a rotten thing to say," Conrad noted with sudden, rising irritation.

"Shut up," Bascal snapped. "I'm doing you a favor. Treat her right and maybe we'll still be friends." And then he melted back into the stands, taking refuge behind Ho and Steve and the others.

Conrad looked at the hand he'd been given, and then at the young woman attached to it. Behind her, Feck was looking on with a sour, wounded expression of his own. Xmary the heartbreaker? Leaving a trail of bodies and shattered dreams in her wake? He could see it in his mind's eye: a Xiomara Li Weng who'd stayed home with her parents on that fateful night, waiting for a secret copy of herself that never came home. Did she suspect she'd met the prince? Been arrested? Smuggled herself to an all-boys summer camp, and then escaped? Who could possibly suspect a thing like that?

But then she'd somehow encountered this Yinebeb Fecre, this runaway who knew people in high places. Who knew *missing* people—revolutionaries on a mysterious voyage. How exciting! How intriguing and suggestive! He tried to imagine what that Xmary would be like, how she might react. That experience was so wildly different than the events aboard *Viridity*—less dirty and smelly and crowded, less frightening. A truly romantic adventure, to balance out the deprivations and indignities of space.

But did he know her well enough to speculate like this? Would his guesses be wildly inaccurate? He was pretty sure the Conrad Mursk on board *Viridity* bore little resemblance to the one that had left Cork County three months before. It was hard to be yourself, in conditions like that. Or perhaps the very notion of "self" was a contextual thing—a collection of learned responses to a particular environment. He found the idea oddly cheering: the human spirit shining through adversity.

"I'll bet reintegration was a shock," he said to her.

A flicker of smile came and went. "That's the most intelligent thing I've ever heard you say."

He glanced over his shoulder at the stands behind them. "So, uh . . . you and Feck?"

She sniffed. "In a manner of speaking, yes. But I believe he had his share of . . . contacts in the underground."

Indeed, the boy was mobbed by female admirers up there, and seemed to know them all. Was that really Feck? Had he and Xmary really . . .

"Oh."

She scratched her neck. "Look, Conrad, it was—"

"Exciting?" he offered sullenly. "Romantic?"

"I was going to say, none of your business."

He nodded. "Okay. I deserved that. And do I inherit this legacy? Am I next in line?"

"Now that wasn't smart," she said, pulling her hand away. Her cheeks reddened—she still had that marvelous blush, so surprsingly easy to trigger. "You can't trade hearts around like coupons, Hero Boy. Or didn't you know? Thanks to you and your friends I've lost my parents and my home. Anyway, what makes you think I want to have this conversation here, in front of the world? I suppose my charms have driven you mad, but believe it or not, we are about to be sentenced."

"Um, right," he said. Then, mustering a bit of sincerity: "Sorry."

That seemed to soften her. She touched his cheek again. "Oh, my. Twenty years, Conrad Mursk. Maybe thirty. They say the heart remembers. Maybe someday, when we're out of prison, a little bird will whisper my name, and you'll think of me, and maybe even look me up. I believe I'd like that."

He could feel his own cheeks coloring now, warming.

How absurd, this myth of his heroism! He'd been selfish and frightened through every minute of an ordeal he'd personally helped to create. And even now, in the relative safety of the Queendom, the touch of a soft hand was all it took to unravel his courage. "I'm an idiot," he warned. "I really am."

"Go. Sit," she said, waving him away with an expression he couldn't read. She moved back, taking a seat among the Denverites, and Conrad had the uncomfortable sense that a piece of him went with her. Blindly, eagerly, heedless of consequence. He hoped she would treat it kindly.

The crowd—tended by half a dozen Tusités—was growing thicker and thicker: not only a Denver section almost two hundred children strong, but a Calcutta section as well, and another smaller one for... Athens? He also recognized the TSA Africans from *Refuge*. They were clothed for the occasion, but even so their blue skin really stood out. And around them stood many dozens of others, in a variety of colors and manners of dress.

Theoretically, the Queendom was one big society, freed by the Nescog from the tyrannies of time and space and geography. That had certainly been Conrad's unexamined view. But he could see now that there were other yokels in other provinces, preserving their own little bubbles of regional culture. These kids over here had a vaguely Martian look: hair teased high over loose-fitting blouses and pastel slacks. Those over there had the squinty, buttoned-down look of Antarcticans—a look he'd had no idea he could even recognize.

It occurred to him that before the start of whatever happened next, this stadium was actually going to fill up. Two thousand people? More?

"What is this?" he asked out loud, of no one in particular. "Who are all these people? Revolutionaries, all of them?"

It was Peter Kolb who answered. "Revolutionaries, all. Not all space pirates, obviously, but rioters and saboteurs."

"But . . . wow, this must be a tenth of the children in the Queendom."

Peter shrugged. "More like a thirtieth. But yeah, it's a lot, and the ranks of sympathizers are even larger. Our exploits really struck a chord."

Conrad nodded, thinking about that. It seemed important: could any society really lock up a thirtieth of its own children? Especially if their crimes were more celebrated than reviled? Maybe there would *have* to be a just solution, a Restoration-style rearchitecting of the social order. And then, in one of those little moments of grown-up awakening, it occurred to him that he didn't really have any idea what that would mean. What did a perfect world look like? If anyone asked him, he could only stare back at them, slack-jawed and simple.

Great. Just great. He'd fought and struggled and made a mark on the universe, for no clear purpose. For the hell of it. Amazingly enough, he had no list of demands to nail over anyone's doorway. Did Bascal? Did any of them? Would Their Majesties even ask, or care?

He took his seat, feeling morose. And since he seemed to be the only one in a crowd of thousands who felt that way, he felt it even more keenly. Did these people imagine some culmination of a prince's clever plan? How disappointing for them.

And the amphitheater really did fill, getting louder and rowdier as it went, until finally the queen's courtier, Tusité, mounted the stage and glared out at them all.

"You! Quiet! Quiet, everyone."

Conrad couldn't tell if the acoustics were natural or wellstone-enhanced, but in any case her voice punched right through the crowd noise like a comet fragment at twenty kips. The conversation splintered, swirling and withering into silence as her gaze swept from one side of the crowd to the other.

"Be silent, everyone. And stand up. Your king and queen will be here shortly."

There were a couple of boos and catcalls at this remark, but they were met with waves of shushing and pushing and even—it looked like—some good, hard punches to the stomach. Whatever they might be guilty of, whatever grievances they had, these myriad kids were mostly loyal citizens at heart. This, Conrad supposed, was the very thing that separated revolutionaries from ordinary criminals: a desire to make things better not for themselves, but for everyone else. Even if the personal cost was high.

"That's right," Tusité said. "If you want respect, you start by giving it. We will now sing 'Praise upon Her.'"

And they did, with Tusité leading them, and the sound of it was beautiful. By the age of ten, everyone in the Queendom had had at least rudimentary voice training, and the tune and lyrics were of course familiar, although a part of Conrad—at once innocent and weirdly alert—felt as though he were really hearing the song for the first time. It didn't take long to get through the first verse, and Tusité didn't lead them through the second. Soon the echoes were dying away, leaving behind only the imprint of memory.

Then the fax machine at the back of the amphitheater crackled, and Conrad turned just in time to see Their Majesties, Tamra-Tamatra Lutui and Bruno de Towaji, step through. They were holding hands at first, but let go almost immediately, commencing a stately walk together down one of the stairways, flanked fore and aft by pairs of Palace Guards. He could distinctly hear their footsteps, the *clump clump* of boot heels on the wellstone marble of the steps.

Her Majesty held the Scepter of Earth in her left

hand. His Majesty held a rolled-up document in his right. The two of them looked grim, unhappy, determined. Their eyes did not survey the crowd, did not make contact, and Conrad was struck by the notion that this man and woman weren't people at all—the parents of his friend, whom he'd spoken with personally—but animate mouthpieces for a civilization of twenty-five billion. And the hairs on his neck stood up, because it was hard enough to explain yourself to two people—to one person. To yourself. Was there any hope of being understood by an entire solar system?

The staircase led all the way down to the base of the stage, whose edge the king and queen followed around until they came to a smaller, narrower staircase leading up onto it. And then, there they were at the focal point, the physical and psychological nexus of the stadium's attention.

The crowd was utterly silent.

"Good afternoon," the queen said. She pointed with her scepter, sweeping it in an arc across the crowd. "You children—and the few dozen legal adults among you—have been very naughty. But you know that."

There was scattered laughter. Ah, Queen Tamra, who always knew what to say.

"Many of your concerns," she went on gravely, "are entirely understandable. However, as you will realize, our understanding does not and cannot equate to forgiveness. The rule of law cannot protect us from each other, and from ourselves, unless it is applied uniformly in all cases. Selective enforcement is the hallmark of a tyranny."

That didn't sound good at all.

She paused to let it sink in, and then continued. "In a very personal sense, we regret that your viewpoints were not presented legally. Our government includes numerous mechanisms for the redress of grievance that have operated effectively for hundreds of years. Granted, these channels are slow, as enlightened social change always should be. But impatience is one of the hallmarks of youth, and in many ways this *is* your argument.

"Childhood is a fleeting condition, and any justice which overruns its boundaries is no justice at all, but a service to the adults you will one day become. And your voices have been very clear on this point: that you will sacrifice the comfort and liberty of those future selves, in order to enjoy a different and more immediate sense of freedom in the here and now. Such a decision should not be—and in our estimation, has not been—made lightly. And again, we understand, even if we do not agree."

She paused again. She had their absolute silence, their absolute attention.

"The matter of your punishment has been the focus of considerable debate and analysis. The solution we've arrived at is not one which comforts us, but justice can be like that sometimes. Please be aware that we love you, and wish no harm upon you. But you have brought this on yourselves."

She pointed the scepter at the sky, and lowered its butt end onto the stage with a soft thump. As gestures went, this one was clear enough: the prosecution rests.

King Bruno unrolled the document in his hand, glanced at it, and then looked up at the audience. "Er, hmm. There's a lot of legalese in this: the whereas and the shall and the by-the-power-vested. Let's skip that part, shall we? And allow me to reiterate: this isn't a desirable solution. But it appears to be a necessary one."

He paused, looking around, and now he wasn't the avatar of a nation, or even the father of a friend, but just some nice man stepping in with bad news. "The gist of it," he said, "is exile. You'll be provided with a starship and the means to form a reasonable settlement in the worlds of the Barnard system, some five-point-nine light-years from Sol, which will be ceded to you for this purpose."

A murmur ran through the crowd.

"And once this ship is commissioned and registered and this land grant is made, you will have forty-eight hours to remove yourselves from the borders of the Queendom, which you may not then reenter for a period of one thousand years."

The murmur became a gasp.

"One thousand years," the king repeated, "*on pain of death and erasure*. I can assure you, this sentence is not imposed lightly, nor in good humor. But your cooperation has been impossible to secure by other means."

He scratched his chin, and tugged lightly at the end of his beard. "The, ah, the course ahead of you is a difficult one, and one I daresay you'll regret. But it is precisely the course you have chosen, and precisely the one you deserve, and if there truly is a God who dwells within us, or is generated through us, or otherwise takes an interest in our affairs, then I pray that he will have mercy on your souls. Because Tamra and I, alas, cannot."

He seemed poised for a moment to ask if there were any questions. But that was the scientist in him, the professor and declarant—an old reflex that sometimes showed through. Today he suppressed it, and remained regal.

"At this point," the queen said, "you are all remanded to the custody of your parents, or parole officers for the adults and emancipated minors among you. We don't yet know how long the preparations will take, as no voyage of this type has ever been attempted. But the expected cost is very high, and any further misbehavior in the meantime will be dealt with"—she peered down her nose at the audience—"very harshly."

She paused for several seconds before adding, "That is all."

And with that, the king and queen turned together, dismounted the stage, and began the climb back up toward the rear of the amphitheater, where the fax gates were. But they didn't get even as far as the third row—Conrad's row—before a purple-clad figure leaped from the stands and threw itself at them with a yell.

The heads of the Palace Guards swiveled, their arms coming partway up, weapon-fingers at the ready. But they made no other move, perhaps sensing that Bascal Edward de Towaji Lutui had no harm in him at this moment. *"I love you!"* the prince screamed, throwing both arms around his parents in an embrace that nearly bowled them over. He was laughing and crying all at once, his strong voice quavering with emotion. "Thank you, thank you! The task of this grievous voyage has been lightly fulfilled, and I am . . . I am . . . pickled with joy!"

Indeed, it was a perfect solution, and Conrad could see that Bascal had been right all along, about everything—even the pushy, malicious stuff. Tantrums and blackmail weren't supposed to work; they just hardened parental and governmental resolve, right? But here the children were, openly reaping the benefits of it. A thousand years of freedom! A whole star system to call their own! Conrad was worldly enough—just barely—to appreciate the irony.

Bruno's answer was soft, personal and private. He knew, probably from long experience, how to shelter his voice from the arena's fine acoustics. But Conrad was only a couple of meters away, and could hear the king's surprised muttering well enough. "It isn't a *reward*, Bascal. It isn't a good thing at all."

"Oh, Father," the prince replied fondly, hugging even harder. And they all lived happily ever after.

Like hell they did.

A: With some parallax view on the subject, I feel
   confident in citing "The Song of Physics" as His
   Majesty's first true masterwork. Here we see the
   culmination not only of literary talent and real-world
   insight, not only of that famous wit, but also of
   generational outreach. The song is fundamentally a
   parting gift from son to father, and should be
   appreciated as such.

Q: It's a much longer poem than anything he'd
   previously attempted, true?

A: Not only longer, but more universal in every sense.
   Here is a piece written with the future—not the
   present—in mind. With an audience which includes
   the Queendom, but is not limited to it. Of course, it's
   the audacity of the project that truly inspires: the
   universe in twenty stanzas, with simple language and
   a compulsively tractable—one might almost say
   childish—cadence of melody.

Q: A gift to all of us, then. To posterity.

A: A parting gift, I would say, on the eve of a perilous
   exile. The poem is ebullient, but the gesture itself
   has an old-fashioned air, of separation and mortality.
   Just in case, we used to say. If this meeting be our
   last, have this token for thy memory of me. And so
   we shall.

—Critic Laureate Julia Aimes,
in a Q299 interview with Fusiliers *magazine*

walking home

By the light of a gas lamp, Radmer takes a final flask of dinite from the chemry and closes its little brass door for the last time. It's a clever device, worthy of its High-rock creators: without electricity, using only catalyst beds and the mechanical energy of a foot pump, it combines the gases in the air with water from the sea, to produce a paste that any spark will explode, even in the vacuum of space. He's been warned not to get this paste on his skin; even the sweet, waxy smell of it sometimes gives him headaches and heart palpitations.

The stuff has a longer name that he can't remember, but the word "dinite" is familiar to any soldier who's ever had shells of it bursting overhead. This formula is a bit tamer than the military equivalent, but only a bit. He sprinkles fine sand into the flask as well—an operation which, in the words of his armorer, Mika, "will reduce the energy and enhance the impulse of each detonation."

The predawn morning has yet to warm up, and finally finishing this chore is a numbing concept; he's been pumping sixteen hours a day for over a week, and his legs feel ready to drop off with exhaustion. From an energy standpoint, it's as if he had to personally hike up out of Varna's gravity well with the space capsule on his back, and then kill enough orbital velocity—with his feet!—for the capsule's path to dip down into Lune's atmosphere for reentry. Actually it's much worse than that, because the pump and the chemry and the mechanics of combustion offer layers and layers of inefficiency. And he's also had to make oxygen candles with a different chemry of similar design, which eats salt water and bits of iron, so really he's had to complete that hike twenty times over. By now he's so sick of it that he's almost relieved at the prospect of returning to space, and thence to the war itself. Almost.

Luckily, the atmosphere here on Varna contains a lot more nitrogen than the plant and microbial life strictly require. As an air thickener, nitrogen leaves a lot to be desired—you need a large planette to contain it over geologic time—but such things had always been a matter of fashion, back when planettes were still being built. Which is fortunate, because the refueling of the brass sphere would have taken a *lot* longer on a noble-gas world. One cannot spin explosives from xenon and neon.

"Handmade," Bruno de Towaji remarks, running his fingers along the lines of the chemry's brass case. "A single device for a single purpose. I see armies of craftsmen, digging ore from the mountainsides, smelting and refining and beating it into shape for this one use. Extraordinary."

He's been around the chemry for days, but now, in the lamplight and the gloom of early morning—their *last* morning—he seems to really notice it for the first time. His tone suggests surprise and admiration, as well as condescension. He might be describing a piece of primitive art. He is wearing the felt johnnysuit Radmer has brought for him, to go beneath the topcoat and leathers that will protect him from the cold of space. It's hardly a garment to be snobby in.

"I've used worse," Radmer tells him as he fishes the

packing trowel from a compartment on the sphere's exterior.

"Yes, I suppose you have. Life in the colonies was—"

"Fine," Radmer tells him, a bit testily. "It was fine. No worse than we have on Lune today. A handmade world *requires* humans in a way that the Queendom never did. Over time, one learns to appreciate this."

Bruno makes a sour face, all shadows and beard. "Requires them as fuel, perhaps. Uses them up. Works them over. Kills them."

Radmer glances at the blue-green half-disc of Lune, hanging peacefully in the starry sky, then favors his one-time king with a hard, unfriendly glare. "Would you rather live forever, Sire? Truly?"

Bruno does not reply, so Radmer—who after all has pressing business on that squozen, half-sized moon up there—gets back to work. He mixes up the grit and paste in the flask, digs a wad of it out with the tip of the trowel, and starts slathering and packing it into the last of his course-correction charges. It's a delicate operation—a slip of his hand could blow a substantial chunk out of the planette—but the danger doesn't faze him. Radmer and danger have been on close, personal terms for longer than he cares to remember.

"We didn't realize what sentence we'd imposed," Bruno muses. His tone is wistful and full of regret.

"No one sees the future, Sire."

"No, I suppose not. But mistakes are supposed to educate us, yes? Instead we have thirteen colonies, thirteen failures, and none of us any wiser for the experience."

"Millions of pages were written on the subject," Radmer points out impatiently.

But Bruno dismisses this with a shake of his head. "Analysis. Rhetoric. Imperfect analogy. None of us understood what was happening. Are there messages which cannot be copied? Organisms which cannot reproduce?

Our Queendom, so simple and inevitable in its logic, rested on a foundation of prior society. There were hidden variables that refused to transcribe to the colony environment. There must have been."

Radmer hasn't had time to consider this subject in recent years, but now with the clarity of hindsight it seems simple enough. "I think it was just a matter of money. A network of collapsiters, spaced every hundred AU from here to Barnard, would have made the Queendom continuous. Or directly connected, at any rate. If the carrying capacity of Planet Two had been higher there'd've been no need for a second colony."

Bruno grimaces. "That's four thousand collapsiters, lad. At least ten-to-the-fourteenth tons. We'd've had to dismantle a moon just to make the neubles to make the black holes—a whole second Nescog, and never mind the energy cost of shipping them."

"Impractical," Radmer agrees. "Perhaps a fleet of cargo ships could have served the same purpose. Sending one vessel—even a fine one—is quite a leap of faith, if you think about it."

"I have," Bruno says. "And the shame will never leave me. You're quite right to despise me for it."

Radmer looks up in surprise. "Sire, have I blamed you for what happened? I don't think anyone ever did. No one knows everything, sees everything."

"A king should," Bruno complains. "A civilization should. We had the wherewithal to reason it out."

"Aye," Radmer says. "That we did."

The correction charge is now fully packed—and wildly explosive—so Radmer drops the trowel into the dinite flask with a clink of metal on glass, and then sets the flask down in the shadows beside the chemry.

"We'll leave this equipment behind," he tells Bruno matter-of-factly. "And more. It's necessary, to compensate for your weight on board the capsule. If you like, we can store it in your cottage rather than littering the ground."

Bruno shrugs. "It hardly matters."

"To the immorbid, Sire, little things always matter. Perhaps you'll return here someday. Or someone will."

He finds the charge housing's end cap nozzle and screws it back on. Several of these have blown out—burst their threads when the dinite charges went off during the outbound leg of the trip. But the charge cases themselves unscrew, so the damaged ones have been removed and the intact ones shuffled around so that the capsule has a reasonable balance of corrections available in each of the six ordinal axes.

"Perhaps I will," Bruno says unconvincingly.

Now Radmer is impatient again. "I'm not taking you to certain death, you know. I've lived down there a long time. The people are as kind and wonderful as people ever are, and they deserve our help."

"Aye, and that's the problem," Bruno agrees, with his own little measure of anger. "They need help and care and kindness, and then they die. And then another generation needs help, and they die as well. On and on it goes. Before the Queendom, keeping dogs was like that: eventually they would exhaust all patience, all love, all grief, until the thought of caring for *one more dog* became an obscenity."

Radmer slams and latches the storage compartment on the skin of the brass sphere and moves to open another, which spills out yards of silk and twine. He says nothing.

Bruno wipes his mouth, and examines the new Timoch boots Radmer has given him. "And yet. And yet, there was always another mutt, wasn't there. Wagging its tail."

"The parachute needs sewing and packing," Radmer says flatly. "After that, we depart. Do you have any personal effects you'd like to bring?"

In spite of everything, Bruno spreads his arms and laughs. "Do I look like a man with personal effects?"

"No. Indeed."

A pang of hunger sounds in Radmer's gut. This is not surprising; working the chemries all week has kept him in a state of constant famishment. In response he has denuded the planette so savagely that he genuinely worries the wild potato and yam and carrot species—and possibly some of the fish—may have been driven to extinction. The fruit trees he's less worried about, since picking them clean doesn't kill them.

But in point of fact, Radmer can digest leaves and grass—all the Olders can, though they don't relish it— and if this long chore were to drag on any longer, the astronomer Rigby would soon notice the color green vanishing from Varna's miniature landscape.

Again, from an energy standpoint, it would have made more sense and been more efficient to feed soil and vegetable matter directly into the chemry, rather than using his own body as the power plant. But that would have required a vastly more complex device, versatile enough to detect and assimilate and reformulate a wide assortment of chemicals. And things simply don't work that way on Lune anymore.

"Can you lead me to some bananas?" he asks Bruno.

Again, there is laughter. "That will be a long walk, my dear architect laureate. But there may still be a bunch or two on the planette's other face."

"Sold," Radmer says. "I can use the break." Then, as they set off, he tells the old king in a more thoughtful tone, "You know, the brevity of a natural life does have its upside. Fifteen years of peace and prosperity may not seem like much to you, but on Lune it's long enough to raise a family. And *fifty* years is a lifetime, literally. I can say, without exaggeration, that my personal actions have brightened the lives of hundreds of millions. This is, of course, dwarfed by your own record, but these are the children of my children, forty generations along."

"This war of theirs," Bruno says, waving off the compliment. "It's a bad one."

"Very bad," Radmer agrees, marveling at how poorly those two words convey the true situation on Lune.

"And you believe I can help."

It's Conrad's turn to laugh, albeit humorlessly. "I've been a fool before, Sire. Many times. But I fear at this point that *only* you can help. Or rather, that if you cannot, then there is no hope at all."

The king's rusty, castaway voice is heavy with irony. "What will you do then? Maroon yourself on a planette? We'll see about this, you and I. There is always hope. Giving it up is a sign of weakness."

"Ah," Radmer says, ignoring all of the easy and obvious retorts.

Ahead, the sun breaks over the round horizon, putting an end to their darkness, and Radmer—who was once Conrad Mursk—chooses to see it as an omen.

When they've winched the sphere over into its launch orientation, when they've donned their leathers and sealed their hatches, when they've bolted the passenger chair into place and peered one final time through the windows at the soil and greenery and cloudy skies of Varna...only then does it begin to feel real. Only then does Radmer feel the relief, the flush, the *excitement*, of success. Hitting Lune will be easy enough, compared to the journey here.

"Will you do the honors, Sire?" he asks, handing the blast chains to Bruno. "One firm tug, on my mark."

"I will, yes," the king says, taking the chains with a weird solemnity.

"It already stinks in here," Radmer notes. "I warn you, it will get much worse."

"Yes, yes. Just give the countdown."

"A countdown!" Radmer exclaims. "How quaint. Yes, that's just what the occasion demands. Five! Four! Three!"

And then he pauses, feeling a tickle of déjà vu at the edges of his mind, like the melody of an old, forgotten song. Or perhaps its lyrics: *She doesn't have an engine and she doesn't have a fax gate...*

"Two? One?" Bruno inquires.

And Radmer answers him. "Sorry, yes. Fire."

So the chains are jerked and the charges detonate, and there's nothing gentle or forgiving about it. Varna departs from the windows, and the sky grows black, and the two men, pressed back savagely into their seats, are hurled toward an uncertain future.

All things considered, it's a hell of a ride.

glossary

This book borrows numerous terms from its prequel, *The Collapsium*. Critical carryovers, plus additional terms first appearing in this volume, are defined below.

Adamantium—(n) The pseudomaterial with the highest known toughness index, and the third-highest hardness. Because it is a poor conductor of electricity, adamantium has a high energy cost to maintain in comparison with other comparable pseudomaterials.

Aft—(adj or adv) One of the ordinal directions on board a ship: along the negative roll axis, perpendicular to the port/starboard and boots/caps directions, and parallel and opposite to fore.

Asteroid belt—(n) A ring-shaped region in the ecliptic plane of any star where the tidal influence of major bodies has prevented the accretion of planetessimals into larger planets. Sol's Asteroid Belt includes the minor planet Ceres, and otherwise consists of irregular rocky bodies (asteroids) smaller than 260 kilometers across. It extends from approximately 2.2 AU at its lower boundary to 3.6 AU at its upper, with a total mass (including Ceres) less than one-tenth that of Luna.

AU—(n) Astronomical unit; the mean distance from the center of Sol to the center of Earth. Equal to 149,604,970 kilometers, or 499.028 light-seconds. The AU is the primary distance unit for interplanetary navigation.

Boots—(adj or adv) One of the six ordinal directions on board a ship: along the positive yaw axis, perpendicular to the port/starboard and fore/aft directions, and parallel and opposite to caps.

Caps—(adj or adv) One of the six ordinal directions on board a ship: along the negative yaw axis, perpendicular to the port/starboard and fore/aft directions, and parallel and opposite to boots.

Cardinal direction—(n) Any of the six main compass points for solar navigation: upsystem, downsystem, north, south, clock, and counter.

Chemry—(n) Any device that employs mechanical energy to drive the chemical synthesis of a product, most typically a food or fuel. Usually applied to human-portable devices; larger versions are more commonly referred to as "factories."

Chondrite—(n) Any stony meteoroid characterized by the presence of chondrules, or round particles of primordial silicate formed during the early heating of a stellar nebula. Chondrites are similar in composition to the photospheres of their parent stars, except in iron content.

Clathrate—(adj) Of or pertaining to a compound formed by the inclusion of molecules of one substance in the crystal lattice of another. In Kuiper and Oort space, methane and noble-gas hydrates (i.e., water ices) are the most typical examples. Literally: "possessing a lattice."

Clock (*also* **Retrograde**)—(adj or adv) One of the six cardinal directions: clockwise when facing down from solar north. In Sol system, a minority of moons and comets orbit clock.

Collapsiter—(n) A high-bandwidth packet-switching transceiver composed exclusively of collapsium. A key component of the Nescog.

Collapsium—(n) A rhombohedral crystalline material composed of neuble-mass black holes. Because the black holes absorb and exclude a broad range of vacuum wavelengths, the interior of the lattice is a supervacuum permitting the supraluminal travel of energy, information, and particulate matter. Collapsium is most commonly employed in telecommunications collapsiters; the materials employed in ertial shielding are sometimes referred to as collapsium, although the term "hypercollapsite" is more correct.

Comet—(n) Any celestial body consisting primarily of ices, clathrates, and chondritic dust. In most star systems, comet diameters are typically 100 kilometers or smaller, and rarely more than 1000 kilometers, although even in Sol system a few are 2000 kilometers or larger.

Converge (*also* **Reconverge**)—(v) To combine two separate entities, or two copies of the same entity, using a fax machine. In practice, rarely applied except to humans.

Counter (*also* **Prograde**)—(adj or adv) One of the six cardinal directions: counterclockwise when facing down from solar north. In Sol system all planets and asteroids, and the vast majority of moons and comets, orbit counter.

Declarant—(n) The highest title accorded by the Queendom of Sol; descended from the Tongan award of Nopélé, or knighthood. Only twenty-nine declarancies were ever issued.

Dinite—(n) Any detonating or deflagrating explosive consisting primarily of ethylene glycol dinitrate.

Downsystem—(adj or adv) One of the six cardinal directions: toward the sun from any orientation.

Duramer—(n) A translucent, gray-white pseudomaterial characterized by flexibility and high strength.

Ertial—(adj) Antonym of inertial, applied to inertially shielded devices. Attributed to Bruno de Towaji.

Fall, The—(prop n) Historical period of the early Queendom, marked by the destruction of the first Ring Collapsiter and the capture of Declarant-Philander Marlon Sykes by the forces of Bruno de Towaji. The Fall both preceded and precipitated de Towaji's involuntary coronation as King of Sol.

Fax—(n) Abbreviated form of "facsimile." A device for reproducing physical objects from stored or transmitted data patterns. By the time of the Restoration, faxing of human beings had become possible, and with the advent of collapsiter-based telecommunications soon afterward, the reliable transmission of human patterns quickly became routine.

Faxation—(n) The act or process of using a fax machine.

Fax Wars, The—(prop n) Historical period of the Late Modern era, characterized by abrupt changes in philosophy, religion, urban planning, and other disciplines following the introduction of practical human teleportation.

Feng shui—(n) A system of spiritual geomancy, dating to the Medieval or possibly the Classical period of East Asia. Under more technical rubric, many principles of feng shui were carried forward into the architectural and matter programming disciplines of the Queendom of Sol.

Ferromagnetism—(n) An attraction between uncharged materials, occurring when atoms of nonzero magnetic moment—containing spin-unpaired electrons and thus behaving as elementary electromagnets—spontaneously align themselves for mutual reinforcement. In atomic matter, ferromagnetism is associated with iron, cobalt, nickel, gadolinium, and certain rare earth elements.

Fetula—(n) Any vehicle propelled or controlled by the pressure of light, including sunlight, starlight, and the radiation of *sila'a* and other artificial sources. The term "solar sail" is sometimes applied colloquially, but in fact solar sails are a subset of fetulae. From the Tongan *fetu'u* (star), and *la* (sail).

Fore (*also* **Forward**)—(adj or adv) One of the six ordinal directions on board a ship: along the positive roll axis, perpendicular to the port/starboard and boots/caps directions, and parallel and opposite to aft.

Freefall—(n) The condition of free travel through any flat or curved spacetime in the absence of perturbing forces. Colloquially, any condition in which gravity or acceleration cannot easily be perceived. Freefall is a theoretical construct that does not occur in nature.

Fressen—(n) A nutritious paste, typically yellow in color, consisting primarily of starches and saturated fats.

Friendly Products Corporation, The—(prop n) Queendom-era supplier of patterns and services for children, parents, and adult recreational facilities, including sports teams.

Gate (*also* **Fax gate, Network gate**)—(n) The physical hardware mediating the transmission of energy, information, and material objects between individual fax machines and the Nescog.

Gee (*also* **g**)—(n) A measure of gravitational or inertial acceleration, equal to the mean surface gravity of Earth at sea level.

Gigaton—(n) One billion metric tons, or 10^{12} kilograms. Equal to the mass of a standard industrial neuble or collapson node (black hole).

Grappleship—(n) Any vehicle propelled by means of electromagnetic grapples. Use of grappleships was considered impractical in the Queendom until the advent of ertial shielding, though high-powered inertial devices were capable of attaining enormous accelerations.

Gravitic—(adj) Of or pertaining to gravity, either natural or artificial.

Holie—(n) Abbreviated form of "hologram." Any three-dimensional image. Colloquially, a projected, dynamic three-dimensional image, or device for producing same.

Hypercomputer—(n) Any computing device capable of altering its internal layout. Colloquially, a computing device made of wellstone.

Immorbid—(adj) Not subject to life-threatening disease or deterioration.

Impervium—(n) Public-domain wellstone substance; the hardest superreflector known.

Instantiate (*also* **Print**)—(v) To produce a single instance of a person or object; to fax from a stored or received pattern.

Invisible—(adj) Incapable by nature of being seen or detected in a particular wavelength range. Invisibility is distinguished from transparency in that a transparent object cannot be used to conceal other objects, whereas an invisible one can. Perfect invisibility (i.e., distortion-free) and universal invisibility (i.e., across all wavelengths) have never been demonstrated and may be physically impossible.

Kaume'a—(n) Tongan word for friend, widely used in the Queendom of Sol.

Kip (*also* **Kips** *or* **KPS**)—(n) Kilometers per second, a measure of velocity useful in interplanetary navigation.

Kuiper Belt—(n) A ring-shaped region in the ecliptic plane of any solar system, in which gravitational perturbations have amplified the concentration of large, icy bodies, or comets. Sol's Kuiper Belt extends from 40 AU at its lower boundary to 1000 AU at its upper, and has approximately one quarter the overall density of the much smaller Asteroid Belt. The total mass of the Kuiper Belt exceeds that of Earth.

Laureate—(n) An honor bestowed by the Queendom for extraordinary service. Descended from the Nobel citation of Swedish monarchy in the Old Modern era.

Light Wars, The—(prop n) Historical period of the Late Modern era, characterized by abrupt changes in architectural and infrastructural design following the introduction of programmable matter. Practices considered exploitive of the general populace continued until the passage of the Architectural Courtesy Edicts in the third year of the Queendom of Sol.

Luna—(prop n) Original name of Earth's moon.

Lune (*also* **The Squozen Moon, The Half Moon**)—(prop n) Name attaching to Earth's moon following the terraforming operations that reduced its diameter from 3500 to 1400 kilometers.

Magtal—(n) A class of lustrous pseudomaterials characterized by high electron mobility and superferromagnetism. Unalloyed magtals can exhibit fixed magnetic flux densities of one million Gauss and higher.

Malo e lelei—Traditional Tongan greeting widely used within the Queendom. Literally: "thank you for coming."

Mass Industries Corporation—(prop n) Queendom-era supplier of neutronium and especially finished neubles. Majority-owned by Bruno de Towaji, MIC at its peak operated a fleet of over five hundred neutronium barges.

Mass wrangler—(n) Term applied to any worker in the neutronium industry, and especially to the maintenance crews of the barges and dredges themselves.

Matter programming—(n) The discipline of arranging, sequencing, and utilizing pseudomaterials in a wellstone or other programmable-matter matrix, often including the in situ management of energy and computing resources.

Microwatt—(n) One-millionth of a watt, a measure of power useful in microelectronics and the application of starlight.

Mulm—(n) An edible polymer of monounsaturated fats, typically served in pellet form.

Nanofiber—(n) Any fiber of nanoscopic dimension. Often refers to the quantum-well-based electron conduits that are woven together to form wellstone and related materials.

Nanoscopic—(adj) Existing or examined on the nanometer (10^{-9} meter) scale of quantum electronics and molecular machinery.

Nescog, The—(prop n) New Systemwide Collapsiter Grid. Successor to the Inner System Collapsiter Grid or Iscog; a high-bandwidth telecommunications network employing numerous supraluminal signal shunts.

Neuble—(n) A diamond-clad neutronium sphere, explosively formed, usually incorporating one or more layers of wellstone for added strength and versatility. A standard industrial neuble masses one billion metric tons, with a radius of 2.67 centimeters.

Neutronium—(n) Matter that has been supercondensed, crushing nuclear protons and orbital electron shells together into a continuous mass of neutrons. Unstable except at very high pressures. Any quantity of neutronium may be considered a single atomic nucleus; however, under most conditions the substance will behave as a fluid.

Neutronium barge (*also* **Neutronium dredge**)—(n) A space vessel, typically one billion cubic meters ($1000 \times 1000 \times 1000$ m) or larger, whose primary function is to gather mass, supercompress it into neutronium, and transport it to a depot or work site. Although less numerous, smaller neutronium barges also existed for transport only.

North—(adj or adv) One of the six cardinal directions: parallel to the positive spin axis of the sun.

Older—(prop n) Informal title or ethnic slur applied to immorbid Queendom residents by the morbid, mortal peoples of Lune.

Oort Cloud—(n) A roughly spherical shell surrounding any solar system, in which gravitational perturbations have amplified the concentration of large, icy bodies, or comets. Sol's Oort Cloud extends from 30,000 AU at its lower boundary to 100,000 AU at its upper, and has approximately 300,000 times the mass and one-billionth the overall density of the much smaller Asteroid Belt. The orbits of Oort bodies can have periods of millions of years, and may be inclined in any direction. The total mass of the Oort Cloud exceeds that of Jupiter.

Ordinal direction—(n) Any of the six orienting points for the interior or exterior of a ship: port, starboard, fore, aft, boots, and caps.

Oxygen candle—(n) A compound of sodium chlorate and iron, typically enclosed in a metal housing, which smolders at 600°C, producing iron oxide, sodium chloride, and approximately 6.5 man-hours of oxygen gas per kilogram of candle. Widely used in spacecraft, submarines, caves, and mines where breathable atmosphere may be intermittently unavailable.

Pandanus—(n) A plant genus characterized by woody trunks supported with numerous aerial prop roots. The pandanus palm or textile screw pine produces large, tough leaves whose fibers were widely employed in Polynesian cultures for thatching, rope, wicker, and basketry. When specially prepared, the fiber of white pandanus, or *kie,* can form a soft, silklike cloth.

Photovoltaic—(adj) Capable of generating an electrical voltage across the junction between dissimilar materials, with the input of light energy, through the liberation of bound electrons in a preferred direction. Many natural materials (e.g., silicon) produce minor photovoltaic effects across grain boundaries. However, the much greater efficiency of quantum-well devices such as wellstone makes them preferable for most applications. In many isolated devices, wellstone pseudomaterials *must* be photovoltaic in order to maintain their other properties using ambient radiation.

Pilinisi—(n) Prince. Traditionally, any Prince of Tonga.

Planet—(n) Any natural satellite of a star whose gravity is sufficient to pull it into spherical shape. Sol system includes hundreds of planets, mainly in the Kuiper Belt and Oort Cloud.

Planette—(n) Any artificial celestial body consisting of a stony or earthy lithosphere surrounding a core or shell of supercondensed (neutronic) matter. The vast majority of planettes are designed for human habitation, and include Earthlike surface gravity and breathable atmospheres.

Port—(adj or adv) One of the six ordinal directions: along the negative pitch axis, perpendicular to the fore/aft and boots/caps directions.

Pseudoatom—(n) The organization of electrons into Schröedinger orbitals and pseudo-orbitals, made possible with great precision in a designer quantum dot. The properties of pseudoatoms do not necessarily mimic those of natural atoms.

Pseudochemistry—(n) Electron shell interactions taking place among pseudoatoms, or between pseudoatoms and natural atomic matter. Also, the systematic study or exploration of pseudochemical interactions.

Pseudomaterial—(n) Any material composed partly of pseudoatoms and existing within the matrix of a programmable substance such as wellstone. "Pure" pseudomaterials cannot exist, since the nanoelectronics required to generate and maintain them must be atomic in nature.

Quantum dot—(n) A device for constraining the position of one or more charge carriers (e.g., electrons) in all three spatial dimensions, such that quantum ("wavelike") effects dominate over classical ("particle-like") effects. Charge carriers trapped in a quantum dot will arrange themselves into standing waveforms analogous to the electron orbitals of an atom. Thus, the waveforms inside a quantum dot may be referred to collectively as a "pseudoatom."

Raw—(adj) Unfinished. Uncooked. In a natural, unrefined, or crude state. Youthful. Colloquially, fashionable or exquisite.

Restoration, The—(prop n) Interglobal election that established the Queendom of Sol under Tamra I. The term derives from the presumption that monarchy is the "natural" state of human beings, owing to a genetic predisposition.

Sila'a—(n) A pinpoint fusion generator or "pocket star" consisting of a wellstone-sheathed neutronium core surrounded by gaseous deuterium. From the Tongan *si'i* (small) and *la'aa* (sun).

Sketchplate—(n) A thin, rectangular block or sheet of wellstone sized and preprogrammed for the portable display and input of text, drawings, and physical simulations.

Sol—(prop n) Formal name for the Earth's sun, derived from the Latin. The Greek *Helios* was considered archaic for most Queendom uses.

South—(adj or adv) One of the six cardinal directions: parallel to the negative spin axis of the sun.

Squozen—(adj) Squeezed. Reduced symmetrically in diameter, as with the Squozen Moon. Attributed to Bruno de Towaji.

Starboard—(adj or adv) One of the six ordinal directions: along the positive pitch axis, perpendicular to the fore/aft and boots/caps directions.

Superabsorber—(n) Any material capable of absorbing 100% of incident light in a given wavelength band. The only known universal superabsorber (i.e., functioning at all wavelengths) is the event horizon of a hypermass. (Approximations of 100% absorption are generally referred to as "black.")

Supercompress (*also* **Supercondense**)—(v) To compress to the point of proton-electron recombination, i.e., until neutronium is formed. Colloquially, to compress beyond any point the speaker finds impressive.

Superferromagnetism—(n) Any ferromagnetism exceeding the field densities possible with atomic matter.

Superreflector—(n) Any material capable of reflecting 100% of incident light in a given wavelength band. No universal superreflectors are known. (Approximations of 100% reflectance are generally referred to as "mirrors.")

Sweetpaper—(n) An edible composite of polymerized and unpolymerized glucose, most typically served as a garnish.

Ta'e fakalao—(adj) Contraband or forbidden by law, as distinct from *tapu* or *taboo* (forbidden by custom or religion).

Talι fiefia—Traditional Tongan welcome, widely employed throughout the Queendom. Literally: "joyous reception."

Tapa—(n) A traditional Polynesian cloth made from the inner bark of the mulberry tree, and decorated in batik floral or faunal patterns using a variety of natural dyes and bleaches. Colloquially, the phrase "tapa pattern" or "tapa style" may refer to any floral print, or to any print in the Tongan or Polynesian style, on any material.

Tazzer—(n) A short-range beam weapon consisting of pulsed, coaxial streams of electrons and metal ions in a guide beam of blue or violet laser light. Tazzers are primarily used to induce temporary incapacity (pain, paralysis, unconsciousness), although lethal versions also exist.

Teleport—(v) To transfer, either instantaneously or at the speed of light, from one location to another. Teleportation can involve either the actual transfer of mass energy, as in a quantum waveform collapse or tunneling event, or alternatively, can involve only the transfer of organizing parameters, which are disrupted at the transmitting location and imposed on an equivalent mass energy at the receiver.

Teleport gun—(n) A short-range beam weapon capable of dispersing the mass in a cone-shaped target region without significant release or expenditure of energy. Teleport guns are notably unreliable, posing a significant risk to users and bystanders alike, and were banned for most uses by Queendom authorities.

Terraform—(v) To make Earthlike. In general, to match the gravity, climate, and atmosphere of a planet or planette to that of Earth, possibly including the imposition of a stable biosphere. Enclosed spaces are "climate-controlled" rather than terraformed.

Timoch—(prop n) Capital city of the Luner nation of Imbria.

Tonga—(n) Former Polynesian kingdom consisting of the Tongatapu, Ha'apai, and Vava'u archipelagoes, and scattered islands occasionally including parts of Samoa and Fiji. Tonga was the only Polynesian nation never to be conquered or colonized by a foreign power, and was the last human monarchy prior to establishment of the Queendom of Sol.

Tongatapu—(n) The largest and most populous island of Tonga; home to its traditional capital at Nuku'alofa.

Train wreck (TW)—(n) A measure of inertial (not gravitational) acceleration, equivalent to 40 gee. In practice, the term is applied only to impulsive accelerations (e.g., collisions, explosions). An unmodified, unprotected human can generally survive a 1 TW impulse lasting several seconds, while 2 TW impulses lasting longer than one second are typically fatal. Survival of millisecond impulses (e.g., vibrational) of up to 4 TW have been recorded. Impact to specific body areas produces highly nonlinear effects, and is rarely recorded or described in this fashion.

Transparent—(adj) Possessing a negligible absorption or reflection spectrum in a particular frequency range (e.g., visible light). Materials with zero absorption and zero index of refraction are referred to as "optical superconductors." Transparency is distinct from invisibility in that a transparent object cannot be used to conceal another object, whereas an invisible one can. Universal transparency (i.e., across all wavelengths) has never been demonstrated and may be physically impossible.

Transuranic—(adj) Beyond uranium. Used to identify natural atoms or ions containing more than 92 protons, or pseudoatoms containing more than 92 electrons. Because pseudoatoms can contain up to several thousand electrons in a wide variety of symmetries, the vast majority of known pseudoatoms are transuranic.

TV—(n) Abbreviation for "television," an archaic telecommunications term revived by the second and third generations of the Queendom of Sol. The term generally referred to any broadcast of audiovisual content, although three-dimensional imagery was still frequently referred to as "holie."

Upsystem—(adj or adv) One of the six cardinal directions: away from the sun in any orientation.

Varna—(prop n) A 640-meter-radius planette constructed in orbit around the Squozen Moon by private investors during the latter years of the Queendom of Sol. Site of the Q1290 Treaty of Varna, granting Right of Return to Barnard refugees.

Wellstone—(n) A substance consisting of fine, semiconductive fibers studded with quantum dots, capable of emulating a broad range of natural, artificial, and hypothetical materials.

Wellwood—(n) An emulation of lignous cellulose (wood), often employed as the default state of wellstone devices.

technical notes

This book owes a great deal to the technical support and advice of Hal Clement, Geoffrey A. Landis, Johnathan Sullivan, Ken Wharton, and the Right Reverend Gary E. Snyder. The idea of diamond-encapsulated neutronium originates with Robert L. Forward, although the term "neuble" is unique to this series.

Wellstone

The wellstone of this book's title is an actual, patent-pending invention, although one that is unlikely to be built or tested in the near future, owing mainly to the nanometer-scale manufacturing tolerances required. Also, for purposes of the story, I've taken a rather generous view of the material's ultimate capabilities.

However, "programmable" substances of much lesser sophistication, but still based on the manipulation of individual electrons in quantum-dot traps, have already been demonstrated in the laboratory. The real-world implications of this are so astounding that I've written a nonfiction book on the subject: *Hacking Matter* (Basic Books, Feb. 2003). Readers interested in a quicker and less comprehensive history of the field are encouraged to check out *Wired* magazine's "Ultimate Alchemy" at http://www.wired.com/wired/archive/9.10/atoms.html

Planettes

A spherical planette sized to hold an Earthlike atmosphere indefinitely, at room temperature, would require a surface escape velocity greater than the average (thermal) molecular velocity of the atmosphere. This requires a mass of well over 10^{19} kilograms (0.02% the mass of Earth's moon), and a diameter of around 20 kilometers, for a surface gravity of 1.0 gee. Paradoxically, lower gravity requires both a larger radius and a larger mass if the high escape velocity is to be preserved.

The atmospheres of planettes like Varna and Camp Friendly are not stable over geologic time, nor even probably over thousands of years, without a replenishment mechanism or possibly a mechanism for keeping the upper atmosphere very cold. Make no mistake: these are technological artifacts, like buildings, and will not persist forever without stewardship.

Lune, the Goliath of planettes, does not have this problem, and will keep its atmosphere indefinitely. With a radius of 707 km, a surface gravity of 1.0 gee, and an unaltered mass of 7.3×10^{22} kg, Lune's escape velocity is a whopping 3.72 kilometers per second (versus 11.9 km/s for Earth). The delta-velocity necessary to reach Varna—in an orbit 50,000 km high—from Lune's surface is very close to the escape velocity:

$$\Delta V = (2\mu/707E3 - \mu/25350E3)^{0.5} = 3{,}697 \text{ m/s}$$

Fortunately, this is achievable through low-tech means, as we shall see in the next volume.

Note that Lune's sphere of influence—the maximum radius of a stable circular orbit—is just over 65,000 km.

Past this point, the gravity of Earth (even murdered Earth) will perturb the orbit of an orbiting object over time, until the object either crashes, is ejected from the Earth-moon system, or becomes a stable satellite of Earth. Of the eight planettes orbiting Lune, Varna is the most remote.

The dimensions of Lune give it a surface area of 6.28 million square kilometers—about 17% of its original area, or 1.7% of Earth's. This is slightly smaller than the continent of Australia, and while it includes ocean as well as land surfaces, it does create a plausible home for hundreds of millions of human beings even at sub-Queendom technology levels.

Fetula (Star Sail) and *Slla'a* (Pocket Star)

Camp Friendly's "star" is a pinpoint fusion generator consisting of a wellstone-sheathed core of industrial neubles surrounded by gaseous deuterium in a state of continuous hot fusion. Orbiting the planette at a distance of 47,500 kilometers and with a period of 24 hours, it requires a total power output of 3.1×10^{13} watts in order to provide Earthlike insolation to the planette.

When focused into a laser beam and shone on a perfect, 1 km^2 light sail, this radiation produces the following maximum forces:

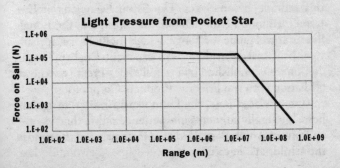

Light Pressure from Pocket Star

In fact, these forces are so high that for the first seconds of the journey it is necessary to throttle the sail's reflectivity in order to avoid crushing the cabin and its passengers. Pushing the star sail (*fetula*) using starlight alone is rather more difficult. The energy flux from starlight is approximately $1E-5$ w/m². If the sail is 100% transparent in one direction and 100% reflective in the other, the resulting force is:

$$f = 2p/c = (6.67E-9 \text{ N/W}) (1e-5 \text{ W/m}^2) (1500\text{m})$$
$$(750\text{m}) = 7.5e-8 \text{ N}$$

Not much, but it does add up over time. If the sail were able to reflect high-energy cosmic rays, with a flux of $2E-4$ W/m², then its maneuvering ability would be about twenty times greater.

Tongan Culture

Some readers may note that I've taken liberties—or Bascal and Conrad have—with the Polynesian fairy tales. Two of three are not from Tonga at all, but from other parts of the South Pacific, and all have been modified to fit your screen.

Similarly, the prince's boastful accounting of Tongan navigational prowess—while accurate—properly belongs to the entire Polynesian culture. Excellent references on this include Bryan Sykes' *The Seven Daughters of Eve*, Jared Diamond's *Guns, Germs, and Steel*, and the Lonely Planet travel guide for Tonga, which includes a surprising wealth of historical detail. An excellent English-Tongan dictionary is published by Friendly Isles Press (no known affiliation with the Friendly Products Corporation).

(On a related note, the Latin word *viriditas*, or "greenness," generally connotes inexperience rather than vigor—an irony of which Bascal Edward is unaware at the time of the Children's Revolt.)

The Cyades

Approximating each body of the near-contact comet pair as a clathrate sphere 100 km in diameter, with the approximate density of liquid water (typical for methane hydrates), yields a mass of 5.2e17 kg (or half a million neubles' worth) apiece. Orbiting their mutual center of mass with an apoapsis of 500 km and periapsis of 50 km (just close enough to collide), the two bodies will complete a revolution in 3.7e9 seconds, or 118 years.

Decelerating with Magnets

The force of a magnet on a ferromagnetic material (such as iron or neutronium) drops off with the square of the distance between them, and is a function of the magnet's residual flux density. The strongest fixed magnets in existence at the time of this writing are alloys of iron, boron, and the rare-earth (lanthanide) element neodymium, with residual flux densities of 13,300 gauss.

The acceleration profile described in this story requires a fixed magnet approximately 100 times more powerful than the NdFeB—speculative but not implausible given the nature of quantum-dot materials.

Observing the Neutronium Barge Telescopically

As any astronomer will tell you, light waves can't be magnified forever. Over large distances, the resolving power of a telescope is constrained by the limit of diffraction, where the light breaks down into interference patterns rather than images. This is a function of wavelength, lens diameter, and range. At a distance of 0.2 AU, the smallest feature resolvable by a 200-meter lens in visible light is around 94 meters, or one-tenth of the barge's diameter.

the fax wars

The very first thing the Fax Wars revealed was the deep-seated desire of every human being to be larger. Not larger in the abstract, with respect to the environment, but larger in relative terms, with respect to his or her peers, on account of the latent genetic programming that equated height, and to a lesser extent muscle mass, with social status.

Simply scaling up the human form was quickly shown to be an unhealthy—and in some cases fatal—oversimplification. You couldn't get more than about ten percent larger without major problems of bone diameter and systolic versus diastolic pressure coming into play. Not that this stopped everyone—among the eighty % of humanity who could afford fax access, average height increased overnight by about fifteen percent, and body mass by around thirty percent and we can only assume that each individual found a balance point between the pain and fatigue of gigantism, and the psychological distress of watching everyone else get larger.

The next wave began in the following year, with the first of many morphing filters that permitted intelligent, systemic changes to the human form under little more than voice command. The enormous mathematical complexity of these filters—which operated on the quantum waveforms themselves—are a testament to the cruel severity of the Old Moderns' dysmorphic yearnings. Once again the change occurred abruptly, with some twenty percent of travelers exiting the system in body forms that could barely fit through the print plate, and most others opting for at least another ten to twenty percent height or mass increase.

The third wave followed close behind, with a series of conformal filters that bent the knees and elbows and neck *just so*, arranging the human body for optimal packing without major redesign of the ligature system. Soon, even larger giants were rolling out of the public faxes in a tight fetal crouch. And then of course came the ligature changes that allowed for tighter packing still.

At this point, regional and national governments (such as they were) applied pressure to the makers and operators of fax hardware, who were themselves greatly troubled by what they had wrought. Hard limits were imposed on the mass of a faxed human being, with no exceptions made even for the natural giants and willful corpulents who still existed here and there in the world. What followed was a brief but intense flurry of exotic body styles designed to circumvent the restrictions: bird-boned women towering over their stocky peers, and men with hollow sacs beneath their falsely bulging muscles.

This was solved with equally inflexible limits on height and volume, and later the ratio between them. As a result, some people refused to travel through the public networks at all, preferring to retain their ill-gotten glamour by traveling the long way around, in vehicles or on foot. However, the rapid disappearance of highways, airports, and other travel infrastructure—no doubt encouraged by the bribes of the early Fax Lords[6]—made such a lifestyle

---

[6] De Towaji himself, supreme among the Fax Lords, is not known to have engaged in this practice, although several attorneys in his employ certainly did.

choice increasingly difficult and austere. And because
it was also associated with religious extremism—the
Murder-Me-Not crowd who believed their souls would
be imperiled by the physical destruction of their original
bodies—the practice was never particularly fashionable.

So for another couple of years, the complaint was that
everyone in the world looked exactly the same: a bland
uniformity of height and weight and physical type. And
the world was too small for these half-giants anyway;
what a bore it was to be constantly bumping your head,
knocking your knees, fitting through spaces nobody had
had the time to redesign for larger humans.

So the wheel of fashion turned, and soon the true indi-
vidualists of the world were turning out in short or skinny
or even midget forms, and everyone was cutting back at
least a little. "Grow your home: shrink yourself!" became
the battle cry, and eventually the maximum-height types
found themselves the butt of good-natured humor and
even, in some cases, less-than-good-natured suspicion.
What good was a tall politician? A burly contract negotia-
tor? Just what were they trying to pull?

Around this same time, it began to dawn on the general populace that they could make copies of themselves.
This quickly resulted in "xeropollution," with some individuals creating as many as ten thousand independent
instantiations, literally overrunning certain urban areas—
most notably Dallas, Texas, the home of the Plural Five.
Governmental and corporate powers took a dim view of
this practice and reacted with harsh measures, including
a three-month, near-total moratorium on faxation, and
the sanctioned mass murder of key individuals to reduce
their numbers. This led—again, primarily in Dallas—to a
number of armed skirmishes that represent the only "hot"
conflict of the Wars, with a definite and easily measured
death toll of 325 individuals. (The mortality rates for instantiations of these individuals is less well known.)

Fortunately, the rapid development of the Lodney Reconvergence Filter permitted human copies to be merged back into single individuals, with all memories and subjective experience intact. Strict limits were soon enthusiastically and bloodlessly enforced, first on total number of copies, and later, more fairly, on aggregate copy-hours over predefined periods of time.

These transient waves took a long time to settle out, and in some sense continued through the Queendom-era fashions of hair color, skin pigmentation, and self-plural cooperation. But for practical purposes, the Fax Wars were over a decade after they had begun, with the vast majority of human beings choosing modest plurality and the convenience of death and rebirth, over the theological virtues of singletonism and walking. And choosing, yes, to embrace their unique physical attributes as symbols of their heritage and identity.

"Clothe thyself in beauty if thou must," the playwright Wenders Rodenbeck instructs us in his satirical classic, *Uncle Lisa's Neutron*. "'Tis charm we find in dreadful short supply."

about the author

Wil McCarthy, after ten years of rocket science with Lockheed Martin, traded the hectic limelight of the space program for the peace and quiet (ha!) of commercial robotics at Omnitech, where he works as a research and development hack.

He writes a monthly column for the SciFi Channel's news magazine (www.scifi.com/sfw), and his less truthful writings have appeared in *Aboriginal SF, Analog, Interzone, Asimov's Science Fiction, Science Fiction Age,* and various anthologies. His most recent novel, *Bloom,* was selected as a *New York Times* Notable Book. Further biographical and bibliographic information is available at:

www.sff.net/people/wmccarth

Once, a generation of children wished to become adults. Now their wish has been granted. With the starship *Newhope* at their command, the worlds around Barnard's Star to settle, and a thousand years of exile before them, can the children of Sol found a glorious new future? Or will this latest attempt at independence ultimately be as disastrous as their last?

Don't miss the answers in

LOST IN TRANSMISSION

the next exciting novel from

Wil McCarthy

"Ah," Bascal said, his eyes lighting on the hologram. "Planet Two. Now there's a site for naive eyes, who've never caught glimpse of a thing undoable. Plotting its takeover, are we? Scheming its subjugation to the fist of Man? Or are we making friends, filling out a shopping list to surprise it with the gift of ourselves? I was going to name the place—such is my privilege, I'm told—but I figure we should wait for the formal introductions. Find out what she's like, how she treats us."

"You need a shave," Conrad observed. It was just an expression; what Bascal really needed was to reprogram the cells in his face to stop producing unsightly hair. Either that, or simply step through a fax machine, commanding it to give him a real beard.

"Do I? Who says?"

"What, are you growing a beard? *Growing* one?"

"The old-fashioned way," Bascal agreed. "It seems more proper than just printing one, or printing myself attached to one. I'm not dressing up, Conrad, I'm growing into a role."

"It's a lucky thing everybody's in storage." Conrad prodded. "You look like you're growing into a pirate again. Or a hobo."

"Ha, Ha. You slay me, sir. A king does need a beard, though, don't you think? It provides a certain sense of gravitas."

Conrad smirked. "Even a king in exile?'

"Especially a king in exile, boyo. I have no real duties here. I command the expedition, but your darling Xmary here commands the ship. My citizens are in a state of quantum slumber, and even when they awaken, they'll be much too busy to look to me for anything more than emotional support. Unlike my parents, I really am a figurehead. I rule myself and nothing more."

Xmary smiled, without much warmth. "It takes more than a beard, Your Majesty."

The smile Bascal returned was equally polite. "I never said otherwise, Captain. It's a grave responsibility, to look good doing nothing. Eternally, no less, for we shall never die! But give me time and I'll do nothing better than anyone has ever done it. I'll be the King of Nothing, and Nothing will bow down before me in admiration."

Coming from Bantam Spectra in spring 2004